THE GIFTED SOCIETY

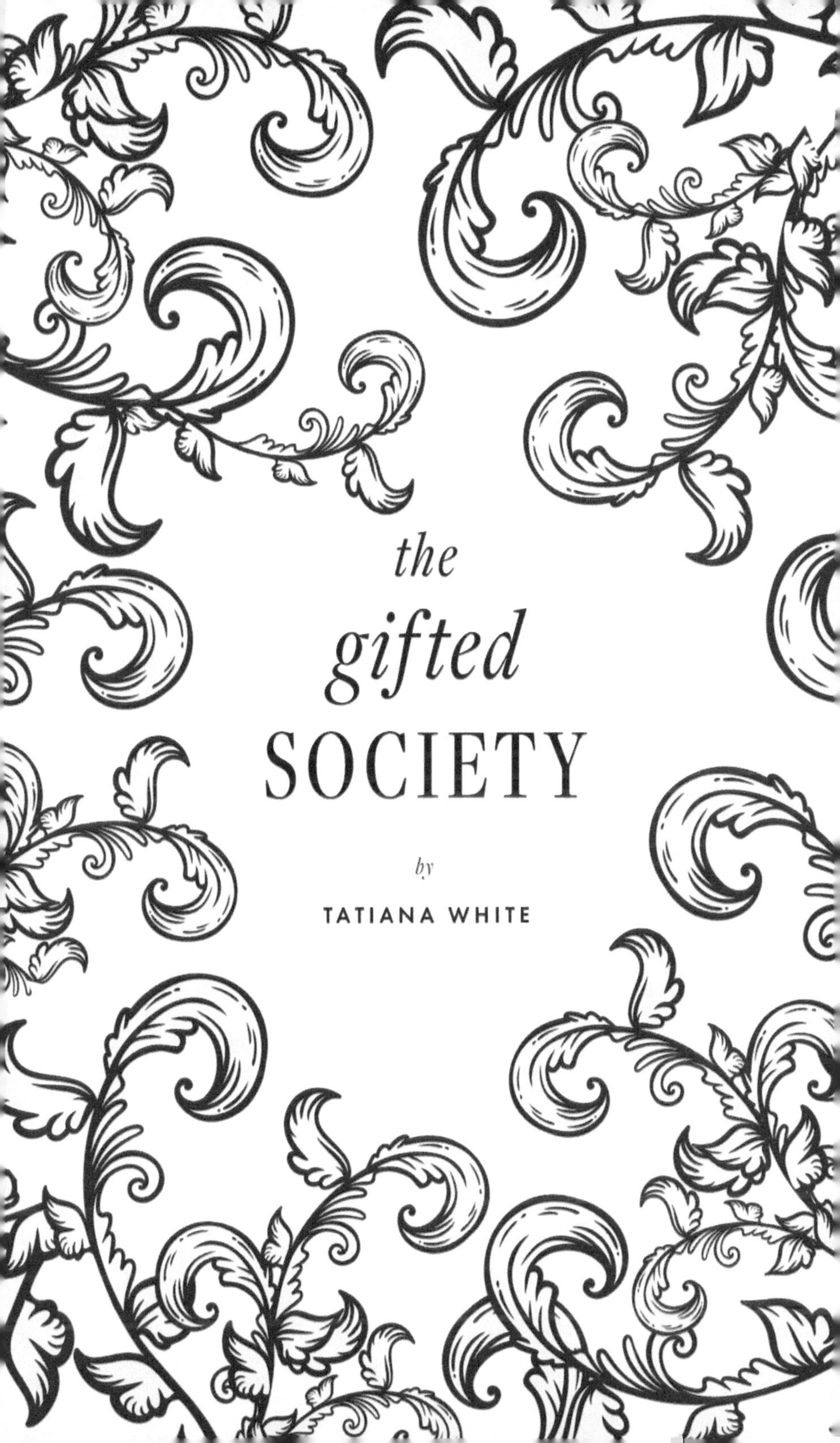

the *gifted* SOCIETY

by

TATIANA WHITE

The
muse papers

For
mom—my backbone.
And dad, who's been my muse all along.

Author's Note

Before you embark on your journey through these pages, please kindly consider the nature of this book's content.

This work of fiction is a fantasy drawn from my imagination. Despite drawing inspiration from reality, it is richly covered in layers of a newly painted world. I drew inspiration from aspects of Christianity but am in no way expressing my own personal moral beliefs of religious history or rewriting it. There are references to the Antebellum South and the Leonid Meteor Shower of 1833. The fantasy elements embellished around these historical periods are for artistic purposes only. This novel also explores psychological and mental health struggles such as anxiety and depression. It also contains depictions of some alcohol consumption, cigarette smoking, grief, monsters, gore, violence (especially within the final battle), elitism, government corruption, systemic oppression, estranged family relationships, wound trauma, and some swearing (as teens do).

Please read with care and awareness. Self-care is most important.

Thank you for reading.

the gifted SOCIETY

T H E   P L A Y E R S

Alexia Jacobs

Kyle Pereira-Phoenix

Alani Akina-Phoenix

Nathan "Nate" Grant

CHAPTER ONE

The Emancipation
will be Televised

ONE HUNDRED TWENTY-ONE CASE files sit on my desk. Neat, crisp with the scent of ink stamped on clean white papers. Collated and stapled, they're sandwiched perfectly in between blue folders. No coffee rings from the last handler, or oil spots from the fingers of a Cheez-It fiend. These files are fresh, unopened by anyone before me. Just the way I like them.

I can scrub through the files within the next forty-five minutes. Not for clout among the interns or making goals, but to find someone. Sarai. My best friend. She was taken away for murder. For slipping her fingers into a man's skull and smearing the walls with his blood.

An annoying figure looms over my desk. "What is that, Alexia? Your third stack of inmates this week?"

"Who's counting?" I don't look up, even though I know the answer to this question.

"Me, actually…"

"Of course, Bryce." I press my fingers into my palm. He's been on my ass since I started this after-school internship a few weeks ago.

"Well, we're to import two stacks a week," Bryce replies. Full condescension in his voice. Hair slicked so clean to his head it looks glued. *This fool thinks he's the Wolf of Wall Street.* "Two is the number, and here you are on a Wednesday on your third. I mean, I understand the way you got this job makes you overzealous, but—"

"How exactly did I get this job, Bryce? Hmm? Nepotism, I guess."

Bryce nods with a knowing look.

I shrug and play dumb. "Sometimes I forget. How did *you* make it on the team?"

"Editor-in-chief of my school paper, repeated swim champion, impeccable GPA, founder of two successful charities that gift underprivileged children toys for the holidays. Basic things."

"Basic." I smack my lips. "Does your father's hefty campaign donation fall under basic, too or nah?" I say, giving a Colgate smile.

He grimaces and drifts back to his cubicle without another word: him, and his suspenders.

I smirk and whisper, "…And don't come back."

Bryce can't ever seem to help himself from butting into my business. He never seems to believe I accomplish things fairly. *Oh no*…there must be *some* unjust reason as to why he's not the best legislative intern at the California State Capitol. But there isn't. I'm pretty much a girl who gets things done for the sheer thrill of crossing out tasks. That's what Sarai and I have in common. She does anything she wants, and she's the best at it. But killing someone? She'd never cross out a task like that.

Sarai can light up any space. No matter the mood. She can be the sun. Always warm. Always so damn optimistic, it's contagious. Sarai is full of good. But maybe all her good doesn't mean anything in light of her bad cells. The concept of those overshadow any good Sarai has to offer this world. And that's because this world isn't made for *people like her.*

I stare outside the window and find the streets of Sacramento filled with Variens. With all this noise in my head, I've almost forgotten about the protest outside. Variens want their rights back, and they won't wait for our country to come around. They will make it happen now. Posters in black, bold letters read: "Sectioned Housing Is Segregation. Kill The California Screen Bill! Senator Jacobs Is A Murderer."

A knot swells inside my throat and I decide it's time to dive into these inmate files and push my pain away. *Focus.*

I open the first folder. The paper is blank. The smell of ink, however, lifts from the page—telling of the words I'll uncover. I hold my pen and click the button on its side. A laser shines through its tip, waking the paper's information and revealing it line by line before my eyes: "Wayne Camden. Twenty-four-year-old male with precognition abilities. Registered at Banneker State Prison for theft by deception. Multistate lottery fraud. Sentenced to fifteen years in prison."

My hand hovers down the page until the laser shows a full-page report. There's nothing left to do but insert my pen into the computer. The file transfers successfully, then I'm on to the next. The last page of the report appears, and I repeat the routine before moving to another file: "Raima Singh. Sixteen-year-old female with glass manipulation abilities. Registered at Crihook Women's Row for committing murder. Sentenced to death."

Every now and then, I stumble across a case like Sarai's. Whether the Varien was justly or wrongfully convicted makes no difference to me. Because every time—every time—murder is listed, so is the sentence of death. I can't help the squeezing I feel in my stomach when it happens. My mouth goes dry and panic comes, and then more panic arrives from the fear of my coworkers seeing me dig myself into a full-blown anxiety attack.

It's the realization that Sarai, my sixteen-year-old best friend, is on death row somewhere with her light blown out. Her soul broken.

It's been ten months since I've seen Sarai. It's been even longer since her body betrayed her—when it turned her Varien. I've never stopped searching for her. I don't think I ever will. She'd never give up on me.

"Ugh, just look at them…" My boss, Stasi, groans as she eyes the protesting crowd from her desk. "Acting out…all because this bill passed. It's scary."

Those voices outside sound like cries to me. A melancholy that pierces through the walls like spears and rattles the windows. Those people stand and march with more grace than any of the cushy "normal" people here. Every day, I see them walk in with sunglasses covering their sleepy eyes, and a thirty-two-ounce coffee with way too many shots to kill their entitled laziness.

The gag is the espresso seems to bring out who they really are. They're full of things—like apathy—that don't make times better, and I'm sick of it all. I need a break.

Stasi draws her attention away from the window and finds me grabbing my purse. "You're leaving? Your dad isn't here to pick you up yet."

I tuck in my bottom lip. Maybe it'll tame the sharp things I want to say. "Yeah, no. Just gonna head out for a quick bite. I forgot to pack my snacks and all I can think about is sweet potato pie."

"In all of that?" Stasi's eyes widen as she points.

"Why not? I mean…it's just a protest."

"A dangerous one," Bryce butts in, again. "Today isn't the day to choose their side, Alexia. Your dad wouldn't want you to."

I should've gagged him and locked him in the janitor's closet before work started. "Seriously, they're just marching and holding signs." My hands slap against the sides of my thighs, and I realize I'm getting worked up. "That's a peaceful protest, guys, First Amendment 101, c'mon." If there weren't hundreds of fed up people outside, we'd be able to hear a pin drop.

There's forced patience in Stasi's voice. "Just be careful, and hurry. Your dad is supposed to pick you up soon. He'll freak out if you get stuck out there."

"I'll be fine," I assure Stasi and the office. They don't think I will be, but they don't say anything else.

I make a fast break for the bathroom and it becomes obvious that I've been on pause all day. Heat rushes to my face then pulses through the rest of my body. The surge is so hot, I check the mirror for any red marks on my face. None. Just the caramel brown hue I wear every day. "You're losing it," I whisper into a pant. My breathing speeds faster and faster as I think of my friend, and when I feel my temperature rising, I begin to reel myself in. "No. No. No…"

I splash water onto my face and wipe my eyes with the backs of my sleeves. *Oh God.* My eyes still show everything I'm trying to hide with their puffy redness, but I give up on fixing them and leave when another person enters the bathroom.

"Hey, sunshine!" a woman with a short brown haircut greets me. Ren Oleynik is her name—or something like that. I barely see her when I work, but boy when I do, she kisses my ass. "How do you stand to look so darling every day?"

"Stress," I play and grin.

Ren gives a country club laugh in her loud red blazer. "I bet, but you know, you're doing great. You've really helped us with getting this California Screen Bill ready. It's like your little baby."

I nod.

"And like a baby, it requires lots of attention, right? But it'll pay off…I'm sure. Everyone will be grateful for it when it hits. You should be proud. I know your father is."

I inch closer to the door as Ren stands in front of a stall. "I am, I feel like a real hero."

My stomach growls and I remember my original plan of getting the heck out of here for a cut of sweet potato pie. I need it bad. A big cold slice of it with a scoop of vanilla ice cream—like Big Mama used to serve it. Even when she didn't have much, she stirred miracles into bowls and baked them in pans, transforming sour days into sweet ones. No one else can mimic her magic, but

Mabel's Sugar Chest, the soul food joint around the way, comes close enough. It used to be Sarai's favorite spot too.

"Senator Jacobs!" a woman standing on top of a bench shouts into a megaphone. "You have led the war on our liberties! Enacting laws that deny us healthcare, safe homes, and now medical confidentiality!"

I cringe. Hot wind blows on my face as I step outside. The sun has been so unforgiving that I wonder if it's angry too—just as fed up with the system as the droves of protesters ahead of me. "We'll march. We'll fight! Give back our civil rights!" they scream.

Side by side, everyone looks the same: human. Like a quilt made of lives wrapped in different shades of skin. I wonder if the powers that be notice it. Without being close enough, there's no way to spot a Varien from afar, making punishment of one—when thousands band together—difficult.

Think again, I say to myself. The Black Coats, the regime in charge of containing Variens, stomp from their armored trucks, armed to the teeth behind their barricade. Guns, huge ones. Batons. Stun guns. Pepper spray. Tranquilizers. And…rot gas.

I gasp. *There are other ways. So many…*

I've witnessed the Black Coats use rot gas once, on a night I'd rather forget, the last time I saw Sarai. They skipped the option of tranquilizing her and went straight to the orange stuff that freezes the nervous system. And they want to do this again…to a crowd of thousands? *They can't.* I watch them uncurl the hose that'll carry the gas. I look out at the crowd and see an ocean of Sarais. Young people who have changed and don't understand why. Girls and boys who've had their childhoods ripped from them. Innocents. I grow anxious, and suddenly, I'm out of my mind. Like I'm some otherworldly being. Like I'm not the girl who spends her days working a job that oppresses Variens. I run into the crowd and push between bodies—heart double-timing, tunnel vision set—till I reach the space where the protesters and Black Coats meet: the police line barricade.

My arms spread out between both parties. My body grows warm. My chest lines up with the nozzle of the rot gas's idle hose. "We'll march, we'll fight. Give back our civil rights!" I tag on to the chant that's grown stronger as the day's gone on. I'm scared to death by what I've just done. Even more afraid of what the Black Coat holding the hose will do.

"We'll march, we'll fight. Give back our civil rights!"

He's not moving, not yet at least. I've got him thinking—which is out of character for a Black Coat. But when his gloved hand lifts the visor on his helmet, I can see his eyes. They're squinting as he reads me. *A Normal. A girl of privilege.* I'm not the kind of person he wants to hurt. I'm not the kind of girl he's *allowed* to hurt. I freeze in shock when he orders his men to stand down.

Two fingers in the air are all it takes to make the protesters cheer and the Black Coats seethe in place.

It's a miracle. A *w* for the right side of the fight. A drop in the sea of change. Maybe our voices, our cries, are making a difference!

I join everyone in celebration, turning the chant stronger with the brightness of my voice. Except, my celebration comes with a price...a consequence I forgot. It stands on the other side. The wrong side. The side covered in uniforms and crisp suits.

Suits?

As I see movement among the Black Coats, I suddenly understand their submission. I see the answer every day, every morning when I'm too tired to stop hitting snooze. When I'd rather stuff my drowsy face with a strudel but give in to the fresh fruit and oatmeal placed in front of me. It's the same answer that waits for me till curfew and has been there when I'm afraid to go to sleep.

I see the cause of all Varien loss and pain: Senator Jacobs.

I see...my dad.

CHAPTER TWO

BURNED BRIDGES

H E'S GOING TO EXPLODE. Not in some extraordinary way, but worse—with a mile of words I can't help but hate already. I hope he keeps them in his throat.

"The hell is wrong with you?" Dad radiates disappointment, and being trapped inside a car with him on the way home is torture.

"Dad," I say through my teeth, like a snake waving the end of its rattled tail.

"What would I have said to your mom? 'At least she's a hero, Solo.' Right over your seized-up body in the hospital."

"Maybe, 'She did the right thing.'" My voice flatlines.

"You think what you did was right?"

"Yes."

"…That's triflin'."

Dad doesn't sound like a senator off the clock. He's a smart man, a guy who's read the dictionary front to back numerous times. But I put this on everything I love, I don't think he ever fully understood the word "triflin'" until Destiny's Child sang it in "Bills, Bills, Bills."

"The right thing…you don't know what that is. You're too young," he says. His brown face folds into a scowl. Even his mustache looks angry.

"So, being young makes me too stupid to understand basic rights? Too young to empathize, or…I don't know…realize that inserting a mandated chip in everyone's body is invasive?"

"At your age, you're unable to make logical decisions for the greater good. You want me to hug every damn Varien as they turn on us. That does nothing."

"The greater good?" My heart feels bruised. "*Sarai* is the greater good." Tears well in my eyes, and I can feel my anger putting pressure on my words. "She was practically a daughter to you… and you just stood there and let them take her away!"

"Alexia, she did—"

"NOTHING!"

The sound of the blinker and my sobs fill the car. "You know Sarai *would've never* hurt anyone."

He shakes his head. "Listen, you don't—"

"Yes, I do!"

"Oh, you're an expert in Varien biology?"

"I know enough."

"Their brain chemistry is different."

"Oh my gosh, you *cannot* brainwash me with all your Salem witch crap…that's why *I* did what I did today."

His nostrils flare, and I brand my side of the argument. "And I'll do it again…"

"No, you won't…not if you're going to be a part of this family."

My eyes begin to burn and my skin feels clammy. "What does that mean?"

"Everything," Dad sighs. "You playing both sides…I can't do this anymore. The back talk and social media rants, the walkouts at your school…and now this. It doesn't match. It's not clean. It's not who you were. We need to give the public a united front. Any more of these scenes…and…I don't know." He pauses as he brakes the car. "Look, I wish I could help protect everyone—even Sarai. It's just not possible and that's…that's scary. Because we don't have time to be scared. All we have time for is a solution."

I freeze.

The solution—to the problem that resides in my own twitching palms. I bite my lip and wonder if he's noticed that my hands don't look the same anymore. Hard, calloused with peeling skin, they house white-hot stars in their veins.

And Dad has no clue. No one does. At least I hope they don't.

"Doesn't a piece of you believe they're scared too? I mean…" I wipe away the tears from my cheeks. "This isn't something Variens want, Dad."

"What they want isn't the safest option," he lightweight snaps back at me. "We need to identify them before they expose themselves. And this chip prevents all of that before any accidents, before the change alters their head, and before the world goes to hell in a damn handbasket. It feels wrong because it's new, but it's exactly what we need to shave down casualties."

"Dad…you're trying to control something that…" I catch the side of Dad's face as he drives. Eyes dead set ahead of him and wrinkles of stubbornness stamped in his skin, he can't be reached. An emptiness somewhere inside me screams, demanding to be filled. Things aren't the same anymore.

My voice softens. "I just think your power should be used for what's right. What if this happened to Nia and Niles…me? What would you do? Send us to a lab to die? To be boarded up in the slums, wrongly convicted of murder? No, you would want us to stay—"

"As normal as possible," he finishes. "And soon, whatever is going on will be cured and destroyed. We'll perfect the treatments. It'll be like curing the common cold. I'll be able to sleep at night then."

"I don't think so," I mumble. "It feels like a forever thing." Today. This evening. This hour. It's all a never-ending struggle. Restraining blazing stars from leaving my body is heavy. Debating Varien rights as I do it is even heavier.

"There's nothing for you to worry about." Dad reaches out to me at a stoplight—before I can think…before I can look outside myself. My insides are ready to release a flood of heat as anxiety rushes into me. But the sound of Dad's ringing phone saves me.

"Am I ever off work?" he groans.

When he looks away, my temperature rockets. And like air slipping from a shaken soda, a small and weak stellar flare jumps around my arm before it disappears back into my skin.

I take a deep breath and glance at Dad. He didn't see anything. He can't even see past his own nose.

Work keeps him away from me until we hit home. You'd think I'd be set to hit the ground running as we pull into our driveway, but when we do, all I want is to stay outside.

"C'mon," Dad says. "Let's go inside." He doesn't move until I move. He must think I'm ready to protest any and everywhere.

"Yeah." I gather my things and step onto the grass.

If perfect were a building, it'd be my house. Mom's little ol' Tudor home. I'm not exactly sure what a Tudor-style home is, all I know is that we have one—with steepled roofs, cream bricks and stones, and double wooden doors. Mom calls me and the house her miracle twins because we were both gifts she was scared would never materialize. She was put on bed rest in her third trimester when she was pregnant with me, all while being caught in a bidding war with twelve other families for our home. Mom and Dad lost the bid, but when the winning couple backed out, their offer shined. The house was won. I was born six weeks later, and the impossible was done.

"All you need is faith as big as a mustard seed, baby girl. God will do the rest," Mom always says when she reminisces on that story. "Because His plans are perfect."

I can see Mom from the porch. Lightly dancing to Sade—her favorite—she's shuffling around, dusting her favorite vases and wiping shelves on the foyer walls. Maintaining her miracle baby of a home. Not one living flaw until I come in.

"Hey, babe," Mom greets Dad.

"Solo, baby." He kisses her. Dad calls Mom "Solo" after all these years. She was a rapper once upon a time in her fly girl days, going hard in colored leather jackets and bamboo earrings. The whole early '90s fit. I'm not sure what the name Solo meant to her, but I'm sure "Sylvia," her government name, didn't cut it.

Mom cranks out a few bars every now and then. I'm always surprised when she does it, like a dog discovering the squeak on a toy. Because all I know is Sylvia, the mom. Not Solo, the hot girl.

"What's up, baby girl?" Mom chimes as she climbs a ladder.

"Hi," I deadpan.

"Oh no, not Wednesday Addams today. I want my sweet child with home training. Now!" She snaps her fingers. "Hey, baby girl!"

"Nothing. Everything's good."

Mom squints and wrinkles her thin eyebrows. "I didn't ask if things were good, but okay—"

"Solo." Dad stands behind me. "I need to talk to you."

"All right," Mom replies. Her squint transforms into a concerned look. "Alexia, go on upstairs. Dinner will be ready in an hour."

I nod, even though it feels too hard to do. Mom passes me and I make way to my room. It's quiet upstairs…unusually quiet. There's no Nia watching her favorite reality shows, and no Niles trolling her for loving said reality shows. There's no Indy either. None of his wildin' meeting me on the stairs. No barking. I peer out the window overlooking the backyard. The pool is clean and still. The grass is unbothered, and no one's swinging on the hammock. So, that means one thing…

I park my feet in front of the door at the end of the upstairs hall and give three strong knocks. "Nia! Is Indy in there?" By the sound of it, not only is Indy behind the door, but so are Timothy Mouse and a magic flying elephant named Dumbo too. Hella noise breaks loose.

"Hang on!" she yells. Nia opens the door, but only enough for me to see the center of her face.

"Open the door!"

"It's open, nerd."

She knows good and damn well this ain't the definition of open. Mom would say the door is cracked. I push so Indy can run out.

"Will you stop?" Nia shouts.

"No!"

"Alexia, get back!" Nia tries her best to close the door, but she's always been weaker than me. One more shove and the door swings back. Nia stumbles and Indy—my furry grey schnauzer—leaps into my arms.

"We'll march! We'll fight! Give back our civil rights!"

That chant. Its cadence gives me goose bumps. The words I spoke only forty minutes ago are running through Nia's room. "Where is that coming from?"

Niles's fingers frantically slam against the keyboard, but he's too late. My face is on his monitor's screen. I look angry, protective, and unafraid—just for that moment. Comments roll up the left side of the screen from strangers all over the world.

"The window won't close!" Niles says.

My mouth goes dry. I'm mortified.

Nia sighs in disappointment, which is nothing new for her; Big Mama always said Nia was born in a bad mood. Who would've thought it'd last nineteen years?

"Just leave it alone, Niles." Nia swats the air. "We shouldn't be embarrassed. We weren't the ones betraying Dad."

She turns to me and gives a curt smile. If I could rearrange her face without my parents knowing, I'd do it right now. I don't need two strikes today, so I meditate on the thought and tell her, "Keep my dog out of your room!"

Settling for those words is hard. There's so much I want to say to my brother and sister. I want them to know that when I fight for

Variens, I'm fighting for myself too. I want to know if love is lost because I am who I am. I want them to know hate hurts.

Except, what I want is very different from what I need. So, I'll continue digging deep graves for these feelings because they can never come out.

CHAPTER THREE

THE KIDS AREN'T ALL RIGHT

THE FIRST THING I see in my room is a picture of Sarai and me. We took it last summer in Atlanta, while scouting Spelman College. We stayed up all night before the tour because we were so excited and got a grip of complaints because of the noise. Mom kept trying to convince us we had allergies—so we'd take Benadryl—which only made us laugh more.

I wish things were still that simple. I wish life was still that light.

I put Indy down and shut the blinds. Weight slips off my shoulders and my hands feel untied. Like a faucet gently turned, my eyes begin to water. I see Sarai's face when the teardrops roll down my cheeks. I see her happy, this beautiful Black girl with smooth, deep brown skin, long lashes, a beauty mark right by her mouth, and the best smile around. I see her changing, her skin dulling and bruising in purples and greens. I see her optimism drained. I see her fears come alive. I see her torn from my hands in the corner of this room.

My knees fold and I crawl into my bed. I'm free in this space to be who I am, to feel how I want to feel, but for some reason, I feel wrong for it. Like I played a part in Sarai's arrest. I wasn't on her side. I played submissive. That's what I do when I work in my dad's office: I empower the oppressor, then blast them for oppressing. And really, that's the worst kind of person to be.

My cries evolve into a sob, which calls Indy to me. He paws at my hands as they cover my face. I squeeze him closer, and he curls his body beside my chest. My teary eyes roam the room and land on the posters of my favorite singers covering the walls. If only SZA could materialize in my room like a fairy godmother and take this pain away. I wish Olivia Rodrigo could turn my cells normal with the strum of some kind of magical guitar.

Four taps hit my door. There's a pause, then two more taps. It's Niles, the only sibling that uses the Morse code Dad taught us to communicate. It's cute, but I'm not in the mood to talk or signal anything. "No!" I groan into my pillow. "Go away!"

The door clicks open, and my brother's head pops in. I chuck a pillow at him. "Still mad, huh? I'm sorry." His voice nears. "I didn't mean for you to see that...I didn't even know that went down today until right before you came home."

"Niles."

"I saw you all over my feed, I had to click."

"Niles, stop!"

He's sitting on the edge of my bed, waiting for me to give him all the answers he wants. "I..." He shakes his head, eyes hesitating, his mouth tucked. "You used to talk to—"

"I know," I whisper as I sit up. The space between us feels bigger than ever before. Biology says Niles is Nia's twin. I've always thought that made him more Nia's brother than mine, but we've always been more compatible in a way. Nia can be too tough for Niles sometimes.

Niles's hands smooth over the curve of his faded hair. "What happened...with Sarai...I wish it didn't. You don't have to say it, but I know it's eating you up." Niles looks right into me, his bronze eyes drawing a rope to my browns. "She didn't do it, did she?"

I'm numb for a minute. No one in our family has talked about what happened with me. No one has been kind enough. No one has really seen me. I break down like an old dam. "It doesn't make sense."

My brother scoots closer and hugs me.

"She's a Varien." Nia leans against the door frame.

"What?" I shudder and break apart from Niles.

Graceful as a crane, Nia walks into my room. The light from my white salt lamp glows against her sweet face—a face Mom says doesn't always align with what's inside. "So, we're living in la-la land now?" she starts. "People can crush things like cars with the flick of a wrist, and we're supposed to be open to that?"

Nia has what western society would deem the better end of the features between us Jacobs girls. A slim nose. Full lips with a cupid's bow bent into her top lip. Mine just rounds out like the Arc de Triomphe. Her curls bounce softer, and mine are coiled like springs. Where I have one dimple, she brags two. She's curvy in the right places, with hips and all. I don't have much of a hump or bump anywhere. Some say I win when it comes to the eyes but there's something about Nia's. They look like autumn, brown with red speckles.

I've always wanted to look and be like my sister, but if we ever pull a *Freaky Friday* and switch bodies, I'd rewire her heart to her brain.

"Alexia?" Nia takes a seat on the other side of me.

I stare at my walls. I look at the albums I have laid beside my record player—Tyler, the Creator's *Igor* and Phoebe Bridgers. If only Tyler were an alchemist responsible for creating a vanishing tincture. If only Phoebe Bridgers could materialize in the corner of my room and use her haunting notes to mute my sister.

Nia doesn't quit. She purses her lips together and looks to Niles for support. "We know you're hurting, but the way you're acting is hurting us even more."

"Nia, c'mon," Niles tells her.

"This attitude you have is not it, Alexia."

"I'm not hurting anyone, Nia."

"Then why does Dad look like a fool? If he can't control his daughter, how can he lead his state? Mom's patients only want to talk about you! Niles and I can't make it through the day without being harassed and followed!"

I bristle. "Your issue should be with the people who can't control themselves."

"It is!"

"Not me!"

Nia's neck looks longer than ever and her nostrils flare. "*You* are one of those people who can't control themselves." She presses a few buttons on her phone and the sound of chanting voices plays. My raised fist and fierce face are on her screen.

Niles snatches Nia's phone. "You need to chill. Get out!"

"See, that's the problem," Nia tells him. "Everyone is on eggshells because of Sarai, but I'm gonna speak up! This is ruining our family." My two siblings argue over me. One is locked in her point of view and the other is trying to shield me from the sharp sword Nia calls a tongue.

"STOP!" I cover my ears, then roll off my bed. They can keep my room for all I care if they don't follow.

"Baby girl? What's going on?"

I stop in the hallway. "Mom…I don't know. Nia is in a mood."

Mom clicks her tongue from the bottom floor. "So, nothing then." She smiles. "Can you come down for a minute?"

"Yeah…I can." I do my best to be sweet, since Mom is nothing less. But it's that sweetness amid a house at odds that makes me nervous to follow her. I don't know what to expect: a great lecture, emancipation papers, tickets, and admission to some random boarding school in Switzerland. It could be anything.

Indy rushes to trot down the wooden stairs with me. He looks up as he moves with his ears perked, almost reassuring me I'm never alone.

CHAPTER FOUR

FATHER OF MINE

"ARE NILES AND NIA coming down?" I ask Mom over a plate of baked ziti. It's a little weird to have dinner—just the three of us.

Mom scoots her chair in. "They'll come eat after we're done talking."

I don't know what to say, but I know I'm not hungry. I drop my fork down.

Mom looks pained. She faces Dad, who frowns, then she closes her eyes. "Baby, you've got to eat."

"…I'm not hungry."

"That's what you said yesterday…and the day before that. Just eat a little," Mom says.

A little. I choose to be petty and stick one tube-shaped pasta noodle in my mouth.

"Eat some more," Dad commands. He's in his lil' king chair across the table, darting his impatient eyes at me like he's Ramesses the Great.

"It makes me nauseous. I can't."

Dad snaps, "Don't talk. Eat!"

"Eddie," Mom warns. She puts her hands together like she's praying. "Okay, baby girl…listen, you've been going through a lot of pain—pain that no sixteen-year-old should be dealing with. I knew you'd be hurt after that night. Your daddy understood this too, but I don't think we've realized how deep that cut you."

Mom's puffy red eyes water. "I thought I knew you inside and out, but your behavior tells me I don't. And um…I hate it because I don't have an answer for you. I don't know how to save you like I'm supposed to."

"That's because you can't," Dad says.

Mom shakes her head.

"I'm just saying…this is not one of those situations. You know?" I can pretty much guarantee that when Dad says, "You know?" in a conversation, he's about to steamroll everyone and own it. "Alexia has to face reality."

I huff. "Can I go back to my room now?"

"No," Dad answers.

"Mom?"

"I'm sorry, baby. Not yet."

"Well, I don't know what y'all want from me."

"Getting rid of that attitude would be the first thing," Mom claps back, a far from seamless jump from sugar to spice. "Your dad says things in a rough way, but the message he's trying to give you is right. Grieving is okay. It's a natural cycle we all go through. What's not okay is you making a lifestyle out of it. You're losing yourself."

Like a good girl, I fight the impulse to rip my ears off and continue listening.

"You can't change who people are. You can't erase things they've done."

"You *can* when they didn't do them."

Dad shakes his head and leaves the table. "This isn't gonna work."

"No, Eddie. It's fine. We just need to be patient with one another."

"Mom, it's all right. We can talk about this later."

"We're talking about this now," Mom affirms.

Dad comes back toward the table. A six-foot-three, massive, tense man in Mom's Zen and bright kitchen. He doesn't fit in this house either.

He slams a leather folder in front of my plate.

"What is this?" I ask him, hoping it's not a one-way ticket to a girls' home in Switzerland. Mom and Dad don't answer. All they do is wait for my next step. I tuck my curly mass of hair behind my ears and breathe. Indy hikes himself up on his hind legs and rests his hands on the table for a good look.

I flip the folder open, and there's no plane ticket or school booklet. All I see is what I've been searching for:

> NAME: SARAI BAKER
>
> AGE: 16
>
> SEX: FEMALE
>
> RACE: AFRICAN-AMERICAN
>
> SPECIES: VARIEN
>
> ABILITY: INTANGIBILITY
>
> PRISON: MERCY BAY PENITENTIARY
>
> CRIME: MURDER
>
> SENTENCE: DEATH

Sarai, my best friend...she's alive. I stare at the paper as my eyes gloss with tears. "How long have you known this?"

"Since the drive home today," Dad responds. "One of my connects at Mercy sent her information."

"Why? Why now after all this time? I've searched for her information for months. You knew that and you could've easily done—"

Dad signals for me to calm down. "Does it matter what I could've done? I did this for you now. I thought it would be good for you to know everything: where she is, how she's doing, what Mercy Bay is like."

My stomach turns. "I just wanted to know she's alive right now. I don't want to read some Normal's biased report on her."

"You don't have to. She's going to tell you herself."

"What?"

"We want you to go see her," Mom adds.

I'm speechless.

"We'll take the day off from everything tomorrow and leave for Mercy Bay in the morning," Dad explains.

I don't know what's gotten into my parents—if I can even call them that. I could be speaking to their tethered.

Mom clasps my hand. Even under the dim light, in all her worry, she's still the most beautiful woman—Nefertiti, if she ever lived today. "Your father felt like this would heal some wounds for you. He loves you…we all do."

Dad nods and bends down. Still in his work clothes, with his keys jingling in his pocket, he kisses my forehead. The big ol' bear—who growled at me in the streets when I challenged him in front of the people he leads. Who saved me from getting gassed as I betrayed his cause. He told those Black Coats to stand down.

And now within hours, he's found my best friend.

If the waters weren't murky before…

"Thank you, Dad."

"You're welcome, baby girl." He doesn't say much more as he retires up the stairs, and he doesn't need to.

Mom gives my hand a squeeze. "Tea sounds good right about now. A nice pot of lemonade tea."

For the first time in a while, I smile back at her and mean it.

Mom heads to the stove and sighs. "I guess I better feed your brother and sister now."

I swallow hard. I've battled Dad, but I've forgotten about Nia.

"Oh, don't worry about your sister," Mom says as she takes a pill from a bottle, cracks it open, and pours it into a teacup. "I've got some holy basil for her mean ass." She winks at me, and I laugh.

I didn't get the slice of sweet potato pie I wanted today. But right here, in the kitchen, I got the kind of soul food I needed.

CHAPTER FIVE

By the Coast

MARLON BRANDO IS ON my iPad screen—and he is everything. The most handsome. The most talented. He had all the essentials and was so perfect at crafting his image and playing different people, I wonder if he did it because he needed to.

I could be like him: a chameleon. I could sell people a dream and be who they want me to be. I don't know why I won't.

"Brando, my boy!" Dad bellows. He's somehow feeding himself wasabi almonds while watching my iPad and driving. Not advisable, being that the highway we're on meets the edge of the ocean. "What's that? That movie *Stella*?"

I roll my eyes. "*A Streetcar Named Desire*?"

"Yeah, that's it."

"Yes."

"Stella! Hey, Stella!" Dad mocks. He laughs at himself. "Dude was on another level, every actor after him was his son."

I slip my ear buds back in, but Dad starts talking again. "Why're you watching that? Ain't that movie a little old for you?"

"Just 'cause."

"Ain't no 'just cause' with you. You do everything with intention." He smiles matter-of-factly, like after yesterday, I should know that.

"It's for the play I'm trying out for. I didn't get the lead in *Our Town* last time, so I figure watching the movie and all other iterations would give me an upper hand this time."

"Knew it."

I squint the sun out of my eyes. For a quick moment, it peeks beyond the endless blanket of clouds in the sky, making Monterey seem like the last place to hold hurt, pain, and slums. It's hard to believe so much of that is here. It's hidden well.

Dad is rapping along to the music playing. You'd think he'd have the blood pressure of a ten-year-old. His attitude is lighter today, less angry, more playful. Maybe he isn't mad anymore. Maybe he understands me. "Did you put Indy in the house?" he asks mid-bar.

"I didn't think I could 'cause that's not 'our place.'"

"It's not, but Ren loves dogs. She's got fifty-leven dogs herself. Pretty sure she'd be cool if he stayed in."

"Well," I say. "It's not like she doesn't have a whole doggie cabana outside."

Dad laughs. "Man, he's gonna have a silk robe on when we get back."

"For real, I think I saw a few dog fits in her guest closet." We share a giggle. It's been too long since the last time we enjoyed each other. I've missed it.

I roll the window down and let the wind wrap around my two-strand twists. The smell of sand and the faint taste of saltwater makes me happy. I wonder if Sarai gets to feel the same breeze. I wonder if they allow her outside.

Should I ask her when we get there? Nah, I think. Even when I pose myself to finish the rest of *Streetcar*, I keep thinking. I haven't seen Sarai in so long. Our friendship has never lived on these terms—except for one night—so I don't know what that'll mean for the two of us going forward.

Dad turns onto a gritty, sandy road. "You nervous?"

"I don't know. I feel weird, I guess."

"…About?"

"About…being here."

The road beneath us roughens. Dad frowns as we bounce in our seats, then glances at the GPS app on his phone. "Well, no one is happy to be here."

Sand blows and dances across the dunes, and just as soon as I start to feel like we're in the middle of nowhere, somewhere appears. "Mercy Bay California State Prison," in iron letters, is fused to two great white boulders. I gape at the huge steel wall beyond the sign. Dozens of Black Coats monitoring and patrolling the area make it clear that nobody assigned to Mercy Bay gets out. The Black Coats stop Dad when he pulls up to their security station. Dressed in all black with breasted armor, they look his car over and request his ID for verification.

"Fingerprint, ma'am," the Black Coat on my right side requests. He's holding a portable scanning device in his right hand.

Breathe. Breathe. My chest begins to surge heat and sting, and within seconds it could travel to my hands to give me away. I try to find his eyes but fail to see anything behind his tinted glasses. "Um…I'm with my dad, why do you—?"

"We try to keep record of everyone who enters, ma'am. Some people are unregistered Variens passing as Normals. We just want to keep things safe."

"Oh." *Shit.* "Well, I can—"

"My daughter doesn't need all that, she's good to go."

"Certainly, sir, as soon as we can clear her scan as normal."

"What's your name, man?" Dad bows his head to see the Black Coat better.

"Corporal!" Another Black Coat comes from her station with Dad's ID. "Stand down!" With her nose turned up, she eyes the corporal as he obeys and walks on. "We apologize for the offense, Senator. He's a transplant."

Dad takes his ID from the female Black Coat. "Thank you. You'll catch him up to speed, right?"

"Yes, sir."

"Good." Dad rolls up his window, and the great massive wall ahead of us rolls open. It creaks as it moves, and rust falls from its top. *Just breathe.* Although the threat of being found out is gone, my anxiety has me fooled, and now I'm not so sure this is the right place to be me.

"You all right?"

"Mmmhmm."

"Doesn't seem like it."

"The Black Coats just scare me…they have too much power."

"Hmm…," Dad says under his breath. He maneuvers the car into a parking space with the palm of his hand. I hear him suck his teeth as I stare out at the Varien slums where a mass of women, men, and children walk the streets—shopping the markets and intersecting. His calm gaze hones in on me. "You didn't seem to feel like this yesterday."

I've never seen Variens live. I've only seen them fight or cry. I've only witnessed their greatness deteriorate as rot gas ate their nervous systems till their noses bleed black. But seeing them live through that is something else.

As I trail behind my dad—who walks through the slum like a king—I see Variens doing things Normals do. Kids play tag and jump rope. Families grill fish, crab, and oysters outside their shanties. Merchants sell homemade goods, upcycled jewelry and clothing. Drums and bluesy guitars are being played by a street band. Variens are still here, a little greyed in the skin, dim in the eyes and contained, but still here.

No one looks at Dad as we head to the ferry port between a trio of Black Coats. At first, I wonder if anyone knows who he is, but as we journey farther through the slums, it's obvious they know exactly who he is.

"Sorry, Senator," a Varien passerby says as he stumbles in my dad's way. His sandals flick sand onto Dad's slacks.

Dad nods indifferently. "You're fine," he tells the young man. The Black Coats hurry him out of the way. A white glare circles his body as the clouds cast away from the sun. The young man keeps his stare to the paved sand as he maneuvers around us. When his eyes pivot to me, he bows his head.

I turn away, and immediately make myself interested in watching the fishmonger on the other side of the street. Seconds go by, and before I can think it through, I stare over my shoulder.

He's still there—several strides behind, talking to another Varien and pointing at...me.

I try to swallow the knot I feel in my throat and reach out for Dad's arm. Dad bends a bit and brings his ear closer.

"Is there a bathroom at the ferry port?" I ask him.

"Yeah, there is." He wraps an arm around me and keeps me close. For the rest of the trek through Mercy Bay's slum, I try to blend in—staying linked to Dad, keeping my gaze down—away from the chances of being met.

CHAPTER SIX

HIDE AND SEEK

"...FOUR, FIVE, SIX," I count in the mirror. Six freckles on my right cheek to match the usual five on my left. "Okay, all right." I exhale, then take to my cheek with a wet paper towel. There's nothing crazy on my face. No discoloration and—thank you, Jesus—no shooting stars in my skin. Everything looks all good.

"What the hell was he staring at then?" I say under my breath. Explanations bloom in my head as I gaze at the slow-draining sink below.

Maybe he saw the viral video? Like everyone else does when they can't figure something out, I turn to my phone. Google is my friend, and maybe it'll have something for me. My thumbs can't flesh out the question fast enough:

Can Variens detect other Variens?

I press enter and the search results begin to load. Except, the loading is slow in this raggedy, old shiplap bathroom.

The ocean's mighty sound enters the bathroom as another person walks in. A woman with a shit ton of stuff on her backpack—camping or hiking gear, I can't really tell. I'm surprised she was able to get any of that through security.

She grins at me. "Good morning."

I throw a quick smile in the name of manners and get back to waiting on my phone.

"It's nice today, isn't it?" the woman adds.

"Mmhmm."

"Ain't much helping us enjoy it, though." She laughs as she checks stalls. "What a location!"

My screen queues up the search results. I scour the list and scroll down:

How To Detect a Varien With DNA

The California Screen Bill: How Senator Jacobs Is Changing Early Varien Detection

Use Thermal Imaging for Varien Detection

No. No. No.

Study: What Variens See When They See One Another

Yes! I bite my bottom lip and click the link. To my luck, it's loading faster this time.

"Jesus, is every stall dirty?" I hear the woman say from behind me, and before I'm aware of anything, her gargantuan backpack jerks me from behind. I lose footing and my phone slips from my hand into the tiny pool of the sink.

"Fuck!" I yelp before my mouth drops at the sight of it.

"I'm sorry." The clumsy woman edges around me. "What's wrong?" She glances at the horror on my face, then the sink. "Oh, your phone took a dive!"

"Yeah! Because of you!" I snatch it from the sink and wipe it with my shirt.

The woman catches herself and tries again. "I should've been paying attention. I forget how to maneuver with all this junk on me sometimes. I'm so sorry."

"You know what? It's all right...I should've moved out the way." Lord knows I have an attitude, so I tag a forced smile on to my reply. The woman isn't quick to say anything back. In fact, she isn't quick to move or go about doing whatever she plans on doing. All she does is stare.

"What?"

She shakes her head. "Nothing." The bangles around her wrists jingle as she glides her hands over the shaved sides of her head. "I just feel so terrible about what I did to you. These phones are so expensive nowadays."

"It's okay, I'll just put it in rice."

"No. No. That phone's probably done for…" The woman rummages through her pockets. "I'd give you my number if I had a phone myself…maybe—" Fast and focused, she hurls her backpack onto the sink, in search of who knows what. "Let's see, I don't have any cash to hand you for the accident. But I've got something even better."

"Honestly…I have phone insurance—"

"Ah! Here we go!"

The thing in her hand—"something even better"—is gold. She holds it in her palm as if it's a living being. "You like lockets? That's 18 karats right there."

"Oh, I can't take that."

"And why not?"

"You're a stranger, duh."

"I'm Greta," she introduces herself, like the conversation isn't beyond that at this point.

"Oh my gosh this is so weird. Look, even knowing your name—"

"Do you like stars?"

"I don't feel comfortable receiving something this expensive and sparkly from someone that knocked me over in the girls' restroom."

Finally, Greta gives it a rest. "Okay…"

I ready myself to walk out the bathroom, but Greta blocks me.

"Please, just listen. I don't expect you to take anything. But where I'm from, we take responsibility for our mistakes, and we pay our debts. I'm a shop owner. I sell antiques. So giving you this is not a loss. It's not weird. You or your parents worked very hard for that phone and in a couple of seconds that literally went down the drain. Now, I'm going to leave this locket right here on the sink. Take it or leave it. It's your choice," she says, backing out of the bathroom slowly. "And should you leave the locket, bear in mind it's probably worth $1,500. Your choice, though…"

"Ummm."

Greta, this tiny, odd bohemian woman, who sounds like wind chimes when she moves, teeters toward the exit and bows her head. "I hope the rest of your day is much better than this."

The sunlight from the cracked door bakes what little I can see of her honey brown skin. The edges of her shine white like a halo. In a matter of seconds, she's gone and I'm alone again.

Monterey's winds beat against the bathroom's paneled windows and the clamor of greedy seagulls quiets. I stand over the golden locket, buzzed by anxiety and something else I don't know how to define. *Leave it. Leave it. Leave it.*

I bounce my heel off the floor like a maniac. "Leave it!" I tell myself as I pull the door handle. And just as it flings open—for me to hurry out of it—I race back to the sink, grab the oval 18-karat locket, and shove it into my back pocket.

CHAPTER SEVEN

NADIR

THE FERRY IS WHERE I want to be and where I don't. It's also where Dad has decided to talk about his business casual sock collection ad nauseum. "The best thing anyone can do for themselves is line dry their socks. They never get lost that way. You can't lose," I hear him say before breaking into a ridiculous laugh. And the Black Coats are laughing too, for the sake of keeping their jobs.

"You put up with this guy? How do you do it," one of them jokes.

"I don't," I fake chuckle. I'm sarcasm incarnate.

I lean my head against the window and watch the ocean's waves crash into bubbles the ferry leaves behind. I wish I would've written some things to say to Sarai. Things I've wanted to tell her since she's been gone—about the world, school, and me. So much has happened, and I don't think we'll have much time to share anything with each other. Maybe I should stick to the big stuff and say: "Sarai, I'm one of you too…"

I cover my face. I don't think Mercy Bay is the right place for that kind of secret. I don't think it'd be the right location for her to tell me the truth either.

"We have a 980 here, Sergeant." A Black Coat's walkie-talkie buzzes. Everyone goes quiet. "The facilities are on lockdown, over."

"Lockdown, what's going on?" Dad asks.

"Not sure, Senator. We'll port at the security belt first. We're closer to the prison at this point than we are to the slum."

"Is it safe, Dad? Maybe we should wait here first. Shouldn't we stay away?"

"I hear you, Miss Jacobs. In these scenarios, the safest place to be is the security belt."

"Then that's where we'll go," Dad agrees. He puts on a brave face—the one he wears every day. Dad has seen a lot in his life, and sometimes, I don't know if there's anything he's afraid of. But being next to him when he's told danger is near means seeing his survival instincts in action. It's all in his eyes. The way he blinks. The way he scans the boat then stares off into space. Dad is working up plans I can't even imagine.

He grabs my wrist. "You remember the code?" The tone in his voice is urgent.

"Y-y-yes. Do I need to use it?"

"Just be ready…like I've always taught you."

"What does 980 mean?"

"…Just be ready, Alexia."

The air in the ferry falls stale. Each Black Coat holds their firearm against their chest. I hear the hum of the ferry's motor; we're moving faster than we were before the emergency alert—like we're running away from something.

The boat cuts through the misty fog like a knife. It's thickening as we glide closer to the port, and every now and then I remind myself we're sailing on water and not the sky.

Black Coats surround us as we walk to the security belt. No one would be able to spot us easily if they were hoping to—not within this human shield. The sounds of their heavy marching boots frazzle me.

The security belt is a dry grey place engulfed in tall security gates and barbed wire. Artificial white light illuminates the halls inside. By the looks of it, not many people are present. The building is cold, full of echoes, and smells like rubbing alcohol.

"Have a seat, Senator," a young Black Coat tells Dad.

Another Black Coat enters the room and locks the door behind him. The rest line up against the walls and salute him. He must be their superior. "Coffee?" he asks. "Hot chocolate?"

Dad pulls a chair for me. "Both, please."

The head Black Coat nods at another to fix the cups.

"How long will we have to be here?" Dad checks.

The head Black Coat takes a seat in the chair across the conference table. He's older than the rest, a lot more confident. "When we no longer deem the threat imminent."

"And what exactly is the threat?"

"Is it Varien related?" I pop in.

Dad frowns.

"Yes. As is everything on this end of the bay." The head Black Coat folds his hands. "I believe you were visiting the premises to meet with an inmate?"

"Correct," Dad says. "Sarai Baker."

I lean forward. "Did she do something?"

The Black Coat holding our drinks serves us. I push the hot chocolate aside. No amount of sweetness can overpower the bitterness of the present.

"She escaped."

I shake my head in disbelief. *What?*

Dad scoffs. "We're talking about a sixteen-year-old escaping a maximum-security prison in the middle of the bay. That's out of her capacity."

"Out of hers, yes," the head Black Coat agrees. "She didn't do this alone."

"This is crazy. Dad…"

"Wait a minute now." Dad holds up his hands. "Someone was with her?"

"In a matter of speaking—"

"With all due respect, I don't need the semantics right now. I want you to lay the facts out like you're supposed to. My daughter is hanging on to everything you say, which is turning out to be a bunch of nothing because you keep beating around the bush. This is a big deal to her. It's a big deal to me too." Dad looks my way and sighs. "So, Captain…tell us everything you know."

The captain shrinks. I pray for him to speak the plain truth, then I pray for the truth to have some sort of hope attached to it. "My apologies, Senator. There's a lot of odd pieces here…I'm trying to make sure I communicate a clear picture. You see, the assailants aren't fellow inmates or prison personnel. We believe them to be outsiders—Variens, which may have something to do with how they infiltrated the facility. The inmate was held in solitary confinement. She's been there the entire time in a padded cell. Her powers have been muted through the water supply—like all the slum residents—she's also been treated with an injected serum. The door to her cell is triple-layered industrial steel. It'd take a lot to try and break her out, but when backup arrived at the scene, the door was pulled right out of the wall."

Dad's eyebrows knit together. "What about security? Was anyone stationed in her corridor?"

"Yes, Senator. Two men. They were the only witnesses."

"Do they recall anything?"

"Unfortunately, one is unavailable for questioning. He's suffered a brutal attack and is in critical condition."

Dad wipes the sweat glossing his forehead. "And the other?"

"Well it seems the Variens spared him. They claimed they wanted him well enough to share a message."

"What kind of message?"

"It's quite cryptic, but the sergeant said the inmate is valuable… for some type of vessel or thing he called 'Nadir.'"

"He?"

"One of the men. The sergeant described him as a Varien with scarring from his face to his chest. Said he wore a duster and it looked like he had a pair of wings underneath. He spotted them as the assailants got away." The Black Coat holds a clear baggie with one yellow gold feather in it.

"And this message…Nadir. I'm not familiar with that, have you spoken to linguistics to find out what that means?"

"We have, Senator, but we didn't have to."

"No?"

"The winged man told the sergeant himself. He said it means our end is near."

CHAPTER EIGHT

GLASS HOUSES

REN OLEYNIK MUST SPEND most of her time alone. Well…I don't know that for sure, it's just a judgment based on the layout of her house. For instance, aside from the weird taxidermized dogs in the living room, it has one master bedroom and three other rooms—one that's completely dedicated to dog furniture, a guest room, and a study. Out of all the cold rooms with glass walls that overlook the beach, Ren's study is the only one concealed. It's the only one filled with books from ceiling to floor, so, it's the only one I really take to after we make it back from Mercy Bay.

Nadir. I haven't stopped trying to find what it means. I haven't stopped reading through tons of books or websites to learn what it is. Nadir is a lot of things. It's a medical term, and also a direction in astronomy. There are hundreds of lingual interpretations of it. It even serves as a noun to describe the lowest point. Rock bottom. I've hit that today.

Sarai is gone again. Not like she was before—gone, but in places I'm familiar with, places I have connections to. Searching for her now feels like chasing a ghost. I let her down.

My feet ache and I finally listen to their plea to sit. I've been reading standing up, too anxious to relax. The currents under my skin have been aggravated. They're desperate to come out.

I've managed to keep them inside by thinking of calmer things in between fits of crying. Petting Indy helps for brief moments. Random dog videos do too. But the tears always return. I'm scared I'm starting to lose my grip.

Indy hops in my lap and I can't help but sob. He's so sweet—this little empath that wants to absorb my sadness. I hug him then release as soon as I notice the warmth building in my stomach. *Take it easy*, I tell myself.

The thought connects me to the brandy on Ren's liquor cart. I've never drank before, but I like the idea of something filling me and my voids. That's what liquor looks like it does to people on TV—except for the ones on Nia's reality shows…they're overboard—so I'll just have a little.

I sulk over to the cart and pour the brandy into a small glass cup. "This is why Ren is alone," I breathe and take in the painted portraits before me: beautiful oil paintings…of her dogs in renaissance clothes. I snicker and hold my face, then take the brandy down the hatch. It burns and I very much want to throw it back up. What a dumb choice.

I stumble to Ren's worktable and see Dad's phone. He was looking for it before he left to grab dinner for us. A nervous pang hits my stomach. *I hope he doesn't need it. I hope he comes back.* The winged Varien is out there somewhere, doing God knows what to Sarai and planning for something to hit us. "*Our end is near*" plays in my head and then I remember what Dad told me before he left.

"*If there's an emergency, hit the panic button immediately. It'll summon the Black Coats and the police. They're patrolling the area and will be here within three minutes.*" I run my fingers over the red button lodged in the wooden table. The concept of it takes some of the edge off…or maybe that's the brandy kicking in.

If only Sarai had had a panic button. If only anyone cared to protect her.

My eyes begin to burn, and I notice a small blinking light out the corner of my eye. It's a device just like the corporal had today, the fingerprint one. Black and boxy, it has a flat screen on its top and a port for users to place their thumb inside. I pick it up and press a finger over the small blinking light.

The screen brightens and a robotic voice tells me what to do. "Please insert your thumb." An arrow on the screen points at the device's port. I know what I am, there's no denying it. Stars shoot from my skin for crying out loud, but sometimes I do wonder if these things work. How can they tell so much with the print of a thumb?

I insert mine and immediately regret it. The device locks my thumb in and starts whirring. "*One moment,*" the robot voice says.

"Oh my gosh, no!"

Indy runs to my side. His ears perk up and he growls.

I try pushing the device off and fail. My thumb is locked in.

"*One moment.*"

"Stop. Stop. Stop!" This time I try wiggling my finger.

"*Varien scanned.*" The screen shows a thermal print of my finger. All red.

My heart shatters, and I cry. I didn't need this confirmation from anyone or anything. The device releases my thumb and I bend to the ground. Indy licks the hot tears off my cheek then perks up at the sound of keys at the front door.

"Alexia!"

Shoot. I scamper. "Dad?"

"I'm back! Come eat!"

"Okay…I'll be down in a minute!" I put the fingerprinting device back on Ren's worktable, next to Dad's phone. "You should probably turn it off, Alexia," I scold myself and press the light on the scanner's corner. When the screen fades back to black, I run to meet Dad downstairs.

"Stop running!" Dad lectures. "There's too much glass in here. Ren was nice enough to let us stay here for the night. I don't think she'll stay nice if we break everything."

"Done." I circle around him. "What'd you get?"

"Your favorite: sushi. I want to make sure you eat something tonight."

"Thanks." I sniffle, and Dad puts his hand on my shoulder, then my face.

"You've been crying?" he asks.

"Yeah."

"I'm sorry, baby girl. I'm so sorry." He hugs me and I feel better than I did without him.

"Have you seen my phone?" He breaks away and pats himself down. "I swore I had it after we got back from Mercy Bay."

"Yeah, you left it in Ren's study with the renaissance dogs." I laugh.

"Ain't that a trip?" Dad starts up the iron stairs. "Set the table for me, will you?"

"Uh-huh."

I forage through the brown paper bag for the to-go boxes, then sneak a couple edamame to eat. Indy gruffs; he'd eat everything I eat if he could. "No. Edamame isn't for schnauzers," I remind him. He hops high to snatch the food from my hand, but I pop it in my mouth before he can.

Dad's heavy feet slow into the kitchen. "Alexia," he says. His voice is low.

I stop chewing. "What?"

"What were you doing upstairs?"

"I rested, pretty much. Packed my bag for tomorrow too."

"No, in the study. What were you doing?"

The edamame I swallow goes down like a shard of glass. "I-I-I had some of Ren's brandy. But just a sip—"

"Oh God, I'm not talking about the brandy!" He raises up the device I wrestled with ten minutes ago. "*Varien scanned,*" it says again.

Damn, I thought I turned it off.

That's my thumb on the screen. My thumb—and not just that, but my name and my date of birth. Two things I hadn't noticed before.

Dad's jaw trembles. He closes his eyes, and the only tear I've ever seen him shed rolls down his brown cheek.

I've broken his heart.

And now…I can't breathe.

CHAPTER NINE

Unarmored

Sᴇᴄᴏɴᴅs ᴄʀᴀᴡʟ ᴀs ᴍʏ father and I stand without speaking. "When did this happen?" he asks me, life inside him dying slowly.

"Don't tell the Coats, please! Please don't tell anyone!"

"When did this happen?" he repeats.

"I'll never leave the house, Dad. No one will know…"

"Alexia, just tell me when—"

"Please listen to me!"

"WHEN DID THIS HAPPEN?"

"Three months ago…I think…I'm sorry…" I cry and cry. I plead and plead. I'm deflated of everything but tears and panic.

"Three months! Why didn't you tell me?"

"Because…because…" I'm completely losing it. It's one thing for me to cry, but to physically react means trouble. This is how the outbursts begin: the lump in my throat, the tingling ears, and hot rushes. I want to pace myself and control my nerves. If I lock those things down, maybe the heat won't reach my hands.

"Why?"

"I-I-I was scared."

"You didn't trust me…"

My nature pulls me to reassure him. That's what I've done all my life whenever I've hurt him. Except, this time, I have nothing to offer but my truth.

He waits for the sugar coating. And I—after months and years of hearing what people like me don't deserve—draw my line in the sand. "I didn't."

Suddenly, my nerves turn cool. Everything frazzled and hot in me simmers. Dad's breathing speeds and he storms out of the kitchen. He heads to the patio—away from me and closer to the ocean. I leave him there even though it hurts. *He needs time*, I think. *Nothing will ever be the same.* I've had my time to accept this. Dad hasn't.

I wipe my face with the back of my wrist, then remember the tissues I usually keep in my back pocket. When I go to reach for them, my fingers find something I don't immediately recognize. The locket. I forgot all about it—thanks to everything that's happened.

The flat oval-shaped gold is thick and shiny. It's a good size, could probably fit some pictures in it. Yet, when I open it, someone's beaten me to the punch. A full moon is painted on the left of the locket, while the right shows off some type of constellation. *Not my style,* I tell myself and shove the antique back in my pocket.

Dad is pacing the patio. He holds his head between his hands, faces the sky for a bit, and breathes like he could will the day away. I know exactly how he feels.

I choose not to stay away from him too long. "Dad?" I call, timidly. The salty breeze whips my twisted hair back as I walk closer.

Dad sits on the patio step and pats the area beside him. An invitation, one I've craved. The steps I take make me feel seven years old again—when losing Dad's respect meant the end of my world.

I sit. Wait for him. *When he's ready, he'll speak*, my mind says.

We watch the sun hide behind the clouds. We listen to the ocean talk.

"True power," Dad finally mumbles. "Your grandma always pushed me to strive for it." He combs through his facial hair with his fingers and contemplates. "She made me promise to do good by you all. And that's all I've ever wanted to do…just work my ass off so you could see privilege I never knew.

"And I thought I got there, to this place where my beautiful Black children want for nothing because they have everything. That really meant something to me." He fiddles with a stick and pokes it into the sand repeatedly. The ends of his mouth droop. "You do all you can as a parent…and you can't protect your own kids."

"I'm all right, Dad." When I reach out to him, he hides his face.

Dad leans forward. "I don't know what to do," he whispers. Little does he know, that's music to my ears. It's not the wall I feared he'd put up when he learned about my change, and it isn't the fence to hide me from society. It's a bridge.

I ease into my reply. "I don't know what to do either…but…I think that's because we're supposed to figure it out together."

"Not that simple." He leans back.

"I think it is."

Dad's brows arch as he second-guesses his retort. It probably consisted of telling me how naïve I am—thanks to all his hard work. "You're probably right." He holds his arms out for me, and I fall into them without a thought. "What a day…what a day…," he mumbles. Pain is laced in his voice. Stress is straining it. "I'll protect you from the world if I have to. Okay?"

"I know."

"I mean it…even death can't stop me from being your father."

"Dad…," I caution in a slight beg. I hate when he talks like this.

"No, listen. I love you. I'm your dad for all time. I need you to understand, Alexia. You need to hear it. Even when I'm gone, I'm still your dad. I just can't be here. But I'll spread my love on the wind," Dad delivers his thoughts to me, tears streaming down his strong face. "Remember the poem?"

The poem. A spur-of-the-moment poem Dad wrote while I was in Mom's womb when they didn't think I'd make it. He recites it to me in bits and pieces of moments—like during hugs.

I nod and wipe my eyes as he recites brief lines.

"And when you're in trouble…when the breeze of your mind blows down your last restraint, and pain comes flooding in, remember you have me, and I've always got you. No adversary is strong enough to break through. Not even time or distance. Remember you have me and I'll move a mountain. Remember you have me, and I'll spread my love on the wind."

We hold each other and watch the ocean's tide rise. I try to savor the moment until I can't. I think of all the days wasted in fear and fights. Days we'll never get back. Cursed times. They're gone and hopefully, they have nothing on what's to come—the progressive era Dad and I will create together. Our united front won't be a front, and I wonder how we'll impact the world. *You see, Alexia?* I say inside my head. *Things will get better.*

Then the doorbell rings.

CHAPTER TEN

CROSSROADS

"WHO IS IT?" I stand behind Dad as he peers through the peephole. He looks out the window when he doesn't see anyone.

"Someone's on the lawn." He squints.

"Ren's gardener?"

Dad shakes his head. "They're messin' around with something out there. Ren didn't say her gardener would be by. Stay here." He grabs at the doorknob.

"It's not that big of a deal. He'll leave."

But Dad's gaze arrows. "Stay here," he repeats.

Indy bounces up on Ren's couch to watch Dad and the stranger through the glass. The hair on his back spikes. Threatened growls roll from his throat. I feel the same when I stare from the oversized window.

"Evenin', brotha," a younger man—whose neatness makes my stomach swim—says. Seeing him dressed in golf attire—bright white polo, crisp chinos, and gloves grasped around a golf club—I can't help but think there's something off about the way he carries it.

"Was walking by and noticed your broken sprinkler," he says and waits for my dad's small talk. Dad nods and the man continues, "Just thought I'd let you know. Water is gold around

47

here." The small talk lowers in volume, and I can't hear. I watch the stranger explain himself. When he pivots, the sun catches his face. My heart lights a fire. His undereyes look like they'd been brushed with soot from the fireplace, but even they can't dim the halo glowing from him…like Greta's.

"Halo…" *Oh my gosh.*

Dad and the stranger start bending toward the broken sprinkler, but when Dad touches the grass, the stranger straightens up, resting both hands on his club as if it's a kickstand. I can't look away. Not until Dad is back in the house.

Indy is still barking. Something is wrong. Indy and I aren't the only ones panicking. Dad is doing the same. One of his massive hands rests on his bent knee—tapping. Tapping. *Tapping!* Morse code. *THE CODE.*

I try to make out the letters. "S…O…S."

The stranger's façade is gone. His face looks like stone, emptiness behind every feature with eyes so dark they mimic a pair of whole black buttons.

"DAD!" I scream and bang on the window. Dad rushes around at the sound of my voice. He makes way to the house, but the stranger whacks his club at Dad's head. "NO!"

I can see blood, and now the man is headed here, marching clean cleated shoes on Ren's lawn. A surge of heat gusts through my shoulders. *What the hell do I do?* Indy is snarling now, scratching his paws against the wood like a triggered bull.

I move to help Dad, but as soon as my fingertips touch the door handle, I hear him. "No, stay there!" I let go and lock the door. There must be something else. Some other way.

I scan Ren's house, and when I peek out the window, I see Dad is back up. Slower, but breathing. He picks up something from the ground near one of Ren's yard props. It's not easy for him to find balance. He wobbles behind the stranger, then lunges after him and stabs a mounting spike into his back. The spike rips into his flesh. Blood soils the once pristine polo. The stranger grits his teeth—a reaction too calm for the pain inflicted. A bone protrudes where the spike ripped his shirt. Dad's hand is still on his weapon. I can see the bone even more now and I wonder why the stranger isn't giving in to the damage. I see the strange man's eyes open as if he's done so for the first time. That sharp grey bone sticking from his back stretches, tearing through deep scarred skin like a possessed deformity. Bones, thick like tree branches, stretch to unfurl a pair of feathered wings. The wings coil around my dad's neck. They squeeze and constrict his windpipe. Both of his feet leave the ground.

Indy is at the door going berserk and all I can think is to let him at the man. Before I can open the door enough to give him some space, Indy bum-rushes through and bullets straight for the man's leg, sinking his teeth into his calf. The branchlike bones choking Dad drop him. The stranger growls. The spike of his cleat stomps into Indy's side and my protective boy scampers away.

And here the man comes again…to the door…to me.

I'm sweating. Out of breath as if I were the one strangled. Those bones are wings…and those feathers, a dim maize, I've seen something like them…today in Mercy Bay, in the Black Coat's hand. That was all that was left from the person who stole Sarai. The person who teased our end is near.

No. The room is spinning, and I feel tipped over. This is how it always begins—the lump in my throat, the tingling ears, and hot rushes. I want to pace myself and control my nerves. If I lock those things down, I can control myself.

A shattering crash comes from the glass part of the door. I tremble. My knees weaken me to Ren's oak floor. The door handle rattles, then booms. He's coming. A tsunami of heat zooms down my arms and into my fingers. The last time the heat reached my hands, I scorched the curtains in my room. And maybe that's it. Maybe it's just what I need right now to fight back: my Varien blood. I won't be fighting against it. This time, it's the answer.

More booms slam at the door.

I bend my fingers into my palms. I flex till I shake. The booms at the door louden and double. When the door bangs open, a rush of air announces the stranger. "Hang on, Dad!" I shout and turn loose. Striking every corner of Ren's living room, a web of cosmic energy sprouts from my fingers. Wood splinters from the floor and cabinets. Glass windows shatter and explode. Vases and picture frames blow over and clatter to the ground as I lose sight of the world. Life becomes a cyclone—a tailspin of floating glass, wood, plastic, and metal. A snow globe of Ren's belongings with a girl at its center. I'm the rage, the fear, and the protector.

A thud rocks the floor. It doesn't sound like an object; it sounds like a body. The stranger. I've got him.

When the last of the buildup that overflowed from me drains, I crawl around on my knees to find the guy. He's lumped a few feet away from me, charred and smoky. Struggled coughs come from him. I crawl closer. The shoes on his feet aren't the cleats that kicked Indy. They're black dress shoes. I see no chinos, only singed and burned blue slacks. *Blue…this is not—*

"Dad?" I cry and gasp. Dad lying on the ground, convulsing with skin swollen and crisp from the tip of his ear, down to his stomach. Half-awake, he mumbles in shock from the burn of my scalding stars.

My Varien blood did this.

I beg for him to hear and see me, like I always have. Except this time, I'd give anything for him to do it his way and not mine. "Dad…no. I'm sorry. I couldn't control it. Please." Tears spill onto Dad's burned skin. I'm afraid to touch him. I don't want to hurt him again. "I'm sorry. I'm so sorry. God…Dad, please say something! Talk to me!" Quick breaths enter and exit Dad's lungs.

"I can get help, okay? Just say something so I know you're with me." I beg from a place of desperate optimism, birthed from the womb of my denial.

Dad fades in and out, and his skin swells more with each second. Both eyes crack open and I'm scared because they tell me

Dad is not here—that there's not much behind the burst vessels and bloodshot whites. They close just as quick as they opened, and I fall apart. Why is this happening?

"Please don't go!" I cry and hold myself. Groans leave Dad's scalded lips. Each one slices into me. "Run...," he whispers.

"What? Dad..." I lean closer, relieved to the heavens to hear him speak. "Don't give up! I'm going to call for help!"

"N-n-no." Shakes plague his body. "Run."

Everything falls grey. All I can hear is the ringing in my ears. And then that same boiling feeling warms my nerves because a shadow grows in Ren's living room. A man grows larger than all my old fears combined once his wings uncoil. The Bible speaks of angels, and how people can feel their protection without ever seeing them, so I know I'm not witnessing kingdom come. This man is not made of God, and he is not here to do His good work.

Those wings build wind, sending a storm through the window I broke. In a matter of seconds, the shadow levitates and hovers closer.

"Run," Dad grunts once more.

I'm up on my feet, racing up the stairs as if the ground beneath me is rotting away. *What about Dad? What am I doing? I have to go back!*

No, he said run, Alexia!

My mind tells me to survive while my heart cries. Dying would be easier than this. Each leg feels like a cylinder of cement, then my brain conquers my heart and I dang near leap into Ren's study. I lock it quick and lodge a chair under the door's handle. I know it won't stop the man, but maybe it'll buy me some seconds. *All I need is three minutes. Three minutes and help will be here.* "Three minutes, three minutes...," I repeat and hit the panic button under Ren's desk. "Three minutes, three minutes..."

A violent pull at the locked door announces the man. Trembles come with every sound. Cold wind wades from his wings. I arm myself with a candle holder, and for once, just this once, I pray for my powers to overcome me again. *Please show up…please!* A shadow bleeds beneath the study door. Slow walking feet. They move on for a moment, then reverse. I step backward with bated breath. The door handle twists down until it can't. I know the lock and chair won't keep the man out. All I need from them is time.

The Black Coats are coming. Just hang on, Alexia. They'll help Dad…

The door handle quivers. Chills rake up my spine. I don't make a sound even though I'm scared out of my mind. A house possessed—the double doors to the study knock back and forth. The chair in front of them falls. All the noise is so loud, like colliding boulders.

A crashing bang echoes through the house. Both doors are ripped off the hinges. I cry when I hear them clatter to the ground. I back away because I don't know what the hell else to do besides try not to die for one more minute. I scamper and crouch behind Ren's wooden desk.

One of the cleats I saw walk through Ren's grass, steps sharply on top of the broken door's debris. Here he comes…my killer.

I've held in so much in these seconds, I'm ready to scream as loud as I can—loud enough for my throat to bleed. But when I open my mouth to do so, two phantom hands clasp around my mouth and chest, yanking me from the study and into nowhere.

CHAPTER ELEVEN

PATHOS

"**D**ON'T MOVE. DON'T SCREAM, got it?" a voice somewhere in the rippling thickness orders. "You'll get sick that way—especially your first time planing."

The hands that held me fall away. There's no hesitating: I make a run for it.

"So, you're just gonna be hardheaded today?" The voice scoffs. "I told you not to move—"

Nausea swirls in my head and stomach. I can't see straight, everything's moving. Crazy of me, but I think I even see Indy. The hair on his body sways like seaweed under the ocean's tide even though it is bone-dry here…wherever *here* is.

I fall to my knees, retching as I try to get a grip on myself. I've got to get back to Dad. Acid crawls up my throat, commanding my watering eyes to shut from the pain.

"Here, try this…," the voice says. A tin can of blush-colored salve appears in front of my face. Indy barks like mad. He growls and bares his teeth to guard me.

"Oh, I've got something for you too, puppy." The voice's owner tosses a treat at the undulating ground. Indy the traitor cancels his protection and races to it.

"Is he real? What is this?" I wince.

"He'll tell you himself," the woman's voice says.

When I put my arm out, Indy comes to it. His hair is under my fingertips and immediately I know all of him is real. The bloody wounds in his fur. The wired hairs among the fine silver strands. "Good boy," I cry and wrap my arms around him. "How did he get here?"

A brown arm comes into my view. "Relax and breathe." Chunky silver cuffs and bangles cover the arm. Instantly in my gut, I know…

"The woman from Mercy Bay," I mumble and look up. "You're—"

"Greta." She smiles. "Breathe this in. It'll help. Then we have to move." There's a tin case in her palm, a salve of crushed flower buds and herbs.

I inch closer to it, think for a bit, and inch away. "Where am I?"

"Alexia…not now—"

"How do you know my name!" I rise, and before I can run, my body cancels all possibilities. Nausea brings me to back to my knees and I throw up. Right here in the middle of nowhere.

"Hard heads make for a soft ass," Greta sighs. She puts the tin can in my face and I breathe with her direction. "In through your nose…and out from your mouth. There you go."

A whiff of smells—woodsy and bright—journey through my nose and into my head. Balance comes to me. The room stops spinning. I can see things clearly—Greta, Indy, and this space. Aquamarine. The reflection of netted waves around us makes me feel like we're hidden at the bottom of a pool. I swipe my hair out of my face and try standing.

"Better?" Greta asks.

"Yes." It only takes a second for me to get a grip. "Dad! I need to get to him!" I run to find a way out of this space. When I reach out and touch the edges, I'm shocked to learn they're solid—even as they ripple. I can't go through like I got in. "Let me out!"

Greta pulls me away from the edge. "The only way out of here, is with me. And I can't let you go."

The blood inside me turns hot. "No! Let me go now! My dad is hurt! He needs me!"

"He needs you to stay alive. Letting you go back would be like serving you on a platter."

"He could be dying! I have to be there!"

Greta places her hand on my shoulder. The sensation of buzzing zips down my arms and I shrug her off me, but it's too late. Cosmic energy is ready to break free. "Let me out!" I scream. Zapping everything in front of me, sparking flares pour from my skin. When I see the same old wall in front of me, I'm moved to tears. "Why are you doing this?" I yell at Greta.

Even after seeing my rage explode, she's centered. She walks over to me and tries to comfort me one more time. "Because if I don't, your father will surely die...as will your mother and your siblings."

I wipe my eyes on the sleeve of my sweater. "What?"

Grief lives in Greta's face. Lifting one finger, she presses into the wavy wall. The crests and troughs rock into greater sizes— changing from blue, to grey, then clear. I can see Ren's house through the mass. The chaos: the broken floor and window glass spilled on the grass, and hordes of armed forces on the scene. "Oh my gosh!" I jog over to where the medics are rolling a stretcher over the lawn. The churning waves from the wall spill under my feet. I'm a foot above the grass, not on it. "Greta, please!" I beg her.

Dad is bleeding, so much so, I can't figure out from where. Wounds are on his head, bones protrude from his arm, swelling has transformed the right side of his face. "My daughter...," he sputters through his busted lips. "My-my...daughter."

"I'm here!" I wave arms for him to see. "Greta, please! Let me go! Please!" I look back at her and there's heaviness in her face. Regret, maybe. She waves her fingers and calls some kind of water from the ground up, stringing bubbles into the air like pearls. One floats by me and locks into the rippling wall. Rushing waves start ahead of me and take the shape of a door. I worry about drowning, but the water stays flat and rolls into the nothing beneath us. It never fills the space. When it's done and the waves have turned to trickling drips over a wet black door, I wait for Greta.

"Go," she says. "Your dad is there."

Hand on the knob, I hesitate, but twist it anyway. On Greta's side, we were in a cave of in between. On this side, there's pavement, grass, and a fence. Someone's backyard. A seagull squawks as it flies. Looking back at the door, it belongs to an old stone and mortared shed. Indy takes off to the gate. I come up behind him. As we pass the window of the house near the shed, I hear a shout. "Hey! Hey!" A man inside drops his mug and book before running after me.

"Shit!" My skinny fingers can't unlatch the gate lock fast enough. And sure enough, beyond it, like Greta said, Dad is here.

Ren's house is across the street. The Black Coats patrol the road and the insides of the house. Indy barks and takes off again. *The ambulance truck. Dad!*

The Black Coats are quick to draw their guns on me. Hands up, I tell them, "I'm Jacobs—Alexia Jacobs! That's my dad!"

Not one Black Coat stands down. Their fingers rest on their triggers.

"Edward Jacobs is my dad! What're you doing? Don't shoot!"

One wrong move and it could be over. I could startle them. Heart beating a mile a minute and eyes bouncing from each Black Coat, I wait for them to recognize me. But seconds stretch and no such thing is happening. What's not clicking? Do I look that different when I'm not at work or next to Dad?

"Wait! Back down! She's telling the truth." A Black Coat eases over to stand in front of me. They finally listen and free me from their aim. I feel like melting down to the asphalt with relief. I know full well situations like this don't always end this way for people who look like me. A path through the Black Coats is cleared and Indy and I beeline to the stretcher outside the ambulance truck.

This man on the stretcher can't be Dad. He looks heavy and beaten, swollen with colored bruises. His face, I can't make out. I can't see the dimple in his nose or the small collection of moles under his eyes. His face is baked. *I did this.*

"Dad…" My hand reaches for his. It sits idly beside his leg on the stretcher. "You're not alone. I'm here." Through his swollen eyes, he peeks.

For a moment, I wonder if he can really see through them. But then Dad jumps from his trance and retracts his hand. "No! No! Help me! Help!" he calls in labored breaths.

A medic steps in front of me. "Excuse me, miss, we don't want the patient upset. He needs to be treated immediately." She and the other EMTs are ready to secure the stretcher inside the truck.

"No…see…he's my dad. I-I should be with him."

A heavy tap on my shoulder jolts me. "Alexia."

"Yes." I turn around.

A Black Coat stands in front of me. "Do you have a moment to answer a few questions about your father?" I glance back at Greta. Worry is all I see.

The EMT hauls Dad up. "We're taking him to St. Mary's. You can meet him there," she tells me. When she swings the ambulance truck door closed, the heaviness in my heart could sink me underground. I've caused enough pain, why stay? Only more will follow. Dad doesn't want that. He's afraid of this. He's preached this. *Variens turn on us*, he'd say.

The Black Coat next to me clears his throat. "Alexia?"

"I have to go, act—"

"This will only take two minutes of your time." As the Black Coat steps closer, my reflection stretches in the shine of his helmet's black visor.

"But—"

"You pressed the emergency alarm?"

"Uh…yes."

"Can you explain what led you to that action?"

"The uh…this man came to the house and rang the doorbell. Dad went out and he got worried suddenly, and then…I want to say they argued and—"

All I can see are bursts of burning light searing Ren's house and Dad's body.

"Miss?"

"Yes. I'm sorry." I shake my head. "I don't remember things that well."

"You don't recall anything else between Senator Jacobs and the man?"

"Well, he grew wings from his back. I saw that. His feathers were gold, just like the feather left behind at Mercy Bay earlier…"

"And did you see him at any point set Senator Jacobs on fire?"

No.

"Or burn him?"

I did it.

"And if so, how?"

I used the blood and cells he gave me against him.

A medic grabs Indy and starts examining his wounds. "Hey, wait! That's my dog!" I shout.

"Miss?" the officer calls. "Everything's fine. They're just going to make sure your pet is okay."

I catch the tears pooling in my eyes before they run down my cheeks. "No. I didn't see anything like that. I was hiding upstairs."

"Don't worry about that. Surveillance footage will fill in those gaps." He types away on his device's screen.

"Are there cameras in the house?"

"Oh yeah. Inside. Outside. All over."

Sweat buds from my skin. "I-I didn't see any in there. Are you sure?"

The Black Coat barely faces me as he walks away. "The dogs."

The stuffed dogs…they were really cameras?

That means the Black Coats will know all about what I did. They'll know who I am before Dad tells them. Naïveté catches me for a second: *Maybe Dad would tell them it wasn't my fault. He'd tell them to leave me alone.* But that's not what he did for Sarai. He left her with the wolves. *No, he wouldn't do that to me.* Maybe not, but if he dies, what he'd do won't matter anymore. No matter how I slice it, I'm headed for the slums. I mean, the Black Coats nearly did away with me without Dad by my side not too long ago.

"On the roof!" a Black Coat shouts.

I scurry to hide behind an armored Black Coat truck. I follow their gaze and guns. My knees weaken at the sight. The scarred man walks atop the neighbor's roof. He's indifferent to all of us, we may as well not even be here.

"I have to go," Greta whispers over my shoulder. "Nothing good is coming."

"Wait," I say to Greta as the scarred man turns his head toward the Black Coats.

"Yes?"

"I'm going with you…I think."

"You sure?"

"I have nothing," I say, thinking of all I've lost and what that means. "I can't stay here if I want to be free, right?" The slums and prison are the only things in my future.

Greta's eyes dash between me and the winged man. "That's right."

"But you're free…"

"I am."

The Black Coats aim at the man. Dozens of them cover the street. The group closest to him holds a hose—something the scarred man twists his mouth at.

He wastes no time and flexes his chest, sprouting those bone wings from his back. The feathers on them are disheveled. Beads of red dust sweep from his chest. They roll through the air like a chainsaw.

The police fire their bullets.

The Black Coats release their rot gas.

Yet, all of it is too late.

Red dust reaches the Black Coat holding the hose. Wet squishing sounds of his bursting flesh touch my ears. Blood-curdling howls follow. Those noises, what death sound like.

The police stand down, but the scarred man doesn't. He hovers above us all in the air—this dark gargoyle that's brought nothing but agony. It's almost like he's begging them to try harder.

"The rest of your family will have the same fate as those men as long as you stay here." Greta's voice gets serious. "You sure you want to risk that and go home?"

A double target on my back. The Black Coats and the winged man. I search the street for the red truck carrying Dad. Relief grows inside me when I don't see it. *I hope they made it to the hospital. I hope Dad knows I got away.*

Greta waits on me. She's patient and in a hurry all at the same time, watching me run through mental montages of my beautiful normal family—my beautiful, *safe*, normal family.

My eyes trail to the fallen Black Coat. Pieces of them are broken apart. Their flesh has been eaten by the chunks. Loose skin hangs out of their ripped clothes. It's everything I wish I could unsee. Everything I never want to happen to Mom, Dad, Niles, or Nia.

"I don't," I answer Greta.

A twinkle circles her eyes, summoning us back into the weird aquamarine space we were in before, except this time, snow trickles from the floor to the sky. Greta holds on to the straps of her backpack as it clanks the gourds looped to its pockets. They make me wonder a lot of things, mostly where she's been, and where we're going.

"C'mon," she orders. "The moon will rise soon."

CHAPTER TWELVE

GRETA'S ANTIQUES

SAFE IS SOMEWHERE I'VE never been before: Greta's Antique Shop, a random setup hidden in trees somewhere near the end of Sacramento like some cottage in a Brothers Grimm tale. Every inch of the shop is covered with jewelry, sculptures, grandfather clocks, and other novelties. A time capsule that smells of wood polish and brown sugar confections. Everything is spotless.

"Let me see…do we have everything?" Greta speaks into her fingers. She says "we," but I don't know if she really means "we." I'm just a moving piece for her and I know nothing about everything that happened today.

"Greta," I say.

She twirls around and changes directions.

"Greta."

She steps into midair, planting her feet into invisible stairs to retrieve a green jewelry box from a stacked shelf. "This, we'll need."

"Greta!"

The box fumbles from her hands. She purses her lips. "What!"

"Are you going to tell me where we're going? Or why that flying asshole attacked my dad? Maybe even how you found me? Are you going to tell me SOMETHING?" I lose control of my temper, and the feverish flow of heat under my skin warns me.

"I understand how you feel, but we don't have the time."

"Tell me what's going on!"

"We have to hurry."

I tease my way to the door. "I'm not going ANYWHERE until you give me something!"

The pink and white neon sign on the wall flickers with my shouts—"You are new again," it reads.

Greta folds her arms. "Well, for one thing, we're going somewhere to fix that right there. These anger fits you've been having…you'll kill someone if you don't figure out who you are."

"I know who I am."

"Could've fooled me." Greta gives a sarcastic smirk. "I read you when I first saw you. You're a wild card. No one knows which side of you they'll get in any given minute. Not even you."

My shoulders drop and I regret demanding the smallest piece of information from her.

"I also saw promise, an aura of violet. Something I've only imagined."

I step slowly to Greta's jade velvet couch.

"My day was rewritten from there. You come first now."

"Why?"

Greta sits before I do. "Because you have a great capacity and we need to keep you safe."

"From who? The guy with wings?"

"Mmmph." Greta covers her mouth. "You'll learn more now that you're on the cusp…"

"Of what?"

"Of you."

She grips a handful of dirt and seashells from a vase and pours it on the coffee table.

"What're you doing?" My voice shakes.

Greta puts her taupe lips together and blows at the dirt. "Waiting for our road, can't leave without one, you know?"

"I don't know," I quip. "I still don't know. I don't know anything about you."

"Honey, this is a job. I work as a Spot Varien for The Grove's Board of Variation—just one out of Varien Country's appointed eleven. We bring Variens to our motherland and get them settled. You'll be on your way to Malveaux. Got it?"

Not sold. My voice breaks free from my lips. "Malveaux? What is that? A Varien slum? Promising safety and a warm home. They used that in the beginning, when Variens started popping up again in the '90s."

"Look, don't be a hard sell now. Just stretching out time you don't have…" The gong of numerous grandfather clocks sounds off all at once, but I can still hear Greta's resilient mumbles. "Well, if I have to…I don't like sending anyone off with bad nerves." From somewhere under the couch cushion, she brings a small grey chest out and places it on the table.

The dirt she sprinkled is still there with particles cycling around like a snow globe.

"Always nice to go down memory lane. Take a look here." Greta passes me a set of old Polaroids.

I check out the first. Two girls, both honey brown with short ebony hair, stand in front of a red brick mansion. Their hands are linked, fists raised in the air.

"We thought we were really doing something, my sister and me. We didn't approve of the Varien Board's dress restrictions for girls." She leans in. "We led a protest right there on the academy's steps. Didn't change much immediately, but a year later the standards were fairly altered. I think that's when it clicked for Maureen…my sister. She knew she wanted to be an agent for change. Now she's head Sage of the academy."

"Sage?"

"Think headmaster meets griot. A Sage must know the odds and ends of history and the world to lead the future. Keep flipping through," she encourages.

I go through the photos one at a time. They're colored with kids dressed in tartan and solid blocks of olive, blue, and cream uniforms, hanging in what looks like a lounge and posing at a school dance. The last depicts a boy in damp clothes, on a dorm room bunk, also doused and dripping in water.

"Andy Navarette. Took a while for him to stop summoning the lake wherever he went. Growing takes time and potential. That's why every runaway doesn't get accepted. Heck, not every Varien is summoned to The Grove." Greta gently slaps her knee.

"…And what's The Grove?"

A subtle smile stretches into her cheeks as she gazes ahead. "A haven…the purest of places—made for us, ruled by us. No hiding. And when you're there, you feel fed. Like the universe is plugged right into your chest. Ain't that something?" When the passion behind her explanation leaves, she shakes her head, almost dismissing herself as silly. "I'd live there if I could, but my purpose has me here. I'm happy with dropping in every full moon, anyway."

"That man…he's there also?"

"…Yes."

"Do you know what he wanted? Why'd he come after us?"

Greta's stare is serious, then she shrugs. "I don't know. Your family is controversial with Variens. Maybe he's had enough."

"And I'm supposed to be safer there than I am here?"

"Yes."

I snort through a laugh. This woman can't be serious. "This is crazy. Do you think I'm stupid?"

"Stupid, no. Ignorant, very."

Greta and I both stare each other down. My mom would knock both my eyes out of my head for twisting my face at an adult. She's not here right now, so in my mind, it's all free game.

"You saw how he did that Black Coat. Sliced them up like a Sunday ham…and that was on a Thursday. The people you need to protect you are the people like you. People who've honed and crafted their gifts to stand a chance, know the systems and ins and out to keep you alive. This is something you need…at least for a few moons. You're not stupid enough to refuse that."

"You think it'll be safe to come back home in what? A few weeks? Months?"

"Moons…just a few moons," Greta repeats. "Then you can go back. I can't speak for your safety from Normals…but you'll have it from ol' brother wings himself."

My eyes glaze over. "That man took my friend too…do you think she's there? In this Grove place?"

"If he came for her, she is."

"What can you do? We have to get her before Nadir! Do you know what that is? That's what he said he needed her for."

Greta's pensive expression brings her eyes to the ceiling. "Hmmm…I don't know. But Maureen would. She knows everything. You should tell her when you get to Malveaux. First thing! She'll help you with everything." A yawn comes over Greta. "Now, I'm tired. I've shown my hand. If you've got any more reservations…well, we ain't got time for that. It's either that out there, or you trust me."

Sarai is still gone. The winged man has her. And like Greta said, if he's in The Grove, Sarai will be with him. I could find her. I could save her. The opportunity is still there, just in a different realm.

"That's all easy to say," I tell her. "It's not so easy for me if you turn out to be on the winged man's side."

Greta arches one eyebrow. "No, it wouldn't be."

"Then how do you expect me to trust you?"

"Because I'm giving you the weapon to kill me if you don't." In her hand, Greta holds a slender green velvet box. I open it. The glare of an overpolished blade glares in the light. "If you don't trust me now…use it."

She exposes her neck by lifting her chin. "Make your move," she tells me with set eyes.

I curl my fingers around the dagger's hilt. It's not heavy at all—easier for me to move with. The point of its blade would make a clean wound. I aim the dagger right where her chest meets her neck. I picture it slicing into Greta in the wash of the pink neon light, but it's not her neck I want to pierce…it's his.

My arm draws down. My defenses stay up. "When can we leave?"

Greta grins and whips her head at the dirt pile. What was, is no more. The old spread of dirt and shells has become a translucent screen. A floating, freaky object that projects the scene of a lonely dark path against the window's incoming moonlight.

"We've got to get there while the full moon still has its kiss on the road. It's the only way in." Greta hurries to the door and motions for me to follow.

CHAPTER THIRTEEN

MOON, TURN THE TIDE

As we walk through moonlit orchards, I pick up the sweet taste of humid air. Navel oranges and apples. My stomach growls. The scent reminds me I haven't eaten much since this morning…and that I may never eat again, thanks to my decision to follow a stranger.

I keep hold of the dagger. If the time to escape comes, I'm ready.

"Stay close," Greta tells me.

"How far out is this place?" My voice cracks over the noise of dirt clumps hitting my sneakers.

"You'll know we're there when we're there. Trust me," Greta replies.

Awesome. Kidnapper rhetoric.

"I just didn't think we'd be traveling on foot. We've been walking for a while now…and where are we? Is this someone's farm? Someone's private property?" I start to panic as the possibilities hit me. *Are we trespassing? Because if so, I don't feel like getting shot at.*

Greta turns back and gives a close-lipped smile. "Oh, it's private property all right. My private property."

"Then why don't you have a vehicle to take us where we're going?"

"Because…you'll miss the sign."

"What sign?" I'm out of breath from trying to keep up with Greta's pace. My calves and my lower back are starting to ache, and the balls of my feet feel sore. There isn't much to see in this spread of land. The road is mostly clear thanks to the moon's kiss. Everything else, the uniform trees on either side of us, washes out with the night sky.

"*Mmmhmm…*" A warm breeze curls a humming sound around me, then it quickly dies. I turn around. Nothing there. Just the empty, long dirt road behind us. Another brush of wind creeps around me and blows the small coils at my neck around. "*Mmmhmm…*"

"Did you hear that?" I shiver and ask Greta. "That humming?"

Greta's pace slows as she looks back at me again.

"*Mhmmm yeh je padu…lout tien jes besquet…,*" An ethereal mashup of rich aged voices sing. They roll out of my ears as fast as they enter them.

"There it goes again."

"What?"

"You don't hear it?"

"I hear something." Greta's waiting on me now. She drops her backpack to the dirt ground and stands in front of me. A knowing expression is on her face. "But what are *you* hearing?"

I look around her for the sources as the singing voices louden. Nothing. No one is anywhere, and that can't be! Because their sounds surround me, becoming stronger as they chant.

"*Mhmmm yeh je padu…lout tien jes besquet…*"

"A song…a chant."

Greta squeezes both of my upper arms. "Stay here."

"Where are you going? What's happening?" I cover my ears but it's no use. The singing continues, and Greta walks to the trees on our right. She sprawls her arms within the branches, searches with her hands for bit, then plucks a piece of the tree.

Her hands prepare whatever she's retrieved as she walks back to me. "Here, you need to eat something. I heard your stomach growling earlier. You're getting light-headed." A peeled orange rests in her palm.

"Is this a Varien thing? This has never happened to me before."

"It is. A little citrus always does the trick," she reassures.

I claw my fingertips into the orange and break it apart. "Want a piece?" I offer some to Greta, not just out of courtesy but confirmation. If she eats the orange, I'll know it's safe for me to do the same.

"Sure. Thank you." Greta takes the orange half I hand over, peels a piece off, and pops it into her mouth.

I watch her for a few seconds and peel a piece off for myself. The chanting I hear has grown faster.

"*Mhmmm yeh je padu…lout tien jes besquet…*"

"It's okay, Alexia." Greta eats another piece.

"*Mhmmm yeh je padu…lout tien jes besquet…*"

For the third time today, I follow her lead and eat the orange. The taste is bold, tart, sweet…and refreshing. I swallow it down and eat another without hesitating, thinking only of the hunger that's being satisfied. I close my eyes and draw my head back. "Mmmph…this orange is hittin'."

"The noise? Is it gone?"

I pause. Those chants of foreign voices…they're gone. Completely gone! Baffled, I feel my jaw drop. "You were right. I just needed food. But what was that about? What were those voices doing?"

"Those voices are your ancestors calling you…welcoming you in the land's old language, Viridian," Greta explains. "Mhmmm, come home now…to The Grove." Beyond her, yellow rolling hills are touched by a fast-rising sun that floods each part of the land with its warm reach. Where it was night, it is now day. The setting isn't what I knew before either. The orchard trees are taller with thicker trunks. Farm workers with large straw hats are peppered among them, searching branches for ripe fruit before placing them in bags. A few of them smile at me. Another, who sits under a tree taking a break, waves. A small mechanical fan windmills and floats in midair to cool her off.

"Harriet! Hey, girl!" Greta shouts at her. "I want some of those watermelons before the season ends. Don't forget!"

Harriet laughs. "You know I didn't!"

I turn back to Harriet as we pass her. She's happier than I've been in months, peeling an apple, with a beaming smile. The other farm worker's sheer halos twinkle under the sun.

Greta and I continue on the road—which is now paved with flat stones and no longer flattened dirt. "Come on!" she shouts. "I've got a ride for you."

She heads toward a tinted glass canopy with a pill-shaped vehicle resting beneath it. A small building—some kind of terminal—stands behind it. Greta opens the door to the terminal and motions for me to hurry. I scurry in.

"Rashad!" she calls. "Rashaaaad!" Greta makes herself comfortable, removing her backpack, and grabbing one of her gourds. "Want some water?"

"Yes…please," I answer as I watch her fill the gourd full of water that shimmers with luminescent silver specks. She chugs the water down, refills the gourd some more before filling a another empty round gourd.

"Here you go." Greta hands the gourd to me.

I study its contents. *Why the shimmering? What is it?*

"Zenith water. It's just lunar dust," Greta educates me.

"Lunar dust? Why would I drink this? It's toxic."

"For Normals…not us. Every year, the moon travels down and pours itself into our waters. We bathe in it, drink it. We have a celebration—we call it the Zenith. This is the stuff that charges us. Makes what we carry inside us weightless. Not the heavy lift of baggage you all have in the Normal realm."

Baggage? "I don't feel heavy."

Greta gazes into my eyes and tilts her head to the side. "Because you don't know anything different." She turns away and calls out, "Rashad!" There's a bell on the counter she springs to and rings repeatedly.

A thirtysomething man appears from a back door behind the counter. His eyes pop when they lay on Greta. "Oh hey, Greta. I thought that was you."

"Good afternoon, Tadashi. Where's Rashad?"

Tadashi, dressed in blue coveralls, grins apprehensively and repositions his goggles to the top of his head. "He's getting the trolley ready."

"Ready with *five* soleils?" There's pressure in her question.

Tadashi bows his head down. "Well…four, but—"

"Ugh! Rashad!"

Finally, the long-awaited Rashad bursts from the same back door Tadashi came from. "You know I can't do five. Four is just enough to get us to Malveaux and back."

Rashad is dressed in coveralls just like Tadashi, but his are singed on the sleeves. Sweat drops glisten on his dark brown forehead as he towers over Greta, looking at her through orange-tinted goggles.

Greta's hand is on her hip now. "Imagine coming home thirteen to fourteen times a year and only being able to enjoy it for half a day."

"I empathize—" Rashad starts.

"No, really! Just imagine how you'd miss it. All I want is to add one more stop on the way back and spend some time in the Belle Rues. That's not asking a lot."

"We have an inventory to account for."

Greta slaps her hands against her thighs.

Tadashi skirts around Rashad and taps him. "We could make it work," he says, full of resolution. "I ran the numbers two nights ago and we have a 10 percent surplus of soleils."

Rashad is tepid, but I can tell he's folding. "Only one stop," he affirms with one arched eyebrow.

"Thank you, *Tadashi*," Greta emphasizes.

"Yeah, of course. I'll go start everything," he replies, aiming a thumb at the side glass door.

"Uh huh, *thanks, Tadashi!*" Rashad mockingly booms. "Let me go help him, sometimes the container door jams, and you need two people to open it. C'mon!"

He holds the door for Greta and she thanks him on the way to the pill-shaped trolley. We pass a weird scent, like melting plastic, as we make our way inside it. There's a wall of heat beating against us when Rashad and Tadashi open a heavy-duty shed. White-hot light flickers from it. With a careful hand, a goggle-eyed Tadashi fishes out a small softball-size sun with a set of black tongs and loads it into a clear canister on the ground. He loads up five, like everyone discussed, then Rashad seals it shut and loads it into the open rounded trolley hood.

"You done with your water?" Greta reaches out for my cup. She frowns when she sees I haven't taken a sip.

"I'm not quite ready for this yet. It's a lot."

"Okay…okay."

We both take a seat, cool under the thick glass roof, relieved by the plush blue seats that wrap around the trolley's insides.

"Greta," I say. "What is a soleil?"

"That's Renauld Malveaux's invention, what they just pulled from the shed. Another renewable energy source we use here. Comes from dust rain—when the stars shed their skin. They come down as little gold flakes on hot days."

Once Tadashi and Rashad are done loading up, they enter the trolley and power it up, bringing its massive weight two feet above the tracks. "Are we flying?" I ask, with my head stuck out the window.

"Hovering," she corrects me.

I don't know how the trolley is doing what it's doing, but I'm amazed and overwhelmed all at once. *Am I doing this? How is this my life? This mess. This tragedy. This surreal event. How do I live in this?* Flashes of my wounded dad intrude into my train of thought. Sarai floats at the top of my combusting mind. I feel like throwing up.

I bring my head to my knees for a moment. A reflection of patterned colors eventually brings me back up. We've entered a bridge unlike any other I've seen before: a kaleidoscope of multi-colored cut glass images of stars raining from the sky, flowers, and exotic birds. The shades strobe over my face and color the inside of the trolley.

"We call this the Retrouvailles Bridge. It makes complete sense when you know that Retrouvailles is the joy of reconnecting after a separation," Greta schools me. "Every piece of glass over us has intention. One, is to tell the story of home. How The Grove came to be after a big meteor shower made holes in the realm barriers. And here she was, home, just waiting." She goes on about how the glass harnesses solar energy—another intention, I guess—and names the bodies of water and ports below us. There are houses along some of the banks with white blimps tied to them. Greta tells me these are wind turbines, another way for Variens to source renewable energy.

"Interesting," I mumble back, trying my best to show attentiveness as my mind struggles to compartmentalize all my trauma. Some things Greta shares stick to my memory. Some don't.

Eventually, something does hold my entire attention: a beautiful forest rich in metallic shades of silver, copper, and gold. Sun rays bounce off their crystallized fruits and flowers. It all looks like something you could only gawk at, and never touch.

"The Virgin Forest, a shard of our creator's Garden of Eden." Greta gazes out her window and inhales the sweet air. "The only forest in the world that's never been plundered or abused. It has all its enchantment. Not one single fruit is plucked for harvest… ever. We wait until the forest chooses to gift us with its vegetation. Respecting its cycle keeps the magic alive."

Rashad continues steering us through The Grove, passing neighborhoods where gigantic trees sprout from the middle of homes, until finally braking at a rod iron gate that shows zero signs of human life beyond it. There's only greenery: cypress trees that tunnel both ends of the gate, vines of ivy choke stone columns and loop around the gate's spindles. The ivy's dominance is so strong, it covers all the spaces in between, except the gold Old English *M* in the center.

"All right, here you are," Rashad says over his shoulder. The trolley floats down and connects to the tracks. "Malveaux Prep Academy and Sanctuary."

I get up slow. Things are happening faster than I'd like them to. There's no time to sit in change, and that's more unnatural to me than the DNA in my body and the moondust in the water supply. I hate it…but I move on. Not because I want to, but because I have to. I linger on the first step of the trolley before stepping down.

"That's it. One step at a time," Rashad swivels around and speaks. His face is warm with the smile of an old uncle. "Everything's gon' be all right."

We nod at one another, and I wonder how Rashad knows this. Did he end up here under the same conditions? Is he living proof? I think about asking him before thanking him and Tadashi for their kindness.

I finally step down and meet Greta in front of the iron gate where her hand presses at the *M* in the center. A clanking and shifting sound echoes as she twists the emblem to the side. The gate slides open, and the cypress trees raise their heavy branches, allowing us to pass.

Like everything else I've seen, Malveaux's spread doesn't disappoint. Past the flower beds of bell-chiming foxgloves and calla lilies, a U-shaped four-story red brick Georgian held up by vine-covered Roman columns casts its shadow over acres of grass. It has everything: manicured lawns, topiaries around a labyrinth, balconies, and a roof crowded with greenery—trees, blossoming flowers, and strings of foliage that spill over their edges. It's almost as if nature has taken the building completely over.

I look over to my right and stare in shock at the biggest natural abnormality: a giant garden of roses clapping their leaves together as they watch a bunch of kids play a game of basketball.

Varien kids are scattered around the property. Some walk through the yard. Others climb trees while the rest of their friends lie beneath them. They're smiling—clean and happy. Free.

A gush of air breezes by. I try to control the silly look of amazement on my face by peering over to the basketball team. A student walks up to one of the coaches on the field and hands him a pink slip. "Phoenix, Sage Cameron needs a campus mentor to show our new student around!" the coach barks into his megaphone.

From the league of ball players in stained jerseys comes a tall and lanky boy with dark wavy hair. I don't know much about basketball except my brother used to play it. He quit after a couple seasons after an injury. That was two years ago, and I don't remember his teammates looking anything like this.

"Hey, Greta! Another runaway, huh?" The boy laughs at his own joke.

I scowl while Greta's brows rise. "Kyle, hun…give us a minute."

"Sure," the dark-haired boy agrees. We turn our backs to him in unison.

"Your locket?" Greta whacks my shoulder. "Where is it?"

"Um…" I haven't seen the damn thing since I left Ren's. It could be anywhere. I pat myself down. Lo and behold, the heavy gold necklace is in my back pocket. "Got it!"

"Put it on. You'll stay protected that way."

"Ah, so the locket has a purpose."

"More than you know. The inside shows you the moon phase over the road. My gifts allow me to find Variens when they use their powers. With this on, I'll have a little more security in locating you."

"That's how you found me at Ren's?"

Greta nods and taps her right temple. "You'll do well here. Oh, and hand me the dagger."

"What?"

"I delivered you safely and kept my promise, but now you're at a school and the dagger is a hazard. Hand it over." Greta wiggles her fingers.

I hand it over, hilt first, with attitude. The routine of my everyday life gnaws at me quick and hard. I should be home now. I trace the school with my eyes. Malveaux is a masterpiece, but it isn't for me. "How long do I have to stay?"

"A few moons." She clicks her tongue. "I wouldn't be so eager to go back home if I were you."

"I just want to know if my dad is okay…how my family is doing. I want them to know I'm not missing."

"I know, girl. I don't think there's a right time for you to tell them anything, though."

"Then…can you tell me? Just check on them. Please."

Greta's chin ruffles as she thinks. Her clean pink nails comb through her hair. "I'll have something for you by the next full moon. Your locket will help you keep track of the moon phases."

The world feels light under my feet, just for a second. "Thank you," I say.

"Now, Alexia, this is Kyle Pereira-Phoenix. He'll be your campus mentor and get you all situated," Greta explains while checking the inside of her backpack.

The boy holds out his hand. "Hey."

"Alexia. Nice to meet you." I shake his hand. His tan skin looks as though it's been baked a hue deeper; he has that golden glow that comes from living under the sun for days on end. I try not to linger on his face for too long, but the vision of his hazel eyes catches me. Beneath bushy brows, they stare back.

"He's an ass ache," Greta interrupts. "Never stops talking. Never knows when something ain't funny. And he doesn't understand personal space eith—"

"Whoa! You're making me look bad."

"You did that your damn self." She smacks her lips. "Over here looking dead on your daddy but not acting like him."

Kyle turns back to me. Even though he isn't running, he breathes like he's out of breath. "Don't listen to her. I'm actually really funny and respectful of everyone's space. See?" He glides back two strides.

I sell him half a smirk.

"Ah! A baby smile!" He turns back to Greta. "How am I doing now?"

"Better." She squeezes him in a hug. "You take care of my girl. I'm serious. I don't care if she cries from a paper cut. I'll be down here in a hot minute."

"You won't be back here any time soon on account of her. Later, Greta."

Before I follow Kyle up the marble steps, Greta gives me a hug. "We'll be in touch."

"Thanks for finding me…I think." What I really want to say is, "*Thanks for not being a murderer.*"

"No need for thanks. Just watch: You're going to have the time of your life here. Welcome home."

CHAPTER FOURTEEN

LEONA HALL

KYLE'S SHOES TRACK NEEDLES of grass and clumps of mud into the academy. He's made the perfect trail from field to marble floor. "After you," he says, pulling another door inside the academy open. "Bet you're excited to take a shower. It's been a long day, yeah?"

I throw all kinds of sass his way. "A shower?"

"Yeah, like…because you came with Greta. Most runaways get to Malveaux after months and weeks of being on their own and sleeping on sidewalks. Stuff like that."

"I'm not *most* runaways."

"*Some* runaways."

"I'm not *some* either." My eyes pierce through him, but the fool is still alive.

An amused grin exposes the ends of his even, white teeth. "Oh, you and I are going to have a lot of fun."

I hum, filling the space of silence with nervous noise and random gazes. "So, this is…a Varien school. Is there anything I need to know?"

"Right!" Kyle claps. "The tour. That's…that's what we're here for. This is the grand foyer of the building." He points. "From here, you've got options. Our dorms and lavatory are on the top floor. The student rec center is up there too for if you want to work out or play some games. That's also where you'll find the art gallery. There's an arboretum on the roof. What else?" He hums. "Oh, Divine Hall is for freshmen and sophomores. Fates Hall is for juniors and seniors. You're a junior, so you'll be in the Fates. Dama Hadley is head of our hall—she's crazy. Classrooms, Great Room, and library are on the bottom two floors. Straight ahead is Leona Hall. You can find the entire faculty there, along with the student store, admissions and records, and the happiest place on earth, the dining hall."

All of it is gorgeous. Cleaner than anything kids should live in. That's what my mom would say. If she could have things her way, our home would be wall-to-wall marble like this place, airy in shades of ivory, sky blue, jade, and gold. But what she wouldn't have are the angelic muraled ceilings with the quote, "Ad Astra per Aspera" circling the base of the dome. Or the stacked arches and Roman columns holding up each story. It'd all be too much. Like heaven's lobby.

"…That's it?" I ask, following Kyle into Leona Hall. "What a grand tour."

"I know. I know. It's just…I have to get back to the court and I'd really like to shower before I show you around. Your meeting with Sage Cameron is the main event anyway. She's gonna set you up. You'll like her."

He swoops open another Victorian door and fans his scent of cut grass and pine in my direction. It smells too much like outside.

"You good?" he checks.

"No, I'm not."

"I'm sorry…I wish I could say exactly what you need to hear."

"Really?" I step one foot into the hall of offices and look back at Kyle.

"Of course."

"Then tell me my dad is okay. Tell me he won't die."

Dumbfounded, Kyle grasps for the right words. "I-I…uh." *They don't exist because no one should ever have to do what I did today.*

"Thanks for showing me around, Kyle," I say in a monotone, perfectly aware of how awkward I've made him feel.

"You're welcome. I'll be back after your meeting…good luck." Grey smoke wraps around his body and ignites a crackling pop as he teleports, and the door between us shuts.

CHAPTER FIFTEEN

STAY

THE DOOR HANDLE TO Sage Cameron's office twists beneath the space of my hand. I freeze and watch the door push away on its own.

"Come in," a voice hums. Through the thinly diffused eucalyptus and lavender vapors, I see shelves of books adorning the wall units. Hanging academic and medical certificates are addressed to Sage Maureen Cameron. *Medical...seems legit.* Then again, Jack the Ripper was most likely a doctor, so—

I hear a giggle. "The prefix before my name is just a formality. So, I hope our meeting will ease any reservations you have."

I look around for the voice's owner and grow mesmerized as she steps away from a bookcase. Her skirt drapes over her feet. With each step, the rhythm of her cowrie-shelled locs and loose clothing create their own Coriolis effect. She moves like the wind.

She clasps my chin between her fingers. "My visions didn't disappoint. You're stunning."

My face goes blank.

"I'm a telepath, Alexia."

"...Like in the comics?"

Sage Cameron gives a half nod. "Maybe. I've never looked into comics from the other realm...where you came from. But, if that's the best way for you to process things, I'll be whoever you think I am."

"The 'other' realm? You don't call it the Normal realm like everyone else?"

"No."

"Why?"

Sage Cameron beams. It's almost as if she's happy I'm asking her this. "Because it's not my normal. It's some other place. *This* is my normal."

My mouth curls in a smile.

"Well, hey, that's better. Have a seat, please."

While Sage Cameron's turquoise-ringed fingers dial the kitchen for mineral water and a light snack, I study the pictures inside her frames. Her photos tell the story of a cultured woman—one whose tawny skin bronzed under the desert sun and rosied during harsh winters. She's done things I'm too afraid to ever do, like riding some sort of exotic elephant with two trunks and walking on hot coals.

"You must be exhausted," Sage Cameron speaks. "I always worry that meeting new students the day they enter The Grove is too much. There's realm lag to deal with—it's night in the other realm. Day here. And then you come into a whole new culture and history. It's a shock."

"It doesn't matter," I say, completely dull. "What's one more thing?"

"Hmm…maybe peace of mind." There's something about her smile after it fades. A genuine happiness. "Of course, given what you've been through, that might take some time develop. And that's completely fine.

"We want to ease you into our culture. Majority of the students here come from generationally gifted families—families that've never seen gaps in their lineage—so they have an advantage over students who share situations like yours. You'll see this as you acclimate but try not to get intimidated: We want to help you transition in the best way possible."

"You think I'm going to acclimate?"

Sage Cameron reads between the lines. "With some ironing out…yes, I do. It's your nature as a Varien."

"Hmph, tell that to my dad," I quip out of habit. Then remember Dad from the last twenty-four hours. He's not the same Dad as yesterday—he's the Dad that knows my secret and the one who suffered for it. I stare at a corner where a hanging glass orb contains a soleil—like the one Tadashi loaded in the trolley—masked in an overcast of clouds. Another unwanted loop of all my tragedies shoehorns its way inside me. *Sarai arrested. The lockdown at Mercy Bay. Telling Dad the truth and living in a small moment of freedom. The winged man atop Ren's roof.* Scenes I don't want to watch.

A rose embroidered handkerchief wipes across my cheeks. Small trails of sadness gather in the corner of my mouth. "Your father loves you," Sage Cameron tells me. "That's something no one can take from the both of you."

A pain rises from inside of me, the worst kind: invisible and hardest to treat. "Then why did he put me in this position? Why has he done everything he could to force Variens into the worst living conditions?"

"Because he's scared…he's just scared."

I scoff. "Well, he should be scared now. He's pissed the wrong guy off. That winged man won't stop until he's taken everything."

Sage Cameron's eyes travel to the other side of the room. She doesn't look like she wants to have this conversation.

I test the waters anyway. "Do you know him?" I ask. "The winged man? Greta told me he may live here… He kidnapped my friend Sarai for something called Nadir and she told me you'd know what that is. We've got to find—"

Sage Cameron sniffs and shakes her head. "It's just like my sister to put twenty on ten."

"What?"

"She talks and she talks…sells folks what they want to hear in an effort to get them here. Smart." I watch Sage Cameron walk back to her desk, fluttering her hand and looking at the basketball team outside her window. Burning in my skin begins.

"Greta didn't seem like she was lying when she said that. She said you're a Sage because you know practically everything anyone could ask you. She said you'd give me the answers. That you'd help me!"

"And I will help you…in realistic ways: mentoring you, protecting you, teaching you about your gifts, and helping you in this process. That is what I can do."

"That wasn't the deal." I grit my teeth.

"But it's the truth." Sage Cameron stands firm. "And my sister cannot speak for me. I would change the circumstances of every runaway if I had the gift to do so. I have other ways of changing things. Choosing the right courses and professors to teach you and guide you. Dama Baptiste, for example, is the finest history professor in The Grove. She will teach you in a way that will inform the present and predict the future. Benito "Ben" Zapata will be your guiding light on mastering your gifts in SIM Class. He will teach you how they work and put you through courses that expose you to weaknesses and memories that can call your power and direct it. We call these spark and steer tokens. They are the key to helping you operate in full control. Once you know these, you'll be at peace. At least a bit more than you are now."

I review myself and release my tight hold on the armrest. Hot turns to warm.

"Life out there, in the other realm, can make you tense… make you build walls inside yourself," Sage Cameron goes on. "It's nothing to beat yourself up about. You do it to survive. Here, you're free to nourish your capabilities because The Grove is a haven for our people. This dark galaxy 'full of undetectable stars. No non-Varien can inhibit you here. That's how it was always intended to be." Sage Cameron takes a small booklet and a manila folder from her desk drawer. She hands me the booklet titled *The Grove: A Quick Guide and Origin Explained*. "Read this when you have some downtime. It has every answer to any question that may come up and it's good to have as a reference."

Mindlessly, I flip through the pages.

"You'll see some info there on the Malveaux brothers: Marcel and Louis, who founded the academy," Sage Cameron shares. I spot their black and white portraits. Two Black men in suits with hair parted at the middle and slicked down. Twins. They share the same pretentious and serious mustache every man from the 1900s donned.

I dog-ear the page and flip forward before getting stuck on a woman's portrait. She's painted in beautiful detail: dark ebony skin with light shining on the cliffs of her round cheekbones. The pleasant smile she gives over her shoulder makes her full lips the focal point. She is regal, donning a silk, copper-colored headwrap that drapes down her back. Tendrils peek from the scarf's edges. I've never seen old paintings of people who look like me in my history books. I rarely meet those whose shoulders I stand on through lessons at school—except the select usuals like Dr. King, Harriet Tubman, and Rosa Parks. A full education of public figures, inventors, activists, and abolitionists came to me after hours, at home with Mom and Dad.

"Who is this?" I ask.

Sage Cameron strains a look into the booklet. "Oh! That's Dama Fabienne Doucet, our founding Mother. She is the reason all of us exist here. She really is the most interesting woman that has probably ever lived."

"Really? How so?"

"You crossed the Retrouvailles Bridge earlier, right?"

"Yes."

"And I'm sure Greta explained the story depicted on the stained-glass."

"She just said it was a meteor shower that made a hole in the realm barrier."

"Yes, that's the beginning of it: the Leonid meteor shower of 1833. It was a sight to see across the other realm…in America. Everyone everywhere could see pieces of the sky shimmering down to Earth. Majestic fireballs raining in every direction for nine hours…that's how it's been described by witnesses. You can imagine that in such a dire and early time, it frightened people to death. I mean, people probably assumed this was the end of the world. But, from where Dama Fabienne stood, in her designated quarters, it was a sign. A sign to flee the imprisonment of chattel slavery, especially as she discovered she'd "turned" into a Varien like a small group on the plantation.

"After hearing stories of enslaved Variens who led rebellions across the country only to be trapped and burned in their homes, or gunned down, fear became a bigger weapon. Propaganda manipulated minds and told everyone Variens were not divine beings, but demons. 'They aren't to be trusted as they can only lead you to death,' is what overseers told them. It poisoned minds. Made brothers and sisters turn against one another…and Dama Fabienne knew it'd be a matter of time till she'd be found out. During the times she could tap in to her gifts, she'd use them to get herself out of trouble as she could manipulate memories with the touch of her hands. She could remove them if something she did angered someone or add them to change the course of events for her benefit. It wasn't worth it to rebel, but it was worth it to run and find a place she could be free and unassuming. A place where she could reinvent herself. So she set out and planned her escape while keeping her gifts a secret.

"And when she finally hit the road, after days and days of traveling arduous paths on foot, she heard a voice. This voice wasn't something she could describe as male or female. It wasn't inside her, or outside her. But it was clear, and it was not hers. She believed it was an angel telling her where to go, keeping her from harm and leading her to the sustenance of an orange grove deep in Louisiana. Roots sprouted from the fallen meteors, making rows of mature fruit trees. Much like the orange you ate, its flesh calmed her hunger and revealed a whole place where the light of day washed out the other realm's night.

"She found The Grove and heard the voice tell her this was her sanctuary, her gift, so long as she could lead others like her to it. And so Dama Fabienne spent her first several months rescuing other enslaved Variens. She did as much as she could, until one day, others started showing up from the realm tears in their states all over the country, and eventually, outside the country—bringing Variens of different colors and cultures to The Grove's doorstep. This stunned Dama Fabienne. She did not know other races and countries were experiencing the 'turning.' You can imagine she didn't trust well—not initially. But the voice told her that she must maintain a loving heart and build a culture she wished for and had not seen. So Dama Fabienne stayed faithful, and The Grove has kept its promise of safety as we built the covenant of working with the land. Not just simply taking but giving. Having a symbiotic relationship. In return, it gives us an abundance of life, energy, purity, resources, and security…since 1833…because of Dama Fabienne."

Speechless. I take a few breaths. "Wow."

"Wow is correct. And that was only a summary of her story. You'll learn all of it in time. Her legacy is ingrained in everything: this school, the infrastructure, our society, government, and technology."

I stare at the soleil lamp beside Sage Cameron's desk, wondering how it works as the small sun floats above the long golden floor stand. She follows the trail of my gaze.

"Even that! Yes, soleils are a product of her foundation. Dama Fabienne always dreamed The Grove would innovate with our environment. She often sought out people with keen minds and vision for architecture and invention. Brilliant people. Renauld

Malveaux, Marcel and Louis's uncle, was one of them. With his ingenuity, he created soleils from the dust rain particles."

"Oh yeah, Greta told me."

Sage Cameron giggles. "Good. I'm glad she told you something accurate. It's important for you to know about this. Renauld's invention is the reason we can house, feed, clothe, and educate children like you. When his nephews opened this school, he vowed to give 30 percent of all profit to refugee students at Malveaux.

"…Anyway, back to getting you started. We'll need a medical exam—both mental and physical—to assess your wellness and powered capability. You'll see Dr. Langley for that. Once the results come back, we will have an official categorization for your gifts, as well as your measured strength. Don't worry, it won't interfere with your studies or place you on a hierarchy. It will inform us of where you are based on a four-tier system: tier 1, tier 2, tier 3, and tier 4. Usually, a refugee from the other realm is a tier 1—as expected. With time and conditioning, your strength, and capability will grow."

Wishing I could sleep instead of dealing, I close my eyes. Sage Cameron's bangles clank. The breeze that creeps from the outside sprays the smell of jasmine in the office. Laughter and playful yells travel from outside.

"Alexia."

Alone. I want to be left alone, I think with my eyes shut.

"Alexia…" Sage Cameron gives way to a sigh. "We offer extensive counseling here. Sometimes students don't need it. I'm just afraid, especially in your situation, if you don't participate, you'll suffer in the long run. I know it's rough to have it mentioned, let alone talk about…but trust, I've seen the most promising people decay because they didn't tame their demons."

Sarai. Mercy Bay. The winged man. Burning Dad. I can't get it out of my head.

"Alexia?" Sage Cameron calls. "I'll give you time to think about it. I'd be happy to do a session with you…if it'd help."

My hands shake. Sage Cameron blankets them with hers. "One step at a time, right?"

"Yeah," I whisper, bracing my sore eyes open.

"I also advise our students who come here, like you, to put off the start of their studies. To fold into The Grove and Malveaux first. Get into the habit of waking up and sleeping here. Eating our food and drinking our water. Digesting how we live and the dynamics of our history. Hearing languages like Viridian and others for the first time."

"So, who would teach me things? How would I learn anything about where Sarai is? Or the fool with the wings?"

"Is that your only focus here?"

I pause. I think about appeasing Sage Cameron, a habit I wish I didn't have.

Sage Cameron sighs. She gets up from her desk to open another window. A paper from Sage Cameron's desk floats in midair and folds itself in half. It draws closer to her, still floating, as though an invisible person is carrying it to her and fans her. "Sorry about the temperature. My office runs hot. Would you like some water? I know I'm thirsty."

She moves around and refills an empty glass—with the same shimmering water I saw Greta drink earlier—from a pitcher.

"I'm good." Truth is, I'm not. I'm hella thirsty. But I'm also hella scared to drink *that* stuff. *Is there anything else around here to drink? Anything moondust free?*

"Okay, next thing…" She comes back to the desk—a wide, live edge, dark wood slab—and taps it before sliding on cat-eyed spectacles and studying the notes in my file. "As far as your rooming arrangements, you'll be in room 242 in the Fates Hall. Kyle will show you around. Alani Akina-Phoenix will be your roommate. Hmph. Let's see if third time's a charm."

It isn't hard to pick up the sarcasm in her idiom. "Third time?" I clear my throat. "Meaning I'm her third roommate?"

"Uh-huh."

"What happened to the other two?"

"One requested a dorm transfer, and the other ended up at a new school. They weren't compatible, I guess."

I'd make it into *The Guinness Book of World Records* for longest eye roll right now. "Listen, I don't want to room with the 'boogeyman.' Okay? I'm barely a Varien. Can I just room alone? I don't care how small it is. I won't be here long. I'd pref—"

"You are *very* much a Varien. And what do you mean you won't be here long?"

"All I need to do is hide out here for a few moons."

"Your words or Greta's?"

"Greta's."

Sage Cameron's head drops but I can still see the disappointment she wears. "I'm really sorry about what my sister told you, but that also is not true. You can't go home in a few moons because we need you safe. We need *everyone* safe. And we can protect you. You'll have to settle with calling The Grove home. It's complicated, and I will explain it to you as emotions settle."

This can't be happening. Greta lied to me.

The heat, it's starting again, rushing through my chest and inching to my arms. I begin to cry. "I can't stay here forever. I *have* to go home. I need…my dad, my family…" I can't speak. My throat tightens the more I envision my old life fading away.

Sage Cameron listens to my curses. She's waiting for me to compose myself—for the star flares to retreat inside my heart. "Hope is still here," her calm voice repeats.

By the umpteenth round of the affirmation, my body cools. I don't understand how she's able to soothe me, but it works like a flood of water over a burning field.

I wipe my cheeks. "So, I've got nothing. That's cool. I'll just adapt to a place that'll remind me of a life I don't want. Not to mention, this psycho roommate you're setting me up with."

"Oh, this is the best place for you to be—with people like yourself. I wouldn't have paired you if I didn't think you and Alani would get along. Yes, she's had trouble with her past roommates, but I chalk those mismatches up to my sabbatical. They have Dama Hadley to thank. I see the potential of a great friendship. Alani has some bite to her, but once she lets you in, she's soft."

"I guess I don't really have a choice."

"You'll never be bored. Both her and her cousin, Kyle, are very entertaining. When you befriend one Phoenix, you're bound to the other by proxy."

"Kyle?" I repeat. "The boy?"

"That's right. Your campus mentor…you've met him," Sage Cameron remembers. "Kyle is…very precocious. Any grey you see on my head came from him. I love him, so, I don't mind the hairs. His dad was very charming when we were in school together. It may not seem like it, but Kyle takes after him a lot physically and personality wise. He'd be a good friend."

She slides a key across the table. "Trust me."

Is trust even possible when you don't have a home? Or when you have to depend on a telepath who can read your mind?

"Do you read people's minds without them knowing?"

Sage Cameron smiles a bit and doesn't hesitate in telling me, "No. I don't think it's moral. But sometimes, thoughts with a high mental volume scream at me. Happens mostly when guilt is present."

"Must be hard for your spouse to get away with a lie," I say with the full intention of prying.

"Ah, that's exactly why he's no longer around. But he is another saga…it's time to start yours."

I think fast—about everything thrown at me in the last few hours and what tomorrow will look like for me. "Umm…Sage Cameron?"

"Yes?"

"What will I do after I get into my room? You said you prefer that I 'fold' myself in to the environment for a bit, but…what does that really look like during the school year?"

Sage Cameron nods as if she understands what I'm getting at. "It can be challenging seeing the world around you move, but once you get into the hang of things and participate in things to improve your wellness, like our therapy groups and campus activities, the edge will soften."

All I see are vignettes of me in quiet. Processing in silence. Unimpressed by this gilded cage. I will lose my mind if I wake up and do therapy and yoga every damn day, and I won't be any closer to figuring out anything about Sarai and where she is. If I want to find her, I'm going to have to dive into The Grove headfirst or I won't be able to sleep.

"That's not going to work for me…"

Sage Cameron clasps her hands together. "Why not?"

"I just think at this point, knowing myself…I need to be busy and social. I will dissolve if I don't. For me, Sage Cameron, this is not folding in. This is soaking in things I don't want to soak in. This is soaking in my trauma. I understand your intentions and recommendations, but every person handles things differently. I think I want to take classes and explore this place with the kids here."

"You bring up good points, but you do understand that this is a survival tactic? It's not actual dealing, but deflection."

"And I don't want to deflect, but I was also tricked into coming here. I thought I would be doing something different and leaving eventually. So please, just hear me when I say I literally can't breathe right now, and if I feel boxed into doing things I'm not ready to do, I will spend my time finding every possible way to leave this place."

Sage Cameron takes a bit. I study her face and read the wrinkles carved in her skin. The crow's feet around her brown eyes pinch, a wear of experience and life, but the eyes they surround communicate something else: empathy.

"I hear you. Processing can't be forced on anyone, especially with such a unique situation. You're exactly right. So, why don't we compromise? Paint a new picture of what your wholeness can look like."

"Okay…" I'm nervous to say more. I'm getting what I want and I need to keep it that way.

"You will be enrolled for SIM Class, but because of the nature of the mental work it takes, I believe it's best to delay your start with it. We will work toward therapy, but I would like to be your mentor and connect with you weekly. Nothing intimidating. Just time spent. You can work with me and learn more about The Grove and the academy through my work and commitments. I can hear about your transition and how things are going."

"Yeah."

"Yeah? I think that's a good balance." She clears her throat and checks her watch. "*Jon bwen!* Time goes so fast. I hope we covered enough, but not too much."

"It's too much," I rain on her parade, her careful approach to my fragility. "But that's not on you. I just…I just think there's no way around it not being 'too much' for me."

Sage Cameron's taupe lips grin and radiate a trusting warmth. "True…I just hope you know that this—what you have and who you are—is not a curse. It's a gift." She turns away, every inch of her musical, like her sister. The shells and beads clasped in her locs, the rings stacked on her fingers. The beaded belts around her waist. The swish of her long, multi-colored skirt. She peeks out the office and perks up. "Kyle! Perfect timing! I was just checking for the stuff I ordered. Would you take Alexia to dinner during your tour?"

"Yeah, first thing." He steps through the doorway. Dressed in a button-up and black slacks, he looks like he's changed more than his clothes. And me, I'm a mess inside and out, still upset with knowing the door is closed on home. No way back to Dad. No road to finding Sarai.

CHAPTER SIXTEEN

WILDER THINGS

WE CARRY ON THE school tour after dinner. I managed to dodge drinking Zenith water for the third time today by swearing by pressed apple juice. Everyone else around us chugged it with no difficulty, but I'm still not convinced. Still a foreigner to The Grove and this body I inhabit. I think of Greta's words: "*Makes what we carry inside us weightless*" every time Kyle takes sips from the canteen he's carrying around. He told me he has to drink at least 120 ounces a day to feel his best. He talks a lot—even for a tour guide. I don't usually like that, but at least I don't have to fill any silent spaces.

"You'll notice there's murals in every hall. Each of them kinda explains the inspiration behind the hall's name." Kyle brushes a finger over his plush bottom lip as a thought comes to him. "Like the Leona Hall, it's supposed to depict the constellation of Leo— where the Leonid meteor shower came from."

"Hmm. Lots of intention."

"Yup. My *favorite* mural is this real nice optimistic layout of scales and possible outcomes of either disaster or paradise. I don't know…seems like the right thing to display for kids who'll embark on adulthood shortly. What do you think?" He stops in front of a wall and brings his right hand back to his mouth.

I follow his gaze and study the mural in front of us. Lit by the warm yellow light of the crystal soleil chandeliers above us, it is realism at its finest. A scale perched in the middle of a meadow. Full on one side where beautiful women, men, and children dance with fruit and branches in hand. And where the scale is high—a crowd of painted people rock distorted faces. Lonely. Toppling from the scale and falling toward doom. Unable to see one another through a mass of dark smoke. In an instant, Kyle's sarcasm translates.

"Oh, wow, yup…very optimistic," I laugh lightly.

"I knew you'd love it."

"Yeah…who wouldn't? I mean, it's a choice. A real…vibe."

"A message: Don't fuck up or your life is over."

My laughter fades on that last one, because that's really what life told me. That's all it takes for me to return to my "shell" as we walk on.

"Are you okay?" Kyle asks, shaking me out of my train of thought. I try my best to perk up, but all I can do is stare at the increasing room numbers on each passing door.

The corners of his hazel eyes wrinkle with his smile. "You're worried about my cousin, aren't you?"

"No, she sounds like bestie material. I'm so excited."

"You're bad at lying…but okay. Alani will like you."

"I'm not worried about *her* liking *me*."

"Ah well, then that's something only you can figure out. Get some rest for tomorrow. We've got a lot to do in the city."

"Yeah. Seven, right?"

"Six, seven…what is time, really? I mean, you're realm lagged, so, I guess one more hour of sleep won't hurt. Seven it is." After a friendly nod, he teleports away—to his dorm, I think.

I turn to mine. My sleepy eyes daze at the numbers on the door. When I turn this knob, I'm on to the next phase of my life, whether I like it or not.

I stand tall, still teetering both realms, my heart with home and my brain with Malveaux Academy. With one final push, the door glides open. I can't back out. Here it is, room 242.

When I enter, every inch of it is cloaked in smoke. My lungs hit me with coughs. As I try to clear through the smoky film, I hear her speak, "Too much?"

I hack and squint. "Yeah, I uh…just like fresh air."

"Well, there's plenty of fresh air for the condescending on the balcony."

The girl opens the sliding door to the balcony. I follow, holding my breath. Nothing irks me more than the smell of smoke after my grandpa died from lung cancer.

The girl flounces to the pearl marble rail and crushes her cigarette against a glass ashtray. "Forgive me for being rude. I usually smoke out here, but there's people in the courtyard. I'm sure one of those losers would snitch on me."

When my eyes widen as the girl leans backward, she leans further. Explaining, "We can't fall. Don't worry. Malveaux wouldn't be Malveaux without an invisible protective netting made of their own patented groundbreaking material." She sits up, laughs at her authoritative mocking tone, then mists perfume across her olive skin then sniffs her hair. It's different, an ombre of flame-colored hues. Maroon roots. Orange body. Blonde tips. "I'm Lalani…but everyone calls me Alani. What's your name?"

I catch myself staring. "Oh, Alexia."

"Alexia…I like it. Pretty girls always have pretty names." Alani perches herself on the balcony's rail. She closes her eyes, dips her head back, and inhales. "I love the smell of autumn here. It's heaven."

When I don't respond, she straightens up. "You can't be comfortable standing. Take a load off." She nods at a plush armchair. I sink into its cushy padding.

"Like a pile of clouds, right? My boyfriend made it for my birthday, strictly for this balcony. Oh, and just an FYI, we're not allowed to smoke here. It's against the rules, but you'll find out I don't always follow them."

I keep my eyes to the stars. "I won't tell anyone about it," I say. And I mean it, if she keeps those damn sticks outside.

"Peachy." Alani smiles. "So, what tier are you?"

"I don't really know what that means."

"Tier, as in strength of gifted capability—or however they describe it. I'm a tier 3…finally. They should've told you after your test. You were tested, right?"

"Not today. I just barely finished touring the academy with Kyle."

Facing the room, she hops on the railing and playfully kicks her legs. Her eyes glint. "Ah! So, you met the parasite, my cousin. Did he get on your nerves?"

I force every sensory function to play it cool. "Not really. Everything is so overwhelming. We didn't really get to interact much."

Alani guffaws. "Lies. Every girl that meets Kyle loses their shit within the first five minutes. There's no way you're immune."

"I mean…yeah. I'm sure he could get annoying, anyone can."

"Annoying isn't even the word." She pans over me. "Are your powers similar to mine? They must be since we're roommates. The school tries to keep all fire abilities together."

I shrug. "Sage Cameron said she made her decision based on intuition."

"Let's hope she's right. Some girls request transfers the next day."

A laugh I don't recognize leaves my mouth.

"They were complete bitches. They had it coming, anyway."

"What'd they do?"

"Well, I have my minor rules and cardinal rules. I only have three major cardinal rules as a roommate. 1.) No snitching. 2.) No keeping tabs on my whereabouts. 3.) No thirsting over my cousin.

No dating my cousin. It just doesn't work well for me. And both of them broke a cardinal rule."

"Oh."

"You can't be my friend if you aren't my friend. Right? That's my thing. A friend wouldn't, excuse me, *shouldn't* be documenting each time I skip out on curfew to see my boyfriend. She shouldn't tell Dama Hadley each and every way I manage to sneak out. It's girl code. But this girl had no couth. She did what she did, so I did what I did."

"And that was?"

"I put blue dye in her showerhead. Big deal. It wore off after three washes."

"Of course."

"And that…" Alani points a finger as she passionately speaks. "That betrayal wasn't as bad as the other broken rule. When the other girl started crushing on Kyle…it put me in a weird place. First, I wondered if she used me to get to him. I didn't like that. He drives me crazy, but he's still my family and I'm really serious about protecting him. She pursued him for a really long time and when he finally let his guard down and got interested, she stood him up one night because she started dating someone else. That was enough for me."

"Enough for you to do what?"

"Douse her clothes in itching powder." She shrugs like it's minor. "I mean who was really the victim in that situation? My cousin, or her?"

I clear my throat. "I think it may be a little more nuanced than that."

Alani smirks in amusement. "I like you. I can tell you aren't like them already," she says, tapping her box of cigarettes. "Sage Cameron may be on to something."

"Maybe."

She shamelessly studies my face. "You look like you've had a rough time."

"I'm not up for talking about any of it, if you don't mind."

"I'm not asking you to. You just had this look on your face, like you didn't want to…never mind." Alani drops from the railing, straightens up, then flourishes a hand of flexed fingers in the most nonchalant fashion. Within seconds, her entire palm erupts in flames.

I sink deeper into Alani's chair.

"Don't freak out. This is my gift. No damage. No burns. No pain. And check this out…" The fire soaks back into her pores—a precursor for her next trick. The strands of her hair ignite into a red blaze. She wears a proud face—one of contentment—as the flames grow and replace her thick, wavy hair.

I admire the fire until the embers cool into a curtain of platinum blond tresses. Like a glamorous shampoo model, Alani flips her hair to one side, living for the gasps and claps I'm giving. "Dang, I wish I'd gotten that power instead. I bet you never have to color your hair."

"Well, I do if I want it to be a wild color. It only changes to blonde and black. Plus, I was born with this crazy setup." She points at her tresses. "So, hair color is kinda boring to me. But, Lex, you don't mind that, do you? If I call you Lex?"

"Yeah, I like it."

"You want to be powerful. Believe me. Whatever happened before was out there. And out there, Normals are threatened by power. Here, you're preyed on for being weak. You have to rise from the ashes that are at your feet now if you want to survive, that's what my family always says during hard times. That's how we got our last name. My great-great-great-grandfather arrived to The Grove as a refugee and changed his last name to Phoenix for a new start, to symbolize the strength and perseverance it took to make it here. He wasn't weak for being in his position. He was brave for finding a way and figuring his new life out." She shares this story with me like it's going to magically make me better and less embarrassed about where I've come from. But I humor her with my manners and let her talk, just like I did with her cousin.

"So," Alani continues. "You can't be a weakling if Sage Cameron paired us. Show me something."

"It's not something I can really call." I flit my eyes. "I used to dream about being cured from it. If it were gone, I wouldn't have to be here."

All Alani's hard edges soften. "It's not going to go away."

Her honesty is free of malice, even though it isn't what I want to hear. I take those words and fight the burning behind my eyes. "Then maybe I'll learn to adjust. I'm sick of breaking out in hives all the time."

"You will. Training and therapy make a world of difference."

My small yawn rolls into a bigger one, pairing well with the redness I feel in my eyes.

"The made bed is yours," Alani points out. "Catch some sleep. Tomorrow, you meet the bloodsuckers. I'm gonna have another smoke. I'll stay out here, don't worry."

I thank her and immediately guilt-trip myself for not wanting to meet her. She doesn't seem all that bad. At least not now.

"Hey, Lex." The huskiness of her voice bounces off my back. I turn around. She savors a long drag from her slim cigarette and blows a lonely smoke ring to me. "You don't have to be scared anymore. You're safe."

CHAPTER SEVENTEEN

ODDITYLAND

DAD VISITS MY NIGHTMARES before he arrives to my dreams. Crying beside Sarai, he wails on about how I've betrayed him. "*You turned on me.*" Dad's weak voice breaks.

Sarai shivers beside his crisped skin. "*And you left me,*" she says icily.

By the time I wake up, I've sweat my sheets to the mattress. "Lovely," I mumble when I catch myself in the mirror. My roots have curled tight on one side of my head from the sweat. Stray coils from my chunky twists stab the air with jagged patterns. They scream for my attention and don't stop until I round them up in a frizzy, ponytail.

"Better throw some new clothes on if you want to grab breakfast," Alani suggests from her vanity, practicing the pyrokinetic lighting and extinguishing of the room's candles.

"You're not ready."

"I've been dressed for an hour," she says. The only large stretch of fabric covering her are frayed denim shorts and the sheer blouse that barely blurs her halter top.

I rub my eyes. "You're wearing that? I mean, it looks nice but…they let you wear stuff like this at school?"

"I'm wearing it," she shoots back. "It's casual day, and I'm sixteen. What do you wear at school? Tunics?"

I shake my head and Alani looks me over. "Need to borrow some clothes?"

"No, it's okay. I can wear this again."

Alani thumbs over my sweater's grey sleeve. It's stained in Dad's blood. "You can…if you're cool with rumors."

When I pause to think, Alani arches one eyebrow. "Varien high school is still high school." She lays out a pile of neatly folded clothes before me: an olive green tank and ripped jeans. Too alien from my usual.

As soon as we step out, I realize just how Normal I am. Between the cross-legged girl floating in a bubble casually reading a comic and the two twins playing kinetic water tag with the spouts of their canteens, I'm burning out on sensory overload.

"Wet T-shirt contest!" one of the twin boys declares, streaming a ribbon of water at Alani. She counters his power using the flames from her hands.

"No horseplay in the halls!" an older woman reprimands.

When is fire ever horseplay?

Alani pops her gum. "Yes, Dama Ghastly…I mean Dama Hadley."

Dama Hadley huffs, looking half-compelled to either keep calm or scalp that pretty head of hair from Alani's crown.

"Move!" an agitated voice crashes into me. I back up and apologize for paying more attention to the hall traffic instead of the path in front of me. But my supernatural distractions are far from over. Especially with an extra set of angry eyes encased in the neck of a six-foot girl. I move away quickly until I no longer see either one of her faces.

"She's an ogre…sorry about that." A pale and dark-haired girl pats my arm. "Should I go 'put a spell' on her?" she jokes with Alani.

Alani pops her gum. "Nah, wouldn't help your cause much." The two laugh and part ways, but Alani clues me in once the girl is out of earshot. "That's Raquel. Everyone thinks she's a witch because she left school awhile back to live on this crazy commune with her parents."

I pause. "Is she?"

Alani swats the air. "I mean…yeah. Anyone would be. But she's cool, I guess. She came back to be regular again. Oh, here we go…are you ready to eat?" she asks with excitement.

The dining hall's interior is even more amazing than when I first witnessed it at last night's dimly lit dinner. Gold caps the ceiling. Limewashed neutrals color every wall. Windows stand from ceiling to floor. Soleil lamps hang, not from chandeliers, but ropes of velvet ivy. I feel like an orphan shoved into a monarchy overnight—completely mesmerized and unfit.

A long buffet table borders a wall, with chefs ready to serve a variety of foods. The menu is impressive—a far cry from frozen pizzas and nuggets—and chock full of some creole dishes I've never heard of. Then there's baked currant doughnuts, sugared roses, cheese grits, honey-glazed biscuits, smoked salmon, breakfast burritos, cinnamon pancakes, butterscotch sticky buns, spinach quiche, artichoke souffle, and eggs. *Hella eggs*. Poached eggs, eggs benedict, and every single egg option that exists.

I inch closer to a tray of scrambled eggs, but a nudge pauses me. When I turn to my left, there's a boy with a crop of short sandy locs with the sides faded. "Them eggs ain't the eggs you're used to. May not wanna mess with 'em," he says.

"What do you mean?"

His brown, deep-set eyes hold secrets and amusement. "The animal products here are cultivated. Lab grown."

I pan back to the eggs then up at the server. "Are these from a farm or…?"

"These are locally fabricated by the Agro-Group."

I stare back at the boy, who's smacking his teeth and raising an eyebrow. We give each other one last telling look.

"Thank you," I say to the server. "I'll go with the cinnamon pancakes."

The boy moves along with me and I grow curious. "Are you from the Normal realm?" I ask.

"Yup," he says smoothly.

"Where?"

"Oakland, California."

"I knew it. I mean, your accent sounds familiar. That's where my mom is from."

"For real?"

"Yeah."

"But you come from?"

"Sac."

"Cool. Cool. I'm Erik, by the way."

"Erik, I'm Alexia. Good looking out. Nice to meet someone from home." I check his tray and he's got a nice hot bowl of plain grits with brown sugar melted on top. "Have you eaten the meat here yet?"

"Yeah. It's not bad. There really isn't a difference…it's just the mental piece. I'm not always good with it. But they've been doing this for decades, I guess. It's how they keep a better balance. Less stress on the environment. And they do get their farm-sourced animal products, it's just limited and regulated. Ain't no free-for-all. That's why mostly everyone here is some kind of plant-based vegan, vegetarian, pescetarian…man…"

I laugh. "And what're you now?"

"A survivor." Erik laughs too.

We approach the drinks and the pitcher of Zenith water taunts me. I pick up the orange juice instead.

"Scared of the water?" Erik's husky voice catches me.

I nod. "Very."

He nods in agreement. "Yup. I was too."

"Was?"

"*Was*. I tried it and it changed my life. I take that water to the neck every time now." He loads up two glasses. "Drink it. Trust me."

As I spot Alani at the table near the arched windows, Erik walks with me. I don't question it. I like him being here. He reminds me of Niles's friends—funny, chill, and cute—another piece of home.

"Hey, Erik," Alani greets him as we both sit around her. "I knew you two would find each other."

Erik laughs.

"He told me about the eggs," I tell her.

"Did he tell you it's okay to eat them? That you won't *die*?"

Erik's full lips scrunch up.

"He just kept it real," I reply, exchanging another knowing look with Erik.

POOF!

A tall and energetic boy materializes through grey smoke and the smell of crackling circuits. There's a mountain of food threatening to fall from his tray as he cops a seat in the chair across from us. I jump while Alani groans. "God help me, Kyle, how much cologne did you put on this morning?"

Kyle sniffs his collar. "Just a spray."

Alani grimaces. "Ugh, I could smell you before you teleported."

"Ah, that must be your third manifestation. I'm starting to think you're becoming a Labrador," he teases between chews.

Alani slams her hand on the table. "Don't start!"

"Woof woof! Ruff ruff!" he mocks and morphs into another form. Right before my eyes are two Alani Akina-Phoenixes. The authentic one on my right side, red in the face and cussing up a storm; and the other, across from me, stuffing her face with a breakfast burrito and barking like a dog.

"Y'all wild," Erik adds, casually eating his bowl of grits.

"I'm just playin'." Kyle molds back into himself and interrupts Alani's rants. "How'd you sleep, Alexia?"

"Terrible, after the shit introduction you gave her," Alani snaps.

"What're you talking about? I'm an excellent campus mentor."

"You're an idiot is what you are."

I work myself up to speak. "I didn't sleep much."

"I'm sorry," Kyle says—just like he did when I met him yesterday, when I almost ate him alive for trying to be nice.

"Phoenix! I told you to wait for me," an approaching tan and tall brawny boy in a basketball uniform says. "Hey, Townsend!" he reaches out to Erik and they do some kind of handshake.

From the switch in Alani's body language, it's clear he's her boyfriend. She stands up to ruffle his shaggy, brownish-blond hair and gives him a kiss. A kiss designed for closed doors. Lord have mercy.

"Get a room before we all get pregnant," Kyle quips.

Erik scrunches his face with me.

Alani cuts her eyes at Kyle until he returns to demolishing his burrito. Her boyfriend's stern face folds into a sweet grin. "Let it go." He kisses her forehead and directs his attention to me. "You the new girl we saw yesterday? Out by the court?"

Erik nods.

"Maybe," I say.

"And you got stuck with this guy?" He points Kyle out.

"Yeah, I guess."

Alani's boyfriend gives Kyle a look—the kind of look that speaks volumes only to those it involves. He scratches his square jaw. "I'm Nate." Nate has a clean-cut swag to him that communicates he's someone important. Yet, he's still seemingly non-threatening with warmth behind his smallish brown eyes.

"Alexia—"

"Jacobs," Kyle finishes.

Boy, if you don't... I'm already over him.

"Do you want that?" Kyle forks into my last pancake. "I'm starving." He laughs as if I'll say, "Well of course, since you're *starving.*"

I turn my nose up. "Go ahead…since you decided to touch it." There's a pricking in my chest every time he bothers me.

"Sweet. These two-a-day practices are getting to me. All I do is eat and sleep, eat then sleep, sleep some more, eat some more—"

"KYLE!" Alani shouts.

"What?" he says with maple dripping from his mouth.

"Are you even chewing?"

Nate gives a toothy smile, exposing a set of dimples. "Bet you'll get a stomachache during practice, Phoenix. I'll put money on it."

"Oh, he'll be dyin' later. Coach'll love that," Erik jokes.

"Why would I make a bet with the heir of one of the great heirloom families? If I lose, I *lose* money. If you lose, you *still* win! You make a few grand every five minutes, right?" Kyle debates.

"All right, if you don't get one, I'll give you 200 fleurs." Nate grins. "In the event you *do* keel over, can I just point at you and laugh? You can afford that, right?"

Kyle pauses mid-chew. "That's the douchiest thing you've ever said to me."

The boys snicker before Erik returns the conversation to me. "So, you're heading out to the Belle Rues today? That'll be a culture shock."

I grin, close-lipped.

Nate adds, "And your classes too…"

"I haven't gotten mine yet."

"I have!" a perky voice chirps. There's a girl squeezing between Alani and me—her and the major bulky machine clipped to her backpack. It beeps and holds a circling bright light. The owner acts like she's needle thin, the way her hips squeeze between us. "We have Varien History, SIM Class, and Engineering together. Three classes!"

I sip the orange juice in my cup. "Oh…I won't be in SIM Class for a bit."

"No?" The girl frowns, concerned.

"Sage Cameron thinks it'd be too much, too soon."

Alani nods. "I agree." She nudges the girl. "And, you know, it's illegal for you to go through the registrar's records?"

"But I didn't…not this time." The girl reaches into her high-waisted pocket. "Here, this fell from Dama Hadley's folder." She hands me a paper. Sure as shit, Varien History, SIM Class, and Engineering are on there with three other courses.

"I'm Lucie, by the way. Lucie Diaz. I lead Malveaux's robotics and forensics teams. Which reminds me, Alani, I know you told me not to bother you, but we need your points on the importance of realm travel without moonlight via Midray. Do you have them?"

"No," Alani snaps. That's when I feel for poor Lucie. All her happy seems to droop.

"Um…you don't have any idea about why it could be fruitful? There are so many—"

"I literally cannot think of one good thing about it. And you know this already, Lucie." Alani brings the frustration in her voice down. "It's never been tested on subjects with our same biology. I love a good rule break but that's not what this is. It's a death wish. And, I don't think our ancestors would approve. Look at how we enter The Grove…through their grace. Based on that, anyone willing to realm travel with this machine is stupid. Put me on the opposition."

Lucie sniffles, pulling herself away from the table. "Yeah. I just thought you'd be up for innovation."

"Not this time, Luce," Alani says.

Lucie smooths her ponytail. "It was nice to meet you, Alexia. If you ever need help in class, or want to explore The Grove's terrain, I'm one message away. Oh, and I can program your school laptop if you want. I could jailbreak it, which would make it run a zillion times faster. It'll get you access to every corner on the IVnet too—even the restricted pages. You can get media you miss from the Normal realm there." She gives me a business card with clouds printed on it.

"Oh. Thank you, Lucie. I definitely will."

"Awesome! Bye, everyone!" she squeaks and power walks away. Her backpack is hiked up so high, the ends of her bouncing ponytail touch it.

Everyone at the table says their goodbyes, and when Lucie is out of earshot, Alani cuts her eyes away and sucks her teeth. "Lex, unless you want to find things like dead invisible manticores and folklore shit, you better keep Lucie out of your school laptop and stay away from her little madshop. Okay?"

"Madshop?"

"Her little hub where she makes crazy shit."

"Okay," I tell Alani.

"Good."

Kyle lifts his tray up and eyes me. "On that note, we better get going. Wouldn't want Alani to worry if you're not back by curfew."

Alani balls up her napkin and throws it at Kyle. "Have fun, Lex. If Kyle acts up, let me know."

"Better start making arrangements then," I say, looking at my plate—evidence of Kyle's premature bugging. Alani, Erik, and Nate seem pleased with my comeback when they giggle. I follow Kyle, indifferent to the land of oddities around me, numb to their emotions, raw as ever with my own.

Inside, I feel like dying. I could cry without warning, and if I have so much as ten seconds to sabotage myself, I may just unzip all that grieving chaos. I'm afraid I'll never come back sane if I do.

But with Kyle, I never get to ten. "You know, I kind of feel betrayed, *Lex*." Kyle rests his hands in his pockets as we exit the academy.

"Do you?"

"Yeah. After meeting yesterday, I thought we'd be friends. Like…a team that Alani would be subtly excluded from." He holds the door open to the trolley and I slide onto its butterscotch seats.

"Hmm…that could still happen."

"Yeah?" Kyle's thick brows perk up. I drop my backpack between us.

"Yeah…when you serve me pancakes." I look out the window, away from Kyle's direction. He holds silent, then sighs.

"That's fair."

CHAPTER EIGHTEEN

THE BELLE RUES

"YOU'RE GOOD LUCK," A voice outside my head says.

"Huh?"

"You're good luck," Kyle repeats, grinning like what he's saying is obvious. "The stars, they're shedding. Dust rain. Only happens on the really hot days. Legend is, if the stars rain on anyone's first journey into town, they're golden." He holds his hand out and little gilded flakes cling to the hairs on his skin.

I stop walking. I've been obsessing over the pits of my life so much, I've forgotten where I am: the Belle Rues. A bustling area full of skinny stone and glass buildings with ornate doors covered in mosses and foliage. Trolley bells ring as drivers wait for passengers to load. Glass orbs float midair to transport people to the tops of vine ridden skyscrapers. The Grove's downtown feels like a shot of vitamin C.

Citrus trees line the sidewalks. Their scent blends with the smell of bakeries, restaurants, and grilled seafood. And the rain, like falling glitter, sticks to anything it touches, piling in the trenches of the curb. It's the most phenomenal thing I've ever seen. A cosmic baptism. I want to be washed in it. I want all the good luck to outweigh my bad, to be anointed. I don't care if it's an old superstition. From head to toe, I brace myself, hoping with all my might to make things better.

"That's the first time I've ever seen anyone wish on dust rain," Kyle says.

Both of my eyes slowly stretch open. "I don't see how that is. It's literally wishing on stars…and besides, we're sort of kin…me and the stars."

I wonder what Dad would say if he saw this. Would he say the universe is dissolving because Variens have thrown it off balance? Would he see this as proof of our curse? To be so far from human that a star's touch feels lukewarm? He'd hate this. So, I dust myself off and walk ahead of Kyle and head into the tailor's shop.

"Wait…wait! How do you even know that's where we're supposed to go?" Kyle waves at me.

I point out the navy-and-green tartan uniforms in the window.

"Oh…well, yeah…like I said, this is where we'll get you fitted."

Fit is an ill word. Especially when you've been waiting on the puberty stork to deliver you a pair of boobs. I try on a grip of skirts, blouses, dresses, and blazers. None of them fit like I want. I feel swallowed by fabric. Tall, narrow, and without hips, I'm a green bean. The only girl without a body in my family. Not once have I ever hit up a family reunion without hearing my aunt yell, "Vince, go on and stack some ribs on a plate for Alexia!"

The Alexia in the mirror eyeballs me. She scarecrows her arms as I do and frowns at the bunching of the blazer's shoulder pads.

"You look like you hate your life in that blazer," Kyle judges.

"I mean…"

"No, like a middle-aged woman who left the job she hates to go home to the family she hates," he jokes.

I find him in the mirror. "Do you want me to tell you what you look like in your clothes?" I retort.

"Only if you apologize after." Kyle lies out on a pink chaise. "Stick with the cardigans."

All it takes is the wrinkling of my nose to signal the tailor away with the blazer. Pulling my knee-highs up, I give in. "Malveaux is just gonna get what I've got."

Kyle rummages through my shopping bags. "What's up with all this girl stuff? Do you like, use all this every day?" He drags his finger into my tub of edge control and applies it to his sideburns. He pats the area down when he's done, and nods in approval. "Oh, that's good stuff."

"*My stuff.*" I snatch the tub from his hands.

Kyle goes from taking my fit with tough skin, to gazing up at me like an awed child. He squints suddenly. "You need uh…help with your tie?"

"I tied my dad's all the time." When we were happy, Dad let me tie his every morning. Mom always says Dad knows how to fix a tie better than anyone, but he lets me think he can't because it's our thing. A father-daughter thing. "I'm fine."

I'm fine…I'm fine. Inside of me, the deepest part of me that wants to scream and mosh, doesn't agree. I'm suddenly hot like a blown fuse, a wick burning down. Scenes of doomsday hit me like channels of static. *Sarai. Mercy Bay. The winged man. Dad. Dad… burned. Dad's skin split by my hand.*

Heaving in little fits, I touch my chest.

"Whoa! Are you okay?" Kyle pops up.

I yank at the collar of my blouse. "I need to go outside…" What I also need is water. It's been too long since I've had some and the stinging in my kidneys feels even worse now.

When Kyle tries to prop me up with his hands, I slip through them. "Hang on," he says. "Put your arm around my neck."

Even though that's the last place I want to put my arm, that's what I do. We walk through the tailor's boutique. Concerned eyes are on us. My body tells me there's not enough time to get out—not enough to keep hold of the supernova inside of me. It's not safe for anyone. I throw myself away from Kyle and bolt out the door. When I fall to the Belle Rues' mosaic sidewalk, my nails dig into the grout. Wrenching up my spine, the heat moves in an unfamiliar way: more wild, potent, and terribly hot. It coils itself up my throat, and God, it's as if I've drank lighter fluid then swallowed a match—like I'm burning from the inside out. I scream and drops of my saliva puddle the ground. Dust rain circles me in a cyclone.

"Just breathe, Alexia," I hear Kyle before he places a hand on my shoulder. I flinch it off.

"Go!" In seconds, the beams of cosmic light—the surreal supernova—inside of me crawl from my throat to the middle of my face. Water fills my eyes as the temperature overwhelms me. I aim my head back to the sky I can't see, and ropes of stars break from my eyes and shoot toward the clouds.

Seconds die, the dust rain settles, and my overflow of nerves and power are balanced again. I'm feeling better, but I'm so tired.

I grimace and wipe my wet mouth. Kyle bends down beside me, looking into me like no one ever has. "Feel better?" he asks. A black bandanna drapes over his palm. "Here."

"You're not freaked out?"

Kyle shrugs with gold flakes of dust rain clinging to his dark hair. "It's not like you're the only one who gets panic attacks."

"You say it like it happens to everyone."

"It does."

"Like that?"

"Not if you don't want it to."

I scoff. "You think I *want* to be like this?"

"Oh my gosh…everything is an argument." Kyle shakes his head and walks off.

"Okay, first of all, you don't know me!" I chase behind him. "Why should I be happy about this? Why should I want to be like this?"

"You have no choice, if you haven't noticed! Take responsibility. Learn your tokens like everyone else so you can spare yourself more drama."

"I've only been here for a damn day. I don't even know what tokens are."

"They're the memories connected to your power. They make it tame."

"And you expect me to just know this? To be up for living on a whole different plane after seeing my dad almost die?"

The record is scratched. Kyle's agitated scowl disappears.

"Alexia…I."

"You know what? Just go—" In the middle of an epic eye roll I manage to scope out something familiar. Something I shouldn't be seeing lives on the other side of a bookshop's window. Small, rectangular, and in full color. Muted gold wings, just like I saw them yesterday. A ragged trench coat. Crops of designs scarred all along his deep brown neck and body. But this time, there's no face of a man on his neck. A skull is in its place, with gritting teeth, and decayed skin that blackens around the valleys of his eyes and cheeks. It's him. The winged man who stole and ruined…on paper.

CHAPTER NINETEEN

LEGENDS

I PUSH BY KYLE's shoulder and storm into the bookshop before he follows me.

"Welcome in," a shop associate greets me. I zoom past her and head to the window. When I get there and hold the book in my hand, more confusion is born.

"A comic?" I say in disbelief.

The shop associate strolls behind me. "Our most popular since we've opened." She's all jolly about it, looking proud as I flip through the pages.

"No…this man is real. I've seen him!"

"Set?" The shop associate giggles. "He's real to ten-year-olds maybe…or anyone who believes in Santa."

Kyle gives her a sharp side-eye.

"Set," I repeat. "What do you know about him?"

"We have to finish up at the tailor," Kyle reminds me.

"Just give me a minute."

The associate gives Kyle a look, almost asking him if I'm serious. "Oh umm…I don't read every issue, but I know he's the leader of the Revenirs."

"The Revenirs." I study the cover. That same word banners the comic in bold: Revenirs Reclaim. "And what do they do?"

Kyle tries to reel me in. "Alexia, c'mon."

"Stop."

The shop associate goes on. "In the comics, they just kill people. People who've committed crimes or done terrible things. In every issue someone comes to the Revenirs for a job, and they take it on. 'Coming back from the dead to reclaim stolen breath!' Remember that line from the cartoon?"

She gushes at Kyle, except he's not amused.

"We have to go. Thanks for your time." Kyle nudges the small of my back.

"I'm staying," I say.

"Seriously? The guarde are right up the street. You keep spewing crazy in here and that woman will call them. She does it for less here."

"I'm not afraid of the police."

"*The guarde*…and you don't know them. You're not from here, remember?"

"Do they serve the public? Taxpayers?"

"Oh my God…yes."

"Then they serve me. I'll go to them myself."

"Sage Cameron is going to flip…Alexia!"

"Go sit somewhere, Kyle!"

"Listen, if you walk in there talking about Set…saying you've seen him…you're going to get committed."

"Because there's a comic based on him and his crew? Normals romanticize killers too. Charles Manson. Jeffrey Dahmer. The Zodiac Killer."

"I don't know who those guys are—you see how that works? But I know what everyone thinks about the Revenirs, and they're complete fantasy. Campfire story crap."

A stab to the heart couldn't hurt more. Sarai wasn't taken by the air. Dad wasn't hit by the wind. The truth is not a fable. "Kyle, I saw Set!"

"You saw someone else."

"Set!" I shout. "He ripped a man apart in broad daylight and didn't flinch. He's a murderer, and I refuse to overlook him by playing story time!"

Down the street, a sign reads: "Grove Guarde." I run to it. The breeze pushes against me—just like Kyle and everyone else.

"You haven't paid any taxes yet!" I hear Kyle shout from down the way.

Crafted designs are embedded in the rusted iron doors hidden beneath the station's porch top. I go to the entrance, but before I can open the doors, a web of charcoal smoke pops and blocks the way. "Alexia." Kyle appears.

"You need to move," I demand.

"I'm begging you, please do not go in there."

"I will scream if you don't move."

"Alexia, please listen. You don't even know how things work or what these guys do. Okay? Community organizations handle smaller scale issues here. Things like theft, noisy neighbors, or property damage. But the guarde handle big issues. Big crime."

"And your point is? Kidnapping is a big crime."

Both of Kyle's tan arms go up. "Not when an imagined character commits it! What're you not getting? Listen, the guarde has changed over the last few years. They're not what they used to be. They ask questions less and punish more."

"Have you seen where you live? This utopia? It can't be worse than what I've seen at home."

"Alexia, I'm begging you."

I take a breath and brace my hands to push him. "For the last time, I'm going to scream."

Kyle's eyes widen. "And I'll teleport and leave you here looking even crazier than you sound."

"I'm sure Sage Cameron and Greta will be pleased with you if you do." *Checkmate.* I smirk as Kyle clears from my way. My hands fit into the door's loose handle. It creaks as though it's rarely opened, and I enter it.

CHAPTER TWENTY

OFF GUARD

THE GUARDE STATION HUMS with the sounds of typing, shredding, and all the other noises I usually heard in the Capitol office. People buzz around with their faces occupied by their tablets and sheets of paperwork. Uniformed guardes sit and listen to the various people in front of them. They're tired, unconvinced, and cynical—not a good sign. But I notice the absence of firearms on each guarde's hip and take that as positive.

I shove my reservations aside. Now is not the time for them, even if Kyle disagrees. After all his failed attempts to get me to turn around and head back to Malveaux, he's still trying. "Do you want to get arrested? That's what's going to happen." He skirts in front of me. I dodge around him, closer to the guarde at the front desk.

"Are you two together?" she asks.

"Yes."

"No!" My brown glare meets Kyle's confident act. "I'd like to file a report."

The guarde removes her gloves and types into a tablet. "What crime are we talking here? Drugs? Assault? Stalking?" She eyeballs Kyle suspiciously.

"Murder," I answer. "Kidnapping and assault."

The guarde's face grows serious. "Date and time?"

"Yesterday, the kidnapping took place early morning. The murder and assault happened that evening."

"In what location?"

I breathe in deep. "Mercy Bay…in the Normal realm."

The guarde drops her finger from the tablet's screen. "We can't help any Normal, nor do we want to. Things out there aren't our problem."

"What if the suspect is from The Grove, though? What if they kidnapped someone and brought them here?"

"Then that's worth reporting," she says. "You saw the suspect?"

"Yes."

"Describe him."

"Male. Over six feet tall. Scars that run up and down his body and face. No hair. Large gold wings."

The guarde glares at me. "You know what you're doing? Reporting a false crime."

"I'm reporting an actual crime. I wouldn't have come all this way to waste time."

She looks me over. "I'll have to pass this report over. Another guarde will see you." With her nose in the air, she motions for us to follow her. We go where she goes, tagging behind her like a train.

"Have a seat," she says and points to the cubicle next to her.

Kyle smiles like an idiot, laying his cheesy charm on thick. "Thank you, ma'am." The guarde leaves as we sit, disappearing into a back door behind us.

"We should leave right now," Kyle freaks out. "It's not too late."

"Then go," I tell him.

He has me thinking he just might as he fidgets. Looking over the cubicle wall, then shrinking down into his chair. "Shit. He's coming." It's obvious before Kyle says it. The old floor shakes under the guarde's steps.

"So, you say you saw a Revenir." His tall height is all that's epic of him. He could've been a titan with it, but that potential source of intimidation is gone, and in its place is a worn out balding man with massive hands and stubby fingers. Very Tony Soprano.

"I did."

The guarde wipes his face down and the bags under his eyes stretch. There are enough rings around them to count all his unslept nights. He puffs out one giggle with a smile that doesn't reach his eyes. "You see all these people in here? They've come to us because of real things."

"Glad no one is wasting your time."

The guarde holds his tongue, staring at me like he wants to cut mine out. "And they're reporting in ways that don't insult the guarde. No fabricated suspects, crimes…none of that."

Kyle, still laid back in his chair, speaks up. "Gold wings, scarred skin…sounds like a proper description to me. One you should listen to and at least write down."

I see him and I don't know who I'm looking at. Kyle is genuinely confident.

The guarde is amused. "I know you, yeah? You play ball, at Malveaux. You're the prick that headbutted my son last season."

Kyle recoils and his jaw clenches.

I check the guarde's name badge. "Rockwell," it reads.

"Don't talk to him like that," I defend. "He's just telling you what I have to say is valid. Something is going down. The men who stole my best friend said so themselves."

Rockwell's face tilts. He glares, out of impatience maybe, but mostly with a message of caution. I jump when his hand closes over mine. The coldness of his black-enameled, gold ring presses into my knuckle. "You should leave."

"Ay! Don't touch her!" Kyle swats his hand away.

In an effortless twist, Rockwell paws Kyle by the arm and folds him face down on the desk table. He's got him locked with his wrist contorted. "Don't fuck with me," he grits over Kyle's groans. "I have no reservations about breaking a kid's wrist." Rockwell bends Kyle's twisted wrist backward.

"Stop! Help us! Please!" I beg at the sight of Kyle's reddening skin. No one in the office looks at me except the civilians. The other guardes ignore me and carry on. Help is something I will not get here. "We'll leave! Just please, let him go!"

Rockwell cuts a glare. He waits the clock out and pushes Kyle's resisting hand further.

"LET HIM GO!"

A guttural cry comes from Kyle. I wonder if he can take more, but I don't have to for much longer. Rockwell releases him. What's left of his thinning hair is splayed across his face.

"Get out." He sneers.

We rush and obey. Kyle holding his injured wrist in one hand, and me with my pride and plan torn to shreds. Our heads keep aim to the floor, yet somehow, we navigate through the station quickly. The attention I so desperately wanted from the other guardes comes as we exit. It isn't the right kind, though.

The air outside the station smells sweet and pure, a big switch from the curls of cigar smoke and staleness of the station.

With his good hand, Kyle punches an advertisement sign near the trolley stop.

"Stop! You want both of your wrists blown out?" I shout in shock.

Kyle darts away from me, shakes his fist till it opens, and rests on the curb of the sidewalk. He's still hurting, and I'm filled with guilt. His head flings his wispy dark hair back and he grunts.

I step closer to him with a small reservoir of apologies. "Is it broken?"

"Another second and it could've been. Are you done now?"

"What do you mean?"

"I mean has all of this sunk into your head?"

"Did you not experience what I experienced? Because clearly they're hiding something."

"Pretty sure I experienced more than what you experienced." He motions to his wrist. "So, thanks."

I could slap the sarcasm out of his face. A deep breath and closed lids work much better for now. But it doesn't get me any closer to answers. It doesn't make up for why I'm here. I've come outside with just as much information and frustration as I had before I went into the station.

My fists ball up and I pivot. I'm ready to run and go my own way—even if I don't know the path. At least no one will tell me I'm wrong or crazy. I sprint away from Kyle like a victim given one shot at escaping her kidnapper. Maybe Sarai is doing the very same thing right now too. I hope she is. My heart beats faster as my legs storm through the Belle Rues. I play a game: The faster I run, the faster Sarai will too. If she gets away, so will I.

Kyle calls after me. I don't answer, and I don't look back. I know I've lost him when the volume of his voice falls out of reach.

CHAPTER TWENTY-ONE

RETROUVAILLES

I COULD RIDE THE wind with how fast I'm running. My feet could lift, and my body would cut its way through the sky. I wish that were me instead: a flier. Not a walking nuclear bomb. Not a daughter who attacked her father. I filled his flesh with hot stars, baking pieces of him, then left half of him alive. I should've stayed no matter the cost…because no matter how I slice it, I deserve to rot. Where Sarai was, is where I should be now.

When the streets of the Belle Rues thin out, I find myself in the Virgin Forest. I stop and crack open my locket. A waning moon appears in the brush strokes of one painted side. Alone and afraid, I break from wandering, allowing myself to cry. Maybe I could hide here till the next full moon. The Grove's entrance shouldn't be too far away. The Virgin Forest was one of the first things I saw when I arrived. I could go home. I could at least try.

You wouldn't survive in the wild till then, I think.

I rest in piles of rustling gold and copper pine needles. Tears water them. It feels good to freely release all of this in an open space. Wind breezes through the lush trees and dries the wet streaks on my face. *Forgiven.* The word blooms in my mind. It dissolves right as it soaks in. Forgiveness isn't something I can fathom right now on my own. No person can without grace, and grace isn't something mankind creates. "*It's from the heavens,*" my Big Mama always said. "*God forgives you. So, forgive yourself.*"

I curl on my side and give my weariness away. "I'm sorry. I'm sorry…" With each iteration, a stitch pierces into my mental wounds. Between the strands of my chunky twists, I spot a pair of sneakers in the distance. They belong to a pair of noodle-like legs. Kyle's legs. I sit up and clear my face with my arms.

"You run way too fast."

Not fast enough, obviously.

Kyle walks over to my cot of pine needles. He's out of breath, and somehow in better spirits. "Need a hand?" he asks.

Drowsy and empty, I hesitate—wondering if I should scamper off again to wait the moon out. But when I see the inflamed ring around Kyle's wrist, I come to my senses and grab hold of his uninjured waiting hand. "Did we miss the trolley?" I look beyond him.

Kyle squints. "Not sure. I think it went back to Malveaux after we bailed."

"You never went back to it?"

Kyle shakes his head. "I had to make sure you were okay first."

The clouds break, and the sun reaches out to us. Wind ribbons around my legs. When I can't move myself to say sorry, it shoves me to take the first step to Malveaux. I look back at the spanning mountains of metallic nature. Gold, silver, and copper treetops. Forest beds of green moss. An autumn dream. The steeples of the Retrouvailles Bridge peek out from them. As much as I ache to walk through it, and leave The Grove, I won't be heading there anytime today.

"Here." Kyle hands me his canteen. "I refilled it for you."

I pause, thinking of all my reservations. Everything is different now, even water. And like the other things, this change isn't something I can outrun. I need it or else I won't survive. Apprehensive, but willing to try, I relent in the battle of Zenith water vs Alexia.

"Thank you," I say to Kyle—which feels wrong to say given what I've put him through. I take the canteen and start drinking slowly, for taste. There's nothing drastically different from the water at home, just a cleaner and brighter feel. Crisp and refreshing with a little hint of coconut. I take more in. The coldness of the water takes my body temperature down. Before I know it, I've drank the entire bottle.

"Dang. You were really thirsty." Kyle takes his bottle back and examines it.

I wipe the sweat from my forehead. "Yeah…I was."

"Feel better?"

A wave of cool drips inside of me from head to toe. A strange sensation, like being doused in liquid menthol. Tension in my shoulders disappears and so do the aches in my back, the stinging in my kidneys die out. It's like every cell I had lost a vise grip. I do suddenly feel lighter, free of gravity, and bondage.

Greta's words come back to mind. *Makes what we carry inside us weightless.* This time she was telling the truth.

"Wanna teleport back? It may throw you at first, but it's the safest way."

"Thanks…I think I need to walk the day off for a bit."

Pine needles crack beneath my sneakers—a satisfying sound bite. It's all I want to hear, the backdrop of the earth's only pristine forest. And with Kyle three paces behind me, it's what I get.

CHAPTER TWENTY-TWO

THE CALL

A s soon as we teleport back to the academy, Dama Hadley meets us on the marble steps. Arms folded to match the tension in her tight freckled face. With her round, oversized glasses, she looks like an owl out in the daytime—too nosy to be bothered with sleeping.

"Sage Cameron will see you first, Kyle," she tells him as though he should expect it. I watch Kyle's shoulders droop and another pang of guilt hits me.

"And you," Dama Hadley goes on, switching her intimidating gaze to me. "Sage Cameron will call you when she's ready."

I rush to open the door for Kyle. "On the phone?" I look back and ask Dama Hadley.

She doesn't say a word. She just taps her temple.

Discipline is coming. I wonder what that looks like in a place like Malveaux. A place that preaches wellness and balance. Are detentions a thing? Is there a three-strike system? The more I think, the more I find myself wondering into wandering—from Leona Hall to the art gallery on the top floor.

Seeing parts of the academy on my own makes things click. Connect. Seep in. It's quiet here. Just the sound of my sneakers squeaking on the grey-and-white marble checkered floor. More paintings of Marcel Malveaux and past Sages are here. There's a wall dedicated to every portrait of Dama Fabienne Doucet ever painted. Her evolution depicts her sweet face in her younger years and her saintlike aura in her old age. Seeing her makes me smile inside—the same feeling I'd get in the presence of my Big Mama. Like everything may just be okay because she's praying for us all still. Watching from above. Protecting.

The sun's rays bleed through the stained-glass window dial and paint me in rainbows. I study its beautiful brilliance, but its appeal draws me to the somber painting below it. The gold plaque beneath the art piece reads, "The Two Madonnas." A tale of a woman split in two. One side of her is perfect, with a gorgeous room serving as her backdrop. An immaculate smile. Neatly braided hair. The other side is in anguish: nothing but dirt and sky behind her. She wears misery on her face. Dark circles under her drooping eyes. Tears rolling down her face and frayed hair. It's how I feel inside. One perfect way on the outside, sick, sad, and broken down on the inside. I am the *The Two Madonnas*.

"Hey," Alani announces herself.

"Hey. How'd you know I was here?"

"Well…Nate saw Kyle getting escorted by Dama Hadley to Leona Hall on the way to the library. That could only mean one thing. Did something happen?"

Lying strikes me as a way to go. For some reason, I never thought of Alani. Never considered her protectiveness or what her wrath could be like when it comes to her cousin. It's hard to imagine this given how they speak to one another. So, how do I tell her I got her cousin twisted up by a guarde?

"I'm going to tell you the truth because I don't know what else to do."

I look down but I can hear Alani taking a breath. "Okay," she exhales.

"I went to the guarde station to report something that happened in the Normal realm. My friend Sarai…she was kidnapped before I came here. I went to report this against Kyle's better judgement."

"Better judgement?" Alani questions—because to her there is no such thing.

"Yes… Sarai was taken by a guy who looks like these urban legends you have here: Revenirs, I think they're called."

"And you went to tell the guarde about it and Kyle told you they'd think you're nuts?"

"Pretty much. And they did think that. I mean, they were very nasty to me. They thought I was filing a false report. One guarde got a little aggressive and Kyle defended me. That's when he assaulted Kyle and twisted his wrist."

Alani's face molds into a concerned frown. "Is he all right?"

"I think so, but he's hurting." I wait for her to say something as her face moves through worry, panic, and surprise. "I feel really horrible even though I didn't intend for this to happen. I just…I just hope you aren't mad at me."

"Mad? You're crazy if you think I'd blame all this on you." She's sitting on a bench in front of the stained-glass window.

"Maybe you should. I'm the reason Kyle went in there."

"Lex, you didn't sprain his wrist yourself."

"But he was trying to protect me. That's all he was doing. I didn't listen. You should be mad about that."

"Well, I'm not. The guarde doesn't believe you, but I do."

"You do? Why?"

"Because Kyle's wrist is sprained. That wouldn't go down over some fake shit. He wouldn't stick his neck out for someone he doesn't respect." Alani has a sharp brown-eyed stare. It's the most intimidating stare I've ever seen on a girl, but it's real. "I believe you," she repeats.

"Thank you," I say. The three words I've wanted to hear from everyone. I've said those words before—to Sarai. They meant the world to her. They mean the world to me.

Her hand taps mine. "C'mon, the kitchen is making pop rouge ice cream with blackberry dumplings."

"I've never had pop…whatever."

"That doesn't surprise me, but you have to try it. Yeah?"

I shrug carelessly. "I'll eat a little."

Alani rolls her eyes and mocks me, "A little." She gives me a hand. "That's all it'll take."

"…For me to throw up."

"For you to be in heaven," Alani playfully corrects.

We laugh and immediately my head goes dark. Thoughts tousled. My mind is now a box, tipped with its contents scattered on the floor. An echoing is loud in my head. *"Alexia, please see me in my office now."* I grip my temples. It's Sage Cameron. The sensation of her voice searing between my ideas and thoughts strikes like an axe wound.

"Lex? What's wrong?"

"Sage Cameron just called me to her office."

"When she could've just had you wait in the admin office till she was ready."

She could've, but after what went down today, subtlety won't be Sage Cameron's style when dealing with me.

"Looks like pop rouge will have to wait," I say.

Alani and I leave the gallery behind and make way to Leona Hall. Alani snaps her fingers and ignites a flame. "Not if I can help it. We're overdue for a fire drill."

I laugh with her but she's serious. Her eyebrows hike up to match her mischievous smirk. "Give me ten minutes," she says.

CHAPTER TWENTY-THREE

DISCIPLINE

THE BELL FROM THE high tower gives three rings at three o'clock. The sound quakes through Malveaux's halls. Oxfords and Mary Janes squeak against the marble floors. Everyone rushes around; their faces are bright—happy to be free from classes for the evening. It's hard to not wonder when I'll have that sort of freedom.

As Kyle walks out of Sage Cameron's office and glares at me, I challenge him back for a moment. But when I catch sight of the brace around his hand, I can't help but feel like the biggest clown alive.

Sage Cameron waits outside her door with a cup of tea. The spoon within it stirs on its own. "Come on," she says, unenthused. *That makes two of us.*

Alani blows raspberries behind me and flashes all her fingers as a reminder. Ten minutes.

"Please shut the door behind you," Sage Cameron says.

I do as she says and sit. "Is everything okay?"

"I think you know it isn't." Sage Cameron twirls to face me. Her grey tie-dye skirt spirals with her legs. "I've never had a student violently injured on a tour before."

"I see Kyle's told you everything." *Snitch.*

"Actually," she goes on with her nostrils flared, "he said he had hurt himself on campus, but I knew he was lying. I couldn't move him to say a word about you or where you went."

"Well, he said what he said."

"Oh, he did." Sage Cameron smirks with amusement. "So did your locket."

"My locket?"

Sage Cameron cocks her head to the side. "Did my sister leave that out too?"

I rewind to the first time I met Greta and flip to the present. "She said she could find me with this…"

"Way to remember. You see, my sister and I are a package deal. When she locates you, so do I. Do you want to tell me what you were doing at the guarde station?"

"No."

"No?" Her eyes pinch. "Being difficult doesn't make you cool here. I can get the answer. I'd rather offer you the respect of speaking up instead of invading your thoughts."

"Fine. I went to get answers after finding out you all glorify psychos."

"That's something you shouldn't have done."

In my head, I can see one of those carnival games with the mallet, the high striker, a game Niles couldn't lose. He'd used all his force to strike the puck up to the bell, and it'd ring like a banshee at its breaking point. That's my brain right now. Ringing. Screaming. Within three seconds, I forget who I'm talking to. "Why not? Because he's real? Because the Revenirs are real? I already know they are. I felt it the moment I reported the incident. And now, looking back on our first meeting, you showed me you knew too. You never acknowledged a word I said about the winged man or the kidnapping."

"Alexia, you don't know anything."

I rise from my chair. Overflowing with frustration, ruddying my cheeks with warmth. How dare she play me like a fool. How dare every damn last adult here. "All of you are liars! Why won't you help me find my friend? Why won't you tell me the truth?"

"Because you're insisting on trouble." Sage Cameron keeps firm.

"What does that even mean?"

"For one, you filed a false report and can be arrested for such. Two, there are things you shouldn't meddle in. Even when something doesn't exist, the mind can make it so."

"You're nuts."

"Excuse me?" Sage Cameron sets her cup of green tea down on her desk beside a stack of blank Malveaux Academy letterhead.

"I'm not going to create Revenirs by asking about them."

"No, but you might open yourself up to the energy that comes with this obsession."

"What?"

"Your safety would be at risk."

"Oh my gosh!" I cover my ears. "Stop. Kyle didn't get his wrist twisted by a guarde for nothing. I'm not stupid!"

"Watch your tone!"

"How can I when I'm not being heard? You say you respect me and then you lie to my face. It was Set who was out hunting me like he did Sarai. That's why I can't come home, isn't it?"

Sage Cameron's gaze is tense. A locked chest I can't crack. "Oh, Alexia. I'm so sorry."

"For what?" I ask.

Sage Cameron sighs, holding her finger to her forehead. "I should've come with you and Kyle this morning. It's not typical because incidents like these don't happen to our students, but so much is affecting you now. You could've used my support. You're very fragile right now."

"Fragile?"

"Yes."

"No!"

"You are."

"No, I'm pissed!" The nosy roses outside peer into the window at the sound of my shout. Without turning, Sage Cameron shuts them out with the blinds.

"Maybe you do need more time."

"To do what?" I throw my arms up.

"To process what's happened to you. Maybe we should scale back on the compromise and fold you in like the other refugee students."

"I don't have time to *process* my way out of depression. I have to find Sarai!"

"You need to let yourself breathe. You need to heal. Everything else is not a priority."

"I told you how I want to do things. That's not going to work."

"Then we have to come to an understanding."

"Which is?"

Sage Cameron is holding on to her patience ever so tightly. "We will keep our first arrangement: weekly check-in, all classes except SIM—because again, you are not ready for that. You will also spend tomorrow morning in the infirmary and complete your lab work."

I grumble quietly. "Whatever."

"And you will not leave Malveaux's premises without me until further notice."

"You can't do that!" Grenades exploding. Doors slamming in my face. That's how Sage Cameron's order hits me.

"I'm your guardian," she huffs. "And I just did." Sage Cameron turns around to the back end of her office, walking her frustration off with both hands on her hips.

My attention darts down to her desk, to those blank letterheads. The teacup beside them has a tide like the ocean. Tiny, crested waves crashing against the china's brim. Sage Cameron's mental storm. I get a quick idea and snatch a blank paper from the pile—folding it up to hide it in the waistband of my jeans.

"When the next full moon comes, I'm out of here." The words are sour on my tongue.

Looking betrayed, Sage Cameron turns around sharply, like I've thrown a dagger at her and missed. "You may not believe what comes from my mouth, but I think you trust me enough to not follow through with that."

"Yeah well, you should trust me enough to listen." One solid stare is all I spend on her. I've had enough talking.

"We aren't done here!" Sage Cameron shouts but no volume is great enough to be heard over the urgent wailing of the fire alarm.

"I think we are," I say.

CHAPTER TWENTY-FOUR

Caution

Labs in The Grove aren't the labs I'm used to. Just like how eggs in The Grove aren't the eggs I'm used to. These labs are very physical. It isn't just bloodwork. It's hair analysis, brain and body scans, skin biopsies, and nerve examination. It's being poked and prodded. It's giving me anxiety. When Sage Cameron ordered me to be here, I didn't think it'd take hours. "Is there anything else on the list?" I check with Dr. Langley.

"Do you have somewhere to go?" he laughs. "People to see?"

Yes, fool, my inner jerk responds. "Other places I want to be." I smile to take the edge off.

"Fair enough. No one ever likes the doctor." He laughs and sighs. "You're all good to go now, actually. We've got everything we need."

"Perfect. When can I expect results? Tomorrow?"

"Results for some tests typically come in fast, but we ran a lot here. A variety of test results will arrive anywhere from tomorrow and others may take up to eight weeks. Just be patient. We'll get it all in."

Eight weeks? Hopefully I won't be here by then, I think.

"Sounds good. Thanks," I say to Dr. Langley. I check the clock on the wall. The timing is perfect. SIM Class starts in fifteen minutes, and if I want to get out of here in time for the full moon, that's where I need to be. Sage Cameron explained spark and steer tokens as tools to help me control my powers. If I learn about them, they could be the key to me going back home and fixing things. I could hold them in and never let them out. I could maybe move somewhere far away and change my name. Especially if helping Sarai isn't possible.

I remember the way to the locker room and find rows of benches and long grey lockers.

"Alexia! Hi!" Lucie waves as she's walking by, drawing attention I'm not sure I want right now.

I wave back and immediately catch Alani's stare down the way. I'm happy to see her, but I don't think she feels the same. Her sharp eyes tell me so. I make a conscious effort to ignore them, moving like everything's business as usual as I search for a locker with my last name on it. When I find it, I stuff my cardigan and loafers inside, but when the door to my locker is slammed, I break from pretending. "The hell is wrong with you?" I snap.

"I could ask you the same. What're you doing here?" Alani asks.

"Getting ready for class."

"I thought SIM Class was on hold for you."

"It was…," I say. I hate lying to Alani. It doesn't feel right, but I don't want to risk her making a scene. Even though she doesn't strike me as a person who'd rat me out, I'm not taking any chances. "Sage Cameron thinks it's okay to give it a try."

Alani's major side-eye hits me. "So soon?"

I pull the SIM Class uniform from my locker. "When Kyle and I were in the Belle Rues, I had a huge panic attack and nearly exploded on the street. I need help now to control myself. I can't wait any longer."

"So you asked Sage Cameron about this when she called you to her office?"

"Yeah."

"And she agreed?"

"Yup."

Alani continues studying me as I zip up my catsuit and boots. "Are you nervous?"

"No."

"Why not? You don't even know what to expect."

My nerves feel agitated by her comment. "I just want to get in and learn so I can get out." Once I finish speaking, I realize I've said too much.

"Get out? Are you leaving?"

I check over Alani's shoulders before looking behind me. Everyone else is moving toward the SIM room after getting dressed.

"Yes," I whisper. "If I can't do anything for Sarai, then there's nothing here for me. My family needs me."

"Your best interest is to stay here," Alani corrects.

"Not if I can control my abilities." Without thinking, I graze my hand over my locket.

"A few SIM classes is all you need, huh? You'll be a master that quick? You'll be terrified by what you find."

"Speaking from experience? I didn't think you were afraid of anything."

"Everyone is afraid of at least one thing…"

"And for you…that is?"

She vaults herself from me, the way a recluse secures their doors upon hearing the faintest noise outside.

"I see." I clear my throat. "Well, you seem to manage just fine with your secrets. I'll manage mine."

"That's not how the SIM works. It has to break you down so you can find your hidden triggers."

"Good thing I'm already broken," I deadpan.

"Whatever."

I slip the letterhead I nabbed from Sage Cameron's office in my sleeve. The bell rings and Alani shuts down. I wonder if I should be worried about what I'm doing, but I can't deny my heart. It isn't here in this school and that's all I need to know.

The locker room empties as the last of us walks out. A parade of olive-green-and-grey catsuits. We don't speak, Alani and I, even as we make our way to the SIM floor. She points in directions, and hands me things without saying a word.

"Thanks," I say timidly. I know she doesn't want to speak, which sucks because I need her to say everything. I'm freaking out over what Alani just placed in my hands. *What do I need an emergency harness, a cuff-like watch, and a knife sheath that carries a bladeless hilt for? How hard-core is this place?* Everyone in class comes behind us and grabs their supplies from the same bins Alani found ours. Alani puts on both items like a veteran. Sheath around the thigh. Harness buckles beneath the ribs. *Got it.* I follow suit.

A dozen girls crowd around us. We're stacked in the neon blue room like an army anticipating a signal. The blond tops in the crowd reflect light, while Alani's entire do is still wild in the cool hue, a blue flame spilling down her shoulders. I can see Lucie Diaz from here. She's a different kind of serious. I wouldn't have pegged her for an athlete—just a brain, but her game face says she's about her shit.

We wait in this dark room. The door in the corner wall unseals itself. Air expels and howls, like the floor of an abandoned house. While it startles me, no one else gives so much as a second glance. They've seen this all before. It's just another day at Malveaux, and we are normal kids, taking an ordinary class.

We roll out the sliding door, single file, into what seems like a never-ending hall. A group of boys spills from a door on the side of us. They make a line parallel to ours and walk on. The ground beneath my boots turns into an auto-walk. Everything is still dark, lit with soleil lamps—little blue orbs hovering in the air. Windows are cut into the wall on the right of us. A glimpse into every SIM room. They're all uniform with padded walls, floors, and ceilings. Safe looking…to me, but not for the ones on the other side of the glass. An acid trip, that's what they look like they're going through. Throwing haymakers and kicks to the air like fools. Climbing walls like mountains. Crying on their knees. Hiding in corners. Lying motionless on the floor. Losing grip on the mass of sparks circling their hands. A cloud of light expands and pops in one room, then smoke explodes. "Was that a bomb?" I blurt and stick my hands to the window.

Alani yanks me away. "Don't get scared now."

My mind challenges her and teases my heart's bravery. *Get scared. Go on. You're not ready.* I fight the anxiety of what will happen when the hall runs out. There's a sourness in my stomach. A knot balling in my chest. *I can't do this.*

Too late. Where our feet press into the ground, circles of white glow until the entire floor illuminates and brightens the room. A man stands at the other end. Our teacher, I guess.

"Afternoon, everyone."

"Hey, Ben," everyone says. They all sound bored.

The teacher stares as we form six lines of four. When I look confused, he steps to me. "Are you lost'?" His thick black eyebrow arches.

I shake my head. "I'm the new student."

Ben checks a screen to his left. "You're Alexia?"

"Yes."

"Alexia, I'm Ben." The hand behind his back reaches to me for a shake. I feel it before I see it. Cold, tough, and smooth. Metal. It whirs as his fingers wrap around my hand. "Not Mr. Zapata Not Damo or sir. Just Ben."

I have a few things to say about that, but Ben interrupts me. "I was told your start time in this class would be delayed."

"Right," I say, pulling the letterhead from my sleeve. "Sage Cameron had a change of heart. She told me to hand this to you."

Ben takes the note and mumbles aloud with a toothpick hanging from his mouth. "As of the fourteenth of October, Alexia Jacobs is permitted to begin training in SIM Class with the rest of her peers. It is of the utmost importance she is offered this course as it may assist her in the prevention of future outbursts and distress.

I trust you will support her in her transition here at Malveaux. Yours in service, Sage Cameron."

Beside me, Alani is taking everything in. I don't know what's on her mind, but I hope she doesn't know I typed the letter myself in the library.

Ben eyeballs me and I think I may faint just before he nods. "Couldn't agree more. Sitting and waiting isn't going to solve anything—at least that's what I tell her. Try your best to keep up in warm-up, I'll explain the rest. Kaur, warm them up!"

Rows away, I spot Erik. He nods and I wave. I wish I could've asked him about SIM Class earlier. It would've given me the perspective I need.

A girl with inches of sleek black hair wrapped in a braid steps in front of us. We follow her for what seems like an eternity doing kneeling squat jumps, reverse lunge leg raises walkout plank jacks…and any other ridiculously hard exercise known to man. I take breaks when my body begs for them, when the burning in my muscles leave me limp. Everyone else goes on.

Ben blows his whistle. "Moving on!" Everyone pops up from a stretch and sharpens their places in line. Ben walks in between each one and lectures. "We're going to do something different today. Something to condition your skill set for the real-world jobs some of you may go into. The Grove needs a strong and safe community, and we can only maintain that with impactful community organizations that respond to crisis. We need calm, clear, resourceful minds. We need innovators. We need passionate and caring individuals. This is how we keep our systems well-oiled and help each other. This is how we will restore a system that has gone off the rails."

Instantly, I think of the guarde and everything Kyle said about them not being the same anymore. I wonder if that's what Ben is referring to.

"I will assign you into teams of three and your mission is to respond to a crisis. You will be given the assignment via your SIM band and you will have to assess the situation, create a plan, and then act. You will tackle all of this and your own personal terrors. Got it?"

Everyone replies, "Yes."

Ben spouts out the teams and Alani's eyes find mine. They aren't so catlike anymore.

She pulls herself back together when her name is called to a group with Lucie and one other girl. "Alexia. Kit. Raquel," Ben finishes grouping and gives his whistle another chirp. The mass of us breaks into our groups.

Kit, who led warm-up, stands beside me. Raquel, the "witch" girl I met my first morning, walks after her. "Are you ready, newbie?" Kit asks me. She's excited—and both oddly energetic and evil for killing me with all those exercises.

"No, but I have to be," I say.

She taps my shoulder. "This will only be difficult it you want it to be." She smiles. "I'm Kit, by the way. Kit Kaur."

"And Kit Kaur is good at everything, so don't listen to her," Raquel chimes in.

"Really, Raquel?" Kit's long braid damn near whips me in my face. "You remember what it was like to do this for the first time. Don't do this to her."

"Well, I don't remember. I'm the freakish cult girl who missed the introduction to all this stuff. I'm just sayin'. You're practically an Olympian. Maybe Alexia should hear something relatable." With light under us, Raquel's face is like a gothic cathedral. Sharp points and steep angles. Eyes as grey as stone. Hair that curtains down like black threads of silk, and casts taupe shadows over the valleys of her eyes and cheekbones. Pink lips that shine like cuts of stained-glass. "Work with us, and you'll be okay. We'll help you."

"Thanks."

Kit sighs and Raquel smiles back. We wait at the back of the line as we watch each group launch themselves into a thing called the veil—a black canvas of inky smoke at the end of a bridge. One by one, each girl runs from the SIM floor and over the bridge to meet the veil's touch. When they do, it swallows them.

"Phoenix!" Ben barks. "Go get 'em!"

I can't see Alani that well from here, but I wonder if she ever gets scared to do this. She was so against me going in, maybe there's a reason for that. Maybe there are things she hasn't conquered yet in the veil. *I should've listened to her.*

Alani searches over her shoulder and finds me. She whispers something to Ben, then walks down the end of the line toward me. "Good luck," she tells me. I want to say so much to her, I could burst into tears. If I didn't feel like two different people, I'd be able to make everyone happy. Maybe I'd treat people better.

CHAPTER TWENTY-FIVE

THE SHADOW

"**I** WANT TO MAKE a few things clear before you enter the veil, okay?" Ben tells me. It's just me and him on the SIM floor. Kit and Raquel have already taken the plunge.

"Yeah." I say, even though I'm confused as hell. Ben circles me, chewing a piece of gum that for sure lost its flavor twenty minutes ago.

"The Malveaux brothers developed SIM Class so young Variens could have the freedom to explore themselves in a safe environment. They believed we held the key to control all along. Sounds like some fairytale bull, but ain't nothing cute about what happens in there. You're new, raw, and here to find your tokens: memories of the invoking emotion of power. Your triggers. Something you will take with you everywhere.

"These are your spark and steer tokens. Everyone has them, and no one is the same. It's the veil's job to deliver them to you. Simple." Ben shrugs. "Some find happiness. Some find trauma, anger, guilt, but there's a method in the madness. It's remembering ourselves at our purest when raw feelings took over. If your token is within your demons…don't run. Let it overwhelm you. There will be these things called terrors, figures in the simulation only you can see. To your peers, they will look like shadows. As you fall in the veil, it'll get inside your psyche and analyze your mind to bring the fears it finds in the form of terrors. So if you're afraid of killer clowns and that causes you a lot of distress, they may pop up. Maybe they're your spark token—a memory or fear that ignites your gift's fuse. Or maybe your spark token is much more traumatic. Sometimes it comes in the memory of a loved one's death…things like that. But your steer token, that's the light. What is your joy? What brings you comfort? Grandma's cookies? A sunset you watched on a vacation in the past? A hug from your mom? Whatever it is, that's what'll help you aim your gifts. With the steer token, you can even decide how much of your gift you want released.

"Spark and steer tokens can evolve over time, and because of this, it's always good to keep training. Even when you become a skilled, top-tiered Varien, it's a muscle you need to condition.

"Last thing I want you to remember is, no one dies here. We want you to be great, but we want you to be safe and have a life worth living, and the veil will show you how to get there. The only way through it, is to run, not walk. *Run.* That hilt inside your sheath will turn into any tool you need it to be. Just press the button and it'll materialize pliers, a saw, or blade…anything. You have a SIM band which acts as another multi-resource tool: a watch, GPS, and Simone—an artificially intelligent assistant to brief you on your missions. Clear?"

"Yes, Mr. Ben." I fidget.

"It's damo, in this realm, not mister. And anyway…Ben is good, okay?" He smirks. "Damo Zapata is my father. You know?"

"I've never called a teacher by their first name. My mom would kill me…Damo Ben."

He cringes. *Nope, "Damo Ben" is a no go.*

"I'll be right over there in that room watching," he tells me. "If you need me or want out, press the button on your harness."

I look at the button on the strap of my harness. There it is: red, round, and itching to be pressed. *BEEP!*

"You haven't even started the simulation!"

"But I—I…"

"Give it a try. You've survived worse things," he says over his shoulder.

I whine and watch the veil. As an active black hole of dancing smoke spews from a round frame, it reeks of intimidation. I study the plumes until my joints stiffen.

"You have to run into it. Remember?" Damo Ben buzzes through the speakers.

Yeah, I remember. He clearly told me that's the only way in.

I breathe and ignore my speeding heart. *I have to do this.* Without a cure, learning my new self is the only way to get better. It's the answer to putting a lid on my abilities, to going home. Before I know it, I'm walking. Each small step sets a pace, one that brings me closer to the veil. Momentum builds as my walk grows into a jog, then finally a sprint. I shoot down the illuminated catwalk until the veil's smoke devours every inch of me. Falling is an icky feeling as it isn't as simple as dropping to my death. There's a presence around me—the feeling of cobwebs catching pieces of my body. Swatting around me, I realize there's nothing to catch, but it doesn't stop the creepy sensation from making my skin crawl. "Help!" I yell. The darkness is a limitless empty space beneath my feet. I scream and flail my limbs in hopes of catching a ledge or rope.

Swoosh.

A beam of light blooms. Gravity drops me on my knees. I hit solid ground and heave. Busted concrete and fire surround me. The silhouette of a broken metropolis stands in the distance. This town must be the ground zero of a battlefield.

"Don't get too comfortable," a voice behind me orders. I spin around and find a struggle going down between a shadowed figure and Kit. Even though it wears no face, the shadowed figure has intimidation down pat, oozing from its shadowed inky mouth. Despite this, Kit is winning the war. She moves smart, fast, and without expectation. "Gotta stay on your guard," she says after palming the shadow in the neck. Weakened by the blow, it freezes still and anchors down into the rubble.

"What is that?" I yell.

The girl cracks her neck. "A terror...they can change shape. But they're always shadowed to the people they aren't meant for."

That's what Damo Ben was talking about, I think.

Kit helps me up from the ground. "How're you feeling? Falling into the veil is pretty crazy, right?"

"Not as bad as I thought," I embellish. "What's next?"

"The end game. See that floating pile above us?" Kit points at a revolving block of metal. Like a Rubik's Cube, each layer of the pyramid staggers and shifts. "That's the ticking pyramid. Once our mission is complete, we make our way to its top and grab the floating sphere. If we grab that, we win." She smiles in a way only an adrenaline junkie can. "First, we've got to assess the crisis of our mission."

"And how're we going to do that?"

"Check your SIM band," she tells me. I do as she says and try to figure it out all by myself. There's only one button on the side of the blank watch's face. I press it and the watch shines a luminescent projection from above it.

"Hello, Alexia. What can I do for you today?" an artificial voice greets me, displaying her words as she speaks. "I'm Simone. I'll be reading your crisis report so that you can respond to an emergency as soon as possible. Are you in a safe place?"

When I look to Kit for assurance, she nods. "Yes," I tell Simone.

"Great. A mother: Lynne Dubois, a Black woman, age forty-one, five foot three, brown hair, green eyes. A daughter: Charity Dubois, a Black girl, age eight, four foot six, brown hair, brown eyes have been reported as missing. They were last seen with a suspect near the Opus Tower Townhomes located two blocks away. A neighborhood resident has called the sighting in. Beware, as you approach the situation, you may find the suspects in the form of terrors."

Kit retrieves a small, flowered barrette from the inside of her sneaker. "I found this right before my terror attacked me. It was inside that empty trolley. This may be what we need," she answers, turning the barrette between her finger and thumb.

"That's going to tell us all we need to know? A barrette?"

Kit keeps a bold fixed gaze on the item. "I can pull memories from objects. Every object has a soul in them. It absorbs the view of the last holder through touch. This may be one of the mom or daughter's items." A tiny strand of smoke leaves the barrette and whirls into Kit's nose before her eyes roll over.

"Kit? Are you okay?"

Completely entranced, her mouth begins to work without making a sound. I look down at the red button on my sleeve. *Should I press it? I don't want the girl to die.*

"The trolley was highjacked…by terrors I can't see. They must not be mine. They let everyone else off and drove the trolley here till its soleil burned out. I can hear the mother speaking. She's begging. The daughter. She's smart. She's taking off the barrette and leaving it on the seat. They snatched her and her mom off the trolley…" The pitch in Kit's voice becomes a deep echo. "The memory ends there, but she may have left other things behind." The soul she extracted from the barrette floats out of her nostrils and vaporizes into the air. Her chest forces out a gust of air and her eyes roll forward. "C'mon! We have to meet Raquel. I told her to wait for us but she left anyway." She sprints ahead, oblivious to my awe-stricken face.

After running down two blocks, we spot Raquel standing outside a busted boarded building—the Opus Townhomes.

"Why'd you leave us?" Kit asks, agitated.

"Because I was being chased by a terror," Raquel answers matter-of-factly.

Kit scoffs. "You let it chase you?"

"You would too if you saw what I saw."

Kit shakes her head. "Don't do what she does, Alexia."

"Noted," I say.

Raquel is amused, but quickly gets back to the matter at hand. "I already searched the building. It's empty."

"You searched the building already? You're going to get us an F."

"Kit, chill. Everything is fine. I can handle myself."

"How do you know no one is inside? Did you search the perimeter or talk to neighbors?"

"This entire mission is stupid." Raquel folds her arms. "I don't want to do it. I don't plan on working for the guarde or the community in any capacity."

Kit is disgusted. "You are setting the worst example today. Aren't you supposed to be more of a follower coming from where you came?"

"What's that supposed to mean?" Raquel frowns.

"Nothing," Kit brushes her off. "Alexia, help me search the area."

"Okay."

Kit nods. "I'll search the front and back. You two search the sides."

"Oh no, no! This is literally the worst idea." I whip my head around. "No one survives when they separate, especially the Black girl. I'm not doing that."

"Well, we're not separating, we're spreading out. We're all outside in the same area."

"You just attacked me for searching a building alone," Raquel adds.

"That's not the same thing…I'll only be a few feet away. And Alexia, this is school. It's not like you're gonna die here," Kit assures me over the windblown sound of the building's banging shutters.

"Kit, no," I tell her.

"We have a grade to fight for. That's all…" She keeps arguing.

"No."

"Will you just at least try it, and see?"

"I said no, Kit!" I lash out, like I've done to anyone who's tried to "help" me at Malveaux.

"I'll go with her." Raquel gives me a look—asking if I'm okay with that. That cathedral face is so fitting—a picture of pity and the promise of sanctuary. "It's her first time. You were scared your first time…we all were."

"I was in middle school. Of course I was scared," Kit retorts.

"And you were lucky to have this right when you needed it. Not everyone does," Raquel says.

I can see Kit calibrating, thinking of a reason to say no, then settling with some sort of empathy she can't deny. "Let's just search each side together."

With alert eyes, we scour the area for anything abnormal. Anything that sticks out in random obvious places, and also the obscure ones. We check barren flowerbeds. We check behind planters and pots. We search bushes for snags and still come up short. I stare beyond the property and down the alley. A hot pink item is on the ground—near boards of lattice propped against the fence. I jog to it. It looks exactly like the barrette Kit pulled a soul from.

"I think I got something," I announce to Kit, who scoops up the barrette from the ground. Like before, she inhales the soul it holds.

"I see the mom and the daughter. You're right, Raquel. I don't think they're here…follow me." Kit takes off down the alley, and Raquel and I tag on to her lead. Not knowing what Kit sees, but faithful in the clues she's picked up with her powers. When the alley lets out to another street, she finds another barrette on the lawn of another abandoned home ahead.

The soul drifts inside of Kit and her eyes roll over again— almost as if they can see the memory from the other side of her eye socket. "This is it. This is the place."

The place. A two-story with boarded windows and tattooed spots of graffiti.

"What's the plan?" Raquel asks, putting on a pair of oversized sporty shades.

"I think we should stay together," I assert. This is my only plan.

Kit gets into the weeds of action. "Let's check the front door. If it's not open, we'll circle around the perimeter for another entry. I'm sure a board must be broken somewhere. Once we get inside, we'll search each room."

"Together," I repeat.

"But we need to be careful. Terrors are most likely in there. Be on your guard. Be prepared to confront them," Kit goes on.

"Always." Raquel nods.

Together, we head to the front door. Of course, it's locked. Nothing is ever that easy. However, things are as Kit predicts: A board on a back window dangles. Raquel inspects the board and whips out her hilt from her sheath. With the press of a button, it lights up and grows, forming itself into the projection of a crowbar. With a few yanks, Raquel is able to pull off the boards, giving us enough space to hop in and land.

Inside the old Victorian house, vines squeeze the patchy walls. Howling winds wrap around hallways. Chipped locked doors lead to rooms. Kit is still our leader, creeping so gracefully atop the rubble and busted stone on the ground.

"Hello?" Raquel eyeballs the house, shouting loud.

Kit shushes her in record time, but Raquel doesn't see the error in her ways.

"We have to hurry," she responds.

A chilling scream from upstairs shakes me. The three of us connect stares.

"Told you," Raquel says.

We race toward the stairs with Kit still ahead. She's so alert, even catching the sudden pouring of blackness on the floor in front of her. It moves in like mist and stretches high—thickening itself into a tsunami that blocks the hallway behind it. I wonder what Kit is seeing. Judging by her stance, straight postured from head to toe, legs apart, with the hilt of her tool in her hand—posed into a long sword—Kit's ready. "Get upstairs!" she shouts at us. "This is mine. I've got this."

Raquel and I work around her and race up the wooden stairs. There are old photos of people nailed to walls with peeling green wallpaper on the way up. None of them have faces. Just bodies, clothed in vintage suits and dresses, holding up heads with no eyes, noses, or mouths.

"What's this about?" I ask Raquel, but she's frozen with one leg on the step in front of her.

"Not you," her voice says with animosity. "I'm not afraid of you." She shakes her head. The black mass in front of her undulates. Even though I don't know what she sees, I can tell her terror has an intimidating presence. The two stare one another down. And just as I exhale, the terror leaps from the top of the stairs and wraps itself around Raquel. Raquel flings to the stairway wall, then the banister.

"Get up there, Alexia!" she manages to tell me through her struggle. "I know what to do!"

I run past her and make it to the second floor where there's nothing but a hall of shut doors. I take a second to catch my breath. The building is full of sounds I want to force from my ears: the scuffling on the first floor, Kit and the terror, they sound like a slide of boulders crashing into asphalt. Then Raquel scrapping with her terror on the steps. It's a lot.

What will my terror look like? I wonder. *What are my worst fears?*

A door down the hall rattles. Could this be it?

The child screams again. This time hollering, "Help!"

Anxiety is building up. I consider tapping the emergency button on my harness, but I think of my purpose: going home. Whatever is behind this door will help me get there. It's the key to being as whole as I can.

As my heart races with the bulging door, I curl my fingertips over the dented brass knob, and twist. A coldness drips over me when the door swings open. The dusty floor planks creak under me, and a stretched shadow grows on the walls. A tormentor of my own. I've let it loose.

Pangs twist my stomach, and I don't move. I don't know how to, and even if I did, I'd forget it all right now. I close my eyes. I'm not ready to face the terror ahead of me, to see its snarling mouth or feel the way it'll gut me with a pain so many say I'm not ready for.

"Alexia?" the terror speaks. That voice. I know it. It's haunted me since it left my life.

"Sarai," I gasp.

CHAPTER TWENTY-SIX

RAPTURE

SARAI IS ALWAYS COLD in my nightmares, grey at the edges of her skin with dull, thin hair, and yellowed eyes. That's who I see in front of me. Behind the door. Wet tears sizzle down my warming face and curve into my parted mouth. We grip on to each other like nothing can ever separate us again.

"How're you here?" I cry as Sarai shudders in my arms.

"Variens can make anything happen," a familiar voice chimes in from the corner of the room. "That's the twist, isn't it?" Dad says plainly. His dark skin is tinted in the room's blue light. The room begins to change and make less sense.

The dusty wooden floor is now carpet—a mix of cream and pepper. The walls around us are colored grey with Frank Ocean and Tyler, the Creator posters on one wall. I let go of Sarai, walk around to feel the sheer chiffon curtains, and head for the hanging mandala tapestry. My hands dive under it, and the cuts and burns I shot into the wood still live. This is my room.

"Dad? What's going on?" Something is off and I don't know what. Where are my terrors? Where is the little girl? "Are you really here? Both of you?"

"I'm always here." Dad taps at his head. "You just don't want to listen." Another glance at Dad and it's clear the SIM is at work—preying on my vulnerabilities to break me down. Dad is barefoot, wearing a wrinkled button up and tattered jeans. He's due for a shave and haircut. I can't help but wonder if he's the real hostage. Him and Sarai.

"Did someone bring you here? With a mother and her child?" I ask him.

His face holds disdain. "Someone." As he says it, he stares right through me. I turn around to see Sarai with a smug grin. The sight chills me before I return my attention to Dad. He takes a deep breath, then walks to his right, revealing two people tied back-to-back in chairs. The missing mother and daughter! They're drooped over, gagged, and—by the looks of their expanding rib cages—breathing.

"Damn…okay! I can fix this. I can help everyone. I'm going to untie you two and get you girls home."

I reach for my knife sheath and remove the hilt. Making a tool appear like Kit did is easier than I thought. What I envision—a knife—comes to life in the same fashion: a projected visual of an actual knife blade. I wave my hand through it with ease. It's not solid, but it will be when I use it to cut the ropes. I move toward the wall to turn on the bedroom light for a better view.

"You're not doin' none of that," Sarai snaps. In the light, I find that Sarai has changed more than I expected: Black tear trails are baked into her face. Neat cuts line her forearms like newly tilled crops. The tips of her fingers look burned, and her hair is stuck in two matted plaits. This is what she looked like when they took her to Mercy Bay.

"What?"

"Drop the knife." Sarai stuns me when she says this. Out of habit, I can't help but look to Dad again for some answers. He doesn't give any. Still, actions speak louder than words: The tension in his clenched jaw shows me I'm in trouble.

"Drop the knife? Are you crazy? A pack of psychos kidnap you all and I'm supposed to be knifeless? I'm helping you out."

"Oh," Sarai says. "You want to help me out now? That's cute. That's real cute, sis." She's condescending. She's never been this way with me.

My heart races, but I carry on with the hilt in my hand. Sarai rushes closer and slaps it out of my grip.

"Sarai! Are you serious?"

"This doesn't look serious to you?" She shrugs heartlessly. "Three hostages. Two of them bound and gagged. The other, a senator who quite literally ruined my life."

I close my eyes for a second. "Three hostages? You kidnapped everyone?"

Sarai smiles like a Cheshire cat.

"Didn't I tell you about her?" Dad says from the corner. "Once she turned, that old Sarai died."

Sarai ignores him and responds to my astonishment. "I didn't kidnap them alone. I had good ol' Eddie here to help me."

"Under duress," Dad responds. "Your control. Tell the truth, Sarai. Tell Alexia you threatened to phase through me and split me open like you did the last guy."

"What?" I breathe. "Why would you do this?"

Sarai's eyes well with anger. "I don't know…maybe to show people like you and your wack-ass dad that these laws and decisions take lives and break families up. I don't have a childhood anymore. Not after they locked my ass up for a murder I never committed! I don't have a regular life! I'm not home with my mom…so why does she get that?" Sarai tilts her head toward the little crying girl. "Why does she get to be a kid? Why does her biology make her worthy of protection and not mine? I'm sixteen. I'm a child too!"

"Children don't kidnap other children," Dad cuts in smooth and quiet. His thumb grazes over his bottom lip. "You stopped being a kid the moment you turned because your brain is no longer what it once was. Variens are vengeful and violent because they can be."

"Dad, stop! Shut up! You made her this way!" I shout.

"If I'm so violent and vengeful, why haven't I killed you?" Sarai quizzes Dad.

"Oh," Dad mocks. "It's only a matter of time."

I shut my eyes and try to grab a hold of myself. My insides feel tangled and a great pressure is building. All the noise around me is feeding it. Sarai and Dad arguing and the crying mother and daughter who squeal and wriggle in their ropes. I grip my head. This is not what I want. This is a nightmare.

Stay calm, Alexia. They're terrors. They aren't real, I tell myself.

"Maybe I should kill you. I'd be doing the world a big favor!" Sarai snaps.

"Because you'd also be signing your death certificate…two birds. One stone!" Dad argues.

I shake my head. "No, no, no, no…NO!"

Life turns black as a warmth scratches my skin. When I check my arms, my flesh flashes like storm clouds. The inside of me feels hotter than ever before, even hotter than that day in the Belle Rues, but this time, it doesn't hurt. It's an itch to scratch. A satisfaction that rolls through my stomach and bones. There's pressure under my skin. *A cosmic storm.*

Hold it in. The pressure ices me with sweat. In a split second, I surrender to the thought of unleashing, and that's all it takes for the wild to tear itself out of me. Wild star flares burn through everyone in the room: Dad, Sarai, and the mother and daughter.

"No!" I scream. Their bodies bend and the voltage incinerates them. Agony stretches their mouths and eyes open. No sound comes from them. It's strange and makes me sick. "No!" Sarai's melting eyes watch me and she dissolves to ash. "Dad?" I race to hold him, but he dies down to grey dust. I fall to the floor. The room around me folds and it's back to the abandoned building.

All I witnessed is gone.

Wind curls and knocks through piles of ash: the people I've killed.

"Alexia?" Kit and Raquel call after me. They find me fused to the floor. Shaking from head to toe.

"Alexia!" Kit kneels beside me. "Did you do this? Did you kill your terrors?" She smiles.

"I killed them." I pour my eyes out, staring at the mounds of ash on the floor. "All of them…"

"All of them? That's good, right?" Kit rests her hands on my shoulders.

"Did you find the mother and daughter?" I hear Raquel say.

My sobs grow with her question. "I didn't mean to explode on them. I was overwhelmed…it just happened."

"It's okay. This was your first SIM…it'll take time," Kit reassures me.

Raquel tries to comfort me. "At least you can rest knowing whatever you saw…it wasn't real." The girls are nice. I like that, but they are weightless where I've suffered, and clear where I'm cluttered.

I rise from my knees. "I don't feel good. I need to get back to the SIM floor," I say with my finger pointed at the button on my harness.

Kit draws my arm to my side. "We still have to get to the pyramid."

"The pyramid?"

"C'mon!" Kit and all her endless energy head outside.

Raquel waits on me. "Are you okay to go on?"

"I…I…I don't know. Normally, I'm sort of empty after an outburst. Feels like there's still something there." Wincing at the fiery pressure, I place my hand on the side of my stomach.

We meet Kit outside and a deep bell ring vibrates through the streets. The sun's light dims as a giant ticking stone-layered pyramid hovers close.

"That's our cue." Kit eyes the structure.

"They really expect us to hike up that death trap?"

"Only way to get full credit for the SIM." She motions for me to follow.

Climb. I have to *climb*. I've never climbed one damn thing in my life—not a tree, hill, rock, ladder, nada. Why not choose a towering pyramid for my first time? Kit and Raquel latch on to its bottom layer like flying squirrels.

"Alexia!" Kit hollers. "Do exactly as I did. Loosen your muscles, jump out, and reach. You got this!"

Not quite sure what's telling her I doubt "having this." Maybe my noodle arms give it away. I trail the floating pyramid, picking up momentum to make the big leap. My feet leave the ground as my hands grasp the first ledge.

"Hurry, it'll float higher once you've made it on." Kit offers me a hand. She hauls me up. I wobble to find my balance and the fullness in my side stabs at me. Block by block, I make my way up the layers, making damn sure not to look down. Just as I ready myself to climb onto the ninth layer, something tugs at my leg.

"YOU LEFT ME TO DIE!" Covered in melting skin, bursting nerves and blood, Dad's here in the skin I scorched. *He isn't really here, Alexia. It's the veil. Focus.* My heart slams a heavy beat through my chest. The pyramid rings, rattles, and shifts its bricks in random directions. "Whoa!" I struggle to keep my upper half on the ledge of a stone.

"C'mon, Alexia!" I hear Kit shout. Her face is no longer hers when I look, it's my father's. Is this part of the SIM? I don't remember anyone saying this would be a possibility.

"This is what I mean to you?" Dad wheezes and coughs up blood. "MURDERER!"

"No. I'm not. I'm not!" The shouts break through me like a hammer. I'm overflowing. Beams of burning energy stretch through my fingertips. They whip at the layer Kit rests on, missing her by inches. I crawl to a corner of the pyramid to calm myself, but light won't stop spouting from my skin.

"Press the button, Alexia! Ours won't work!" Raquel yells to me, slamming at the button in her harness without any result. "The SIM has gone crazy!"

It sounds so easy, but I can't get a hold of myself. Not with Dad's face where hers used to be. From behind me, his sizzled body rises to my level. The lower half of his face is seared—charred gums and a mouth that doesn't close. His left eye is melted shut. I've done this to him. I've destroyed him.

"LOOK WHAT YOU DID TO ME!" Dad squeezes both of my arms and pins me down. "I HATE YOU!"

"No! No!" More currents of energy are called from my veins. Shooting stars circle the pyramid. Everything I've held in breaks free, and it feels good. I channel a wave of energy into the terror that's hurting me and light it up till it breaks apart. The more I release, the higher I feel. Cosmic white flares lift me to the sky and circle me in a cocoon. I'm free.

But it's here that I can't stop thinking of my flaws, the skin that harmed my dad and doused him in starfire. *How could I have done that after earning his trust? He was right. He was right all along... and I fought against him.* A rod of crooked, yellow light shoots from my eyes. Anger turns to pain, pain turns into energy—an exciting energy, all fulfilling. Screams storm through my mouth as my skin welcomes the eruption of several currents. The wind roars. A mirrored piece of atmosphere shatters and rains down. I think I've cracked the sky.

"Alexia!" Sage Cameron calls from the roof of a building across from me. Her arms are splayed like a starfish. Some sort of glass medallion dangles from her hand. It catches the light from the sun and glares. "Pull through! Think of light," she shouts to me, but sadness is all I feel. I've burned my father and severed my family. I let Sarai slip through my hands, not once, but twice.

Sage Cameron raises her medallion over her head. Light…the lifting of a weight so heavy. Those feelings, they're flowing right through me. Washing out my bad blood and cleansing it. I see the sky in my mind. My entire body under the bluest water breaking the surface for air. I drink it in. The Grove's forest surrounds me. Just me. A peaceful place redirecting its energy back to me. The high is gone. The rage is gone. Everything is suddenly quiet. My muscles fall limp as peace flows through me. Energy ropes seep back into my pores and the entire simulated city goes dark. Blackness returns as I fall back to the veil's surface. The velocity of the pull burns my eyes until the SIM room's illuminating light is back into view.

I'm glued to the neon floor—weak and drained, sopped in sweat. Sage Cameron comes into focus. She kneels to me as the rest of the class crowds her. Damo Ben must've called her once I lost control. "That was a lot," she says with my chin in her palm. "You see now?"

"I'm sorry," I rasp. "I don't know how it got so bad. The SIM kept coming after me." The bell of Sage Cameron's white sleeve grazes my face. She tilts her head a bit so I can see her better.

"Just like I warned you…," Sage Cameron gently scolds. Even with a delivery like that, my guilt and shame rise. She did warn me. Alani did too.

Rocked to my core, I have nothing to say—except I wish my abilities could make me invisible. So, I close my eyes and breathe. It's just enough at this moment. And the closest thing to disappearing.

CHAPTER TWENTY-SEVEN

T H E S E T U P

S AGE CAMERON HAS WATCHED me like a hawk since my big failing scheme in SIM Class. Discipline followed the incident, of course: a lecture from Sage Cameron and Damo Ben, and also a space for me to explain my thought or emotional process. Not only did I put myself and other people at risk in the SIM, I also forged a signature and stole a Sage's official letterhead. Big trouble. I would be expelled in the Normal realm, but here it's not so easy. Not when expulsion for runaways can lead to homelessness. So, Sage Cameron designed a different path of punishment: no SIM Class—as expected—with the added luxury of Dama Hadley escorting me to every class from the first bell to the last. After which, I report to Sage Cameron's office to be under the wing of her shawl. We study botany and talk Varien history. I've been well-behaved, and the steady routine has grown on me, but the thought of going home hasn't left my mind as I wait for the moon to fill itself every day. Only two days left in its cycle before I can get home. Maybe I'll be worthy enough for it this time.

"That looks lovely…what you've done over there." Sage Cameron eyes my wild flower bouquets. It's the last harvest before the first frost starts having its way. Lavender, dandelions, and chamomile—there's something about them, how they bloom without the help of human hands, and shimmer like gems in the glare of the sun. There's so much of that here. I'll miss this piece of The Grove.

"Thank you," I say.

Sage Cameron places her clippers down on the table. "Here, better tie them with twine. I'm going to dry hang them…use them for teas and sachets."

"Okay." I take the twine from her hands and wrap it around the bushels.

Sage Cameron's gaze is loud. I can sense it without looking up. "You seem happier."

"Really?"

"Yes, you've been a little…buoyant."

"It's nothing. Just more settled these last few days."

"Oh, that could be it." Her bony fingers clip through flower stalks. "Sure there isn't anything else to it?"

Don't look at her. Don't look at her. "Nope. That's all."

"I see." Sage Cameron props her top hat up. "Are you enjoying yourself with your schedule like this? I know it began on such rough terms…after your rapture." Rapture. That's how Sage Cameron always refers to my loss of control. She always makes it sound specific to me. Like it only happens to me. I replay the incident in my head all the time with my other haunting memories. The more I gave in to my fear and released my abilities, the crazier the SIM acted and the more dangerous it became for everyone. That's messed with me and made me feel different around the people I should find common ground with.

"We've come a long way since your first week. I could be wrong, but I feel you're rested and a lot more settled. Am I off to think you're finding things a bit easier?"

"No," I tell her. "It's been a nice change of pace. I feel like… someone I still don't know much about but will."

"Great. As long as you *stay* here, I can promise you will." If her eyes could turn me to stone, I'd fuse to the marble under my feet.

Sage Cameron points. "Do me a favor, run me that mint hatbox from the closet."

"Sure." I head to the back of her office. A stranger would think the closet belongs to a ringmaster at first glance. Like, a unicycle. I mean, really, what the hell does she need that for?

"Do you see it? Just at the top on the right side there."

The box, I see it, three shelves higher than I can reach. "Perfect," I huff under my breath. Making the most out of the tools around me, I scoot the unicycle over and step on its seat. When I reach and pull at the box's brim, the unicycle rolls back, and I go with it. A flailing simp. Things topple down and papers rain, but at least the hatbox does me a solid and falls flat on the floor.

"Is everything okay?"

"Yeah. Umm…," I drag on, picking up papers. "The hatbox fell down."

"Oh, be careful, okay? One moment," Sage Cameron says to the knock at her door. "Yes, Lorraine?"

Under the weak golden light, I organize the scattered pages into a stack. The lot of them are random things: music notes (what does Sage Cameron play?), instruction manuals (she's a hoarder), blueprints for a giant cup with a mount sticking out of it (weird), and old notarized documents (a hoarder, I say!), and a black box with something silver glaring against the light. I remove the top of the box entirely and find a dagger—the one Greta gave me at her shop. I think for a moment, then tuck it under my waistband. I may need this when I leave The Grove. Having it did make me feel better. I put all the weird things back in their places and set Sage Cameron's hatbox on her desk. She clips the end of another flower. Her face looks pained.

"Is that the wrong box?" I ask.

"…No."

"Then what's up? You seem bothered."

"Sure *you* aren't a telepath?"

I raise my hands and shrug.

"Well," Sage Cameron goes on. "It's just…I've been thinking about things: that day in the Belle Rues and SIM Class."

"Oh. What about them?"

"I'm trying my best to put myself in your shoes. I have a thirteen-year-old daughter. I know a thing or two about reinforcing rules. Sometimes it works and sometimes it backfires. Sometimes there's no way around it all."

I fiddle with the bushels like I'm still sorting them.

Sage Cameron finishes snipping the leaves on a stalk before continuing, "That's how rebellion is born. And while I don't believe I was wrong to reinforce our agreement after the two events transpired, I don't think it's sustainable. I always knew it wouldn't be and that at some point I'd have to reevaluate everything."

I nod. "Okay, Sage Cameron, you're making me nervous."

"Don't be. Let's be honest here." She sets her hands flat on the table. "All I've heard from you about SIM Cass is why you did it. But we've never discussed how you felt about it. How you started and finished. What did the rapture feel like for you?"

I breathe out slowly. "Whoa…umm. It was a few weeks ago, so I'm not as sharp on the details but, I remember starting it and feeling determined but intimidated. Then when the SIM got going, I felt out of my league. Standing next to Raquel and Kit…I looked like a baby. I never had to deal with that before. So, I was embarrassed and frustrated before I even met my terrors. And then when I met them…I couldn't think clearly under the pressure which made me more afraid and upset. And then on the pyramid, I saw my dad's face on Kit. The terrors wouldn't end."

Sage Cameron is struck curious. "That's not how terrors appear. They don't tag onto living people."

"Well, that's what I saw."

"Interesting. How did you feel after that?"

"By that point, I had to release what was building up. There was no other way. But it didn't feel like all my other outbursts, it felt…good. I know that sounds bad, but I do feel like that SIM did something to me—even though I failed it. Maybe because I was able to confront things in a way I won't be able to."

Now Sage Cameron is nodding. "This is why I call it a rapture. Release can be exciting. That's exactly what SIM Class can be good for. It is therapy in its own way—exposure therapy. Well, our version of it. You're in a safe environment with exposure to situations that spur fear. I couldn't help but think about how this may have benefited you in ways I couldn't grasp. I was so frustrated; I couldn't see the forest for the trees. I'm there now and I want you to know I'm sorry for not listening to you. I have my reasons for denying things, but that doesn't negate your need to be heard."

"Thank you."

"We need to build trust and I believe that's possible with time and action. How can you obey a person you don't trust? How can you depend on someone who hasn't earned it?

"I know all too well that we as people need to act more than we speak. So, to show you that I mean what I say, if it's okay with you, I am lifting your ban on SIM Class. You can start as soon as you feel ready. Take it at your own discretion, though. Just because you start it doesn't mean you must stay the course. Communicate with Ben and me if you're uncomfortable. We'll hear you out and go from there."

I can feel my face reacting with surprise. "Really? Wow… thank you, Sage Cameron."

"You're welcome. In addition to that, I've arranged for you to take a break from Malveaux for a few hours today. A real treat." She grins.

"Thank you, that means a lot, Sage Cameron."

She smells like rose oil when she hugs me. "You're welcome. I can't be the old hippie that kills everyone's joy. I refuse. So, I figure a day at the Montparnasse Museum is a perfect change of pace to learn more about your new home. I learn from seeing and touching things more than I do hearing them, myself."

"That's how I am too. When am I going?"

Sage Cameron squints at her wristwatch. "Umm…now actually. He'll be down in a few minutes to accompany you to the trolley."

"He?"

Right when I pose the question, I already know the answer.

He steps into the office.

My stomach flips.

"Since you two have already gotten to know each other some, I figure it'll be an easy outing for the both of you. A Get Out of Jail Free card. No pun intended." Sage Cameron laughs. I'd laugh too if she weren't lightweight messy.

Kyle's face tenses. This isn't what he wants either.

"Okay, bye, kids! The trolley will depart in ten minutes. Another won't be available for an hour. So, you two really need to get going because *I've* got a game of bocce ball to catch. Have a good weekend!"

We both fumble our words for any reason to stay at Malveaux. Sage Cameron shoves us out. The die is cast, and our stupid fate is sealed. Kyle and I will spend the day together.

CHAPTER TWENTY-EIGHT

SOMETHING IN THE WAY

"So..."

"...So," Kyle repeats.

I dig deep into my social bag of ice breakers and find nothing, not even the tiniest crumb. The purr of the trolley's soleil-powered engine is the perfect white noise. Still, it doesn't distract me from the elephant in the car. I should apologize.

"Hey…about that scene I made the other day. I'm sor—"

Kyle darts his eyes from his phone. "Scene?"

"In the Belle Rues. When I went off on you…like a hella crazy—"

"Banshee," he interrupts.

"Yes…wait, huh?" I pause. "I don't think you deserved that. You were just trying to help."

Kyle places his phone down. "Alexia, you don't have to kiss my ass. I accept your apology. Want some gum? It's the best flavor in the world." He offers me a stick like nothing happened.

"Thanks." There isn't much to discuss now, but at least the air is clear.

Kyle's phone rings and he antes up the awkward. There's a girl on the line. He entertains her by making it clear to me there's no talking, no moving, no blinking, and no nothing while she's on the phone. "Hey, I gotta go," he finally tells her. "We just got to the Montparnasse."

I hear a scoff through the speaker.

Kyle glances at me. "I'll call you as soon as our tour is over."

"How long is the tour? We need to talk about things."

"Not sure. I promise I'll call you as soon as it's done," he replies, but it seems like the other person has already hung up.

I smirk my way out the trolley. "How loving, maybe you should lower the volume so I won't hear bits of your belittling conversations."

Kyle exits after me and greets the driver. His tongue lingers on the ends of words. "Benien non meli."

"Is that Viridian?" I ask him.

"Yeah."

"You're fluent in Viridian?"

"Is that a shock?"

"No…yes. I mean, I haven't heard anyone our age speaking it since I got here. I thought it was more of an old tongue."

"It's sort of a family requirement." He ushers me to a gliding walkway beneath a tunnel of flowered arches.

"So, that means Alani is fluent too?"

Kyle cracks up. "You kidding? Alani can barely speak English. She can keep up in some ways, but she's better at speaking Japanese and Hawaiian because of her mom. Our great-great-great-grandfather immigrated here and changed his last name for a new start. Wiped the entire slate clean. The language he picked up here stuck around with each generation. Just another way to honor our history."

"Yes, Alani told me. That's a lot. Do you speak any other languages?"

"Portuguese from my mom. But I'm a little out of practice. It's been years since I've spoken it."

A thick gust of smoke pops in his place and he reappears ahead of me. "You got any family traditions?" he inquires, holding open a large glass door.

"I wish. Sometimes we celebrate Juneteenth, and even though I love our Sunday dinners after church, it'd be nice to have a kept language. I like the idea of it."

His shoulder brushes against mine. "Well, if you stick around Alani, she'll teach you all the dirty Viridian words she knows. That'll look good on your college application."

The Montparnasse, a slanted abstract building of glass, reclaimed wood, and metal, is a time capsule that sits on a river with trickles of spilling water flowing from its sloped roofs. Kyle plays like he's lost his balance on the stones leading to the entrance.

"Can you please stop?" I say.

"Why?"

"Because."

"You're worried?"

"No."

Only the top half of his profile is visible, menacing eyes that tease me through the mess of his floppy hair. *Watch this*, they say. Springing off the balls of his feet, he jumps on stones planted in the river. The water is so deep, so thickly colored—a fluid citrine—I can't see the bottom.

"Wait." I almost slip atop a stone. "Just…wait!"

Kyle's tongue cuts to the side of his mouth and he wobbles.

"Oh!" I can't help but shout when his body falls closer to the river. But the air swallows him and pops, then sells his secret a few feet away. A sparking charcoal cloud bubbles and drops a lanky boy from its haze.

Chills curl down my back. "Are you serious?"

"Never. Sure you aren't worried?"

I finish walking across the stones and push through his shrugging arms. "You're annoying."

Kyle's smile lets out into a giggle he can't let go of. He opens the door for me and a man that could make tips as Bill Murray's doppelganger bows in the Montparnasse lobby. "Bwenien, kids! Please make sure you hurry from out there. Saw a few gators earlier." He doesn't have to tell me twice; I haul ass up the lobby's steps.

"Well, that's too far, ma'am. You're already inside. A gator can't make it through this door."

"It can if it's a Varien." I eye around him.

Kyle's eyebrows raise and the museum man points at me with his thumb. "Only the best from Malveaux…what a joy." His voice flatlines. "I'm Andre Navarette, your curator and educator for the day. You two are Kyle and Alexia, I'm sure."

"Correct," Kyle responds.

"Wonderful." Andre claps. "Those names partner well together like their own work of art. I gotta tell ya, I really like the flow of it." Reading the signals of my sighs, Andre seamlessly moves on. "It rolls off the tongue nicely, kind of like the background history of this living monument. There's not one person who loathes hearing it, not even me…after reciting it every day of my life."

My eyes skip from wall-to-wall in search for a clock. It will be a long day.

Kyle whispers to me as we walk into an exhibit, "I like this guy…he's weird."

I don't appreciate his weirdness, just the real Bill Murray. The bland seems less bland that way. Speaking of bland, I don't know if that's something The Grove could ever be considering its beginning. Here, at the Montparnasse Museum, paintings of the 1833 Leonid meteor shower greet us. Below them are actual accounts of the sight secured in clear glass cases on columns. We walk on, and a panoramic map shows all of the international locations the Leonid shower fell on. The map sparkles with locations around the globe. All of them brought Variens from their homes to The Grove's gate, asking Dama Fabienne Doucet to give them a safe place to exist, live, and thrive.

Every time Andre says the word "sanctuary," it fires into me like a bullet. The Grove was created by the faith of refugees who saw their loved ones die as they fled from persecution. Their names are etched in slabs of granite. Stacked in rows. As we walk between them, I hear their cold death cries and the clicking of Andre's dress shoes. I reach out and touch the last slab we pass. The bottom half of its slate is blank and smooth. My name could've been here.

"You all right?" Kyle checks in.

"Mmhmm."

Andre is the only one smiling after that gloomy walk through the memorial. "And that, kids, is the reason I hope you will always remember why we proffer grace the way that we do. Sanctuary is woven and carved into our culture. As you can see to your right, the first Zenith baskets were woven to depict what sanctuary is."

Kyle steps over to the glass case before me. Circles with crosses in the middle, the sanctuary symbol, are woven in the baskets. As we continue, some baskets depict paintings with an elegant lion on them.

"The lion symbol came later to represent all refugees and Variens born to The Grove in 1908. The lion is specific to the Leonid shower—which hailed from the constellation Leo. As you'll see more art detail throughout the tour. This symbol is a fitting reflection of the art nouveau themes of this time," Andre elaborates.

"What's a Zenith?" I ask. "I heard about it before, but a simplified version."

"Hmm," Andre mumbles. "I feel foolish explaining it because experiencing it is the only way you'll understand it. Not just anyone knows what it's like to have the moon pour itself into them. It doesn't do that for anyone but us…because after all we've survived and suffered, we're still here and humble. We proffer grace on the last evening of our body's charge—when the weight of our gifts becomes heavier than we're used to, and the moon is at her highest point. She comes down to fill us, then we are sustained for another year…speaking plainly of course."

Andre walks on, Kyle follows, but I am stuck on what I just heard. I walk past the labeled captions in the display case. The definition of zenith is printed on laminate.

Zenith: the time at which something is most powerful or successful.

synonyms: highest point, height, top, acme, peak, pinnacle, apex, apogee, vertex, tip, crown, crest

antonyms: nadir, bottom

Nadir. Nadir. The word hugs my mind like a stranger. The sense of it is buried beneath a mountain of "just gotta make it to tomorrow" kind of days.

The hairs on my neck spike when Kyle creeps behind me. "You'll get to see it next year."

"It sounds unreal."

"Would you want to see it next summer?"

"Next…summer?"

"What, you're already booked?"

Andre claps from behind us. "*I* am the only one booked here…with you, for another hour before lunch. I'd like to shave that down to forty-five minutes if we could. There's a bottle of tawny port and apple pie waiting for me. Shall we?"

"No thank you, I despise the taste of port." Kyle sophisticatedly clears his throat, a ritzy tone in his voice.

"Young man, port despises the inside of your mouth. You're underage. Let's go."

"Yeah, okay." Kyle snickers back at me as we walk. His humor is kind of refreshing in between serious things. There are heavy items and big attractions: replicas of the first bungalows built from the Virgin Forest's dropped wood.

"My ancestors," Andre adds, his nose turned high, "built the first general store in The Grove from fallen white oak."

"Get out of here? Your folks did that?" Kyle fakes amusement.

"Yes. Yes. The entire process took them twenty years to complete. They don't make stores like that anymore. Everything's rushed together."

"Yeah, because who waits decades to nail one wall?" Kyle mutters.

"Ahem…" Andre's throat clearing should've knocked us back in our place, but I fall out even more. I go from stifling my laughs to catching them from my open mouth.

"Sugar rush…she ate a lot of candy on the way here," Kyle covers. We go on and enter the roaring twenties timeline of the exhibit. I don't get any quieter, Kyle gets mouthier, and by the time we reach the exhibit's exit, Andre has given up on us.

"Ooh, can we take pictures?" Kyle stalls at the sight of a vintage photo op a few feet away.

"Children, we've been touring for forty minutes and haven't even scratched the surface of this building. What do you think? But please, don't let me harsh your mellow." Andre flashes his hands.

We look at each other, Kyle and I. "Okay…," Kyle sings. Stoked, he runs to the set—without Andre's permission—and tacks on a curled mustache prop. After two kleptomaniac attempts to run off with the fake mustache, the photographer caves and allows Kyle to keep it. He wears it proudly through the next exhibit and twists its ends like he's grown it himself.

Andre acts surprised when the clock reads fifteen minutes till lunch. "Time flies with good times. What do you say we break for lunch?"

"It's a little early," I say.

"Lunch is at noon, yes. And actually," Andre says and points to his wrist, "my watch says it's noon now and it's pretty accurate. I tune it every day for precision. I don't want to be a second off when it comes to time. So, lunch. You two are fine with lunch?" He never stops nodding as he asks, and we find ourselves nodding with him. "Great," he says. "See you back here in one hour."

CHAPTER TWENTY-NINE

The Missing Piece

THE MENU IN FRONT of me has nothing I'm familiar with on it. I've never heard of any it. Kyle insists on ordering for me, even though I've howled "no" repeatedly. I agree to give him a shot if he lets me do the same.

"Stand over there. I want you to recoil in fear of my decision," I tell him.

"I'm not going anywhere. You just heard what I ordered."

"Like I know what rete…plantan ve lio is. Go!" I point. Kyle turns on the heels of his feet. I scan down the Virdian menu once again. All its fancy words make it hard to choose. I put faith in the meal item with the prettiest name, jele marane.

"What the heck did you get me?" Kyle teases, still facing the opposite wall. "I heard you stammering over there." I laugh at the mental playback of my wrecked pronunciation. Kyle grabs our drinks, chooses a table, and pulls out my chair. "I heard you trying to say rete. It sounded like 'reed.'"

"No, I think I said it correctly."

"You said it three different ways. All wrong." He morphs into my image. "I'll have the reed—reetee—ray tay plantan ve lio?"

I give my straw a nibble. "You like to make fun of people, don't you?"

"It's *reh-tay*," he eggs on. "And I've never tried any dessert with bananas, so you better pray this is good." He notices my blank face. "What?"

"You didn't answer my question. Do you like to make fun of people?"

"Not exactly." He thinks. "I think I'm a heavy-hearted person who tries to make light of every situation. Laughing about things is better for everyone. It doesn't come from a heartless place, which you probably don't believe. So…yeah."

"I don't think you're heartless at all. A little obnoxious, yes, but far from heartless."

"That was your first impression of me? Seriously, don't answer too quick!"

"Yes."

A giggle chokes him.

"I don't even want to hear what you thought of me." I poke through my shake with my straw.

Kyle flattens his faux mustache. "You hearing it isn't the problem…me saying it seems to be."

There. The thick, webby silence I hate plants itself between us. It's brief but it feels like an eternity. Happy to move to a new subject, I dish another nagging question. "You're not going to eat with that thing on, are you?"

"Alexia, I'm going to live the rest of my life with this 'stache. I can barely grow one."

We dig into our pastries, placing a bookmark on the conversation until further notice. I break the floral pattern of thin sliced apples by the forkful. Mine is simple, a glorified apple pie.

Kyle plops his spoon down. "Okay. I'm coming clean. At first, I was pissed at you for ordering a banana dessert but honestly… this is out of the park." His spoon arrows to my lips. "Try some." *He wants to feed me. From his spoon. While holding it. Gosh.*

A sensation of needles tickles my chest as I open my mouth. It's a sort of crazy banana pudding, but with crepes added to it. Damn good, and so perfect.

"All this sugar…we're about to crash. Andre is going to kill us."

"Peter Venkman? Nah."

"How do you know about *Ghostbusters*?"

"How does anyone not?"

Right as he asks, I find myself fidgeting. "Isn't that a Normal thing?"

Kyle scoffs. "That's the kind of stuff that keeps us divided."

"I-I-I didn't mean it that way."

Ever the actor, Kyle breaks his façade when he's ready. "It's nice to see you tripping over your words for once."

"Oh, I'm getting you back…watch." I fold my arms. I mean every word. "But be for real, how do you know about *Ghostbusters*? I haven't seen any pop culture connection to home and it's making me scream internally."

"That's because you're at Malveaux. It's a fortress from the outside noise, even Varien pop culture. At least, for the students. Outside of that place you can find stuff bootleggers bring in from the Normal realm. Some Variens feel like it's beneath us but we always have refugees coming in and making a market for old comforts from their old lives. It's not as black and white as you think. We have a neighbor who came to The Grove in 1989, and he has this crazy collection of movies. He introduced me to *Ghostbusters* and a whole bunch of other Normal movies. *The Goonies*. *Big*. I'm fascinated by it. Can't lie."

"So…you're like the little mermaid?"

"Who?"

"Ariel?"

Kyle's face is blank.

"The mermaid with red hair?"

"Not ringing a bell. C'mon, we better go. Andre will down that entire bottle of port if we don't." *Good idea. Responsible even.*

But when we get back to the exhibit, we find that Andre has drowned in his tawny port. In a hall of oil paintings, sculptures, and relics, he's smacking his lips and peering at the world with heavy lids. "Roam wherever you want. The museum is yours… ours. The public." He directs us in a sweaty haze.

So, we roam. Kyle takes to the oil paintings while I grasp for straws to find meaning in a preserved encyclopedia. "Nadir. Nadir. Nadir…where are you?" It must be somewhere in the aged pages.

"You…what're you scouring for over there?" Andre sways closer to me.

"Don't really know. Could be anything, a person, place…this Nadir thing."

"It's legendspeak," he blurts and wobbles, in the face of a sculpted block of tourmaline. "The lowest point in the fortunes of a person or organization…or…a ritual set in the winter solstice on the night of the hunter's blood moon. A turnstile of death to seed all life…legendspeak." A burp seals his sentence. Andre looks at me, but he doesn't see me. His glossy eyes go through me. Behind me. To a bust that commands the room.

My blood chills. Carved in stone is a man ripping his solemn, sleeping face off. Roaring underneath, his teeth bare like human fangs. Strings of ripped skin dangle from his skull. He's part man and part monster.

"A Revenir. A debt collector. The only payment he accepts is your last breath." Andre circles the sculpture. "'And before spring reaps that which is sewn, rare blood will pour on the soil so that all will soak in its possessions and restore balance.'—*The Varien Revival*, by Niro Oxley, 1905."

Sarai. Mercy Bay. The small moment of happiness with Dad. The winged man…and Nadir. They all go back to the Revenirs. Nadir is what they said they needed Sarai for!

Kyle is stuck, biting his lip with his fists balled. "That's pretty disturbing."

Andre slaps his hands on our shoulders. "There are worse things to be afraid of as you grow up. Real things…like the tax man."

"Rare blood. What makes one's blood rare?" I inquire.

"Same condition as the mother. The Eden gene. A limitless Varien gene believed to grant several capabilities over a lifetime. Not just one or three like most Variens. There's no cap on this gene. And it is this gene the Revenirs will consume to have inside of them. This way, they'll reclaim our realm and the Normal realm as the righteous superiors." Andre hiccups. "This is all folklore of course. Who has the time?"

"We should get back now," I say, ignoring everything else but the target in my head. "I have a lot of homework…I don't want to be up too late." Guilt fills me for having the slightest amount of fun. I didn't forget Sarai today—God, I could never. But I covered her for a moment. Like one throws a sheet over a pile of laundry before company visits. My focus has been on going home during the full moon. Now, with this information, I'm not so sure that's what I want to do.

"Okay, yeah." Kyle frowns but doesn't push.

"No, no, no…you have to stay," Andre stalls us. "We can do the photos again. I'll be a little more tolerant this time. I'll take a few with you."

"It's been great, man. We just have to head out. I'm kind of tired myself." Kyle steps to shake Andre's hand, but the gesture does nothing for him.

"Oh, c'mon…all right, kids. Well, come back anytime. I'll be here," Andre says to our backs.

I almost feel sorry for him, then I hear *Nadir. Sarai. Nadir. Sarai* in my head, and I can't get out of the museum fast enough.

On our way back to the Montparnasse's front door, Kyle pivots toward the gift shop. "C'mon, I wanna check something out."

I tug at Kyle's arm. "Umm…I was thinking we could just go."

"What's wrong?"

"Nothing, I just don't want to go shopping right now."

"Did I do something wrong? You're acting different."

When a pang of heat flares in my stomach, I try thinking of happier things. "No, no…you've been nice. I just want to leave."

"Alexia, it'll only be a few minutes."

"Then I'll go back myself!" I lick my lips as though I can mop up the verbal mess I made. But I can't because anxiety kills, and I've already stormed off to find the trolley outside. Kyle sticks to his guns too. He still leaves to check out the gift shop and meets me minutes later with a shopping bag in hand. I'm silent. I've ruined the vibes and I don't know how to stop, or how to say sorry twice in one day.

Our driver cruises us back to the academy via a winding route through the Belle Rues and Virgin Forest. The sights are soothing, but I'm tense in their shaded shadows. I've got to figure all this out. I have to get to Sarai before Nadir. Except the Revenirs are as real to The Grove as Paul Bunyan and John Henry are to the Normal world. Finding them may be half my battle.

"Alexia," he calls my name as he removes his faux mustache and smushes it between the seats. "You don't have to tell me what's wrong. Just tell me you're okay."

I think for a bit. What does okay mean? Without sadness and anxiety? Is it only having one or the other? Is it being free of physical pain? All those things?

"I'm—"

Kyle's phone rings and my turn to speak is a dead-end. It's the girl from earlier again. I roll my eyes and tuck my hands between seats, grab Kyle's fake mustache and jam it in my pocket. "Don't worry, I won't speak while your girlfriend is on the phone." And I don't. I keep it mum even when they hang up.

When we get back to Malveaux, I rush to the steps of the school to rid myself of further embarrassment with Kyle.

"Hold on a sec." He taps my shoulder. "This is going to sound lame but…I got something for you." I fight the urge to smile.

"Today was a better day for you, I think. I figure you should come away with something to remember it by."

With a bashful grin, he reaches inside his backpack and gives me a round and flat glass item. "It's not much. I remember you saying you wish you had some sort of cultural tradition passed down. Maybe this will change things. It's a pathigram. A Varien tradition."

I dangle the pathigram from my finger. I've seen this before. It's like a personal stained-glass window, colored with a picture of the land. Sage Cameron had something like this when I was in my rapture. "Isn't this problematic?"

"Problematic?"

"With your girlfriend and stuff?"

Kyle laughs. "What girlfriend?"

"The girl on the phone. The one you wouldn't let me speak around."

"Oh! No! *Lucie?* She's not even close to being anything like that to me."

"Then why were you so serious with her?"

"Because she's serious. We have a project together and Alani has already kind of screwed it up. It's hard to explain…they're both alpha dogs and I'm just trying to keep things civil so Lucie doesn't go rogue and start working on the IVnet in her madshop with all her conspiracies. We'll be the laughingstock of Malveaux."

Lucie, the techie. I remember her. She's the one who wore that huge machine on her back on my first day. She gave me her business card if I ever needed help with my school laptop. Alani didn't like that. *"Lex, unless you want to find things like dead invisible manticores and folklore shit, you better keep Lucie out of your school laptop. Okay?"*

"Well, in that case…thank you. I love it."

Kyle takes one step closer to me. "It's a map of The Grove. It's supposed to push the negativity coming to you out of the realm. Maybe it'll keep whatever's in your way out. Maybe you'll stay then."

"Alani told you I'm leaving?"

"She didn't openly tell me. I asked. She was really upset the other day and I'm nosy so…yeah, I know."

My eyes close shut from the electric feel of his attention.

"Well, Alexia, I had fun today," Kyle says, beating me to the punch. "Thanks for letting me be your mentor…despite the obvious roadblocks."

"I really didn't have a choice," I say. "But you made it easy. And ummm…you're forgetting something." I take his beloved mustache from my pocket and tack it above his top lip. The right side of his mouth curls.

"Does this mean we're friends now?"

I stop myself from snort laughing. "You give that title up so easy, huh?"

"I'm just going off what you said."

"And that was?"

His body molds like clay until I see another me in my uniform and jumbo hair twists. "Yeah, when you serve me pancakes," he says in my voice.

That's cute. Nice try. "Still waiting on those flapjacks…so I guess not."

"You had crepes today…in the food court."

My head shakes. "A crepe—"

"Is a French pancake."

Embarrassment doesn't look good on me. But damnit, it's not something I can hide right now. Kyle nudges me. "It's all right. I'm smart enough to know that if we're going to stay friends, you're always right, even when you're wrong."

I welcome the rush of every reacting nerve in my body, even the prickling he gives me. It's a detour from my depression, which hasn't haunted me as much today. Not till Andre explained Nadir.

Kyle holds the sun behind his eyes and is blessed with the kind of smile that makes me feel like I'd never hurt again.

I give a gentle slap to the side of his face before running to my dorm. "See you tomorrow in class!" With each step up the academy's stairs, Kyle's figure shrinks. Even from a distance, I can sense the static warmth of his gaze. A piece of me believes he wants to make sure I get to my dorm unbothered. Another piece wants him to share what I'm feeling. Despite everything, most of me can't help but hope for the latter.

CHAPTER THIRTY

ALEXIA VS THE UNIVERSE

"TODAY," DAMO BEN SPEAKS dramatically before his students, "oh today…we're gonna do some heart work."

Above the white neon floor, I tremble, wondering what heart work means. I catch a grip fast. *No spiraling, Alexia,* I say in my mind. *You are here to be better.* I fix my sight on the industrial background behind Damo Ben: the cords, vents, and pipes.

"For your task, I'm putting you in teams of two, and the veil will feed on the biggest bruise between the two of you. Now, what it pulls isn't a judge of what is most tragic. It's not a metric of trauma. It's simply a draw of the most tender memory. If you're wearing it on your sleeve, it'll read it and push you toward some revelation. Some mental strength. A token. Closure. The point is to not lose control through the memory. Okay? Now, I understand this is a tough one…so I want to remind everyone…" He says everyone but drags his focus to me. I can't tell if I'm on his least favorite list still since my first SIM episode. Then in a split second, his bushy arched eyebrow calms and his expression softens. "That as always, we have therapists available for trauma-informed care after class. Once your task is done, your challenge is to take on the ol' pyramid against another pair from class. You gotta make it to the top together, not alone. The pair that makes it, passes. The pair that doesn't, fails."

Everyone groans.

"Ay, I've got a job to do. I've gotta grade you."

"Pass or fail?" I hear Kit shout from the back.

"Clearly he wants some of us to die," Raquel laments, dragging a finger across her neck. "Things are going to get cutthroat."

Damo Ben claps. "That is *not* how Malveaux is. We do not step on people. We take our L and we learn from it. Right?"

None of us respond.

"Right?" Damo Ben tries again.

"YES," we say in unison.

"That's better!" Damo Ben scratches at his dark beard and moves on to announcing our pairs. Erik is my partner today. A relief.

"Jacobs!" Damo Ben calls out and motions for me to meet him in the glass control room.

"Yeah," I say after jogging over.

Damo Ben takes two steps back and turns a silver knob near him on a panel adorned in dozens of identical knobs and buttons. His brown skin is colored an onyx blue in the light. "Sage Cameron told me she agrees with your desire to take this class. I agree with her, you've got a unique amount of promise when it comes to your gifts. I've never seen anything like it, you almost shut the entire SIM room down, but what I can't have is another situation. You know what I'm talking about, right?"

"Y-y-yes."

"The lying. I like the determination; I don't like the deception. I'm not a traditional person, but I like to think I'm a stand-up guy. I want to make stand-up students. Okay?"

"Yes, of course. I'm sorry."

Damo Ben nods. "You don't have to apologize…not for that. Maybe for calling me Mr. Ben, but not that."

Before I edge out of the control room, I look back and smile at the joke. "Thanks, Damo Ben."

On my way back to the SIM floor, I take my place next to Erik and Damo Ben whistles. The veil and I are about to have our second round. It's been some time since the first, but the mental beating it gave me feels fresh—like it happened yesterday. The goal I had has shifted. I'm not going home just yet. Sarai needs me, and I think I can find her. I just have to look in other places, and in the process, I could get to know myself while I'm still in The Grove. I'll be even more ready to be who I need to be when I go home. No outbursts ever. Just Alexia as she was.

"You scared?" Erik stands beside me and asks.

"I hate that I am," I reply.

"Don't be…you'll get to that spark token faster."

"Really?"

"Bet. That's how it was for me." Erik tightens his harness as he reassures me. "I got you."

When he says it, I know he means it. There's something about having another refugee from home to guide me on this task. Something that makes me feel covered, connected, and safe.

"All right, here I go." I breathe. Close my eyes. Breathe in deep, then out again. I wipe my mind as clear as I can. Fear of falling into the veil still clouds my head, but I do the damn thing anyway. I run down the catwalk, then fall. The drop is just as suffocating and even more webby than the last time. Except I know what's coming now. I can be present. Aware of all the subtle stars stuck in the canvas of infinite blackness. Wind runs through the rows of my cornrows. I keep my mind still. I tell myself, *You're almost there*. To the bottom…to the spark. *You're almost there.*

The veil is on time. Turning me right side up to gently land on my feet. I grip my head. My insides feel like a thrown box of breakable items. Contents spilled and thrown back into place.

Nighttime's black glow paints the setting like a filter. Grass is beneath my boots. Familiar grass with thick blades. Grass my mother always bragged about with our neighbor. I look up and the Tudor home I've grown up in is in front me. Immaculate as always, it's like I'm really there. The gardenias near the front porch perfume the air. Haunting. The veil has given me what I want most, and what I am most afraid of.

"This you? I've never seen this place before," Erik says from behind me.

"Yeah, it's my home."

"Nice crib."

"Thanks," I say, unsure if it's a compliment I can even reply to. It's not my home anymore. But it's the only one I've known, so I lead us up the concrete steps and inside the door.

Clean and new. That's how everything smells. There's no dust on the fixtures and tables. No grime on the baseboards. The slim wood-paneled floor looks freshly polished. My mom keeps a very tidy home. She fixes every snag on the couches and refreshes the art, florals, and pillows as the seasons change. All I see is her winter décor. Her carefully curated palette of neutrals, cranberry, purple, and matte gold.

Gold sleigh bells hanging from the front door chime as Erik closes it. "Smells good in here." He sniffs. "Someone's cooking… and everything is all perfect and decorated. You were rich!"

"No, I wasn't. Upper middle class…maybe."

"That sounds like one step away from rich to me."

A tight smile is all I can give as I watch Erik explore the photo wall in the formal living room.

"Were you student of the year every year? Damn." He points at my certificates. The sight of them makes me embarrassed. I don't know why. All I know is how far I feel from that version of myself.

"Unfortunately," I answer.

"What do your parents do?"

His curiosity is natural, but I don't want to answer. It's written on the walls anyway. As Erik eyes the framed photos, it becomes clear. "Oh," I hear him say quietly. A reaction to the photo of my dad with the president at the US Senate ceremonial swearing-in. I wonder what "oh" means. How layered is it? Is it a surprise? Does it come with a judgement? I can't tell.

"They had you in that Annie wig performing?" Erik laughs, an easy cover-up.

"Well yeah… I was Annie. What else would I have on my head?"

"I don't know. Maybe your own afro. It's just kinda funny." He giggles and keeps panning down the wall. "Dang, how many plays have you done?"

"I don't know…maybe thirty. Stopped counting a while ago."

As I decide to check around the house, Erik makes himself comfortable on Mom's formal couch. I almost stop him out of habit.

"Wish I could've had it like this," he mumbles and collides back first onto the cushions.

"Enjoy the couch…I never got to. I'm gonna go peek around the wall into the kitchen. I think I hear someone talking." I move through the living room, feeling guilty about wearing shoes—even in my simulated home—as I cross into the formal dining room. I lean sideways to see around the dining room wall into the kitchen. Niles is there drinking out of a mug, doomscrolling through his phone.

"Erik," I whisper. "Get up. Come here."

Erik sits up, ready to join me, but there's a thick cloudy shadow racing toward him. His terror!

"Erik, look out!"

"Oh shoot!" He falls back. I run closer, just enough to keep eyes on him.

Erik's lips are folded tight. His muscles are tense as he balls his fists and flexes his arms. The shadowed mass of a terror creeps up his legs and crowds its way to his chest and shoulders. Erik is shaking. His skin turns into a ruddy sienna brown.

"Get off me!" He swats at the terrors on his chest. "Ah!"

"Erik! Fight! Fight it!"

Erik clenches his jaw and tenses back up. His body is still shaking—still signaling a summoning from inside him. Both of his eyes are closed beneath his knit brows. He's focusing, working his way through whatever fear is scurrying over him. In seconds, he's tapped in, erupting in needlelike thorns all over his body. Erik's teeth are gritting as he growls and the terror goes stiff before dying out and fading.

The both of us catch our breath.

"Are you okay? You did amazing…really good," I say, sitting beside him.

Erik wipes the sweat from his forehead with his arm. "Rats. I hate them." He sniffs and shakes a chill off.

"How did you do that?"

"What?"

"Get your power out. You freaked out for a minute, but you zeroed in and schoomp!" I imitate the thorns emerging from his skin.

"The tokens. I just go through my memory all over again, and then it's like an on switch."

"But how did you know your token was the right one?"

Looking serious, Erik turns to me. "Can't speak for everyone, but I knew mine because it was when my granny died. She was like my mom, the closest I've ever had to one. After she passed, it was foster home after foster home for me. That's when my heart broke. You just gotta live in that one place you never want to relive, I think. The first heartbreak you ever had. I don't know what it's like for the Variens born here in The Grove, but for people like us… we've got a lot of shit buried on top of us. That first heartbreak splits us in two. All that's left is the before and after versions of us."

Reading between the lines, I think of his terror and wonder what Erik has gone through. What has he braved before getting here? How did he get here? Did Greta save him from a chaotic situation? A toxic one? Instantly, I feel seen. "I think I'm in it…"

"In what?"

"The night my heart broke." Tears puddle in my eyes.

Erik straightens up. "How do you know?"

"Everything looks the same…the Christmas decorations. The Kwanzaa kinara is out. Everything smells the same as it did that night, like pot roast. All of it makes me sick…seeing it, smelling it. This was the night."

Erik removes his hilt from his sheath. "Then we're gonna get you through this. Me and the brave Alexia you got inside you. We got you. I know how it feels to be in your position, so I'll walk you through."

"Okay." I wipe my eyes and Erik helps me up.

"I'm sure you need your privacy. So, I'll stay here. But just remember to keep a cool head, you'll need your better memories to get you through a bad one. The steer token. Okay?"

"Yeah."

Erik pats my shoulder and I return to the kitchen, curious about what SIM Niles is doing and what he has for me.

"Niles?" I call to my brother. Seeing this fake one's face light up when he sees me makes me miss my brother more than ever. Niles has the best smile. Clean white teeth that are all the same length with no ridges, dimples, and a mouth that curls at the corners. When he smiles, he really means it.

"Alexia," he says brightly. He lifts the mug in his hand. "You want some hot cocoa?"

"I would love some," I say, fighting brewing tears. "Would you make me a cup?"

"Of course. Almond milk, right?"

I wipe my eyes and sniff. "Yes. Almond milk, please."

"Mom bought some pirouettes to go in them. Don't tell her I put two in mine." Niles laughs and I tell him I won't snitch. Everything feels like home until he turns back to me from the refrigerator. "Hey, you don't have to wait. I'll bring this to your room."

My heart beats faster.

We never eat or drink anything in our room, not with the mom we have in charge. Niles saying that snaps me back in to place. *This is about a task. I can't forget.* The SIM will only work if I go to my room.

"Oh," I act surprised. "That's so sweet. Thanks, Niles."

"Bet."

I leave SIM Niles and take my time getting up the curved staircase. I pass Nia's room—where music blares through the walls. I meet a sleepy Indy—who leaves his dog bed in the upstairs family room to follow me to my room.

Inside, everything is as it was that night. My pink Christmas tree is lit and positioned next to my desk. Christmas lights are wrapped around my canopy bed. Wrapping paper scraps are scattered on the floor from my horrible attempts at wrapping presents for my family. Staring at my collage wall, I sit on my bed. "Why am I doing this?" I say aloud.

I can't help my bouncing feet, so I sit on my hands to help. Somehow that triggers Simone to speak from my arm band. *"Your heart rate is considerably high. Please remember, this is only a simulation. Breathe, and remember, you are in a safe place. If you are hurt or distressed and would like to end the SIM, press the red button on your harness."*

I consider tapping the button on my harness for a brief minute. *No, Sarai will be here any minute. You can do this. You've done it before.* I shake my head and stare at my window. Any minute may as well be any hour. That's how time passes. Slow like honey.

The SIM Indy resting beside me perks up. His ears stiffen and his head tilts. A gruff rumbles through his snout. Sarai is here. Indy can hear her phasing through half of my window and wall.

I jump.

A hooded figure crawls out the solid wall with ease—as if it were made of paper. I can't believe I'm living through this again. I never thought I'd make it another day when it happened. This was the beginning of my bad luck. The crack that lodged a separation between old Alexia and new Alexia—like Erik put it.

Sarai's voice is tight. Her breath is heavy. "Alexia," she whispers.

"Hey…how did you get in here? What'd you just do?"

In a panic, she strings her words together like she doesn't hear me, just like I remember her doing. "Oh, thank God. Can I stay here?" She falls on the floor before my feet.

Trying to pace myself, I keep playing along. "You can always stay here…but did something happ—?"

"Nothing happened," she cuts me off. "I didn't do anything… but they think I did. They were coming to get me—"

"They?"

"I was at home, and I snuck out the back. They were questioning my mom at the door. One of them saw me and they started following me, but I think I lost them. And if they find me here, they can't do anything, right? I'm good here. Your dad won't let anything happen…right? He knows me."

That question is a punch to the gut. A literal definition of "hits different." Knowing what I know now, Sarai's question and the desperation in her voice is enough to unravel me. I fight the sensation by exhaling. A tear travels down the slope of my nose. I wish I didn't have to lie to SIM Sarai. I wish my answer could be true.

"Yes. You know he will."

Sarai curls up in a fetal position on her knees. Cries break from her like a busted pipe. I come down to the floor and place a hand on her back. Heat is churning in my stomach. I try to separate myself from this current version of me, so I think of happier times. I remember that I loved Dad's summer crab feeds in our backyard. Family and friends were there. Sarai was always there. It was nothing but good food, vibes, and good weather. Light. I remember feeling very light then.

"*Your heart rate is stabilizing,*" Simone reports.

Sarai rests her head on my lap. "I didn't do it, Alexia. I didn't kill him. I never wanted this to happen to me."

Both of us never said the word "Varien." It was just something she alluded to, and something I put together. Maybe she figured her phasing through my wall would be enough of an answer. I draw her close to me. Thinking a hug could remedy her spirit. But it only makes her more brittle—a clump of dry clay crumbling in my hands. "Just save me. They want me dead. Alexia, please."

"They? Sarai, tell me what's going on. I can help you."

"I don't know what to do…" Her sobs are loud, and the hallway light flicks on. Its brightness spills under my door.

"Alexia?" my dad calls.

Sarai sits up and puts her sobs on hold.

"Everything good?" I hear his weight bending the wood panels beneath his feet.

Both my heart and head fight the urge to hug him. "Yeah. I'm good, Dad."

"Okay." I hear him walk away.

"He doesn't believe you," Sarai whispers.

Breaking the memory, I go off script and forget the part I'm supposed to play. "I know," I say, sniffing my tears back.

"How do you know?"

"Because…I've been here before."

Sarai is confused, then paranoia seeps in. "…I gotta go."

And she almost does. I catch her hand before her body slips through the walls.

"I shouldn't have come here—"

"*Your heart rate is increasing*," Simone warns.

I go digging through my mental closet of good memories. Where's the joy? Niles's smile? Mom screaming and cheering for me at the end of my performances? The rush of an audience's applause flowing through me?

"Sarai, just wait," I beg.

"No. Unh-uh, this was a bad idea."

"What do you mean you didn't kill someone? Why do they think it was you? What happened?"

"I can't get into this."

"Tell me now."

"No."

"We're best friends, right?"

Sarai stops. Her head shakes, but she sighs like she agrees. "Don't use that against me. I can't right now." Sarai stares off. "I was in the wrong place at the wrong time. That's all. I don't even know what happened, really. You believe me…right?"

"I know who you are—" A ball of metal crashes through my bedroom window. It rolls on the carpet, spewing orange gas from its sides, a Black Coat signature.

"*Your heart rate is considerably high…,*" Simone recites the same script as I react. Breathe in. Breathe out. Dad's hugs slide at the forefront of my thoughts. The way he'd palm me by the head and bring me in is my happy place. That and his scent of fresh rain on leather. The rising heat inside of me cools and stays in my stomach.

Green lights flash through the windows. "Sarai?" I look for her in the smoke.

"I can't feel my powers anymore."

"I'm going to find you, I promise." A thought to try something comes to mind. "Tell me where you are now? The Grove? Can you tell me?" I leap to her as she tries to push herself through the wall.

"Alexia, I can't. I'm not working."

"Answer me!"

"The gas. Go before it hurts you too!"

"No!" I pull her away with me. Then a train of voices moves closer to us with the sound of stomping boots.

Sarai's face grows tired. "Don't believe them…no matter what they say." She squeezes my hand so tight it hurts. I cry because I know what happens next. I got no answers then, and I'm not getting them now. I'm losing Sarai all over again. The Black Coats break through my door, shouting things at us and pointing their guns. I hold on to Sarai, like a leech, as if I can make her body new again by transferring all I have into her. She'd phase us both through the walls if I could.

Dad. Think of Dad. Dad's hugs.

"Alexia! C'mon!" Dad's arms wrap around me and pry me from my best friend. I hear my mother cry from the hallway.

"No!" I kick behind me.

Sarai cries, "I didn't do it!" Fear rains down her face, the early markers of a mental hurricane. Her hand reaches for mine before her body gives in to the gas. Before her nerves fry. Before her veins freeze. Before black blood drips from her eyes and mouth. Before the gas fills her lungs and powers her brain to sleep.

Before I feel those same things too…

Dad. I envision Dad hugging me tight, and I'm okay. I'm safe.

All the walls around me fall and wipe away into another landscape. A meadow thick with wild flowers.

I'm safe…and I didn't lose control. I didn't outburst.

The realization gives me permission to pour out all I held in. I release and cry until Erik's boots step into view.

"I made it…I made it through." I rise and bring my hands to my face. "No outbursts."

"No outbursts," Erik repeats proudly. "What did it feel like when you were holding it in?"

A cool breeze curves around my face to dry my tear-stained cheeks. "Liquid fire in my stomach. Rising up my chest, then back down when I tried to think of something else. The heat never went away, though. It stayed; it just never came out."

Erik goes into deep thought, peeking cool stares between the tips of his locs. "Well, I hate to be the one to break it to you…but that sounds like your spark token."

"What? Really?" An electrical feeling revives me.

"I'm no expert. I just know that feeling. I don't feel liquid fire. Mine is more of a scratching in my stomach. The sensation is different for everyone, but the location of it is the same. Right here." He points to his stomach. "Next time you get a chance, run that memory back, see if it brings your gifts out."

"Okay…" I shut my eyes, ready to try things out while they're fresh.

"Ay! Not now," Erik laughs. "We gotta challenge ahead. C'mon!" He motions at the stone pyramid covered in moss behind me. Tired and drained, I carry on, not knowing how I should feel. I'm closer to the other side of whatever all this is. One step closer. A broken-down, old Alexia being made anew.

CHAPTER THIRTY-ONE

99 SHOTS

THE PYRAMID LOOKS A lot less industrial this time. Covered in moss and wild flowers that climb and curve around each step. Nature dominating it makes it less threatening. That, and the absence of it flying midair for us to leap onto it. I feel better about this challenge.

When Erik puts gloves on, I wonder why I don't have any.

"I say we stay together. Edge up the sides, the stones are bigger over here. It'll be a little easier to grip and step and probably save us some time," Erik explains. When I don't respond, he waves a hand in front of my eyes to kill my doom loop.

"Yeah, I'm okay with that."

Raquel comes around the corner of the pyramid. "Good, because you'll both be failing today."

"Hi, Erik!" Lucie comes behind her, adjusting her curled bangs.

"Oh hey, Lucie. I'm here too," I remind her.

"Yes, hi." Even though she seems at a loss for words, she's still smiling.

"Nah, we won't be losing," Erik tells Raquel. The two of them start to race their way toward the first step.

I straggle behind to get a word in with Lucie. "Hey, umm…Lucie?"

"Yeah?"

"I need to talk to you about something. I need your help."

"Right now?"

"After class. Meet me in the locker room?"

"Okay, sure."

"Thanks…good luck."

"Good luck to you too."

We break away to meet our teammates. One foot on the first stone, I glance up at Erik.

"Follow my path," he shouts a few steps up. As an ounce of confidence moves through me, a ticking sound starts. The challenge has started. The game is on.

I make smart and stable strides, sticking my foot on even-sized ledges and pushing up before grabbing at another layer. Once I'm closer to Erik, he gets going, and based on Raquel and Lucie's location, we're making good time. They aren't lagging by any means, but there's a decent space between us, and if Erik and I keep this pace up, we can beat them and pass.

Gripping on to another stone, I look behind me. A seed of anxiety blooms once I see how much higher we've gotten. There's a vibration I feel underneath my palm growing stronger and stronger. The pyramid! It's ejecting from the ground to take flight…just like my first SIM challenge. *Oh lord.*

The memories of the last disaster—my outburst that gave way to the rapture of power release and the haunting wounds of killing SIM Sarai, my SIM father, and their two hostages—return to my mind. A fuel to my anxiety.

I'm hesitant to keep moving the higher the pyramid ascends. I take a moment to breathe and notice Erik's gloved hand on mine. He's come down to my level.

"Don't look down, sis. C'mon. Get in front of me," he encourages.

Hesitant, I take a moment to acknowledge him, then I maneuver around him to take my place ahead of him.

"Good. Don't trip about anything. I'm right behind you, okay?"

"Okay!"

He's right behind me, but Lucie and Raquel are parallel to us on the other side of the pyramid. Shit. I messed us up. I ruined our lead.

"Take a step!" Erik shouts to snap me out of my spiral.

I step as he says, once, twice…then three, and four times. I'm moving better, getting back into the hang of things. As my foot pushes off the next level, the step beneath me feels unusual. Less solid…and a bit mushy. The odd texture drives me to check under my boot. I tilt my head toward the pyramid and aim my chin down, staring past my chest and stomach. A body. I stepped on a body. I blink hard and reopen my eyes at the brown-skinned person. I think it's Erik for a moment, but as my eyes come in to focus there's no deceiving. It's Sarai. A dead Sarai with a lifeless stare and a crooked, gaping mouth stained in black blood. Nausea comes to swirl me around and I grow weak—almost letting go of the stone in my grasp.

"Got you!" Erik holds my back. There's nothing behind me when I see him. No dead Sarai. She's disappeared.

I gather my wits and breathe. *Just take one more stone. One stone at a time,* I tell myself. One stone happens, then the second. On the third, I pick up a handful of hair in my grip—strings of box braids. I pan up and dead Sarai's face flops to the side looking me square in the eyes. Sickness and the replay of the night she was taken away by the Black Coats collide. Sarai dead, my biggest fear, sends me into a horror. I scream from the pit of my stomach and light the liquid fire inside of me.

I tense and retreat closer to the stones. Voices whisper around me, "She's dead. You're too late. It's all your fault."

"No! No!" I cry. The heat rising into my chest warns me of my power's exit. I look for Erik to warn him, and find him in a sea of dead Sarais. "Erik, get away from me!"

"Why?"

"The terrors…I don't know. I'm seeing things!"

Erik looks confused. "There are no terrors on the pyramid!" He catches Raquel and Lucie up ahead and shoots thorns at them to delay their path.

The Sarais that once covered the pyramid vanish, but the damage has been done. "Erik, move!" I demand.

He looks confused again until the heat flushes into my eyes, dousing them in starfire. Erik scurries to the side and I look up quickly to release at the sky where no one can get hurt. White and yellow flares burn from my eyes until I'm emptied. The heat drops and I can see everything clearly again. The blue sky, the clouds… Raquel and Lucie at the top with the sphere in hand.

Another punch to the gut hits me. *Fail.* I failed. Erik failed this SIM challenge because of me.

The scenery around us collapses and we ascend to the veil, then the SIM floor. Erik helps me to my feet and Damo Ben rushes over. "I just don't understand," he shakes his head and says. Using his mechanical arm, he makes a screwdriver and tinkers with the control panel. "Why were you seeing terrors on the pyramid? That's not supposed to happen."

He doesn't want to lean toward the fact that each time I take SIM Class, I experience a haunting on the pyramid. It's an issue significant to me…and maybe in my own head. I don't know. I'm sure he'll tell Sage Cameron before I can.

Erik pats me on the shoulder. "Don't be hard on yourself."

"Easier said," I reply. "Sorry I didn't pull myself together. Thanks for the help, though." I walk off and leave for my locker room.

Behind me, I can hear Erik smacking his lips. "Wait…hold up! Alexia!"

I'm too embarrassed to look at him right now. I just want the day to end. I got what I needed out of class…time will tell if it's worth it.

Alani picks up on my energy as we change from our SIM Class catsuit back to our uniform. "Do you want to talk about it?"

"Not really."

"Did the veil bring up one of your memories?"

"I'm okay, Alani. I promise." I shove my catsuit in my locker with my boots.

Raquel comes down our aisle, sympathy in that cathedral-like bone structure of hers. "Hey, I wanted to come check on you. I asked Ben if he could rethink your grade…considering what happened."

Alani's eyes pop, saying, *What happened?!* in her body's language.

"That wasn't really necessary, Raquel." I shake my head.

"Way to rub it in." Alani scrunches her nose. I don't know what she's picked up, but I can tell she's read between the lines. "I'll see you in the dorm?"

I nod softly before she heads out. Raquel trails off behind her with a bad taste in her mouth. I don't care to sweeten it. Too much is on my mind right now.

When I close my locker, Lucie pops up. "Hey," she speaks softly. "Are you okay?"

Gosh I hate this. Here she is with the same clunky light-flashing machine on her back. Satellites are spinning as she walks and giant tubes of smoke are aimed at her face and she wants to know *if I'm okay?*

"I wish everyone would stop asking me that," I huff. "Umm…" I swat the vapor blowing into my face. "What are these things for?" I point to the large tubes.

Lucie glances at her equipment. "Oh these? Oxygen infused humidifiers, that's all."

"Oxygen infused? Isn't there air in water?"

"There is…but this water was canned straight from the clouds over Serpentine Peaks. Wrung out like a sponge." Her nails clink against a jar of purple water taped to the left of her backpack. "The air is always too dry in Malveaux for me."

"Well, I'm glad you found a solution."

"Me too."

I look around before continuing. "Umm…Lucie, I need access on my laptop. I remember you saying you could help me with this if I needed."

Lucie squints her eyes. "Access to what?"

"Information."

"What kind of information? You might have the perfect software installed already."

For real, Lucie? I move close to her ear, ensuring I'm out of everyone's earshot. "Not if I, uh…want to know what manticores eat."

From the pop of her eyes and flicker in her freckles, she's caught on. "You're a believer too?"

"Proud of it." I nod with an acting smile. "And soon, everyone else will be too, if I can catch one of those damn things. We won't be laughed at then, will we?"

"No, they'll be the fools then." Lucie grins and taps a button behind her ear. A set of clean lenses builds a shield before her eyes. "You'll need the IVnet then, *and* something with the metal alloy ballan to cut through the vinman netting barrier on the balcony if you plan to get out that way." She holds her hands out and I place my laptop in them.

"Do you think you can jailbreak that before the night bell?"

Lucie stalls. "The night bell? That gives me a few hours and I have homework and robotics club…dinner. I can do this for sure, but I need more time."

"I don't have more time. If I'm going to catch one, I need the info tonight. Winter will sneak up on us." I pause and try not to laugh. How am I this good at sounding ridiculous? "They won't be out for much longer before hibernation."

"Manticores don't hibernate." Lucie's eyebrows dart at me and I swallow a gumball-sized serving of anxiety. "Everyone knows that."

Everyone. "Yeah, but I'm not talking basic manticores. I'm looking to catch a new breed, super rare. Studies show there's a slew of manticores born with bear in their blood. That's what I'm going to find."

And just like that, Lucie is back to salivating. "I'll have this done by the end of period."

"Great."

"Was that all?" Lucie's sweet doe eyes wait on me.

"Yeah, why?"

"Oh, I was thinking you would ask for some tutoring in Engineering. I saw you got a D on our last test."

I pat at the crown of my braids in frustration. My former title Student of the Year has now been replaced with Biggest Idiot in Malveaux Academy. What a fall from grace. "Thanks for looking over my shoulder, Lucie."

"Sorry, I wasn't trying to."

"It's okay. You can make up for it by hooking me up."

"Yeah," Lucie assures me. "I will make up for it…but, there's just one thing you have to promise me."

"What is it?"

"If you want to keep the IVnet on your computer, you'll wait till everyone is sleep to get on."

"What? No way."

"Then I can't help you."

"Lucie!"

"Promise me. Promise me you'll wait till bed checks are done."

I huff.

"Alexia, I could face expulsion for this. This is not a harmless favor. Promise me."

"Yes, all right. I promise you."

She goes back to normal in seconds. "Perfect! I'll have everything ready before the night bell. Meet me in the library a quarter before it rings." Lucie's freckles twinkle and a ton of alarms—hailing from both her backpack and watch beep. "I better get to robotics. It's tournament day."

"Right. Well, good luck and thank you."

Her and the mist of pregnant clouds whisk off—just as happy to go kick some robot dog's ass as I am to find Sarai. The visions I had of her—dead with ashen skin—are all I can think about. I have to get to her before it's too late. I hope it isn't too late. I'll never forgive myself if it is, but I won't be able to live with myself if I don't try.

CHAPTER THIRTY-TWO

BURNING IN THE QUIET

THANKS TO LUCIE AND her ability to manipulate technology, my computer can operate outside Malveaux's firewall—granting open access to the weirdest corners of the IVnet. I rule the keyboard, digging through the IVnet for morsels of Revenir information. My mental shovel hits a treasure trove of legends two feet in—well, two minutes in. The Revenirs don't feel so distant now, and in two more minutes, I'll be watching some of their looney admirers go live: the DeuxCadets. I'm not sure why they call themselves that. None of their videos explain why, but I've fallen down their rabbit hole because they're intensely devoted to being Revenirs one day.

I set my earbuds in each ear. The screen is black as I wait, then a light in the dorm flicks on.

"Lex, why are you still up?"

I press my laptop down. "Alani! you scared me."

"Because you're suddenly seven years old? Go back to sleep. What assignment are you even working on? Surviving Armageddon? No assignment is this important at 2 a.m."

Lying through my teeth, I tell her, "If I'm going to stay here, I need the grades to do so…"

"Stay?" Alani's tired head bounces. A smile warmer than soleil lamps brightens the room.

"Yes…stay." I check the screen. The DeuxCadets have started their live session—mouthing words and adjusting their camera.

"When did you decide? Wh—" Alani holds her hand out and flexes it into a wave. "If we go into detail, I'll never sleep. *But* you've got to explain all of this first thing in the morning!"

"Okay, I will." The light clicks off and Alani rolls over. The rustle of her plush white comforter makes me want to fall into mine. *Soon…not now.* There are more answers out there for Sarai. I turn the volume on my laptop up so I can hear the two guys on camera.

Paler and gaunter than I saw them in their last uploaded video. They were searching for clues and deciphering codes for an event they call Passage—a night for Revenir recruitment and networking. It happens once a year and clues are sprinkled throughout The Grove for the quickest Revenir admirers to catch on. Anyone who can gather every riddle, is welcome to attend Passage and sign their name up as a Revenir recruit. DeuxCadets have found messages in commercials and news reports. They've seen politicians throw up signs during speeches. Things have been planted in the Virgin Forest for them to find, and even the Belle Rues. Looking for these gems is a full-time job, one that is never complete until twelve months have spanned. "Medi len jue?" the DeuxCadets say in unison. They pause and stare at the typed letters queuing up the sides. More words in Viridian I don't know.

"Good. Good. Tonight, we've found the final piece to the Passage equation," one boy says, staring out of focus. He shuts his eyes and brushes his wavy golden hair back. "I'm happy to say that Jaime and I are on our way to Passage this year. First time."

The guy named Jaime pats his shoulder—a signal to rest and let him speak. "Croix is exhausted from sleuthing the hours away. He'd rather be sleeping right now, so would I…I'm sure all of you would like to. So, thank you all for joining us. As we move on with our announcement, we think…well, we promise you'll be happy you logged in." Jaime fiddles through something. "Now, on our last live, we deciphered the date of Passage—the night of a full moon—but not where. We'd been stumped on that for about eight months, because as you know, every theme of Passage differs from the last—which has kept us out of the running of attending one. But Croix here became the master of all riddles this year. In our last video, we found an item in the Belle Rues that led us to the time of Passage: 10 p.m., November 10th thanks to your help." I scribble the date down and stay tuned to Jaime's voice. "And in some sweet twist of luck, we found another item in the Belle Rues."

"Rare," Croix jumps in. "Two items in the same location just doesn't happen with these guys."

"Never," Jaime affirms. A noise scrapes behind them and the two turn around. Croix blows at the space in front of him, a stone mortared room lit by two fading soleil lamps. White waves funnel off the walls then disappear.

"Must've been a bird." Jaime squints above while Croix laughs the scare off.

"I need sleep, man, my head is fried," Croix says.

"Here." Jaime hands over a cigarette, lights Croix's, then lights his own. "We'll make it fast then."

"Bette's Book Nook had an interesting display for all to see," Croix picks up. The smoke from his cigarette curls into an upward vine. "Hard to catch for the ignorant. Loud to all of us." Croix holds up a book in front of him and my throat numbs. It's the same comic book I saw in the Belle Rues. The same one I held. "Okay, you'll see Set front and center, dropping from the sky in midair with a pipe in hand. Nothing peculiar there. Right? Okay but when you take the display's props into consideration, things start clicking."

"A pipe cutter! Right beside the comic," Jaime says at the camera. "I mean, it doesn't get more obvious. Set with an old pipe in grip and one industrial pipe cutter for display. I couldn't have conjured a better clue. And it wasn't just any pipe cutter, it's an iron cutter from the early 1900s."

"Which led us to many places around The Grove, places that employed the use of these pipes in the early 1900s," Croix adds. "We learned this pipe derives from the only location with cast-iron pipes still installed."

"And because we've made progress on our journeys thanks to the collective effort of our followers, we felt this to be a team reward, not just something we keep to ourselves. So…" Jaime removes a heavily corroded pipe from a box. "We will tell you where this pipe derives from thus the location of the Passage."

"That's right! We're all getting there together."

More words clamor to up the side of the screen. Ecstatic followers type exclamation marks and dynamite emojis. *I can't believe it. I can't fucking believe it.*

Jamie holds up a finger. "There's only one place that utilizes this type of plumbing, and it's hard to make out on the side…too much sediment buildup. But the embossed design—" Jaime and Croix seize. The bar at the bottom stops counting the minutes.

"No! Don't do this!" I press play and nothing happens. I try refresh and everything goes black. "No!"

Alani springs out of bed. "What? What is it?" Flames grow from her hands.

"I lost it! All my work. I spent so much time studying, reading, and watching videos. I took notes. I cross-examined and I got close to being there. To getting an answer and this stupid piece of crap just broke down!" I throw all my notebooks on the floor and curse more.

I fold into my bed. The mattress dips where Alani sits beside me. "Lex, it's all right."

"No, it isn't." I sob into my comforter. "I can't get anywhere without the last bit of information. I can't close my thesis."

"You can."

"I can't."

"Yes, you can." Alani grabs me by my shoulders. "Look at me. This is just school. Shit happens and we fail, and we learn from it. We're supposed to mess up and lose things. All of our teachers expect us to, anyway. You won't die because of this. Trust me, you'll get better. You'll get smarter. You'll find the answers on your own—without a computer."

"I will?"

"Of course," she rasps. "After you get some sleep, though. There's so much information out there. We have the biggest library in The Grove, here. Did you know that? Go there. Go to where that leads you. Check out the museum. The greenhouse."

"The museum," I mumble. "Yes! Alani, you're so right."

"My quote in the yearbook," she quips.

"I'm sorry I woke you up."

"You should be."

I sniff and gush out a giggle. "Why do you say that?"

"Because I'm never this sweet to anyone who wakes me up without returning the favor one day." Alani winks and gives my hand a squeeze. "Cocoon up and get some sleep. And on your side, please. You snore when you're on your back."

"Right." I roll my eyes in the dark, behind her back, where she can't see me. Inside the covers, I should find peace and contentment, but I don't. Not because my computer screwed me out of an easy answer. No. I can't sleep because all I can think of is whether Andre is working a shift at the Montparnasse tomorrow.

CHAPTER THIRTY-THREE

SERENDIPITY

DAMA BATISTE SLAPS THE end of her ruler on my desk, and if I had less of a mind, I'd tell her where she can stick that ruler. But since I'm me, Alexia Jacobs, daughter of Sylvia "Solo" Jacobs—grand master of home training and discipline—I exercise restraint and battle dozing off.

"Hey." Kyle pokes at my side with his highlighter. "What's wrong?" We're supposed to interpret the divide between the academy's founders: Marcel and Louis Malveaux.

"I pulled an all-nighter. Stayed up to work on something and my computer malfunctioned before I could finish."

"It wasn't due today, was it?"

"It's not something that can wait," I say.

There are glimmers of ideas in his eyes, just like there were in Alani's last night. "You can still get it done without your computer. There are ways."

"Well, I know that. It's just...I'm not exactly able to leave campus and go chill at the Montparnasse again."

"The Montparnasse?"

"Yeah."

"For what?"

"There's something I need to ask Andre about." When I see Kyle open his mouth with another question, I bulldoze. "Face-to-face. The phone won't do."

Kyle leans closer, the bass in his whisper tickles my ears. "I could go with you. We could do that."

"Really?"

He nods, and for some seconds, I forget we're in class.

I pretend to yawn and notice the spaces of Kyle's work sheet. "You're leaving it blank?"

Kyle shrugs. "She never collects these free writes. I've got an answer for every question anyway."

As if she could detect the mention of herself, Dama Batiste walks by our corner. She shadows Kyle's shoulders and spots his ink-free paper. "Kyle," her call almost warns. "Care to write your answers instead of blabbering to Bel Jacobs?"

He makes a face to hold in his attitude and fails. "Nah, I think I'm good, seeing as you'll probably forget to collect our assignments for the millionth time."

The class "oohs."

Dama Batiste's lips purse. "Ah, I should've seen that coming. You've been on my nerves since freshman year. All right, motormouth, have it your way. Share your knowledge with the rest of us. C'mon…up, up." Her eyes point at me. "You too, Bel Jacobs."

"Me?"

The thud of Kyle's dropping pen joins the screech of his scooting chair. "I'd first like to thank Dama Batiste for the opportunity she's given me to verbally touch all your hearts this morning. It's always good to check if you still have one. Correct, Dama Batiste?"

"Kyle," she thins out his name. Laughter infects other students.

But Kyle makes damn sure his own voice is the loudest. "The war of brothers! Sounds dramatic when it's thrown around, but if you give its history some time and attention, the name fits. These brothers—Marcel and Louis Malveaux—founded this academy in the early 1900s, hoping to trailblaze a path to engineering, innovation, self-control, and potential. Ironically enough, those goals tore them apart. Marcel went one way and Louis, went the other."

Dama Batiste hums. "And Jacobs?"

Kyle turns to me. I freeze like a deer facing an eighteen-wheeler. Everything I'll say will probably sound dumb and Normalish.

"You're good," Kyle whispers. His lips barely move.

I think of all I've learned so far, in the manual Sage Cameron gave me on my first day, and the museum tour. "Yeah…umm. I guess Marcel believed Variens were stronger when in control of themselves: mind, body, and soul. He believed that if one could achieve control of those, they'd possess a potent clarity that'd unlock the full potential of their powers over the years. Louis argued against this. To him, talent was the only way."

"And a Varien either has it or they don't, right?" Kyle builds on my input. "The strong aren't made. They aren't trained. They aren't taught. They just are. Louis felt certain restrictions must be set on admitted students. They needed to be advanced Variens in skill and potency. Anything less held our culture back. Louis was deeply disturbed by the marginalization Variens experienced at the hands of Normals or Wonts—as he called them. Even with a realm of our own, he didn't understand why we were satisfied with designated spaces of preserved land. The Normals occupy a majority of Earth, and under their care, they've abused it. We should always be ready to take back what's ours. He even stated in one of his essays…" Kyle stares above him, as if the answer is attached to an invisible cloud.

"'The Harbinger,'" I answer for him.

"Yeah, that's the one. Louis stated that The Grove was even mismanaged by what he called Fledges, or 'weaker' Variens, and in desperate need of a political revival—some crazy means to avoid becoming another Normal-majority realm. That's what he was all about. Nothing was too crazy if it meant making the Varien revival happen. Not even physically harming students if they didn't meet his testing standards."

"Because any student or Varien who measured tier 3 and below was a waste to him."

"He was nuts."

"This ended Louis and Marcel's brotherhood…"

"Pretty much for good."

"Especially after Louis changed his last name to Knox to sever ties with his brother. After this, he partnered with Niro Oxley to form a new militant school."

"The Knox-Oxley Institute. Home of elitist ass clowns and robot militants."

I laugh. "Is that etched somewhere on their crest?"

"Since 1915. Everyone there is a tier 4, yet, somehow, they still can't see us on the court."

"Something Louis is probably rolling in his grave over…if he has a grave. The Malveaux family banned the use of their patented soileil energy from being used, which moved Louis to depend on kinetic energy to power his school. He also disappeared after this epic and bloody duel with his brother. No one ever found him, he just vanished."

"Can you speed past this part of the story? Freaks me out."

"It is kind of creepy, isn't it?"

"I've got goose bumps." Kyle rolls up his sleeve. "Can you imagine hating your brother so much you break all of his ribs, puncture a lung, and tuck him into a nice yearlong coma?"

"No. I can't imagine that or wiping him from existence, which is what some conspiracists believe Marcel did to Louis."

"Not me."

"Of course not, I thought you didn't want to talk about this?"

"I don't." He claps. "But Dama Batiste insisted that I do, and I just pray it's enough to make her happy. How'd we do, Dama Batiste?" Kyle gives a grand and dramatic bow. The class is quiet. A church house instead of a school. Pens aren't scribbling and whispers don't live. Maybe everyone is afraid of Dama Batiste. I am. The woman has nearly carved half-moons in her arm by now.

"You two work well together…*when* you work. Yes, class?" Dama Batiste gazes around the room, eyes circling over her pearl framed glasses. "I'd much rather enjoy this dynamic on paper," she says. "So, please, Jacobs, keep it quiet. Phoenix, is that even possible?"

Without a thought, Kyle gathers his book bag and fusses under his breath. He loosens his tie and surprises me with a set of words. "Let's go."

"Me?" I look around. "Where?" Either I didn't give a quick enough response, or I gave the wrong one, because his back is traveling away from me.

Dama Batiste props a hand on her hip. "You think you're leaving unexcused?"

"Looks that way." Kyle pushes through the door. "I'll escort myself to Sage Cameron's."

Kyle's whisper of "Let's go" plays on repeat in my head. My toes flex. My knees brace. I feel my thighs cinch in with my core. Step-by-step, I walk the path Kyle walked. None of it is logic, or even a loud thought. Like a moving piece in a game, it all doesn't involve me. I'm in the deep of something so filling. That, or hormonal insanity.

I repeat, "This is the first and last time," in a low voice until Kyle's head turns at the clicking of my oxfords.

"Are you crazy?" he asks.

"I should be asking you the same."

"I didn't think you'd actually listen to me."

"Well, I did, so now what? Are you really going to Sage Cameron's?" I smile from the rush.

"Not anymore." Kyle relieves my backpack from my shoulder. "The Montparnasse?"

The space between us closes as he wraps his hand around mine. I nod. His skin is gentle, and soft where callouses ought to be. Just as I settle into what's happening, his thumb massages the back of my hand—sparking an explosion of chills. He makes me feel like Disneyland after dark. Safe, excited, and shadowed with the mist of adventure. All of which keeps me from wanting to break away. I see Sarai in my head, grinning at me as I shed my armored skin for once and follow my heart. *"Girl, you're down bad."*

Then there's Alani weighing heavy on my heart. Her cardinal rule of no roommate of hers is allowed to have a romance with her cousin is battling my moral compass. But I didn't plan on liking Kyle, and I don't know when it started. It just happened.

Kyle gives me a look—the kind of look someone gives you when they want to see all of you all the time. I smile at the rush he gives me and throw Alani's rule away for a bit.

Yeah, I'm totally losing it.

"Hold tight," Kyle tells me, teleporting us out of Malveaux.

CHAPTER THIRTY-FOUR

DIZZY

ANYONE'S NOTHING CAN BECOME something in a second. My aunties and older cousins used to say this on sunny days when one of them was worried. They'd sit on the porch beautifully sun-kissed, sipping iced tea while watching me and Nia play. "When you're headed on the right road, your heart will feel dizzy," I'd overhear.

I feel that. A nothing morphing into something. A road farther from the land of pain I felt. An answer to the blankness. Maybe even healing.

En route to who knows where, Kyle's soleil-powered Sportster drifts us through the dirt roads of The Grove. "Hold on a little tighter, I want to show you something!" he shouts over the engine. I melt into his back and squeeze my arms. We head into a section of the Virgin Forest, and to my surprise, we aren't slowing down.

"Kyle?" a smidge of apprehension coats my voice. The road ends. There's no path for a motorcycle pushing 120 mph. Clearly, this boy has a death wish for us both.

Schwack! Whoosh!

The Virgin Forest comes alive, swiping and lifting metallic trees and branches out of harm's way. I hold my breath like it's enough to keep me in one piece. My nails press into Kyle's chest, digging deeper at the sound of violent foliage. At this rate, my grip will kill him before a sequoia. "We have to get out of here!"

"Nah, we're nearly there. Hang on!" He revs his engine and braces forward. The ground ahead of us bulges into a mound, throbbing like a beating heart until it shapes into a great hill.

A mighty branch swerves over me, tossing my braids over my eyes. Kyle revs his engine again. We're accelerating even faster now, but with resistance. The tilt of my body blows my hair from my eyes and I don't breathe until we stop moving. "Thank goodness that's over."

Kyle throws a smirk over his shoulder. *That look…as if my heart can't beat any faster.*

A sobering breeze points out the drop ahead. *No! No! No!*

Kyle's feet teeter on the ground before returning to the pedals. "Kyle…wait!"

There's no waiting, just the roar of air as we zoom into a spread of bare land. The bike's engine purrs loud against my screams. After clenching every muscle in my body, it's finally time to breathe again.

"Are you dumb? Did you bring me here to die?" I pound my fists into Kyle's shoulder. He laughs through the blows and holds my arms. "You said we were going to the Montparnasse!"

"I wanted to make a pit stop."

"In hell?"

"Chill. The Virgin Forest does this to everyone. It's a defense mechanism. Making it so hard to get here is its deterrent, keeps the land pure. Now, if we had a bad agenda, it'd read that loud and clear…and kill us."

I mock his nervous laugh and freak out some more. He deserves it. "You couldn't teleport us in?"

"It's more fun this way," Kyle tries to convince me.

"You're a loser."

"Alexia."

"What?" I snap.

"Calm down and turn around."

I spin fast, too pissed to cool off. "Whoa." I gasp. "What is this place?" *Mount Olympus.* It has to be. Scenes this divine could only exist for gods. The sky, a smear of peach, orange, and gold, hangs above us. Exotic birds, unlike any I've ever seen, dip their webbed feet into the water. Their tails leave behind streaks of iridescent colors.

"Welcome to Adieu Lagoon." Kyle guides me forward. I stare in awe of a waterfall. Its power is mighty and its beauty is ethereal. Like an abalone shell, the lagoon's waves are ever-changing, shifting colors with each churn.

"This is my favorite place in The Grove. Did you have something like this back at home?" he asks.

"There's nothing like *this* around."

Kyle rests against the trunk of a silver willow. "Well, where do Normals go to clear their head?"

"They don't really ever get clear." I sit in the waxy moss beside him. "Camping…or the movies helps, I guess."

"Where did you go?" He pokes at the dimple in my left cheek.

"The stage. I'm a theater kid. So, I like escaping into stories and becoming someone else for a while, I guess. I never went there to make sense of anything. Just sing and dance."

"You know, I used to dance?" He looks more amused by that fact than me.

"*You* can dance?"

"Yeah, but that doesn't mean I should. I haven't danced since I was a kid, when my mother was a classical dancer. I still know a lot of tricks."

"Why'd you quit?"

Kyle's face turns dim. "My parents died."

My heart sinks. I didn't expect those irreversible words. "How old were you?"

"Six. I had them for a while, I guess. It's hard to remember a lot about them. But the memories I have are enough." He takes out a brown wallet and flips it open to a photo of a woman who could've given Audrey Hepburn a run for her money. "My mom was this beautiful Brazilian woman with a head of bone-straight black hair. Every time she hugged me it smelled like peppermint."

The next photo he shares is one of two men at a bar enjoying their mugs of beer. One has a fair-skinned complexion and dark hair with wavy ends that touch the sleeves of his a vintage graphic T-shirt. The other reminds me of my godfather—tall, brown skinned with a strong nose. His hairstyle and facial hair are a unique set-up: a beard and thick sideburns trailing to a silver streak of hair on his head.

"I don't know who this other guy is, but that's my dad." He points to the one in the vintage jersey. "He cooked the most amazing things…like, works of art. Pancake volcanoes. Waffle teepees. It was his idea to live in a camper for a while. He sort of believed in living off the land as much as he could to connect with nature. Deeper than your average Varien. He taught me and my brother that very early during those trips. I even lost my first tooth here."

"You have a brother?" I ask.

"He passed along with my parents."

A flaring sting cuts my throat. *Why am I asking questions? They're making things worse.*

"My younger brother…Adam. No one was able to figure out exactly what happened to him. He was just gone. My parents were murdered while I was at school. Police found the bodies in their bedroom and that was it. Nothing's ever been solved."

"That's horrible. I'm sorry."

"Ah, it's all right. 'Mel neut beni awhem en len' as my dad used to say. All is well within me. I've gotten by."

I want to somehow make up for everything he's missed over the years, but what can I give? What, if anything, could fill a void so deep?

"It's weird that I'm talking like this to you. I'm getting a little too comfortable." Kyle shrugs and smiles.

"You can talk to me," I assure him.

He springs a coil hanging over my brow. "You make me forget we just met. I never thought I'd talk like this to a stranger."

"Stranger?"

"Okay, maybe you're not a stranger. That's a weird word, isn't it? Stranger…" The bass in his voice stretches out the last syllable. "I can't complain about my life, though. I really lucked out. My aunt and uncle took me in. They never thought twice about it. I can't picture growing up with anyone else…they're all I've known. What about you? I told you my little downer story, what's yours? How did you find out you were a Varien?"

"Like everyone else…I guess."

"Everyone else?" His ruffled brows make it clear that his idea of everyone else involves Grove-born Variens—people who know nothing but the other side of Normal.

"I mean, manifesting was a shock." My cheeks warm. No one knows my past…well, maybe Sage Cameron does. But at least she pretends she doesn't. I want to keep things this way. They don't need to know I broke my father. Would they believe it was an accident when I tell them the story? Would I sound innocent after they find out that biologically, my father hated my guts? Does it sound like an accident then? Juicing high-powered bolts into my dad as soon as I came out to him. It all plays like the perfect premeditated murder plot gone wrong when you're not the one who lived it.

If Kyle could read what's behind my eyes, he'd find skeletons. But he's so new. He walks right by them. I clear my throat. "Especially with my dad being a senator…he couldn't deal with me. You know? I soiled his clean quilt. This immaculate family he patched together."

"So, he was against you?"

"Mmhmm." I nod, my mind carefully dancing around its own land mines. "Well, Sarai first, but it might as well have been me. She turned, then ran away to my house…said she wanted me to save her. But…I couldn't make that happen. My dad could've. He had all the power to do that, and he didn't." I stare off, fighting the taste of bitterness creeping up my throat. "So, the Black Coats ended up taking Sarai. They said she'd done something bad… that she'd committed murder." My eyes begin to puddle. "I just remember her screaming like she was dying. They pulled her away from me…and that was it. She was gone. And then, strangely, my manifestation happened months later. I didn't even know it. It started with a fever. My mom had me pop a few fever reducers and take a cold bath to break it. Thank goodness for that—if we'd gone to the doctor, I would've been like Sarai."

"Man, Normals are brutal," Kyle sighs.

"Yeah." I take a moment to catch my breath. Sweating as I devise a lie to cover my most unforgivable act. The words are getting harder to say. I hate reliving this. I hate lying, but I can't have anyone knowing what I did. I just can't. Not now. "I kind of…hid in my room after my first outburst…only coming out to eat, nothing more. But Dad knew still. He always knew things about me. And when he went off on me, he pretty much said we were done. Life as I knew it was done. The next day, he was going to send me to Mercy Bay's slums. Then, Set kidnapped Sarai from the prison and tried finishing off my dad a few hours later…and I found out I wasn't the only person mad at my dad for his beliefs and laws. He destroyed him. I had no choice but to leave at that point. Greta saved my life, but I thought I'd be home again at some point. Not here to stay. And now, I don't even know how my dad is. Is he alive? Is he in the hospital still? What does he look like? What does he think about everything?"

Can Kyle find the seam where lie and reality meet? I don't think so. My performance is worthy of an Oscar.

Kyle wipes the sadness from the side of my face with his hands. "We shouldn't talk about these things today, they're a little too heavy," he says. "C'mon…I want to show you something."

We hike up the hill that houses Adieu's waterfall. It's the perfect scenic view of the lagoon. "I can feel the rumble of the water under my feet," I gush.

"That's not what you think it is," he says, wrapping his arms around mine. "That's the heart of The Grove pumping."

My mouth hangs open as he guides my hands beneath the moss and into the soil. The beating heart, buried down in layers of rock, pulses strong and freakish. "Crazy," I gush again, waiting for Kyle to tell me more about The Grove's secrets. When I look around, he's moving in a funny way. "Oh my gosh! What are you doing?" I hide behind my hands at the sight of his skin.

Removing his clothes, he chuckles. "We're going swimming."

"Unh-uh. Heck no! We don't have any clothes to change into, and I'm not down with jumping to my death."

"Do you always worry this much? Most of the girls that come here—"

"*Most* of the girls?"

Kyle raises his hands. "I didn't mean it in that way. I mean when people come here unplanned…they improvise. You're the only person I've brought here—"

I throw his blazer and hoodie at him. "Just put your clothes back on." Peeking through my eyelids, I see him inching closer. I can't handle what's happening. I want Kyle to put his clothes on because this is strange…and I can't stop ogling. He has the perfect stretch of golden skin. *Seriously perfect.* "I play basketball with my shirt off every day" perfect.

"Fine. But that doesn't get you off the hook." Kyle reverses his steps and buttons his dress shirt but leaves his hoodie and blazer on the dirt. Looking over the edge of the waterfall, he asks, "What're you afraid of?"

"I'm not afraid of water. I don't swim in clothes and I'm afraid of—ahh!" Chained together by the lock of his hand, we plummet into the blue. I float to the surface, fighting through my boiling skin and temper. I suck in as much air as I can before lashing out. "Jerk! You bum-rushed me!"

Kyle pops through the surface, grinning from ear to ear like a big dumb idiot. "Okay, that may have been too impulsive." Noticing my trouble with treading, he hooks me by the waist.

I flail my arms in the water. "Did you not hear me say I didn't want to jump? I'm afraid of heights!"

"But you survived." He smirks.

"Shut up!"

Kyle apologizes.

"Sorry doesn't help my hair," I snap, stressing over its soon-to-be-frizz potential.

"Did I ruin it?"

"Of course you did. These are fresh braids."

"But it's beautiful no matter how you do it. Braids…those twists…I liked how you did it that day in the Belle Rues."

I claw into his shoulder for dear life and splash him. "The day you said I sounded crazy?"

"I definitely deserved that. Give me one more."

He doesn't have to tell me twice. I splash him repeatedly.

"Okay! I got it!" he hollers through toppling drops of water.

I swim to the land. Kyle catches me by my skirt and braves through a few more of my vengeful splashes. "Did I sell you out, though?" he says. "Did I?" I don't stop splashing. It's funny until he can't open his eyes.

"Stop being stupid and let me take a look," I demand.

Kyle flinches and fights my arms before giving in to the touch of my hands around his face. I blow softly into his eye. "Is that better?"

"You don't think I had your back in the guarde station?" he goes on, towering over me.

"Shh."

"And with Sage Cameron?"

"I know you did." My bones rest like lead in my flesh. "But, why?"

"Because…maybe I believe you."

Those words. Oh, I've never realized how much I've craved them until Alani first said them. How different the world looks now knowing another person hears me. Alani and her cardinal rule strike my mind again, but I think I'm too far gone now. I'm acting without thinking. My hand slides down his jaw and collects the fresh drops of water rolling down his face. The tips of our fingers touch, with mine transferring mild static into his. Kyle flinches. *Easy, Alexia. Don't light the boy up.*

He nuzzles his lips against my neck, and now, *all* of me feels prickly and excited. I want him to kiss me.

His mouth moves up my neck, making a trail to the anxious nerve endings in my lips. Endorphins. Dopamine. The hug of his kiss, so sweet and addicting, lifts me. With this layer of ice between us broken, we make each peck longer than the last. I'd live happily ever after if this feeling could play on loop. But, as with everything, nothing lasts forever. A cold chill comes over me as we separate. Adrenaline dissolves, and now we've got to figure out what the heck just happened.

"You're freezing. We should start heading for the Montparnasse." Kyle guides me to shore, then teleports to the waterfall's hill where he collects the dry clothes he left there. He cloaks me in his blazer and puts his hoodie over his wet shirt. "I definitely didn't expect any of this to happen."

"That makes two of us…Alani is going to kill me."

Tension takes hold of Kyle, hitting him in the chest, as he remembers who his cousin is. "I totally forgot about her…I'm sure everything will be okay."

I feel stupid and sober. "This shouldn't have happened."

"I'm glad it did, though." Kyle circles around the tree and smiles, almost daring himself to come closer. "I've wanted to kiss you since the first day you came to the academy."

I tug his tie. My temptation and attraction are growing stronger than my worries again. "That explains your playground behavior."

We both drop down to the moss.

I lean against the tree's bark and take in its draping silver canopy. Offering protection, the fringed branches enclose us and swing in the breeze.

Kyle faces me. "There's just something I can't explain. Is it like that for you? This absorbing state of…something?"

"Something," I nod and notice my locket's shine beneath my blouse. "Absolutely."

"Everything in my head is quiet," he muses. "Being around you is different in that way. It trips me out…"

Unable to hide my truest self, I beam bright. The braids draping down my back are sponged with ounces of water. My naked feet warm in the sun's piercing rays. Happiness avoids me at all hours of the day, except in this moment, it becomes mine.

"I really like being around you…," Kyle says. "And even when I'm not, all I do is plot ways to get around you again. Like, should I get my other wrist twisted because you're so damn hardheaded? Yeah, it'd be worth it. I feel like I'm rambling. Am I?"

"No."

His pupils catch mine and expand. "I like you, Alexia…a lot. I know you're worried about Alani, but I'll handle her. She's just overprotective of me because of what happened to my parents. All she wants is for me to be happy and in a good place."

"Are you happy and in a good place now?" I reach for his hand.

"Yeah," he says softly, coming closer. "I really am."

Everything loses its sound, just like Kyle explained—even the booming waterfall. Not only have we taken a pit stop from the road to the Montparnasse, but we've also managed to detour from the heaviness that threatens to sink us every day. All that matters is us. We don't need to define things on our own, we create the answer together.

So, I kiss him without shame and throw the world out.

CHAPTER THIRTY-FIVE

All the Best Places to be a Plumber

WHEN WE STEP INTO the Montparnasse, the place we plant our feet garners disgusted frowns from the adults peppered in the lobby. Ladies in tweed suits whisper near the elevator. Men in ties give us double takes. The receptionist sneaks looks. A woman with dainty white gloves walks to us. Her eyes cut around us, never connecting to our own. "The group home is located south of the Belle Rues," she says to us. "Do you need someone to show you the way?"

Kyle grimaces. "DeBeers? We're not looking for a group home."

"Yeah, excuse you. We have every right to be here," I go off.

The woman is snide. "Not dressed like that. I'm afraid we must exercise our right to reject service." She's the snootiest of snooty curators. Her nose is so high, it cuts through clouds.

"And what's wrong with our clothes?" I retort, knowing good and well what we look like: wet and wrinkled with our Malveaux crested shirts untucked.

The curator folds her hands. "Well, for one, you both are disheveled."

It's not fun to be referred to in this way. Especially not after making out for minutes on end. Even though I'm not wearing lipstick, I wipe the corners of my mouth to hide evidence of my

226

fun, because I can still feel those kisses on my mouth and neck. I shudder from the playback of those moments, and the cool breeze that meets my wet threads.

Kyle's voice booms through. "Because our clothes are wet?"

"My, that private school education is doing you good. Yes, young man. Your clothes are wet."

"Have you looked around?" he retorts. "Your stupid building is in the middle of a river. It's not our fault we fell in on our way up."

"You expect me to believe that?"

"Umm…we're customers, so yeah," I say. "Who's your manager?" *That's right, Alexia. Turn the tables on her.*

"Yeah," Kyle adds.

The woman's mouth hikes, and by the lazy glimmer in her eye, I can tell she's enjoying herself. "I'm happy to say *I* am the manager."

"Damn," Kyle mumbles under his breath. Within one blink, the museum snob ushers us back toward the entrance and starts closing the door on us. I inch my shoulder in the crack between the threshold and the heavy wood.

"Can you at least tell Andre we're out here to see him?"

"Andre?" The snob pushes back but I've got her in strength. The door is pushing open. "Security! Security!"

Kyle is shocked. "Alexia, what're you doing?"

"I'm getting answers," I grunt. "I need them now."

"For your report? We can go somewhere else? The library."

"No! I need Andre!"

"Maybe we can catch him another time. It's okay."

"You believe me, right?" I pant. "You said you did. I'll explain all of this later…just help."

There's a moment of hesitation, maybe to calibrate, maybe to give the logical piece of his brain a chance to reason why bum-rushing a blocked entrance is a bad idea. Lucky for me, it passes quickly. Zero to sixty. Kyle grabs my hand and teleports us into the Montparnasse's lobby. Our wet shoes slip on the polished tiles and bring us to the strong hands of security. They loop their arms under ours and shout for us to get down.

"HEY! GET OFF!" Kyle and I throw out demands. There's scuffling and all kinds of ruckus going around. I can't keep my eyes on Kyle because all I can feel is the pain of my arms getting twisted.

"Oh, whoa! Whoa! Whoa! Whoa!" a deadpan tone nears and grows panicked. Venkman till the end. "Don't handle them like that! These are kids!"

"Who've trespassed! Stand back," one of the security guards says.

When I force my chin up, I see Andre—patron saint rescuer—staring back at me as he bends to my level. "Alexia, what're you doing?" he sighs before rising to the security guards. "I know these kids! They're good. Let them go!"

The snob scoffs. "Are you claiming responsibility?"

Andre shrugs. "Indirectly, perhaps."

The snob is surprised yet too tired to continue battle. "Well, then, Andre, you won't mind being escorted from the premises *with* them." She points outside and the guards lug us by the shoulder till we're ankle deep in river water. All three of us.

"Oh," Andre puffs as he assesses his soaked feet. "I need a bottle of wine."

"Bottle?" I ask.

"I was just thinking the same thing." Kyle trails beside him, bringing Andre to stop with agitation.

"There's cider in my cottage…and dry clothes. Just up the stream." Andre directs his finger to a tiny two-story cottage among wild redwoods. "It'll kill the chills…maybe you can tell me what this is all about too. Maybe, I don't know. What do you kids think?"

Kyle checks with me, our eyes negotiating things we can't say in front of Andre. I'd only say one thing, because Sarai is out there and she still needs me. Because the Revenirs are working, and I can't stop.

"Okay," I respond.

CHAPTER THIRTY-SIX

The Navarette Cottage

"You know, I don't ever wake up in the morning hoping to get thrown out of my place of work," Andre quips as he zips around his cottage's kitchen. He reaches for glass liquor bottles tucked in obscure places—the oven, a cereal box, under the sink—and a bag of salt and vinegar chips. The way he slams them down makes me think they'll break.

"You said you had dry clothes here for us," I whine through chattered teeth.

Kyle shivers. "And cider."

Andre frowns. "Your generation is so self-centered. You have no boundaries. You aren't afraid of anything. That's just not compatible with the real world."

"Andre."

Kyle's call is ignored. Andre is too busy pouring a healthy serving of scotch in his glass. Guess he's skipping wine. "You see, the real world is a dark draining hole. And there's a place for people who don't want to follow its rules. So pick a side." Andre's right arm flails and the bottle of scotch spits out some of its contents. "Either conform and go to college for something you'll never make a living from or get used to wearing a horrid shade of orange for the rest of your life."

I clear my throat. "Andre."

"No! I'm talking!" This time he washes his helping of scotch down his throat.

"We are so sorry."

"Oh really?"

"Yes, we are," I say it again, hoping it'll sink in. "The last thing we want to do is embarrass you or ourselves. But none of this would've happened if we didn't need you. You're the only one who can help me with what I need. I know that for a fact."

The sentiment sobers him instantly. "Well…" He pours the rest of his drink out, then takes sips of air from the empty glass. "I gather it must be important."

"Very."

"Mmhmm." Andre takes another airy sip. "And it pertains to?"

"I'll get into that, but I really need to get out of these clothes. I'm dying."

"*We're* dying!" Kyle corrects.

"It's not really that cold in here, kids."

"Says the guy wearing dry clothes." Kyle is snippy, and so far, capable of getting every jab in at the right time. Andre would've barked at this earlier, but his inner raging Hulk is shrinking, and I've got to keep it that way.

"I picked out some dry clothes for you both laid on the couch in the guestroom. Change into them and bring the wet ones to me. I'll remove the water myself. Go on." Andre points.

"And cider?"

Biting his fingertips, Andre eyes his kitchen full of peeling wallpaper roses on cabinet doors. A large bird cage with no bird sits in the corner where dust collects next to a pillar of newspapers. "Looking for that kettle. I don't use it much these days."

Kyle's face lights. "Shocker, hot toddies aren't your style?"

Dishes tumble in the cabinet Andre closes and he leers. "Alexia, if you want him to live, which of course you do, get a hold of him," he says.

"Right. Come on, let's go change." I say. Kyle listens, not happily, but he walks with me—and thank God. Andre's hallway is bordered with toddler-size dolls. All in knitted pastel garments, their smiles are frozen and tinged in the corners. Their hair is stiff and poised into linted curls. I wonder if they're watching us walk for a moment. They're all tilted, posed toward the end of the hall, pointing their lollipops at our backs.

Anytime my siblings and I had to look into anything scary in our house, we'd line up single file with me sandwiched between them. I miss that. Right now my back could be a bullseye for a psycho with a dagger. *Andre's dagger.* And I'm the bright one who got us in the center of his web. So dumb. I'm practically glued to Kyle when we enter the guestroom.

"What're you doing?" He frowns.

"I don't know if this was a good idea."

"What?"

I pace back and forth in front of a futon bed. "I should've thought this through more, but there's not enough time. There's never enough time. What if Andre is one of them?"

"Alexia, who's them? Hey." Kyle waves in front of me.

I blink heavily and spit out the truth. "The Revenirs."

"Wait, huh?"

"Them is the Revenirs."

"And you think Andre is one?" Kyle looks like he's set to laugh.

"No…maybe…I don't know. I'm afraid. I don't have any other option and I just spent the last night learning about every Revenir conspiracy known to man and now I'm too freaked out to be in Andre's dusty house. What if he drugs our cider? What if he kidnaps us? I-I-I'll never crack the code and rescue Sarai then. We won't ever get to go home."

"Lex, calm down." Kyle's hand takes mine. "I need you to start over for me. Okay? Can you do that? Can you tell me why we're here?"

Somehow, when he speaks, my nerves cool. I lay it out for him. From A, everything that happened at Mercy Bay, everything that happened at Ren's minus me murking Dad, to Z, my IVnet date with the DeuxCadets and Nadir.

"This is a lot." Kyle's brows perk up. "Are you sure about this?"

"Never mind." I flounce to the bedroom door.

Kyle's voice begs me to stay. "Wait…I know you're telling the truth. It's just—you think you can stop this from happening?"

"Do I really have a choice?" Like he did in the lagoon, he stands over me. A curious tickling washes through me. Everything around him blurs. How does he pull this from me?

"When it comes to your best friend? No…you don't." He's got our change of clothes in his hands—his are the color of saffron and mine are mint. He hands me the dress and smirks. "The moment we've all been waiting for but can wait even longer for."

I laugh and hide behind the wooden room divider in the corner.

"Should I head out or…?" Kyle fidgets.

"No, I don't want to be by myself."

He nods stiffly.

"Just turn around?"

"Yeah." His back faces me and I feel secure enough to peel the wet clothes off. It's colder in the room when the air touches my skin, and still cold when the drape of this mint dress falls over me. It's practically all ruffles.

Kyle's high-waisted zoot-styled pants make him look like a loud crime boss. We get a kick out of what we look like after changing clothes and hold tight, so Andre doesn't suspect us of laughing at him.

"You don't like the clothes." He sucks his teeth as he waits for us to return to the living room. The look of his heavy brow chokes my giggling fit.

"No, no!" Kyle explains, handing Andre our wet clothes. "We were uh…creeped out by the hall of dolls back there. How do you deal with those? Scary."

"My mother made them."

Kyle scratches at the back of his head. "They've held up well. I mean…most dolls don't even manage to keep their faces over time. You know because of the sun damage and oxidation. Does she live here? I'd love to meet her."

"She's deceased," Andre says.

I gulp. The more Kyle talks, the itchier he seems to get.

"We're sorry," I tell him, but sorry doesn't seem to cut it. Arms crossed and bundled in his dingy beige robe, Andre goes past us and finds an ironing board to set our clothes on.

"Everything here was hers, and she left it for me. Said she knew I wouldn't have myself a partner once she left, and she was right. That's what those dolls are for…some company when it gets lonely."

I frown. "But they don't talk to you."

"And I hope you don't talk to them," Kyle quips. I ice him and take a spot on the loveseat.

"No, they don't. But they give me something to do. I tend to them like Mother did. I repaint their features when they fade. Clip loosened hairs and dry-clean their clothes. Mother was a great seamstress. She always made matching sets of clothes for potential buyers. Kids…adults…collectors of all ages." His eyes point to our threads and linger there with some sort of smart smile.

"Well, thank the lord for that," I say and Kyle snorts.

Andre cocks his head. A sigh straggles from his mouth. "Anyway, children, you didn't commit a misdemeanor just to talk about Mother."

A whistling scream from the kettle interrupts my chance to answer.

"Right! The cider." Andre points a finger and springs toward the kitchen.

Kyle faces me and I meet him with the same antsy mood I had in the guestroom. "Thanks, man," Kyle says. "We're not too cold anymore, it's kinda warm actually, so I think we're good on the cider."

The kettle calms while Andre clatters dishes around the cupboards. "I disagree, young man. The cider is done, and you were both soaked for some time. A cup will do you good."

We exchange more nervous stares. "He may pour the cups, but we don't have to drink them," Kyle whispers. "I think it's all right, though."

"This recipe was Mother's," Andre brags. "Cloves, a twist of lemon, some allspice, brown sugar syrup, house rum usually—but I'm holding it because you're minors—and seven apples courtesy of the Virgin Forest. Very seasonal." He beams over his product and sets a tray of mugs with cinnamon sticks on the coffee table in front of us. "Drink up!"

"Thank you, Andre," I say. "I'm going to wait for mine to cool."

"You're very welcome."

"So, I guess I came to you to find out about the plumbing system in The Grove. The history of it at least."

"Plumbing. Uh-huh," Andre mumbles.

I run my palm over my knees, determined to somehow iron a wrinkle out from the fabric. "For an assignment at school, of course."

"What class would this be for?"

My mind races. "History. I've decided to do a report on The Grove's innovations and to do that, I have to start at the beginning. I was wondering if you could tell me when The Grove first used cast iron pipes for plumbing, and when they moved to using other materials."

Andre is stoic while laying hands on our garments—gliding them across and summoning the water from the threads till they become bone dry. "That's very boring stuff. There wasn't anything else to study?"

"That's what I said." Kyle grins.

"It's not a total snoozer," I explain. "Some of it is interesting, seeing how an idea is born. It's all pretty much out of necessity and that makes for good stories. And, unlike the both of you, I'm an infant to this place. I know nothing about it. So, everything seems to fascinate me."

Andre raises one brow. "Well, that's where you're right. Growing up with Normals would put me to sleep. Cast iron plumbing was pretty common, even for them. What made it cutting edge was what flowed through it."

"Which was?" I ask.

"Zenith water."

I shrug. "I don't get what's so special about that."

Andre laughs as though it should be obvious. "Zenith water contains moondust. Moondust is highly abrasive like sand, except sand is subject to erosion, which helps smoothen it out. Moondust, as it traveled through those cast iron pipes, ravished our plumbing system. So, we moved to ductile pipes sometime in the nineteenth century. They're still made of iron and some Varien innovated material, but aren't casted—which, I'm not understanding of the science of it all, but I believe makes it a stronger material."

"And are there any locations that don't run ductile plumbing?"

"Well, there very well could be. Cast iron is an exemplary material. It isn't loud and can last for over 100 years or so if it isn't running Zenith water. It's very durable, but for me to say where those babies are still employed, I haven't the faintest idea. Perhaps an actual plumber." He shrugs. "Your cider should be room temp now."

"Do you have any books that might be helpful?" I go on, ignoring him. "Or any idea where we can find documents related to this?"

"Of course, I have helpful books and things. I've got copies of the community newsletter dating back to the first years of The Grove and an archive of Grove history notated by my family. But

I still think a plumber would be best as my family's historical documents were never published for public record."

I walk around, checking out the cottage for Andre's description. "Where's the archive?"

Andre's lips draw a hard and plain line. He grabs his keys from his pocket and stares at the rusted lantern hooked to the hallway wall. "In a place I'd rather not go."

CHAPTER THIRTY-SEVEN

The Cellar

AFTER KYLE AND I change back into our dry uniforms, Andre takes us two stories under the house. The stairs that guide us are made of poorly plastered cement. I can't find my bearing on every other step it seems, and the damp air just makes it worse.

"Please explain why you have an underground lair." Kyle sounds as cool as he can, but I know he's anything but. He doesn't know whether it's safer for me to follow behind Andre, sandwiched between them, or lag at the end. So he's positioned beside me, his hand grazing mine.

"That I won't do. But I can tell you all about my cellar." Andre stops at the last stair and flips a handled switch lodged in the stone wall. The dark is washed out in dim yellow light. Barrels rest in formation like soldiers waiting for war. There are tons of them around us, and where there aren't barrels, there are shelves of books in the walls.

Kyle and I both gawk.

"Your drinking makes sense now," Kyle quips. "Been doing it your whole life."

Andre clicks his tongue. "Hardly. My parents weren't vagrants. A little whiskey and port did me good during a cold, but that was about it."

"That's all it took," Kyle jokes.

"So what do you do with all this stuff? You can't just keep it for yourself," I interrupt.

"I sell it when the time calls for it." Andre shrugs. "There are some hundred-year-old barrels here and probably hundred-year-old spiders and heavens knows what else."

"You don't like coming down here?"

"Never have," Andre's answer echoes. "Never will."

"I'm sorry."

"No. No, Alexia. Clearly you need something beyond school papers and projects, right?" A web of a smirk catches Kyle and me. We're slightly shook, but still listening. "And since I descend from a long line of bad hoarders, I wouldn't be surprised if the morsel of info you need is here in the Navarette family archive." With half of his body inked in a dark corner, Andre flicks one more light switch. A ladder is laid against a book-covered wall. It goes on for what seems like miles and the mere sight of it turns my breathing offbeat. *Needle in a damn haystack.* "Good luck."

The cellar walls groan. "You're not staying?" I quickly ask Andre.

"I promised I'd take you down, didn't say I'd stay. Come up if you need me." His exiting steps are loud and cold. Suddenly, the cellar doesn't feel as welcoming and the groans we just heard turn angry.

"What is that?" Kyle says.

Andre stops on the third step. "Pipes. Coincidence, yes?" Every nervous feeling I had before fills me again. We're alone now. Two stories below a stranger's house and no one knows.

Kyle's voice goes low. "I can teleport us out of here quick if something happens. Don't worry."

"'Kay."

"Start on this half." He eyes the wall. "I'll tackle the other… we'll meet in the middle."

It feels good to loosen my hands on the wheel a bit, to not be in this on my own.

"I'm thinking we should check the table of contents in each book. Look for anything related to plumbing, maps, or architecture."

Sounds simple. Easy. But Kyle and I both know we stand before a mountain. Together we sigh, shaking our heads and shrinking in the shadow of the shelves. My grit shrinks as another sudden sound wails and creaks, then I remember the perseverance of my ancestors, the wit of my mother, and the love my father has for his people.

This wall may be a mountain, but I stand on the shoulders of giants.

CHAPTER THIRTY-EIGHT

NEEDLE

I WANT SO BADLY to hold the answer in my hand. For it to warm me and point me right where I need to go. I just hope it's not somewhere below me, overlooked. The pile is deep. Not stacked— but a thrown hill of hard-spined Varien fiction and nonfiction books with splayed pages. Some on their sides, others on their backs. We've done work.

Kyle glances down. "This fool has first editions all locked up for the air to read. It's crazy."

"I was just thinking the same thing."

"And all this wine too. If he sold this room, he'd be eating good forever."

"I don't know…" I look over the cover of an original copy of *The Classic Tale of Mera Hare.* A cute rabbit with bows in her hair dons the cover. It's interesting to remember there's an entire world of Varien pop culture to discover. "I wouldn't be able to part with them if they were my family keepsakes."

"You mean to tell me you'd be fine living paycheck to paycheck when you have first editions collecting dust in a cellar?"

"Yes, I really think so."

"You've never even read these books. They mean nothing to you. It's all Varien literature."

"I know, I'm just saying I'd rather be a collector than a seller."

He frowns—somewhat disgusted, surprised, and interested. All of it intrigues him and encourages him to irritate me as he goes through his side of the shelves, asking if I'd consider selling different titles. "*Valley of The Twin Palms?*"

"No."

"*The Fury of Fire?*"

"Kyle, I already gave you my answer."

"*Rogue River?*"

"Stop."

"*It Happened in Autumn?*"

"Ugh…you're a troll. Are you even listening to me?"

This time Kyle laughs. "Says the girl who refuses to see the wealth in selling all these books."

"I couldn't care less about money with things like this."

"Because you've always had it?"

"No."

"Then what's the reason?"

"Collecting things and making them survive the test of time for your loved ones…it's sweet. You don't think so?"

"I would want my loved ones to cash these puppies in."

I shake my head. "Because you're obviously not capable of loving words."

Kyle's faint smile doesn't cower. "Pull a book from the shelf."

"Why?"

"Just pick a book for me."

"Which book?"

"Any one of them."

There are so many, so I do what I always do and pick the prettiest one. A deep forest green book with a gold-foiled spine. "*Remy and Rosette of Enracine.*" When I see Kyle perk an eyebrow up, I clarify. "It says it's by Genevieve DeWitt."

"Oh," he responds. An airy look is in his eyes and he giggles.

"Ring a bell?" I skim the table of contents and flip through the pages.

Kyle squints. "Ah...," he mumbles. "'Chapter Two: When Rosette gave you her time, you felt special. It was like she had the gift of healing in her skin. And the night I met her, I shed all the hard shit my father plastered on me. A boy of concrete. She cut all of that. With her eyes, the soft curve of her rounded nose, and those lips—damn...those lips that could send me into a forever type of sleep. My favorite mix of poison. "Do you love me, Remy, as much as I do you?" She'd ask, yet she knew the answer. And I would never answer, because ties speak louder than words, and my soul promised her the property of my heart—in this life and what comes after. It was hers for the beating.'"

The glisten in his hazel eyes catches my tongue. I clear my throat and check the first page of Chapter Two, and there it is: the monologue he just recited inked in the first paragraph of browned pages.

"Does that count as a 'love of words' or...am I delusional?" He grins.

I can't help but curl my mouth. "Troll," I say. "Keep looking."

"Yes." He clutches a flimsy book to his chest. "Ay yi, captain!"

We comb through more covers, pages, and spines. Our fingers pointing the way around the words. There are so many, and so far, not one of them says one thing about plumbing or iron. Kyle isn't a quiet reader. He mumbles everything he reads. Low and soft, but I can still hear him.

"What will you do when you find it?" he says, tossing a book over his shoulder. I neatly drop the one in my hand to the pile near me.

"Are you talking to me?"

"Is there anyone else here?"

"Hard to tell when you never stop talking." I smirk.

For a second, he laughs. "You mean the reading?"

"The reading aloud, yes."

"It just helps everything sink in better. You'll be able to hear me when I find something that way too."

"I guess…"

"And then what will happen after that?"

I shake another book for loose papers. "I'm going to get her."

"Just like that?"

"Yeah."

"You're just gonna walk in like, 'Hey! Sarai…Wilkerson. Where are you?'"

"Her last name's Baker, and no, I'm not. I'm going to look like everyone else at the Passage and steal her from under their noses."

In the deep amber light, Kyle looks confused. "How?"

"I don't really know yet. But that's my life right now. Moment to moment, you know?"

"Yeah."

When I find his eyes, they don't cower. "I don't think you should do this—"

"Well, I'm going to," I snap.

Kyle's hand gently waves. "That's not what I was saying. I mean, you shouldn't do this by yourself. These kinds of people aren't the kind you want to piss off alone."

My heart starts skipping. "I know that, but I don't have anyone."

"You got me." He says it, and I want to say, "No, I don't" out of routine and defense. Except the truth is, I'm so damn tired of feeling like no one cares. So, I don't say anything. "I'll go with you. I think I should…I know a little something. All this stuff, I've heard from my uncle over the years about the Revenirs. He's one of those conspiracists, I guess. Full of information he can't do anything with because either you believe in them or you don't. And if you do, you're crazy."

"Why did you pretend then? When I saw their comic in the Belle Rues?" I ask.

Kyle shrugs. "I didn't want you to get sucked into this stuff. I didn't want to start down the rabbit hole either…it's not a healthy thing to open your eyes to. It's an ugly thing and it seems like this cancer that can't be cured from The Grove because no one believes it. So I never knew what to do with the information, but it always made me wonder. You know? I've been everywhere with you on this thing. I'm here now." He shrugs and moves closer to me. One hand on the spine of a worn book on the shelf, and the other sneaking itself into mine.

I hesitate, then I let go, closing the gap between us for the second time today. I don't know what's wrong with me, but I like not wanting to figure it out.

It's cold down here, but the press of Kyle's lips on mine is warm. The pad of his thumb strikes against the end of my jaw like a match, and I'm warm all over. He lets go of the book and it topples to the floor like a shot pheasant. Both of his hands hold me now, and mine crawl up his neck and into the draping of his messy, dark hair. I'm not alone anymore. We are alone.

Then a scraping noise, the sound of rock against rock says otherwise. "What was that?" I gasp. Kyle startles and moves just enough for me to see past him.

The air is icier. The light weakens.

"You see that?" Kyle inspects. "A piece of the shelf sunk back."

Blackness is all I see where a portion of the wall once was. The lantern's light doesn't reach the space's end. "Must be some sort of hall…path. Something. Where do you think it goes?"

A chill tickles me. "I don't know. Put the book back."

Kyle looks at the pile around us. "I can't remember which one it is."

"It doesn't matter. Let's just put a book back in that spot and close this space."

"Okay, just hang on."

But I don't, because who would want a dark passage to open so that whatever is in it can have its way? Not me. While Kyle searches for the correct book, I choose a random one, *The Thursday That Never Ended*. The ground rumbles a bit, and the scraping noise returns as the shelf fits back into place and closes the gaping hall behind it.

"Oh, thank you, God." I breathe. "Maybe we should go? Try again tomorrow?"

Kyle doesn't answer me, not with what I want to hear.

"I think I found it," he says instead.

"Found what? We need to go. I don't know what's going on in here, or who Andre or his family really are, but we need to do something other than stay here."

"This was the book that fell from this spot." Kyle points behind him. He flips the leather cover open and starts reading aloud again.

"KYLE, do you hear me? Let's go!" I lunge and grab his wrist.

He rocks a little and keeps reading, "Behold, the last works of Harrison. The heirloom Navarette's eldest son…"

"KYLE!"

"And The Grove's most notable cartographer."

I pull harder this time and the book frisbees from his palm. This time, a page rips loose from it. "Just leave it!" I command. But he doesn't. He keeps going—reaching for the page from his knees. Another electric chill shocks my spine and my need to leave increases.

"Please don't make me leave you," I say.

"You won't," Kyle replies.

"I will if it means I won't die."

Whatever trance he was once in, he snaps out of. He's intrigued again, playful with something good behind those eyes of his. "I think you're forgetting something."

"What?" I fold my arms.

"You need me."

"Like water in my lungs…"

"Or…air."

"Are you going to tell me why so we can leave?"

"We can leave safely anytime, remember? I'm a teleporter." He swallows himself in grey smoke then reappears right in front of me, smelling like fresh smoke and cologne. "And the answer, was right in front us." Kyle unfolds the fallen piece of paper, the page that tore from the book. It's large and filled with blocks of color, veins of tangled blue lines inked onto the paper.

"A map?" I'm breathless.

Kyle smiles and nods. "Not just any map. An infrastructure map of The Grove from 1931."

CHAPTER THIRTY-NINE

BARE BONES

THE NEXT DAY, I can't stop my brain from deciphering the hand drawn blueprints and maps from the book Kyle and I found. I haggle Lucie before SIM Class to repair my computer as soon as she can. She isn't excited to take on the task, so I wrap my request in another lie about manticore hunting. "Don't forget the mission, Lucie. We have a point to prove," I remind her. The bait is all she needs to take my computer back for tinkering.

"I'll have it ready for you later today," she replies confidently.

"I have detention with Dama Batiste after school."

"Okay, I'll deliver it to you there."

"No," I whisper to Lucie—who's already in motion to her SIM locker by the time I try to tell her not to. I watch her walk off and mumble my thoughts: "Why would she deliver something to me during detention?"

Alani sneaks up behind me and looks over my shoulder. "Oh, you got your test results?"

I glance at her and trace her sight to the reminder beeping and blinking from my watch. It's from the school clinic. "Yeah...I guess so."

"You haven't checked them?"

Uninterested, I shrug. "I've just been really busy. Can't be anything too crazy. I'm a girl that shoots stars through her body. That's as wild as it gets."

"Don't you wanna know how that works or what tier you are?"

"Ugh," I groan. "Honestly, no. I suck at SIM Class, so I have an idea. I don't need to see how much of a baby I am on paper."

"You don't suck." Alani folds her arms. "You literally shut things down when you're in power. There's no way you'd be anything below tier 3. It's the sparking and the steering you need help with."

"Don't remind me." I scribble notes down in the margins of the book, then set it down in the locker.

"Why're you so obsessed with school?" Alani picks it up and thumbs the pages like a flip book. Neon tabs blow raspberries as she does it. "What class is this? Dying Art II?"

"Alani," I huff and take the book back. "This is for my project. Remember?"

Alani rests her head against the locker beside mine. "How could I forget? You only woke me up at 2 a.m. bitching and moaning about the damn thing."

Where I would bicker with Alani, I keep my mouth shut. No gasoline on this fire.

"You should be a kid right now, Lex. Kids don't care about blueprints. We change our minds every other day and do what we want because we can. You can't do what you want when you're thirty-five, you've got too much shit to float. You know? A place, maybe children, maybe a marriage, and a ton of bills. It's messed up. But that's why you shouldn't care about anything right now… especially after running away here. You need to take it easy."

"Alani…you're the most high-strung person I know."

"That's because you don't know yourself." She zips her boots. "I'm going to make you take charge of your life."

"I'm already in charge."

"No." Her eyebrows hike up. "Like, really in charge."

After finally getting my foot through the pant leg of my bodysuit, I zip the front up. "How?"

"You'll see…"

"Oh, you should be scared," Raquel throws her deadpan comment in from behind me. "Following the Book of Alani has been known to cause drama all over Malveaux. Get influenced at your own risk." Raquel winks and Alani isn't impressed.

"Says the girl with her foot in a boot," Alani claps back and frowns at the clunky black brace Raquel's foot is encased in. "How'd you screw that up?"

"I didn't screw it up. I played volleyball after school one day and my ankle just started aching. I don't even know what really caused it. I just woke up and it was sore."

"That sucks. I hope you heal fast," I say.

"Why are you even here? You can't participate," Alani says it with an obvious air.

"I know," Raquel answers. "Ben says I have to sit with him and observe. Guess I'll be hanging out in the panel room."

Always one to get her point across, Alani walks with her head high, nose aimed up. "You know, if you followed that so-called Book of Alani, you wouldn't have to be under Ben's armpit all period. You'd be clear from attending SIM Class entirely…but go off."

Before Raquel can say anything back, Alani taps me. "Come on, Lex. Ben will be pissed if we're late."

We leave hobbling Raquel behind and venture to the SIM room. When the door opens, Damo Ben does his same ol' same. He drills. He watches. He examines with an arched brow. He orders us to start again when our form is wrong in martial arts. He assigns us target practice to sharpen our access to spark and steer tokens. I call my spark successfully most times, it's the steer token I haven't found yet—causing me to miss each holographic target while Alani nabs a perfect ten out of ten score. I don't think I have any more fuel to fight through the rest of the SIM, but I power forward and fall into the veil before Alani.

Coolness spills over me. A beautiful waterfront breeze. Long-haired grass and the rush of water my heart once silenced.

"Why're we in Adieu Lagoon?" Alani says after touching down. I can sense her frown without turning back. "This isn't from me."

Don't think of him. Don't think of him.

"Have you been here before?"

Remnants of memories bleed like watercolors in my mind. The water droplets hanging from his doused hair were like pearls. Sneaky tints of red where his skin is the thinnest. His softness to counter my sharp edges. I'd give in again and again...

"You know I haven't," I bluff.

"Weird."

Smoke trails mark the sky, puffing higher and higher. There are a lot more trees here than I remember. Some of them are brown and green like the forests I'm used to.

"Is this weird to you?" Alani asks. Thick branches sweep at her hips as we trek our way deeper into the veil's game.

I struggle to squeeze by. The trees are thickening as we go. Even crawling won't help at this point. I've got a solution, but even to Alani, the very sound of the blade leaving my sheath offends her.

She gasps. "You can't do that here."

"These trees wouldn't be earth colored if this were really Adieu."

"But wait—"

"It's all right." I cut away. "God knows my heart. C'mon, there's smoke beyond these. Then we can be done."

Alani nods apprehensively at my side. She trims at the left and I go for the right. The foliage is impossible, resisting to break in one blow like metal is hidden in its bones. We swipe numerous times at one, and others surrender in one swoop. By the time the trees thin out, the climate isn't enough to keep me chilled. The inside of my arms ache from the burn of labor.

"Man. That was hard." Alani is out of breath too. There's a cottage in the clear of a meadow. Andre's cottage. "The veil is messing with us."

"We haven't even really started."

Alani whips a flask from her bra.

"What the hell are you drinking?"

"Calm down. It's water." She waves the open flask under my nose. "I'm not a full hellcat."

"Where'd you even get a flask?"

"It's my dad's. Holds just enough water. Easy to hide during SIM." She winks and takes a swig. "But listen, we're beat, okay? Fuckin' tenderized meat too tired to shield what the veil is going to throw at us. We need to steer our powers effectively. We've got to be smart. Let's stay out of our feelings."

I don't know what that's like. My life as I've known it, is all about feeling everything. Fine time to try. We come up to the creek, where I splash my face and grow weary as the sun begins to set in a matter of seconds. The change is just as volatile as the last time it did this. The woods around us are manipulative. The Virgin Forest's overzealous twin.

When we get to the cottage, I picture Andre sitting in his dingy armchair surrounded by his dolls. Maybe they'll be my terrors. Maybe one will come creeping from the cellar.

Alani has my back and we cross the threshold into a place that shapeshifts into something new again...a place I've only ever seen once.

A place I'd rather forget.

Splintered wood and shattered glass litter the floor. There's a smell. Ugh. Charred wood and the scent of a blown circuit. *Me.*

"Is this you, Lex?" Alani studies Ren's house.

Isn't it obvious? Ren's items are mixed with pieces of my deepest psyche. Her framed pictures are replaced with those of my family. My father with the president. All of us on stage upon his win on election day. Dad, Mom, and me—weighted by bouquets of sorbet-colored roses after a performance. The veil has given me away, I just hope it doesn't tell the rest.

Alani notices the photos and doesn't breathe a word. She grins with sympathy, not knowing if this is the right time for consoling, but she's Alani so she writes her own rules. "The only thing that matters is right now. Okay? That's what they want us to learn. The past can be the present if we're not aware. And that's when we're our weakest."

I practice breathing, like Sage Cameron's exercises. "Why can't I be as strong as you?"

"Because I'm me, and that's exactly who the world needs me to be. You stay you." The top of her red head gently bumps into mine. "I'll cover. I don't think there are any shadows here for me."

There isn't anything anyone could do to make me feel covered. Anxiety taps my chest and suddenly the sun seems to be under my skin. We walk to the kitchen and the heat travels to my ears.

The sight of the ocean from Ren's kitchen should be soothing, but the hot needles pricking at my flesh rush with the rattling of a pantry door. There it is, my shadow.

The four paneled door shakes. Pushes from the other side of it grow violent. Worse than the last SIM, but just as forceful and fervent as Set's attempts to break through Ren's study.

"Nothing behind that door can actually hurt you," Alani's voice rasps in my favorite way. It isn't until she speaks that I realize I've been still. "It's okay to be afraid. Just don't let it stop you."

I close my eyes and breathe the swooping salt air in from the windows, blindly taking hold of the handle ahead of me. The door opens with ease, as if nothing or no one were waiting to explode from it. The peculiar scene ahead startles my eyes wide open. Silk threads make a webbed bed and cocoon around dainty ankles, knees, hips, and shoulders. A girl rests. Her pallor is enough for me to think her dead. Her mouth is barred open with crisscrossing silk strings.

Alani winces for a closer look. "What the? Is it breathing?" She takes a step. "It's sweating…"

A gust of breath sounds from the deep of the cadaver's stomach. *Auhhh…*it starts and breaks into groaning spurts I've only ever heard in horror movies. Vomit filled with worms, newts, and centipedes crawl from the cave of her mouth and up her face. A stiff arm breaks from the web and reaches out for Alani. She tries to jump back but she's caught in the pinch of the girl's forearm and elbow. I scream and reach for my sheath. This isn't my terror. It doesn't make sense. And if it's Alani's, how am I seeing this?

Alani grunts and pats around for the button in the harness. "What the hell is she?" I hear her yell.

"The skeleton in your own fucking closet," the girl spits, rough handling Alani loose and kicking her square in her back.

"What?" I recognize the figure, a doppelganger duplicate of Alani with dark hair. I go to help the actual Alani find her balance. A rustle in the chimney tells me things won't be so easy. It's wind, I think, but wind doesn't have color. It wouldn't be this tangled mass of strings crawling through the fireplace. Vines and roots swirl around one another, building little by little into a shape I can't make out yet. In mid-stare, Alani yanks down at my shoulder and swings a right hook into the doppelganger's face. Her palms glow with flames.

"Alani, don't! Wait!" I order from the floor. "She's not a terror! I can see her too." Alani couldn't care less as she pummels into different parts of the girl. They grapple and sneer insults between their teeth. When I check behind me, the growing roots have intertwined in the shape of a man.

"God, no…"

Hundreds of roots extend and crawl over each other, sculpting their pointed ends into an open hand. The leaf of a vine folds. Its leathered texture evolves into mahogany lips. "I told you this would happen," he says.

"You're not Dad." I shake my head. "It's never you."

"Not your dad," he scoffs. "You made that clear weeks ago. Didn't you?" His eyes are holders of the poison he wishes I'd drink. He raises the sleeve of his blue button-up, revealing burned skin that patterns like the bottom of a drought-starved lake. Those arms used to give protection and the fullest hugs.

"You want to shoot through me again, huh?" Dad sneers.

My jaw trembles. Hot water pools in my eyes. "Dad, no. I just want to be with you."

"Till you can pay me with what you think I deserve."

Warm. Hot. Hotter. A temperature I've grown fearful of circulates inside of me. I run off to the next room, but when I turn around, Dad is right behind me.

"There you go…running off. Running off! Face me! FACE WHAT YOU DID!" Dad's mouth hangs with abnormal wideness. Veins protrude and match the onyx his irises adopt. Smoke curls from him. Layers of skin grow weak and wither from his face like the bark of a decayed tree. I turn away.

"LOOK AT ME!"

I close my eyes to wipe my mind and find those feel-good thoughts. His roaring blows my hair back. "LOOK! YOU CAN'T BECAUSE YOU'RE A COWARD! YOU WILL NEVER MAKE THINGS RIGHT! WITH ME OR SARAI!"

My hands clench into fists and I open my eyes. "Shut up!"

"SHE'S GOOD AS DEAD BECAUSE YOU PLAY THE FENCE! ALL YOU DO IS CRY AND WAIT!"

"Lex, focus," I hear. That rasp I love, warm honey to a raw wound. "You can find that steer token. You've got the control."

"That's what she calls it?" Dad's snicker looks more sinister than ever. A tarry grout appears between his teeth. "Control? You control yourself to create pain. That's what you're good at. That's the only thing!"

Dad's hugs. Remember Dad's hugs, Alexia! I think. As I fight the flood of heat, visions of our last hug invade me. It's not working, not even a little.

I scream, and my outsides flash out of me again…*not again.* Alani jumps to soothe me. A bright ray races toward her, soaring into a flaring star. *Hold tight.* I squeeze my muscles. Close my eyes.

"I'll never be gone, babe." There's Dad…my real dad, in my mind, on the patio at Ren's beach house, live and gracious. He smells like the city, old leather, and cologne. The bittersweet smile I remember is there. *"No, listen. I love you. I'm your dad for all time. I need you to understand, Alexia. You need to hear it. Even when I'm gone, I'm still your dad. I just can't be here. But I'll spread my love on the wind,"* Dad's voice echoes. *"Don't forget that part of our poem."*

In the turn of a second, both my mind and heart push everything I have to maneuver that flare. It misses Alani by centimeters, turning left on its brakes, then crash-landing right into the chest of my SIM father. Energy zaps and whips the terror into a charred form, then finally a mound of ash.

I fall back against a wall and cry. Alani is panting. She doesn't hesitate to hold me. "Listen to me, okay? I have your back, all the way."

"I almost hurt you."

"Yeah." She grabs my face. "But you didn't…because you have my back too. You're a good person, and a damn legend. I don't see a lot of runaways tapping into their tokens this early. You found the steer token, yeah?"

"Finally…yes." I smile and the cold absence of what just happened gnaws at me. "Those weren't terrors, were they?"

"I don't really know."

"You could see mine?"

"Yeah."

As soon as shame fills inside me, Alani cuts the faucet. "You don't have to explain what I saw. Your story belongs to you. It doesn't change things."

I nod in thanks. "You fought yourself…and you were scared. I didn't think you could fear anything."

Alani leans back. A sigh edges from her lips. "I'm a twin…I used to be."

Hairs on the back of my neck stand. "What?"

"It's crazy, I know. But not what you think. The other baby didn't make it through birth and that's where the story ends. Except…sometimes I get the feeling a piece of me is somewhere else. In some spiritual way, it's true but I don't know how to deal with that. Gives me the creeps, you know?"

It creeps me out too, so I nod, hoping we'll both never see Alani, the unborn, again. "Do you think you conquered that fear?"

"I'd say so." She gives me a sealed smile and sprawls her legs out. The ocean's breeze curls around us, and I think of my dad. Only the good things this time.

A tumbleweed of black hair rolls across the grey wood floor.

I laugh a little. Alani glances at me, chuckles, then rests her head on the wall. "Almost made that bitch bald."

CHAPTER FORTY

Iron Sharpens Iron

A BEEPING NOISE FROM my watch hijacks my attention. The pen I'm scribbling notes with writes jagged as I study my wrist. "What the heck?" REMINDER: YOUR LAB RESULTS ARE AVAILABLE flashes on its round screen. I suck my teeth and swipe the message away.

"Do you have to go?" Kyle checks.

"I don't…I *should*…later."

Not sold, he sets the cartography book we took from Andre's cellar down to show he's serious. "I can stay and work on things if you have somewhere to be."

I drop my pen and look him square in the eye. "Kyle, it's fine. Lucie synced my school calendar and message box to my watch when she jailbroke it. I can read my labs another time. It's not important now."

"It is important, though."

"Yes." I pick up my pen, ready to move on from this conversation. Kyle for some reason is still shuffling around for ways to keep it breathing.

"It doesn't take long."

I sigh. "Fine. I'll skim through them now, okay? Happy?"

"Yeah, actually." He grins.

With my watch, I log on to my school mailbox and click the link to my results. When it asks for my fingerprint, I timidly place it on the watch's glass screen and unlock my information.

"It's okay," Kyle reassures me. "If there was anything serious, Dr. Langley and Sage Cameron would've called you."

That's true, I guess. Silence is a good thing. I finally turn back to read the results. "Gifted ability: stellarkinesis… I don't really understand most of this stuff about my blood and cell structure."

"Just skip over that stuff," Kyle says. "What does it say about your tier?"

I scroll down to search for any mention of it. "Tier…4."

"Tier *4*? You're kidding."

"No. Look…"

Kyle zones into the screen and reads it for himself. "*Shit.* When did you manifest again?"

"A few months ago. Why? What's wrong?"

"Oh, nothing's wrong. Your capability for a new manifester is pretty much unheard of. Everyone starts at tier 1 when they first manifest, an heirloom family kid like Nate and Lucie *might* manifest at tier 2. For us, that happens in middle school and our families throw these big grandiose parties to celebrate—"

"Like a bar mitzvah?"

Kyle shuts his mouth and his eyes trace up to the sky. "Basically."

"Wow."

"Anyway." He shrugs. "Our gifts have aged through maturity as we've grown and worked with them. That's how it works. It's like an extension of our physical bodies. When our gifts are newborn, they're clumsy of course, but they don't pack much punch. It takes time for them to age. But you, you're already there. You're ahead of people who've had their gifts since they were twelve. I *just* tested as tier 4 this summer—and that's with using my tokens. You just started using yours."

"What?"

"It makes sense. I saw your outburst that day in the Belle Rues and I thought you were going to light up the entire town."

I shake my head. The more I think of it, the more it freaks me out. All this power so soon. What does it mean? What will things feel like as my powers mature? More feral than they already feel? Will I feel out of control forever? "This stuff doesn't matter to me. Let's get back to work."

Kyle's stare lingers on me as I lock my watch screen. I know he can read my deflection. He's nice enough to honor it and go along with the plan.

Being tucked away in the hedges of the Knaves Labyrinth is almost as good as being in Adieu Lagoon. It brings a level of escapism I want to get back to and his company makes it even sweeter.

"Here, check this out." Kyle hands the book to me. "There are two places: either the mausoleum or the canals. Both were the last to switch out their cast iron pipes according to the book."

Giving the map a once-over, I already know that's not it. "I feel like that's too easy."

"Easy? It wasn't easy to find this kind of information."

"For us…"

Kyle's brows perk to agree.

"Think like a Revenir. Would you leave a clue to give a half-ass answer? We checked all the modern cartography collections and none of them feature any building with cast iron pipes."

"Well, maybe that's what it is. Maybe the answer is the last building to convert."

"But that's a soft answer. Wouldn't it make more sense for this pipe cutter to derive from a place that still has cast iron inside of it? A place that can't run Zenith water because it'd shred through the pipes over time."

The pen Kyle holds rests on the edge of his lip. "So, you think—"

"There's a building we're missing. Something that's probably not even named in these books or lists. And look…" I reach inside my book bag for the pipe cutter Kyle nabbed from the bookstore the DeuxCadets found the clues in. A quick teleporting trip during lunch did the trick. Benefits of having a teleporter on your side. "It has The Grove's symbol on it."

Those dreamy pools of hazel lock onto the plank of the handle. "The lion…the reestablished one that represents all Variens: originals and refugees…"

"From 1908."

I get a kick out of his bugging eyes and watch him skim through the most recent cartography log. "The canals were the last to convert in 1922."

"So, there's something out there. I'm thinking the best way to find it now is to cross-reference what we have. Pin every commercial location or reserve in The Grove that's upgraded and see what's left."

"You're good," he says, cradling his chin. "Let's do it!"

I still have to pinch myself because how do I have this person down for my insane journey? "Already started." I hand him a stack of pages. "Got all the way down to places that start with *L*. Almost there."

Kyle turns, surprised, and scoots closer to me. Giant roses stretch their shadows to shade us from the glaring sun. They favor us for bringing music today, specifically Kyle's playlist of Varien alt R&B that mixes English with Viridian. I grab Kyle's small speaker and turn it off. The roses huff along with Kyle. "Hey! Leave it on," Kyle demands.

"Stop whining, I want to show you something." I log back in to an illegal app Lucie uploaded that plays music from my realm. It's been a long time since I've heard the sounds of home: Sade serenading us all through cleaning. I've missed it so much. And SZA, who sang my emotions to the surface so I wouldn't explode. She saved me so many times, my brain craves her voice. It's a weird dependency and my withdrawals have peaked. I play SZA's "Ghost in the Machine," entrancing the roses to sway.

"This is my favorite singer from home."

Nodding in rhythm with the melancholy beats, Kyle brightens. "I like her. This is good."

"Yeah?"

"Yeah."

The roses carry on and move as if they could uproot themselves and do a contemporary dance. Amused, Kyle and I laugh.

"Too good. Well, here, let me take the other half and contribute…or something," Kyle says.

"You know you're appreciated. Stop."

"I kinda feel…not as exemplary with this sleuthing lately. Off my game."

"You're a drama king."

"For real."

"Oh, really?"

"Yeah."

"So, what is it? Why is your focus off?"

"Ahhh, you wouldn't understand. This girl keeps following me around and making me kiss her."

I roll my eyes and nudge into his amusement.

"Are you serious?" a voice that could only belong to Alani squeaks. "We've been looking for you both all lunch hour. What're you doing?"

Kyle pushes his hair back. "Last time I checked you didn't own me."

"Well, it's hard to prove after throwing away the receipt." Alani stands in the center of the labyrinth. Her arms are folded, her hair is in the most underwhelming bun and she's wearing pearls with a pastel argyle sweater. The kitten heels on her feet are the insult to injury. Nate is behind her, equally as *Riverdale* clean as her.

Kyle gives her a once-over. "What are you wearing? You look like Dama Hadley."

"Because this is how Dama Hadley wanted us to dress for Blossom Royal training today. It's required for Blossom Ball candidates," Alani says.

Kyle lies out on the grass, resting his head in his hand. Quick and hardy giggles turn his mood. "Best laugh ever." He exhales. "I still don't get why you're going so hard for this."

Shaking her hair from a bun, Alani replies, "The top three law schools are more likely to accept Blossom Royals. It's called getting ahead."

"Whatever," Kyle snaps

"How'd you find us?" I ask.

As soon as I verbalize it, I regret it. Nate is cheesing like a brother watching his sister on the receiving end of a lecture. "The roses," Alani answers. But the roses, still humming to SZA, turn their budded heads away when we face them.

"Can't say we're surprised after hearing you ditched class together." Nate grins like a fool.

Alani tacks on another question. "Where did you two go?"

"It's none of your business because you don't own me!" Kyle shouts.

"Okay, you're right, I guess Alexia does now," Alani says.

"You sound like a stalker." Kyle points. "How about you worry about the king of dorks over there behind you instead of me?"

"Ay!" Nate booms, holding up a large gold coin in his hand. "I had an heirloom meeting."

"Right, I forgot The Grove governing board promoted you from bootlicker to water boy. Sorry," Kyle quips.

These three could go on all day if I let them, so I don't. "You guys need to chill. Kyle and I were just catching up on the extra literature classwork we were assigned because of ditching. We have detention later, but we thought we'd get a head start on the work now." When I lock my watch screen, the roses start to wilt and beg me to keep the song playing. "Sorry, y'all," I tell them.

Alani's glare is skeptical, but the bell robs her of the opportunity to say anything else.

I gather my things. "I've gotta get to Engineering, my grade is already crap. I can't be late. See you in detention." I nod to Kyle. "Bye, guys."

Alani and Nate mumble their "see yous" and "byes" to me and linger behind. I'm not sure if the adrenaline I feel comes from them possibly knowing the truth about us or being so close to finding the location of Passage.

What I know is, both will happen soon.

CHAPTER FORTY-ONE

FIGHTING TIME

"**A**IR CONDITIONING IS A luxury, and since this is detention, there will be no luxury up in here." Dama Batiste would rather see herself choke on the odd fall humidity before getting us napkins from outside the classroom. All eyes on me. All eyes on Kyle. That's how she's kept it since detention started. That's how she's going to keep it. Her made-up face has all but melted to the floor. Sweat has turned her silkened edges coarse and coated her face like a butterscotch drizzled chocolate sundae. I know she's hot. She'll never show it, though. She's too stubborn, too dead set on making us sorry for cutting class. Her only saving grace being her church fan with an airbrushed Black Jesus on it.

Kyle's lips rumble with the low sounds of lines from his history book.

"Mute it, please." Dama Batiste twists her head. "Use that inner voice."

I slide Kyle a jailed grin. It never latches to him, his attitude acts as a gate.

Kyle flops over his desk. "Can we have water or something? Some towels, at least? No way are we lasting like this for another hour." Asking and telling at the same time.

"We can open the window," Dama Batiste says proudly.

As his nails dig into the desk, I know his insides are itching to make him vanish. "So, what happens if Alexia faints from these conditions?"

"Don't start." Dama Batiste bats her eyes.

"I'm serious. She's stellarkinetic—she runs hot. She's also vulnerable to outbursts as a newly manifested Varien. Having her in such conditions in a place she's told she's safe doesn't sound humane to me. I don't think Sage Cameron would disagree either."

We're going to have detention for a month now.

Dama Batiste waves her fan faster. "Always motorin'. Always. Water I can do. I was just becoming parched myself."

Kyle stares up at a standing Dama Batiste, a prep school puppy dog. "Chilled would be nice."

"I'm sure it would."

"And some towels…"

Dama Batiste darts a stare back mid-walk.

Kyle shrugs. "Asking too much?"

Two things at the same time—holy and angry, polite and rude—Dama Batiste continues her quest to appease a child she'd rather strike with a switch. She limps her big behind out of the door and raises one last stern brow through the window.

Kyle presses his praying hands together. "Good looking out," he speaks to the air above.

"You're good," I can't help but gush.

But instead of gushing back, Kyle grows serious. "Lucie's coming here, right?"

"She said she would."

Kyle bounces his nervous knees. "All right, let's hope she does," he says, then goes mute the moment heavy feet are heard outside the room. Nate, the teenage behemoth, peers inside. He eyes the empty teacher's chair then mimes a make out session with the window.

"Is that supposed to be me and you?"

"Kinda hard to tell. Neither one of us is flat and clear without a soul, arms, and legs…a mouth to kiss back with."

Nate is all teeth when Kyle shoos him away. The big dolt simmers down, hesitates on wiping his saliva from the glass before moving on.

"Isn't he the best?" Kyle laughs.

When the door cracks, we expect to see Nate or Dama Batiste enter the classroom, but grow surprised when we catch our short friend and kid genius.

"Why is Dama Batiste in the kitchen?" Lucie walks in.

"Thirsty, I guess," I reply. Surely my heart hates me for the roller coaster it's going through.

"Weird," Lucie chirps. "But perfect! I couldn't wait to give this to you!" She slides my laptop onto my desk. "Everything is back on it. Everything you asked for." She winks a most obvious wink. "I even got the device to restore all sessions. Rare, but how cool?"

"You restored everything?" *What I really mean is "You saw everything?"*

"Affirmative. All you have to do is open the screen, sign in, and pick up where you left off…for Engineering." She dodges looks between me and Kyle. So nervous and obvious with our "secret."

Kyle twiddles his thumbs and speaks in the most sarcastic tone. "*Oh*, you two have Engineering together. I forgot."

"Yup. I just downloaded a sophisticated program on there for her blueprint layouts. It's expensive, but I jailbroke it for free." Lucie wipes sweat from her brow. "Don't tell anyone."

"On you, Luce? Never."

"Thanks, Kyle." Lucie does some sort of awkward bow and backs out of the room. "Alexia…if you find that thing, maybe keep me posted. I could help you with supplies. Anything you can think of, I have it."

"Wow, yeah…I totally will."

She waves and finally leaves.

"If you find that *thing*?" Kyle leans on his desk, arms folded.

"A crossbred manticore…it was the only way."

"Of course it was." He smiles. "We don't have a lot of time, okay? Well, we have some cushion. I asked for chilled waters, which means Dama Batiste will get them from the kitchen. Chef Epps is cooking today so I think they'll go on a few tangents from the Bible study they had yesterday evening. And she'll have to pass Dama Hadley for the towels, she hates my guts too. A few minutes of Kyle bashing is pretty much guaranteed."

"You've planned this out?"

"During geometry. Only took a couple minutes. Now, check this out…" From his pocket he unfolds a cluster of yellow tablet paper. "I went through every listing of the past and cross-referenced with the map like you said. I got down to it and you're right, there's one place that isn't named with updated plumbing: Pynman's Den."

Suddenly, thirst and heat exhaustion are nonexistent. "What? You found it?"

"I think so!" He points around the map. Pynman's Den, a stone covered building, is circled in blue marker.

"Pynman's," I breathe, heart beating so fast I can't think.

"Pynman's," Kyle repeats. "It's some sort of abandoned water treatment facility. Blaise Hensley owns it now, but the building isn't in operation, so it doesn't run Zenith water. No repairs are on record. And the craziest thing is there's a cavern sitting underneath this thing."

Fireworks crackle in my brain. Butterflies flitter in my stomach for other reasons I shouldn't be thinking about right now. Because that's not what this moment is about. This is about being one step closer to getting Sarai. Never mind the fact that I could kiss Kyle so hard for helping me get there.

Kyle mirrors what I'm thinking and scoots closer. I dive right into my laptop for access to the DeuxCadets and their confirmation. Everything is as Lucie said it would be. Except when I hit play on the DeuxCadets paused live recording, a message informs me the link is no longer active.

"All good," Kyle eases my panic. "Maybe there's others. There has to be. It's been a while."

"Okay." Through shaking hands, I type and scroll through their channel. There are other videos…too many.

Kyle warns me. "Chill. Chill. Chill. Slow down, I can't see."

"We don't have time," I reply.

"We'll get it. If not now, then later today…we'll get it regardless."

"I need to know now."

"Wait, what was that?" His finger slides up the screen. "'Passage Survival Kit.' Click that."

I fumble between checking the door and choosing a video, so much so, I click the wrong one. "Damn."

Kyle sweeps up the mistake and presses the correct thumbnail. The video loads fast.

"This video is five minutes long. Ugh," I huff.

"Just hold on."

In the same mortared dark room, the cadets introduce themselves and excuse their drained appearance. "Been an even rougher week," Jaime explains. "I'm sure for all of us. We hope marauding has been easier for you than it has been for us."

Croix sighs. "The worst is over though, yeah?"

"I don't wanna jinx it." Jaime crosses his fingers.

"No, we're good now…we've got everything we need to get into Pynman's," Croix says.

"Yes!" The DeuxCadets cheer, joining hands and rejoicing in some kind of shake.

Wow. Pynman's. PYNMAN'S. PYNMAN'S DEN is confirmed! Kyle and I figured it out!

In the corner of my eye, the cadets are holding something gilded in the camera shot. "Now, if you don't have access to an original heirloom entry to Pynman's like most recruit hopefuls, this is the price of admission," Croix explains. "It has the Revenir crest on it…hopefully that's coming through clear. It's a bit old-fashioned, but the tomb we took it from happened to belong to a Revenir from the 1920s. We suspect many of yours will look like this."

"What's he saying?" Kyle asks. He takes the map from me.

"That's what we need to get through the door. A ring from the finger of a dead Revenir. How the heck are we supposed to find one and raid a grave in five days?" I practically rub my face off in frustration. I've come this far, and this is it. *This* is the barrier I won't be able to break.

"Can you believe this?" I poke at Kyle. "We're screwed." His shoulder blades are hunched, sharp enough to make me think he could sprout wings just like Set. "Did you hear what they said?" I try again.

When he finally turns, there's no lack of hope in his face, just focus. "I heard them but they're wrong."

"What do you mean? These guys know everything."

"No one knows everything," he corrects with his pen dangling from his mouth. "You see this map? Harrison Navarette made this for his family. None of this was published by anyone, it was in Andre's cellar for private record, just for the family."

Kyle pauses to hold the map up. "Andre is a Navarette. So, it's no surprise this map shows some kind of tunnel going from his cottage to Pynman's."

"What?"

"Look: I thought it was a road, but the lines are dotted. All the other roads on this map are solid lines. It goes straight to Pynman's."

And off I go, staring into space. "The cellar…it had that trap door behind the shelves."

"Exactly." Kyle nods. "That's it!"

Before I can ascend into joy, God clips my own wings. "But why would…Kyle, I'm afraid of what that could really mean."

Heels are approaching the door. Dama Batiste is back. I know the sound of that gait anywhere.

"It means that's our only way," Kyle whispers.

I shudder at the thought. The feeling I had deep in the core of my bones that evening at the cottage sends aftershocks. Something wasn't right then. The house wasn't welcoming, and Andre was eerily helpful. And last but not least, the hidden passage. The DeuxCadets just said entries to Pynman's are heirloom passageways. I hide my laptop in my book bag, turning back to aim a reply. "Not if Andre is a Revenir himself."

CHAPTER FORTY-TWO

Dark to Light

IN BOTANY AND HERBALISM, every growing second with Sage Cameron pushes me into paranoia. How easy is it for her to pull Passage plans from my mental chest? Would I know? Does she always keep her word? How easy would it be to access my mind? And what do the layers of thoughts sound like to her? Do they crowd against each other like the people in Times Square? Would that make it difficult to hear the gist of one? What does she know? Would she tell me?

Her brown fingers grasp at grouped bushels of herbs we've harvested and laid on the table. Sage Cameron refers to them as life-forces because they keep Variens vibrant, second to the moon. She's so peaceful when she speaks. Hard to paint her as calculating or invasive. But nevertheless, I keep dodging any thoughts about Passage or Kyle. They slip in, until I chase them out by singing my way through the whole damn *Hamilton* soundtrack.

"These we'll use for the sports department. Turmeric is in high demand with them. Propolis and echinacea for cold season…" She shrugs with her hands on her hips. Her gaze tight with examination. "Let's add St. John's wort too. Midterms are around the corner. You'll beg me for it. Alani is a lot of *fun* then."

"You forgot about Blossom Ball. What about adding holy basil too?"

"I like your style." Sage Cameron winks. "That'll be all for this week's tinctures. Let's prep. Set out the alcohol and glass jars. I'd like to stay away from vinegar this time since there's no culinary use. We'll have a longer shelf life this way."

"Okay," I say, taking note of the five plants we're working with, and one we've missed. A red tipped plant bundled in a bin of its own. "Wait, Sage Cameron, what about that one…rhute leaf?"

"Oh no, I think it'd be safer if I processed that tincture myself. Rhute leaf is a miracle worker, but the seeds are dangerous. Just leave it there. I have a jar of cloved and fermented virgin forest apples to keep myself in the safe zone just in case."

I do as she says and gather the others on a propped table that holds my open textbook. Dama Fabienne's sweet memory tincture takes up one whole page. I haven't stopped thinking about this particular tincture since I got the book. A tincture to give others the power of memory stripping, the very power Dama Fabienne possessed herself, is the only one of its kind.

"Do you ever use Dama Fabienne's memory tincture?" I inquire. "There's nothing else like it in this book."

Sage Cameron soaks in my question and seems proud of my curiosity. "You're right, there isn't. It's not a common thing to offer a gifted ability in a bottle, so to speak. But Dama Fabienne was a heart worker. As you know, she helped so many people find new homes here, but that was not where the struggle ended. For some, moving on was just enough to heal. For others, the threat of those traumatic wounds from their past was all-consuming. They'd come to Dama Fabienne and ask her to rid them of those memories. She'd oblige and it granted them the reset they not only desired but needed. Nothing but positive outcomes came from it, so Dama Fabienne created a tincture formula to have the same effect for Variens in The Grove living beyond her time. She was truly lovely. Saintlike."

I skim over the list. The wheels in my brain turn faster as I eye each ingredient: crimsonweed, goldhusk hemlock, retu mushroom, saffron. I could use this, not for myself, but for protection. "Yeah. She really was."

When I look up, Sage Cameron's photo wall catches my eyes. For a moment, the strong blend of botanical smells dulls when I roam over each picture. Specifically, the ones starring a teenage Sage Cameron. She seemed bold and heart strong. A '90s version of Angela Davis wielding fists of power and peace, making front-page news as a table shaker. She's the reason Malveaux's dress code isn't biased against girls anymore, the fire under the banning of toxic foods in schools. She's the maverick who became the first headmistress of a historic Varien prep academy. I can't help but wonder if all that fire is still there now that she's gone through the glass ceiling. "Sage Cameron?"

"Yes?"

"Were you ever afraid?"

"Afraid? Afraid of what?"

"To do these things…to stand up." I point to the news clippings.

In the mid-tying of her apron, she spends little time thinking. "Hmm…yes and no. Everything I stuck my neck out for felt intimidating, like a David and Goliath battle. The trick is when you feel fear…keep going anyway. Being afraid is very different from being a coward. I was always afraid, but living in complacency scared me more." She helps me with the jars. They clang like brash chimes. "Knowing who I am is part of that. Feeling it so deep inside. I don't need a mirror to show me. I don't need another person to explain it. I've done the work to recognize Maureen and know her limits and talents…her calling. That's one reason why we have labs done here. It's sustenance, really."

All I can do is snip at echinacea leaves. Queue another *Hamilton* song.

"Do you have any questions about your lab results?"

"…No."

"No? They're quite impressive. Measuring in at tier 4 when you've newly manifested…it's remarkable."

"I heard that," I deflect. "But I keep forgetting what a big deal it is."

The shearing of branches and stems slices the air. "A certain Phoenix will do that to you—get you to ditch class and forget about yourself."

"That's not what it is—"

"I know he's charming."

"Oh my gah, no!"

"But you have to focus on you."

I set the scissors down and flail my hands to explain myself. "It's not him. It's not anything or anyone else. It's me. I'm in my own way because I don't want any of this to define me or make this a real thing…for it to be all I am and make me an anomaly among people I'm supposed to fit in with." There's a fire burning behind my eyes. "Even in SIM Class…I'm different. Something always goes wrong and I outburst in front of everyone. And these surges I have, they're enough to burn the school down or hurt someone."

"You are growing and learning, Alexia. It's not like you're not improving."

"No one else's powers look like mine. Mine are wild and extra. I don't want to be that way. I don't want to start off at a tier 4." I shake my head.

Sage Cameron places her gloved hands in mine. "Why would you want to be anything else when you've been gifted by God?"

Embarrassment colors me stupid. I shouldn't be this way.

"There's nothing wrong with you. You belong here, and you need to say that to yourself. Make time to be anxious and accept yourself in that moment, then say who you are. The lab is just a piece of it. You decide who you are and what you want to stand for." She gives my hands a squeeze and I smile. Still cracked in big places, I get back to holding myself together with mental scotch tape.

We cut all the herbs, stuff them in jars, fill them with alcohol, top them with parchment, and label them. We talk of Sage Cameron's days as a kid and what Malveaux was like in the '90s. "Very different from now," she shares. "Less free. Which is why I made my own freedom." And when our cleanup is done and the bells ring for me to grab dinner, she calls my name before I leave.

"Yeah?"

"I forgot to mention something. Me being brave wasn't just because of myself. I didn't do anything alone. That's been the pillar in my life. It's the greatest one you can have." Tingling pricks my skin. The place where my locket and chest meet warms.

"I agree." I grin back, and when I open the door, Kyle is leaning against the frame—dirty basketball uniform, a wrinkled book in his hand, and a million smiles to stitch me solid.

"Ah, there it is. *En chamer cel shene*." He throws back a wave of dark hair from his eyes.

"English, please."

"You smell like a hippie?"

"Much better."

"I love her smile too," Sage Cameron sneaks a Viridian translation of what Kyle really said.

Kyle waves faintly to Sage Cameron and spends the next few minutes fantasizing about the ways to eat the potpies being served for dinner. "Crust mashed in, or crust eaten as I go. It's all so serious, you know? We never got to celebrate our last day of detention. So today is the day."

"We don't have time right now," I remind him.

"Dinner won't be served for another couple hours and there's *always* time to eat."

"No...you know what I mean. We can't play all evening. We have to go over our plan, finish the cloaks and stash them."

Smug and up to no good as ever, Kyle smirks. "Done and done."

"Done?" I frown.

"I finished sewing the cloaks last night when Nate and the boys went out to the Belle Rues."

"But I thought you went with them?"

"Nah. I just said that in front of Alani. Got in the trolley with them, said I felt sick, teleported out."

"And you stashed the cloaks? When?"

"Yeah, right before I came to get you."

"Oh." My heart thuds and my stomach churns. "You hid the cloaks in the Great Room a few minutes ago?"

"Yeah?"

"You didn't teleport inside the room?"

"No. What's wrong with that?"

"Everything." I place a hand to my head. "Alani has Blossom Royal training before dinner…in the ballroom. It faces the Great Room! It has windows!"

He swallows his spit like he just ingested a gumball. "She didn't see me, though."

"Are you sure?"

The beeping of his watch answers everything. Kyle holds his wrist up. "It's Alani."

MEET ME IN THE GREAT ROOM NOW, the screen reads.

CHAPTER FORTY-THREE

Truth and Shadows

WALKING INTO THE GREAT Room is a walk across a plank. Try as we might to avoid it, the fall still comes. Nate is here, sans the basketball uniform Kyle dons. His mood is heavy. He's in a suit—probably had another one of his heirloom meetings. Money is what he looks like, a trust fund brat. The navy threads of his suit mesh with the paisley cerulean wallpaper, and taupe drapings. The gold soleil chandelier above flickers like a hundred embers. And beneath it, near the mouth of the giant fireplace, is Alani. Hair so red I can't find the seam of flame and silhouette.

Kyle is tense. "I'm here."

Alani's jaw juts. Her dark eyes claw onto him. I don't even exist. "Like you were earlier."

"You're spying on me now?"

"Can't call it that when you don't mind being seen." Alani lifts the corner of the Persian rug in front her, scanning the wood planks till she spots the place—our place—beneath two knotted planks. All it takes is a push and one side dips down. Alani repeats this action on five more planks, and before our eyes, she removes the wood pieces till a square hole shows in the floor. "Dama Hadley saw you go in during Blossom Royal training. She wanted to come after you and report you to Sage Cameron. I told her I'd take care of it and get you out of there." Alani crisscrosses her legs. "You were so focused on getting these planks reconnected, you didn't even hear me come in. You didn't catch me hiding behind the curtains. There are notes in here…your handwriting's all over them, Lex." A twitch in her brow works like a spotlight, one that burns.

Kyle steps in front of me. "Don't blame this on her."

"I wasn't, but now I'm wondering if I should."

"You should mind your business," Kyle snaps.

"*You* are my business!"

"Please. All you care about are quickies with Nate after bed checks."

Nate, who's lying quiet on the love seat, cautions the cousins by clearing his throat.

"Kyle," I call.

"I care. I've cared since Uncle Calum and Tia Lecia died!" Alani's voice raises.

Suddenly, Kyle unhinges. "Then stop caring! If this is what caring is, stop! You're driving me crazy!"

"No! No! Both of you…don't do this. Don't fight." I wave between them. "It's me. All of this, everything Kyle has been doing is to help me." In a matter of seconds, I've successfully managed to sic Alani on myself.

Kyle is doing all he can to keep me out of her crosshairs. "Lex…you don't have to," he breathes into my ear.

"Oh yes, let's act like I haven't been lied to for weeks on end," Alani snaps.

"See? This is exactly why I can't talk to you…you don't know how speak to anyone!" Kyle yells. "Especially when it comes to me! I love you, Alani, but you love me *too* much sometimes."

The bottom lids of Alani's eyes start to puff. "*Too much?*"

"Kyle, don't push," I say.

Streaming tears gloss Alani's rouging cheeks. She's vulnerable, in a way I never knew she could be. "That's a nice way of thanking me for protecting you. I know what this is! The hooded cloaks.

This black fabric, coal mud, and shell paste! Do you think I'm stupid? Dad told you to leave this Revenir stuff alone!"

What? Kyle catches my confusion, and in this moment, his silence is confirmation. A cold shame freezes his eyes. He's always believed in Revenirs…and he never told me.

"This is for me!" I go on anyway. "I have to get my best friend back." I explain everything to her—from A to Nadir. I could turn to ice right now. The longer I speak, the more I feel my muscles seize. When I'm done, I brace for her brunt.

"You two are nuts." Nate's voice breaks. He's still a perfect picture with the window behind him overlooking Lake Moody. "You really think you're going to walk into some secret society and save the day?"

Two bony fingers to his lips, Kyle elaborates, "We're a bit iffy on the walking in and those logistics…but, yeah."

"Funny." Nate fakes a laugh. "Because let's say they don't exist like everyone else knows…you're giving yourselves up as the sacrificial lambs to demented people who choose to believe they do. That's just as dangerous."

There's a trace of condescension that makes Alani uncomfortable. "Nate," she breathes.

"Let him say it, Alani." Kyle's eyes turn to stone. "Let him say what his rich-ass parents think about us and our family, what we've been through, what we believe…"

"Calm down. That's not what he's saying," Alani pleads.

Nate shakes his head. "You're not hearing me, Kyle."

"I've got you loud and clear."

"Kyle! Stop!" Alani shouts.

Kyle's jaw clenches. "Tell me Revenirs didn't kill my family! Just say we're crazy and leave!"

Nate rises when Kyle steps to him. The two can't even meet nose-to-nose with Nate's height, but Kyle's anger tells me this wouldn't be an easy fight. "Don't go there, Phoenix," Nate warns. "Don't make this something it isn't. You know what I mean. I'm not knockin' what your family believes. I'm not saying I haven't believed it either, but there's no proof."

None of that makes a difference to Kyle. He's still immovable. Seconds away from letting his anger get the best of him. I take Kyle's fist and hold it like we're back in Adieu Lagoon. His pulse beats in my palm—fast—and with no powers, no magic, no words, just my skin on his, Kyle's fist blooms into a hand that holds mine back. Breaths of frustration start to settle, and he finds my eyes. I feel like I've never understood him more.

"We're going to Passage," I tell them. "Our minds are made up. We're prepared and will plan everything as tight as we can. I'm sorry we hurt you, Alani."

Alani's hands cover her eyes. Mascara smears onto her palms as she brings them down.

"We couldn't tell anyone because I can't have anyone in my way," I continue. "This is something I *have* to do, something that *will* happen. I had no idea it would start a fight between you two."

"It was bound to happen." The grip of Kyle's hand tightens. "My parents are dead, Alani. I've accepted it. But I'm not dead. You may think controlling every aspect of my life will save me, but you can't protect me from the world…not like you used to." When Alani's sobs rain, Kyle reaches for her. "Alani."

"I am terrified of life stealing anything else from you." Her voice hoarsens. "Probably more than you are. When Uncle Calum and Tia Lecia passed away, it was like we were all robbed. But the pain you went through…it can't happen again. I have to protect you. If I don't, I lose you. Don't you get it?"

"If I didn't get it, I would've stopped you a long time ago." Kyle unwraps himself from me. He and his cousin embrace, clinging on to each other for dear life.

Alani peeks through the strands of her hair. "Lex, I owe you an apology."

"No. You did nothing wrong," I say.

Alani gives a somber chuckle. "I'm working on myself every day...a lot more since you came. You're the only best friend I've ever had. I don't want to lose you because of some dumb cardinal rule I made up."

"You won't." She hugs me. The understanding we have is the relief I've wanted for weeks.

Nate hums. "Are you saying that because you and Kyle are getting married, or?"

"Shut up," scoffs Kyle.

As if they weren't at one another's necks minutes ago, Nate fishes through painted candy dishes and chucks something wrapped in gold at Kyle. "Everyone's been talking about it, man."

"Everyone but me," Alani murmurs under her breath. "I don't get how this all went down."

Kyle props his knee on the arm of the couch. "Well, Alani, when a man and woman get together—"

Nate chucks a velvet pillow at his head. "No way, virgin!"

"So, this is a thing? A *real* thing?" Alani asks.

One look at Kyle and I know. "Yeah, I just like having him around...for some reason," I joke.

Kyle laughs then aims praise at the ceiling.

"Well, you know realm jumping has been known to cause long-term delirium," Nate jokes and plants a noogie on the crown of my two cornrows.

"Nate, if you don't get out my hair..."

"Sorry." He releases me. "In all seriousness, I like this...you two together."

"Me too," Alani says. Light in the apples of her cheeks, dusk behind the eyes. "But not at Passage."

"What?" Kyle says.

"The two of you can't go to Passage...not alone."

"Alani...no." Kyle shakes his head.

"Yes," she affirms. The big boss is back. "I'm going with you. If you tell me no, if you leave without me, I'm telling Sage Cameron."

"Oh, c'mon," I groan.

"You're not a snitch," Kyle adds.

"I could be for things that matter. You're going to need help. Whether it be with brains, street smarts, or control. One of you has anger issues and the other is one panic attack away from nuking the world. You need me."

"What the fuck?" I whisper.

Kyle shakes his head. "No way. You stay here. You stay safe. You stay quiet."

"Not a chance."

Scoffs and sighs puff from Kyle and me. He surrenders the decision to me. For a split second, I hate him for it. "Fine, but you have to put the work in," I sigh.

"No one works harder." Alani grins.

"You have to study their customs, history, and rules. You have to drink the chasm," I tell her.

"What's that?" Alani asks.

"Don't worry. I'll teach you everything I know soon," I explain.

Alani won't let up. "Let's crank it out now," she says as she cozies down to the floor and sits.

"B-b-but dinner," Kyle stammers.

I roll my eyes. "Honestly, you ate six tacos at lunch. You're not running on fumes."

"How're you gonna tell me?" Kyle smacks his lips.

I meet Alani on the floor, face-to-face with the shadows and warmth of the fire.

"Teach me," she says.

The floor shakes when Nate dunks down beside us. When we give him a dead stare, he mugs back. "What? Can you three knock ten people out at once?"

Kyle sighs and finds a place in the circle.

"Didn't think so," Nate says.

I wait for Kyle to clap back; you can never be too sure you have the mic in this crew. I shrug when he doesn't and get straight to it. "Nate, since you volunteered yourself. We need you to answer something."

Alani and Nate look on with anticipation. Even Kyle is suspicious of what I'm fixing to ask. "The admission to Passage is a ring from Revenir alumni. Apparently, some have gotten theirs from digging up a dead Revenir's grave. Obviously, that isn't an option for us. We wouldn't know where to start with that."

"Okay?" Nate's brows rise with his voice.

"So, the other option is coming in from the entrance of an heirloom family home. Do you have…is there anything like that at your home?"

"Hell no!" he bursts out. "My family aren't Revenirs. They don't even like hearing …conspiracies about them." I can tell he's choosing his words wisely for Kyle and me. I wonder what he really thinks. Does he believe his parents or us? Or is he in the middle somewhere, just along for the ride?

Kyle encourages me to move on. "Trust me. There wouldn't be anything like that at Grant Manor. Our best bet is to go through Andre's cellar."

"Whose cellar?" Alani butts in.

"This museum guide from the Montparnasse Museum," Kyle explains. "He let us search his archive when I asked him about the plumbing history of The Grove. We found this weird secret passage behind the bookshelves and he's part of an heirloom family. The Navarettes."

Nate's brows knit even more. "The Navarettes. I've never heard of them or met them before. There's no Navarette member at our heirloom meetings."

Kyle and I check with one another. "Weird," I say. "Because their family have deep roots here. They made the first general store…and the secret door does lead straight into Pynman's."

I get chills the more I think of it, but Kyle shakes me out of it by rubbing my back. "We've got a solid plan, and we're going to stick to that plan. Let's move on and tell them about the chasm," he says.

"Right." I take a big breath and say, "The chasm is an elixir pledges must drink during Passage." I flip through my notes and recite them. "According to the DeuxCadets and some other sources on the IVnet, chasm is a liquid that works to separate the soul from the body. It keeps the mind of the person but relies on the psychoactive effects of its ingredients—woodrose, gob tar, rhute leaf, and milldanum, a fungi grown in the Serpentine Peaks—to enhance the rage and abilities of the Revenir during their hits. This is what turns their appearance to the wraiths they become on assignment. It splits them and allows this creature form to take over. The sole purpose of serving pledges this drink is to see how well it sits in them."

"Why the hell are we gonna drink that?" Nate frowns.

"Because the chasm doesn't take effect with one dose. It takes many. The ingredients have to build up. We can spare one night. Also, we don't have a choice, Nate. They'll make us drink," I say.

Alani is already thinking ahead. "Do you know anything about those ingredients? Maybe there's an antidote."

"I did learn something about rhute leaf…Sage Cameron had that in her office during my Botany lesson. She was so careful with it; she wouldn't allow me to handle it." I snap my fingers. "She named something, though…to make it safer in case things went bad. It's escaping me."

"The one thing that shouldn't escape you…," Nate sighs.

"Don't worry. I'll remember it. For now, place your hands in front of you like you're holding a bowl or cupping water."

Before I can correct Nate's ill-placed hands, Kyle has a laugh. "Whoa! No!" He swats at Nate's hands. "Less sexually offensive, Nate…if that's even possible for you."

Nate clicks his tongue, folds his lips, and brings his palms closer to each other.

"Good," I praise him. "We need to be open to receiving the chasm—a drink. This is very important to a Revenir. It's what makes them."

"What else?" Alani rasps over the crackling fire.

Sarai's imprisoned figure is in my heart's target. Everything is for her. "There's the face paint. We have to paint our faces to look like skulls for Passage. All black attire for all, with black veils for you and me, Alani," I respond.

"Okay, no problem," Alani says.

Between the two of us, Kyle and I tell Alani and Nate everything else we've learned about Revenirs on the IVnet, how we figured out where Passage will be taking place, and how we'll be getting in without the price of admission: through the secret path in Andre's cellar.

We don't know much about Passage and what the ceremony will be like, but, with four heads put together, we devise a plan to get us back to Andre's cottage.

For a moment, guilt doesn't live in me, only selfishness. I'm drunk on it after being alone, then carrying secrets around with Kyle. Having a team changes things. Having a team may just make this mission work.

CHAPTER FORTY-FOUR

Creepers

TONIGHT, IS THE NIGHT of Passage. The night I find Sarai by squeezing out of Malveaux. Halls are not dark. They're lit and bright like the floors of a hotel. With security posted at exits and entrances, being caught is easy, walking out is a hard feat. But as Mom would say, ain't a damn thing impossible.

The crew and I have a plan, one we've fussed over from dawn to dead hours. We know the ins and outs of Malveaux Academy and one out happens to be our best bet at a clean vanish. The only trouble is, along the way, there's nowhere to hide. Just bending dormitory halls and shut doors. Alani and I couldn't appear any more out of place: dressed in all black, against the school's gaudiness. My gosh, I've never noticed it more. We have artwork sprinkled in almost every hall. Real pieces by painters I've never heard of. Variens, maybe. They're framed in gold above wooden board and batten. And it's all this that has the two of us looking like we're ready to rob the Louvre. God help us.

Heavy feet take to the floor up the way. Alani and I find a corridor to hide into. Steps are nearing. "Hadley," Alani whispers. As if she could see through walls, sure enough, walking slow in the thickest night gown I've ever seen with rollers wrapped in her greys, is the head of the Fates Hall: the Hadley Monster.

"All right now, whoever is out of bed better get in it. I won't be repeating myself. Not tonight." She's speaking to an empty hall when all she has to do is face her left and find us in the dark. A dramatic and whimsical romantic television instrumental whips her hunched back straight. She smacks her lips. "I'm not playing with these kids. My stories are on." Just like that she retreats to her quarters.

"Damn, she must really like her stories," I snicker.

"Name one old lady who doesn't."

With Hadley back in her lair, our destination is a straight beeline ahead. We're too close to risk anything, so to increase the chances of making it, we take our shoes off. Every stride kicks my heart up. *Almost, almost, almost,* till we've arrived.

"You got the pick?" I whisper.

"Don't I always?" Leave it to Alani to know her way through a damn lock. She slips two bobby pins from her hair, shapes one into an *L*, flattens the other, then rigs them into the lock. A little shake and the door yields.

"Always?"

"I've gotta hook up somewhere." Alani winks. The fragrant clean smell of laundry is thick in our noses. The boys are perched on a steel folding table, legs swinging from the sides.

"Close it gently, Lex." Alani glances back.

I ease the door in slowly, keeping hold of the handle so it doesn't twist back into place.

"Took you long enough." Nate hops from the table and swings Alani onto it. "Run into Hadley?"

"Hid from her." In four seconds flat, Kyle and I are subjected to the tongue-entangled couple known as Natlani.

Kyle's face goes sour. "And I'm nauseous…"

"Do they even care about us seeing them?" I turn up my nose.

"Ummm…no. I think they feel right at home."

When I laugh, Kyle hops from the table. A wave of seriousness comes rushing to his face. "You ready to do this?"

"I can't believe *we're* doing this," I say, emotion closing my throat. I don't feel any nervous stellar energy as he holds my hand. I feel bonded and safe, even in the face of our Revenir agenda.

"Believe it, because we're going." Kyle checks his watch. "Now!"

Nate comes up for air and brushes his hair back with his fingers. "Sorry, we haven't seen each other all day."

"That's what goes down when you don't?" I quip.

"Lex, don't get judgy. We were just kissing," Alani says.

"It was more like mauling," Kyle claps back.

Alani latches on to his free arm like it's something she's done for years. "Is that how you classify what you and Lex did when you cut school?"

I clear my throat.

Nate lugs a duffel bag over his shoulder before taking hold of Kyle's shoulder.

"Nope...I call that romance," Kyle responds.

"Oh, you'll have to tell me what your idea of romance is." Alani rolls her eyes. "I'm sure it swept Lex off her feet."

Out of habit, Kyle and I catch one another staring. We dodge a little only to remember being with each other is a thing now. "Yeah..." He bites his lip as his gaze pours memories into mine.

My feet vibrate into tiny particles scattering around to become grey smoke. Everything feels like the peak of a roller coaster just before the fall, like it did the first day Kyle kissed me, like it feels every time I free my heart to return to him. My locket shimmers, dancing reflections onto his skin. We both smile knowing we have nothing holding us back from this mission. *We* are doing this.

CHAPTER FORTY-FIVE

MASK

WE PLANNED FOR NO surprises. Meeting in the laundry room. Kyle teleporting us from Malveaux into the Virgin Forest. Yet, no one told me I'd spend my first few minutes in Adieu Lagoon the only one blindfolded.

"Just a few more steps," Kyle directs, guiding me by the arm.

"Remind me why you're doing this?" I imagine what Alani looks like just from hearing her alone: over it and kicking her boots through the long-haired grass with annoyance.

"Because I've played third wheel to you both since I was an embryo. Okay, stop right here." Kyle halts me.

"Ay! Phoenix…what're you doing, man?" I hear Nate shout. "Put your shirt back on!"

"Shut up." Kyle rolls his eyes.

"What? Not again," I panic.

Alani gasps. "Not the shorts too. Please!"

I rip the bandanna from my eyes. "Wait, no! I'm not getting in that water this time." Alani and Nate erupt in laughter.

"Thanks for being jerks. It was really helpful." Kyle slow claps.

I skip through the damp grass. "This is your surprise? Adieu? I've seen it all…with you."

"Yes, but you haven't seen it at *night*," Kyle clarifies, directing his flashlight to the scene ahead. "C'mon!" We run in the wild darkness. Laughing and scaring each other, stopping for nothing except the luring glow of Adieu's waterfall and lazy rivers. Where it used to mirror abalone, it now glows like a swirl of poured paint. Kyle's right. I've never seen anything like it.

The silhouette of a wonky-looking tree sharpens in the distance. Barren of leaves, its naked branches droop with tulip-like buds at its ends. Like flies to honey we run to it and gawk at its weirdness. In his best ghoul impression, Kyle lights his face with the flashlight. "Give me your hand."

I grimace, too scared of what he "needs" it for.

"Seriously, let me see your hand," he repeats.

I raise my arm slowly.

"Don't be a wimp, you're okay." He kisses the back of my palm. Finger by finger, he shapes my hand, leaving only the pointer flexed. He directs it to the dormant buds. With each soft touch, they bloom, releasing butterfly-winged flying creatures from their centers. They're like fireflies, but not.

"Is this real?" I gasp.

Kyle marvels at the fluttering creatures. "That'd be the only way to explain it." I go around the tree and open flowers by the dozen. Before I know it, the sky twinkles with flying sparkles of light. An illuminated creature floats by and plants a small kiss on my cheek. It lets out a squeaky giggle when I gasp. "Periwings," Kyle says. "Their wings shine blue in the night, clear in the day."

I twirl beneath their light. "They stunt at night, huh?" I say to myself. "Does the wonder never end?"

"Unfortunately, yes." Alani folds her legs atop the grass. "Business first."

Business is our mechanism of movement. All the points which will drive us right into Pynman's Den. "We're going to go over it one last time." We gather round as she unfolds a poster-size paper littered with smaller pieces of tacked paper—fine details. Periwings make the lines and writings visible. Alani points to her hand drawn map. "From here, we go to Andre's. Kyle, you're still good to be our ruse?"

"That was my plan."

"Nate, you have the wine?"

"A nice Cabernet Sauvignon, courtesy of the faculty." He nods with a silly grin.

"And the sedative?"

"Mixed in one and a half doses to buy us time. Resealed the cork myself," Nate confirms.

"A handsome criminal…I love it." Alani winks.

I take the reins before Kyle and I have to survive through another make out mauling. "Then from there, Kyle, you get him to drink. Once he's sleep, you let us in and we enter the cellar to Pynman's. We'll lay low—"

"And drink the chasm," Alani cuts in. "Lex, did you ever find out anything about that antidote?"

I drop my head. "Sage Cameron was out of office when I went to track her down and there's nothing about it on the IVnet or in our Herbalism textbook."

Periwings swirl and chase around the treetop, making a still moment a little more frantic. Kyle gently places his hand at my back. "It's okay if you can't remember right now. The chasm won't affect us." He looks to Alani. "We'll drink this one-time dose and that's it, keep blending in, and find Sarai."

I nod and breathe nervously. "But I did remember something else…" I reach into my bag as the gang's eyes wait on me. "I learned about this in Herbalism with Sage Cameron: Dama Fabienne's sweet memory tincture. It's used to erase traumatic memories as Dama Fabienne did for refugees. But I thought it may come in handy if we get in a pinch." I pass out the tiny bottles of tincture. One for each of us, small enough to hide away in our clothing.

"A pinch?" Kyle asks as I place a vial in his palm.

"This is perfect," Alani says. "If someone is on to us, this could come in handy."

Nate isn't completely sold. Not yet. "But how will we even apply this? We'd have to be close."

I sigh. "That's the dilemma. We'll have to figure that out on the spot, but it can work in multiple ways: intravenous, mixed with food or drink, inhaled…"

"Intravenous?" Kyle questions.

"Yes…but that doesn't seem possible tonight, does it?" I giggle through my nerves, wondering how stupid I must sound to everyone, but Alani smiles anyway.

"Thank you, Lex. The more in our arsenal, the better," she says.

"Oh and lastly," I say, remembering the most important detail. "We are looking for Sarai. She's a little taller than me. A Black girl that's maybe five foot eight with brown eyes and dark brown hair. It'll probably be hard to find her if her face is painted too…but she has a scar on her left eyebrow from when her dog bit her as a kid. So it always looks arched…I hope we find her."

An awkward silence follows. I don't think anyone knows what to say.

"We will," Kyle finally says. "We should start painting our faces. Time is running close."

The gang all agrees. Nate rummages through his duffel and lays out the small round cans of coal paint and shell paste.

"I, umm…actually, do you mind if we paint ours separate?" I set my eyes on Kyle. "Kinda want to talk to you about something."

Nate mouths, "Already?" to him and they laugh while we pass on to the willow tree that observed some of our first kisses.

"What's going on?" he talks down to a whisper.

"Everything…" I harpoon straight to the point. "Why didn't you tell me about your family and the Revenirs? That would've helped me so much."

"I know," he says, scoping across the way to make sure we don't have an audience. "I didn't want to make it complicated."

"Complicated? How on earth would that make things complicated? We could've turned the Revenirs upside down by now."

"That right there. You wouldn't have wanted to wait…and neither would I. But this is the smarter route. We blend this way. We learn more this way."

I shake my head. "Did you know all these answers? Or did I just waste my time?"

"No. No. I've been honest about everything else. I wanted to tell you, Lex. I was going to tell you…I was just afraid of ruining things for you." He zones out ahead at Alani. "She always knows when I spiral. I don't know how, but she does. She knew a little this time, but I wasn't invested enough for her to catch on early. I played it smart. All the other times, Revenir hunting was all I did. All I'd ever think about."

"Because…you think they killed your parents?"

I've never seen Kyle's face more serious. A whole new person answers, "I know they did. My mom was stalked the entire last two years of her life by Revenirs. She couldn't get help from the guarde, just like you couldn't. All their reports mark her delusional because of it, but she would see them haunting her on her walks home. My uncle said she once saw their face in the pool of her sink, telling her she'd be theirs."

"Theirs?" A chill dances up my spine.

"They wanted her gifts…"

Ringing sounds turn my ears hot. I can't believe this. How are these things able to happen? I search for Kyle's hand in the dark. The Periwings fly over to lend their brightness, making the willow something of a live lampshade.

Kyle squeezes me before going for the can of shell paste. "It's why we moved a lot for a while."

"It's all so horrible. I'm sorry."

"Don't be." He takes a brush and paints my skin with the cold, gritty thickness of the paste. "You're on the right side of things. We'll get in there and do this for Sarai, and my parents."

"Are you nervous?"

"No."

"Why not? What if we get caught? Aren't you scared of that?" I wriggle my nose to fend off a sneeze.

"Well, if you think like that…we will be caught."

"Has anyone you know seen them? Besides your mom?"

"Nope." Kyle shakes his head. "Conspiracists think they've 'sighted' them. That they look like living wraiths, half-dead, but really strong when they kill."

"My gosh…"

"Even scarier is how their leadership has changed. My uncle says Set, the guy with wings, he's completely reshaped the Revenirs. They're in all branches of The Grove's functions to make headway in their mission. And they splice still, taking genes from lower-tiered Variens and implanting them into themselves."

"Have they ever taken anyone from Malveaux?"

"Legend has it that Malveaux is sacred property per a blood pact between Louis and Marcel. The school is off-limits. No one can be harmed there. Marcel fought for it to stay a sanctuary in the spirit of Dama Fabienne. He won and Louis had no choice but to honor it. Nothing's ever happened there, so it must be true." Kyle breaks the spookiness with a scoff. "We'll find out if all these stories are real tonight, won't we? Sometimes I just don't want to believe everything. Maybe because I don't see how a group of Variens could want their kind to suffer that much. Did you get the answer you expected?" Kyle awkwardly giggles. He sets a smaller brush inside the coal paint, then circles my eyes, smears the tip of my nose, and lines my ashen mouth with stitches.

"Not at all…I could use a few laughs now," I say, sighing my way out of an anxiety spiral. "How do I look?"

"Like the belle of the brawl." He closes a kiss on my hand. "I'm up."

I pay him fine attention, coating him in shell paste and turning his most beautiful features sinister. "You could pass for a third cadet," I joke.

"TroisCadets? No."

"Hey, that was me nudging you for a laugh." Acting like an antsy child, I grab his arm to shake the blue from his insides. "Let's dance."

Kyle's arm drops like lead. He shakes his head. "We have to get mentally prepared."

"So, you don't want to dance?"

"Lex, we're about to do the craziest mission in an hour—"

"Oh, so what you're saying is, you don't know how to dance?"

Kyle blows raspberries. "You're not talking to me. Because I swear I've told you I'm a pro."

Hook. Line. Sinker.

"Oh, that's right. Where are my manners?" I say in a dry tone. "What will I be learning from you today, Damo Pereira-Phoenix?"

Kyle scoops my hands and sways his wiry body back and forth. "We could always foxtrot. Man-oh-man do I love a good foxtrot."

"*This* is *not* the foxtrot."

"Clearly, you lack the rhythmic sophistication to even recognize the foxtrot so…we'll move on." He sticks his nose in the air. "Now which one of *my* signature dances do you want… or should I say *can* you learn? There's just so many. I don't know where to start. Oh-oh, what about some pole dan—" He licks his finger and drags it down his chest.

"No pole dancing lessons, please. Not tonight. Maybe on a Friday, but on a Monday…no." I stick my foot out and trip him. Thinking faster than I ever could, he teleports himself back up and tackles me into a mound of leaves. We dull down our laughter and admire one another.

"Can we stay like this forever?" he whispers.

"No. I can't kiss you like this. We'd be two clowns."

"That's not what I mean. Can we stay here? Leave Malveaux?"

"Malveaux is home." My mind goes blank after I say it. I'm shocked. When did I flip? When and how did Malveaux go from a glorified prison to the place I feel safest? When did my old home become part of my past?

"It is home but…this is us. This space right here." He points at my heart, then the willow's cape. "This is all my home…with you. We can build a safe house and name it Fort Jacobs-Pereira-Phoenix. Sounds pretty badass if you ask me."

I wrinkle my nose at the sound of the word "fort."

"You're killing me, Jacobs," he huffs, checks his watch. "Thirty minutes left. Can we rest here and fall asleep? You know, get lost for a few minutes and pretend like nothing on the other side of that hill exists?"

The pillow of leaves rustles beneath my agreeing head.

Kyle unzips his black jacket and lays it over the both of us like a blanket. I rest my head in the nook between his arm and chest—feeling safe and worried, all at once. Side by side, we lose ourselves in our wild home: staring at the stars that peek through the willow branches, saying nothing, while somehow, still sharing our fears. I listen really close—to the regular but forced exhales of Kyle and notice his tight chest. The skin of his hand bakes clammy in mine. I rest my eyes. *I've got you*, he seems to say from deep inside.

CHAPTER FORTY-SIX

THE RUSE

WHEN MY FEET PRESS into the dirt around Andre's cottage, they make soft impressions like fingers to fresh-baked goods. Smells of sulfur and fish violate my nose. I work to remember the paint on my face every time the urge to cover my nostrils comes.

"Is this cool?" Kyle's frame morphs from a painted skull-faced Revenir hopeful, to the tousle-haired, wiry boy I see every day after school, sans the makeup.

"I'd never guess you were up to no good," I quip.

"You know you don't have much time?" Alani says.

Kyle frowns. "Time? What is time exactly? Is it the longest distance between two places? Is it an illusion?"

Nate pops the crown of his head.

"What the hell?" Kyle faces Nate.

Alani comes through with another.

"Damn!" Kyle flinches. "I'm ready. I'm going," he yells into a whisper. When his arms outstretch, Nate places the wine bottle in his grip. "You think he has to drink the whole bottle?"

Nate is startled. "No, we don't want to kill him."

"Kill him?" I damn near flop over. "Nate, you weren't supposed to put that much in there."

"We need enough to take him out in one cup. I had to." Nate shrugs.

"I cannot go to prison in The Grove," I affirm.

But Nate is too confident. "You won't."

"Tuh! I don't have the privilege not to. Meanwhile I'm sure your parents own the damn thing."

"Lex, it's all right." Alani slices between us. "Just one cup," she reminds Kyle. We leave him at Andre's doorstep and take cover beneath a cluster of redwoods and bushes. What a bunch of weirdos we are: smothered in face paint like botched sugar skulls camouflaging in shadows behind leaves.

After Kyle rings the bell, he waits in darkness till a yellow light in the cottage flicks on. More lights liven the house as they burn closer to the door. "Andre?" Kyle Cheshire grins at the peephole. "It's your favorite person."

In the most cliché scenario, dealing with a quirky person like Andre, I'd expect to hear a dozen locks shift and turn. There's none of that. Just the sound of heavy items scooting about and very few clicks.

"Kyle…what're you doing here? A little late, isn't it?" I hear Andre through the now cracked door.

"I come bearing gifts. Felt really bad about the other day at the Montparnasse. You stuck your neck out for me and Alexia. It's the least I could do."

Wind talks in place of their voices. There's a pause and Andre opens the door wider. "Thank you. You should get back to Malveaux. I don't expect Maureen to let you off easy if you're caught." Wine in hand, Andre starts to close the door.

I feel panicked, wishing I could hurl ideas into Kyle's head, but he blocks the door from closing just in time.

"Do you think I could use the bathroom before I go? Teleporting shakes my bladder up." More pause. More singing wind. More skipping beats in the center of my chest. The rest I can't hear. All I see are Kyle's feet leaving Andre's porch as he enters the cottage.

CHAPTER FORTY-SEVEN

The Bottle

ME. ALANI. NATE. WE are sitting ducks in the shrubs. And Kyle? The mere seventeen-minute absence of him has us on edge.

"We should go in there." Alani's voice is ripe with nerves.

"Give him three more minutes. Then I'll rip the door from the hinges," Nate replies.

I know it's not good enough for Alani because it isn't good enough for me. "If we wait three minutes, we could also be three minutes too late."

"We need to go now, Nate," I say.

"Just give it a little." When his hand acts as a gate, Alani breaks past it. Nate looks me square in the eyes—as if I have the water to douse Alani's fire.

I stall and stay with him between the bushes and trees, watching my feisty friend lurk carefully around Andre's small windows. She goes from creeping around the window's edges to staring straight through their center. There must be nothing there.

A loud thump from inside makes her scared.

I rise to my feet.

Nate cautions us. "Stay back! Get away from there."

"Something's not right!" Alani panics.

I point to the cottage. "You heard that, didn't you?"

Nate lowers his voice, a signal for us to do the same if we want to stay under the radar. "Yeah, but what good are we if we stand in line to get killed? Get back!"

This time we get with the plan and take cover behind Nate.

"Someone's coming," he whispers.

We dread the anticipation of that "someone." What if someone came through the cellar's secret door to stop us? There's no telling who it may be.

Air cracks before us. It's Kyle. "Please tell me you won't talk this loudly when we get to Pynman's. I could hear every word."

Alani lets out a sigh of relief. "What took you so long?"

"Can we go in? We can talk about this later," I cut in.

In the pearled moonlight, Kyle's skin ripples back into black and white curves and valleys. "Yeah. C'mon."

With Kyle's blessing we trek into Andre's cottage. It's as warm as I remember, a cozy hodgepodge of things new and old: stained-glass lamps to match the stained-glass windows, a big flat screen, knitted blankets to cover all couches and chairs…Andre's lifeless body on the cherry wood floor.

Alani curses. I yelp a little.

"What the hell is this, man?" Nate asks.

"Keep calm, he's only sleeping," Kyle explains.

I bend down and place a finger under Andre's nose. "He's breathing."

Alani doesn't look too convinced, neither does Nate.

"Listen," Kyle readies to explain. "Out of all the days to pull off a stunt, this fool chooses to enact wineless Wednesday and make bonds over a cup of cider. I had to get creative."

"Cider again?" I shout.

"What the hell does 'get creative' even mean?" Alani snaps.

Kyle folds his hands. "Persuasion. After he told me this bottle of wine was some rare Cabernet Mignon—"

"Sauvignon," Alani corrects.

Kyle swats the air. "Whatever. I just egged him on and told him even with his experience, he probably couldn't handle this high of a proof."

"How much did Andre drink?" I ask firmly.

Kyle plays nonchalantly and scrunches his lips together. "Sips. He had some sips from one glass."

"Okay, good," I breathe.

"Question." Kyle raises a finger. "Should we be concerned if the glass is more on the large side?"

"Kyle, you didn't…," I say.

"I didn't." Kyle twitches. "Nate added too much sedative. I merely watched Andre pour the drink…into this humongous wine glass."

The three of us look at the empty fishbowl-sized wine glass on the table with our jaws dropped.

"Me? You should've stopped him!" Nate snaps.

"And then what? Pique his suspicion? It'd be game over."

I rush to turn off the kettle of whistling cider and roll my fingertips over my freshly plaited cornrows. "There's nothing we can do about it now. Kyle's right. He would've just given himself away."

Andre is out cold, wrapped in a red silk robe with holed sweatpants for an ensemble.

"We can't leave him like this. We should at least sit him up in the armchair. It'd help his breathing," Alani tells us. "Nate, lug him over there." Our big tree of a friend does what he's asked and sets a floppy Andre in the oversized comfort of his worn armchair. "You think he'll be alive when we get back?"

"Not sure, but I'm putting it into the universe," I say.

Kyle nods. "That's right. Manifest that shit, Lex."

Alani pops him and the two bicker in brief whispers. Then the crew and I take our eyes off Andre, reluctantly, and make way for the cellar.

In the night, the hall of dolls feels more sinister, even with the additional protection and eyes of two friends. They're disturbed too.

The cellar is unlocked, and without Andre to flip the right switch, we employ Alani to be our sun. She brightens herself just enough in her hands, guiding us down the stairs and over to the wall of first edition prose and poems. "Which book was it again?" She wades her flamed palms in front of the shelves. Splayed books from our last visit still lie in a messy heap.

"*The Thursday That Never Ended*, I put it right back before we left. It was closer to the right."

Kyle takes the reins. The fire from Alani's hands intensify, touching us with much-needed heat. Kyle is just a shadow till the flames mask him in gold. A nimble finger slides the book away, and the door scrapes against the ceiling and floor as it moves to the side.

A hall of black awaits us. "We're in." Kyle says.

CHAPTER FORTY-EIGHT

The Toll

"L EX, YOU GOT THE map?" Alani checks.

"Yeah." I rummage in the pockets of my black pants. My heart sinks when I fail to feel it, but ah, there it is.

I've never known air to be so damp without a trace of rain, yet here we are, in this cold corridor of a secret path. Brick from wall to floor. Five feet across and, by the looks of Nate's hooked neck, a little under six feet high. Here is not where we want to be, it's where we need to be. Hopefully, it won't be where we stay.

I unfold the map, and the dark black lines re-ink themselves neon yellow. My heart drops as I try to figure out what the hell is happening.

I spot Kyle fidgeting next to me. "Dust rain has a pretty cool luminescent effect when liquified."

"Whose idea was it to retrace the map, though?" Alani snaps.

Kyle rolls his eyes. "I don't know…I just got the idea. Almost like I had this nagging axe wound on my back telling me to do it every half hour."

"We need to move. I'm gonna wreck this tunnel if we don't." Nate pushes his hands against the ceiling.

Kyle pats him. "This never happens when Alani sucks the oxygen from your mouth?"

"Kyle, please," I call out. "No comedy bits till we're at least out of here. Everyone, follow me." As I navigate, all I can think of is Sarai. She's the only motivation keeping one foot in front of another. There's an overload of filth—cobwebs, rats, and their waste, and another stench I can't quite pin down. Alani and I squeal when the critters scurry over our feet, dragging their thick tails behind them.

"I hate this," Alani mumbles. We walk closer now. Not by choice, but force. The room is narrowing.

"The hall is squeezing in," Nate says from behind me.

"Getting shorter too," Alani adds. Her flamed hands dimly show a mortared wall at the end.

She's right. The map shows we've entered the canals, yet there's nothing beyond these stone walls. The ground is steep now, and the hall only allows for a single file line. At the mouth of the dead-end, our hall opens into a circular alcove.

Blue flames hatch behind stone votives. Alani folds her hands and extinguishes her fire. "So, what now? Is there a button we're supposed to press?"

Nothing on the map gives the answer. I search for something that stands out but there's nothing special.

Nate comes closer and tries to read the map. "Man, I hope we're not stuck." A clinking sound of metal against a surface chimes under his feet. "Wait…"

Nate bends down, shuffles around some more. "There's a pulley down here…or something?"

The three of us crowd to inspect it, but as Nate pulls on it, a loud scraping noise pushes a pedestal up from the floor's center.

Soaked with the sapphire glow of the alcove, the altar sits on rough cuts of beautiful stone with an inscription around its brim.

Alani lends her powers again and hovers her light to make out the words: "Drainem jen a'herit." Her hands go cold.

"What does it mean?" I ask.

She and Kyle pass morose looks. "Drain the heirloom blood."

"What?" I fidget.

"There's more," Kyle says. "Fairer trel jen y'ame…soak the soul."

Every single one of us stares at Nate, hearts somewhat in arrest. Fear bubbling in the pit of our stomachs. I can't help but feel responsible, convicted, and selfish.

"Listen, you don't have to do this. We can just go back the way we came," I tell him. "I'll find another way."

I'm not sure what Nate is thinking or what he's staring at in the ceiling. I just know I don't want him to get hurt. "Does anyone have a knife?" Nate says.

"I do," I say. "But I don't want you to use it. I didn't want anyone to come. I can't have anyone's blood on my hands."

Kyle squints. "You have a knife?"

"More of a dagger, Greta gave it to me when we realm jumped."

"There's so much I don't know about you," he mumbles in shock.

"Nate, listen, please don't feel pressured. Let's just go." Nothing I say is working. "Alani, help me!"

One and the same, she wears a long face, but does nothing. "Give him the dagger."

"Alani?" I gasp at the sight of Nate's begging hand.

"Hand it to me. I'm a strong guy, I can handle it. I'll be all right."

"You're crazy," I tell him.

"*I am*. And so are you, and her, and him." He points. "We're literally in some type of cave or whatever the hell this is because we're crazy enough to rescue your friend from traffickers. I want to be crazy."

"Don't you want to know why it's asking for your blood specifically?" I reply.

"I'll ask those questions later, Lex. Give me the dagger."

We stare off for a bit, but it ends with me honoring his request, and placing the black and gold hilt in his grip.

"This is a ballan dagger," Nate tells us as he studies the detail. "They don't make these anymore. This thing will cut through anything." With a steady hand he aims the blade. Pressure is applied and out comes a stream of red life. I squint and squirm. Kyle looks away. Nate takes it up a notch by squeezing his fingers into a fist, grimacing as more blood wrings out. Down the altar the drops go, into a clear flute that travels to the ground. "Now what?" He sniffs.

The altar gurgles with the sound of flooding water.

"Soak the soul." Alani laces her hand around Nate's wrist and drives his hand into the dip of the altar's bowl. Murky water surfaces and coils over Nate's fingers like a snake.

"The chasm…" I watch the bowl fill with it. Licorice floats in the air, an ugly scent for an evil thing. Nate winces and even though his arm is flinching, he holds tight.

"Hang on, babe," Alani soothes him.

Then, the mile-long seconds end and the chasm clears back to where it came from. Nate shivers down to the ground, where the altar retreats. We huddle around him and find his wound is miraculously healed.

Just as soon as we catch our breath, the block beneath us breaks from the alcove. The wall ahead of us cracks like a shell. Water is beneath us, and we are moving along—four teenagers on a stone raft.

Frantic, I check the map. Rumbles almost jerk Kyle off the stone.

Alani grabs him just in time. "Lex, what's happening?"

"I don't know! The map doesn't say anything about water. Just that the alcove opens to Pynman's!" We float on with water trickling where we sit. A force is pulling us. It's not buoyancy or a current collaborating to drift us through open water. We are being hauled.

Our slab of stone, our black threads, and the shining dark water are a monochromatic nightmare. All I can see are the whites of our shell-pasted faces. Eye sockets and noses missing like aged corpses. Ahead, a figure in white stands in the water with nothing behind it except the horizon of onyx—a matte sky and water crests that shine like patterned leather. I can see other painted faces around us nearing, closer and closer till their rafts hook to the back of ours. A line of Revenir hopefuls being led by infiltrators. It's getting real.

The crew and I sit close as our raft connects with a flat pier like a magnet.

The pale figure stands before us. A statue, I think, but as I see their rib cage letting in breaths, I think otherwise. Alani nudges us all to our feet. She draws her black veil over her face, and I follow. Finally, the person in white meets our eyes. Theirs are not concealed like ours. Pink, radiant, and piercing, they almost entrance as we near. I've never seen skin so white that even the dark can't swallow it. Almost like an internal halo. But with no sun here, how could that be?

Although the figure doesn't smile, they appear pleasant. Their hands are clasped in front of a steel breastplate. A metal contour band fits snug where their gold hair and forehead meet, and curves over their nose, lips, and chin. Their frame shrinks down to ours.

Here we are, toe-to-toe.

"Medi len jue?" they say to us, proud and strong.

Alani acts as if the words have passed her by like they did to me. And on my right, Kyle has stiffened. Then after a beat, he replies, "Mel…mel neut beni awhem en len."

Nate follows Kyle's lead. "Mel neut beni awhem en len."

The figure grins with pleasure and splits themselves at the seam of the middle of their body. Both figures step aside and welcome us to walk on.

CHAPTER FORTY-NINE

PASSAGE

A HALL OF MASKS flash at us. Carved in black stones, their illuminations pulse as we pass. Each expression is different. They start prideful, almost bursting with heart. Now, they're worn, weary, and worried.

Alani gives my hand a squeeze in the dark. Her touch startles me. I settle when I catch her gaze, knowing she's just as scared yet determined to follow through. The eyes on the next mask flash empty. No life. Our shoes scuff against slated stone as we notice the mask take a new form. It's hardened where innocence was. A mouth is pinned by anger only to flash on into what we know as a raging Revenir. A death for a rebirth.

The walkway gives into an old ruin of a statue. I recognize what's left of it: a cracked lower half of a wraith's face, roaring in transformation with teeth bared and veins protruding. A larger version of the bust I saw at the Montparnasse. Water drips from its broken edges. We enter through its mouth. Warm, orange light is there, and my heart flutters as I spot bodies congregating in its shine.

You are here. You made it here. You stuck to a side, I repeat in my mind.

I can hear the buzzing of conversation. I can smell the staleness of old water. A parade of black draping is before us now—other hopefuls.

"Medi len jue?" one painted boy greets us.

Kyle takes the lead again, nodding.

"Mel neut beni awhem en len!" I repeat the phrase quickly, while it's fresh in my mind.

The measure stuns Kyle, and as Alani sets to speak those words, he claps. "Glad to make it!"

My teeth clench. *A slow clap at a secret society initiation. What is he thinking?* Others in the room pause and look up. *Shit.*

With surprising grace, the painted boy bows. "Yes. It is an honor, brother."

"Absolutely." Kyle nods.

We find a corner in the raw stone room to claim. A place to look on without calling too much attention to ourselves. "What the hell was that?" Alani sneers in a low tone. "I know Viridian! You're sabotaging us."

"Lex sounds like an amateur. You know how to read it better than you speak it. I saved us." Kyle adjusts his hood.

Prickling settles beneath my locket. I clutch it and scan the room.

"Do you see her?" Kyle's breath tickles my ear through my veil.

"Hard to tell. Everyone looks the same here." Smeared in coal and ivory painted skulls. Silhouettes faded in basic clothes. Hands gloved.

"Aren't those the cadets?" He points. "Croix and Jaime?"

I search for myself, and yes, I recognize them all too well. Some profiles are too strong with noses too unique. Croix. And some smiles, like Jaime's—gapped near the incisor—can't be mistaken. "They get an A for effort, yeah?" Kyle says.

The stares of recruits unnerve me. "C'mon, let's mingle."

The crew follows in synch when a paunchy man blocks me. He's drinking from a silver cup. I see a diamond symbol filled with five stripes sewn to his sleeve. The insignia of a Grand Skull. "You kids make it here okay?" He smiles curtly. Showing teeth behind the skeletal ones painted on his lips.

"Just a hop, skip, and a jump for us," Kyle replies.

The man is amused. "Is that so? Even through the obstacles, huh? The puzzles, messaging, and riddles. A hop, skip, and a jump?"

Kyle doesn't break confidence. "When you really want something, the work isn't so hard."

"I like that," the tall stocky man laughs, waving down the server holding flutes on a tray. "Drinks?"

With my nerves aflutter, I battle hot flashes with the memory of my token. *Not here. Not now. Steer yourself.* We all grab a flute. Not because we want to, but because the stocky man's eyes tell us we better. My friends drink without missing a beat, but I'm apprehensive and take my time. Holding the drink like an accessory and fidgeting as I attempt a sip.

"It's just pear cider," the man catches on to my nerves and reassures. That small fact is enough for me to release some worry. I don't need to be underage and tipsy while undercover at the recruit night of a secret society.

"Thank you." With relief loosening my spine, I bow and sip the cider.

"What school do you come from?"

"That's against the rules, isn't it, Grand Skull?" Alani lends her voice. She teases a curled brow as she sips under her veil. "Initiations aren't to be manipulated by identities."

The man points and grins right as I fear she's gone too far. "This is a good batch. I can feel it already." We join with smiles that look as inauthentic as his.

"I could always guess anyway," the man says.

"Oh, is it that easy?" Kyle inquires.

"Well," the man sighs. "There are characteristics...many of which relate to academy insignia, believe it or not. All the public-school students usually appear quiet, but then they warm up. They have this need to be accepted. So, it's almost inevitable. If you're a

Crowneheart you're most likely to speak when spoken to. Keen on listening…which makes sense. They're artists, so they spend their time studying first. Knox-Oxley's students command the room. They know they've got it and they want next because the only thing standing between them and us is opportunity. That's true Knight spirit. Now, Malveaux Mavericks…they wouldn't be here."

Cold and hot pour inside me all at once.

"Not without purpose. Their own purpose. They'd be harder to pick out. Cause, you see, they are a little of both. Louis may have left Marcel to his devices, but his foundation is all in that school." The man bends his head back to finish his drink. A ring on his finger clangs against the silver cup. "You can cut branches, not roots."

"Interesting," Kyle says. "We're not prep age anymore…we're college freshmen."

"Fair enough," the man responds.

Alani is still seamless. "Thank you for the drinks, Grand Skull. We'll see you inside."

The paunchy Revenir bows his head. I can't tell if he's satisfied with ending the conversation or not, but we move on as he watches and make small talk with the DeuxCadets.

Alani's best friend radar picks up. "You okay? Did you spot Sarai?"

"No. I saw someone else." That gold ring on the stocky man— the black enamel and gold crest. It lives in my memories.

"Who?"

I peek around Croix and Jaime. "The guarde that twisted Kyle's arm. He's the Grand Skull."

Alani's face would flush red as her hair if her skin weren't painted. I can see her reaction in her eyes and the stretching of her nostrils.

A wall in the front of the room slides apart as drums welcome recruits inside. There's a tall man revealed in the middle. He's painted in the same fashion as the other Revenirs. "Anyone who wishes to leave must do so now. Remaining passengers, continue."

CHAPTER FIFTY

STALACTITES SPILL CLOSE TO us like melted candle wax. Streams of water trickle from the deep of the cavern and pool in the middle of the den. Revenirs are like Reapers. It's hard to tell the paint from the person. From what I've learned, paint is child's play vs when Revenirs actually turn.

We're instructed to fill in the space of the pond. Our feet sink into the cold water, walking timidly to make the rows we're instructed to make. I lead my bunch. Kyle is at my back, then Alani, then Nate. I wonder what they're thinking—if they regret committing to a death wish, if that's what this turns out to be.

I can't find Sarai anywhere like I should. *Since she likely has the Eden gene, shouldn't she be here? Wouldn't they brag about their new property?* I can barely stand to wait for what's coming, but I have to, for her.

The rest of the recruits stack up. Young soldiers. New idiots. Sheep hoping to run with wolves. I look under me, where ripples grow from my restless ankles to the edge of large rock. Carved stairs curve behind a cavern wall with a rounded balcony carved into it. Eyelets between show someone watching. No wings, but I remember those scars: a map of illustrated brandings in his skin. How he wore them with pride when he destroyed my life. He wants us to see all that's inscribed on his chest and arms. Names, designs, tally marks. Graffiti on a canvas of skin. His watchful eyes test us. So many around me care to impress him. I can hear them sucking in air as they fix their posture and stances.

Behind me, Kyle is solid. A perfect actor. It's clear he's been waiting on this his entire life. His eagle eyes have found Set as well.

Barefaced, the circles around Set's eyes are even darker than I remember. His sockets are their own caves, homing two predatory eyes isolated from happier things and sunlight. On the way to the steps, he cops a white button-up from a podium. The effort toward professionalism is slim, though. Set puts his arms through the sleeves and stops there.

Set bows his head in acknowledgement. Scanning. Pacing. "I see a lot of faces this year. Maybe we made it too easy. Maybe… you were just hungry enough to find us this time. The smell of prey in the air, rattling of grass…you sensed it. A special blood in the water. It's here." Set points down to the ground. "In homeland, in The Grove. And if y'all are worth making it, you'll feel her blood running through your veins soon. Not in your tenure like some of my partners, but in your prime. You will be part of the revival in ways Louis himself could only dream about."

Slow-dripping water echoes. The cavern's attendants are quiet. Set stares back over his shoulder. "Right, Phil?"

A bespectacled man with a black eye is at the end of his gaze. His blood-stained shirt is stretched at the collar. Phil is bewildered, sitting at a random desk with a pen and paper.

"Is it the writer's block, man?" Set pats his hands on Phil's shoulder. "This is our guest, Phil, a staff writer for *The Vine and Times Chronicle*. He wants to cover our operation, and so, Phil looked in places he shouldn't have to expose our plans and lab. He wants to tell the public we take genes from wasteful Variens and implant them into our soldiers. He's a smart cat—won a bunch of medals and prizes—but he made one huge mistake." From his hand slides a thick curved blade.

Phil's breathing turns frantic. He trembles and begs. "No, no, no…please! I won't write the piece! Trust me!"

There's no mercy in Set's face. No acknowledgement of Phil's sounds. Just a seething anger overflowing at the surface. "The pen ain't mightier than the sword." He slams the blade down and shrieks of pain come from Phil's mouth and blood gushes from his hand.

"Write that down," Set spits, and swats Phil's severed thumb off the desk. It bounces to the floor and rolls to the edge of the pond.

Phil breaks into a cry.

"Take him out." However, "take him out" doesn't mean what I expect it to in my little Disney brain. It's a hard one hitter quitter to the jaw that flops Phil's head over before he's dragged away by his arms to who knows where.

"Spoiled blood." Set sucks his teeth. "Phils. Rats. Fledges. We don't want y'all and if you're in here…we'll sniff you out. We always do." Four Revenirs line up behind him. Their hands hold scallop-edged bowls. "Run the oath, now. If it's worth bleeding and facing war, pledge to me now. Offer this piece of yourself."

I'm not all the way in my mind. I know this because my friends walk up to Set in synch while my feet are fused to the pond's floor. Visions of Sarai clinging to me as plumes of smoke put us in a temporary death flood me. I wake up quickly and loop my steer token to calm down. The thought of Dad's hug fails hard as I stand before Set. He's proof I couldn't be saved from a nightmare. When I catch up to my friends, Set strikes a match and lights the chasm sitting in each bowl. Blue flames dance atop the liquid.

A nod from Set sends the Revenirs to us. They demand we kneel, and when we do, they place the bowl in our hands.

"Now, your turn." Set swallows the burning match. "Recite."

In a somber unison, Revenirs recite an oath, and line by line, we all repeat it. The oath is clear, all the words are there, except I can't hear or see anything but my dad when I say them. His mangled body is blood on my Varien hands, and now I'm committing more of a crime against him. What am I doing?

Finally, the script runs out. The last words have been said, and although Set stands on the other end, in front of Nate, his glare arrows me. "Are you here?"

My teeth chatter. "Y-yes."

"Forgive her, Damo," Alani pleads. "Our colleague has motion sickness from our journey. No one is more grateful to be here than her."

"Is she lying?" Set makes his way to me.

"No, Damo," I mumble.

I toe the line of melting Set down to bones with an outburst and quieting my mind. It's getting harder as his hands peel back my veil. He locks eyes on me. "Prove it to me," he says, and when I hesitate, he waves his knife in my face. "The price is your tongue and hers."

Visioning Dad isn't working this time. So, I hone in on joy that's fresh and healthy inside of me. Adieu Lagoon. Kyle and I fusing energies together. Dizzy. Suddenly, I'm clear. With Set's direction, I take the oath:

"My life, reclaiming life. My mind, one with the soul.

This flesh I dedicate an advocate

Of land, the chosen, the innocent

To preserve and restore, clean the blood and avenge.

I will turn and be of guarded conscious no more.

I declare in the hour of night and now, a Revenir becomes my vow."

There are people who are never meant to smile, and Set is one of them. Pleasure doesn't reside in his mouth, it's in his eyes. He takes the bowl from my hands and aims the edge to my lips. I consciously force myself from dodging the heat of the fire and close my eyes. The chasm burns the repulsive fragrance and flavor of licorice inside me. Gasoline is what it tastes like, yet I show little trace of my discomfort. Set is still at my eye level. He folds his knife back. "Thanks, Bel. I would've been sad to cut you."

"Ruem nadat," Kyle whispers.

Set cuts his eyes to him.

I rush to pick up Kyle's lead. "Ruem nadat, Damo."

"Same place." Set goes on. "Same time. The last Friday before Nadir…you three."

The crew thanks him in a mash of Viridian and English. I know better than to attempt words I've only just heard again, so I bow, and that seems to be enough. Set brings forward the cover of my veil. His eyes never separate from mine.

CHAPTER FIFTY-ONE

STRAYS

THE MEMORY OF SET'S stare feels like walking through a cobweb. Thick. Cringey. Faintly there, but very much there. He stared too hard, like he knew me.

Alani catches up to me—my phantom with a soothing voice. "Breathe," she reminds me. Her dainty hands secure her veil. "We're almost out." The very definition of out being back to the path that leads to the canals: a doorway connected to the lobby we're standing in.

Kyle stalls in frustration ahead of us. "It's locked." He pulls at the handle.

"There's only one exit," I hear from behind. The Grand Skull from earlier stalks closer. His crooked smile gets the best of us. "Leaving so soon?"

Alani turns on her charm. "We were dismissed so we're heading home. Have a good evening, Grand Skull." We turn away, seeking that one exit.

"Well, that's what's interesting to me: home," the Revenir responds. The pad of his thumb rotates his gaudy ring around. "You know earlier, you were relieved to find ciders in your glass. Eighteen is the legal drinking age. Relief is alarming to see in a bunch of college kids…I let that go." He shrugs before pointing

318

a stubby finger. "But then I get to talking to you. I talk the three schools here. You don't bite. I get it…anonymity. Do you know what a Revenir does before we turn for a job?"

The four of us go mute.

"It's a very tasking, tactful practice. You gotta learn your kill in a way no one has ever known that person. Not even their mother. See, because people have sides to them. Not everyone gets to see all of them. But we do. We see all seven deadly sins in that one person. We see them when they think no one does. And sometimes, we break bread with them. Mix in, you know? A Revenir becomes a human lie detector. So, when a group of college kids fidget, I know they ain't Crownheart alumni. I know that if they came from Knox-Oxley alumni, they'd wear it with pride because this is what they've dreamed of."

Kyle makes a fist behind his back.

Alani steps forward. "Grand Skull, not everyone from those places you named is a monolith. Those are generalizations."

"Yeah, but generalizations come from truths, don't they?"

"Not in this instance, no," Alani answers.

We walk on through the music of our hurried feet, the dead quiet of the lobby. "Well then it ain't true Malveaux kids have remnants of Louis's courage. Just more of an idiotic hippie schtick suited in tartan," the Grand Skull tells us.

Our walking hasn't stopped, yet the load is lighter. Kyle is standing back a few paces. "Does courage mean psycho now?"

The Grand Skull chuckles. A real smile lights his gapped teeth. "Go home. Wherever home is…wouldn't want anyone to worry." That last word ripples in my ears to my feet. We've got to disappear immediately or get him in contact with Dama Fabienne's memory tincture. This could happen if shadowed bodies weren't near the door. Hooded and painted like their counterparts, they nod at the Grand Skull's new orders. "Make sure our recruits touch down." I race to understand the meaning of touch down and how cryptic it is. Making it home? Touching the dirt once we die?

The two Revenirs open double doors to another exit—one that's unfamiliar from our watery entrance and filled with forest.

As I observe the two Revenirs, one moves behind me, the other at the end of Alani and Nate, I can see the same panic in my friends. A little less in Nate, although something tells me he isn't all right. His eyes squint, and one side of his mouth hangs like he can't help it. Sweat streaks through his coal and ivory, but the night's darkness conceals it once we're outside.

Pine and dead redwood needles snap under our weight. There are no lights, only the moon. "Keep up," the Revenir behind me commands Kyle.

"How far is the main road?" Kyle asks. I grow nervous as I notice the regularity of the trees. There's no shine in them. No sanctuary.

"There's no main road."

Kyle and I exchange worried looks as the weight of the meaning sinks in. I can't end the flickering heat waves inside me. Maybe I should be happy about that and focus on steering that energy instead. How many volts could lay out a Revenir? One scared glance at the size of one's head tells me not nearly enough. Not when their bouldered bodies are bottled with dozens of powers—a couple of theirs, the rest probably from expendable dead and "unworthy" Variens. We could be deemed unworthy tonight. It takes a doubled pace to keep up with their steps. Even Nate is having difficulty. He stumbles into the brush of the forest. His hunching back coils like he's close to vomiting. Alani runs to him and the Revenir near Kyle and me holds his arm out. *Don't,* the gesture says. The other Revenir throws Alani back and pulls Nate up with a one-handed grip. "Walk!"

Nate sways. "I can't see straight." He tries to go on, then pauses.

This angers the Revenir. "Come on!" He kicks into the back of Nate's knees.

His partner shakes his head, disgusted. "Let's get it done here and move them later."

"We're too close." The Revenir's eyes go bright like headlights when he peers at Nate's back. "If you won't walk, I'll move you." He jerks Nate's shoulder. Those beaming eyes catch the side of what should be Nate's face. There's a monster on the left of his face. Cracked, decayed skin and bloodshot eyes alarm us. A wraith.

"Leave me!" Nate roars, reaching a screeching decibel that's half banshee and beast. The Revenirs step back.

A cloud of smoke crackles next to me. Kyle is gone with the smell of a burned fuse in his place. "What was that?" Both Revenirs make a protective stance and root to the ground. "The kid…he disappeared." When we all look around for Kyle, we notice Nate is gone also. Not even the Revenir's high beam eyes can spot him in the wild. They sniff the air around them. "The big one is out there," one of them says. "He's not close, but he's out there. We'll entertain him…play a little hide-and-seek game. Get the girl!"

My windpipe is pinched as one Revenir vices me in his forearm.

"Let her go!" Alani shouts.

The Revenir growls while his partner speeds off into the woods, he leaves a wind tunnel behind that we brace to withstand. I can feel the bulk of his muscle cutting my life off. I don't want Alani to be worried and scared, but I am. She yells like a powerless child, and the fear I hear sends a sole tear down my face. Yet, as Alani commands the Revenir, an orange flicker, a burning ember glows in her face.

I raise my chin and nod. Letting her know I'm fine with whatever defense she has in mind.

Alani pops forward and spits a cluster of sparks in front of the Revenir and me. He drops me instantly and shields his eyes. The sparks curve around him, manifest into a rotating ball, and rocket to the stars.

The dirt is wet and cold beneath me, but I roll in it and hop on my feet to haul off with Alani. "Where are we going?" I pant to her.

"Follow the phoenix!"

"What?"

Above us, flames blaze from the wings of a giant firebird. It cries into the sky, forging on and showing us the way.

In the distance are two men, one towering over the shorter one, fighting. The Revenir and Nate. It's not an equal fight. Even from far away it seems brutal for my friend. The firebird hovers and circles them as the Revenir serves Nate a rock-fisted punch. Alani and I stop ahead once the Revenir catches us in his scope. He stalks closer and closer to us before breaking into his supernatural sprint.

"Alani, what do we do?"

"Hang on!"

Heavy stomps alert me to check over my shoulder. The other Revenir is charging at us. We're being closed in.

"What do you mean hang on?"

"Just trust me."

"I do, but we have no time!"

The Revenir ahead of us is flying from his feet, a few more seconds and he'll meet us.

"Alani!"

"Down!" Alani yanks at my arm and we fall into dead leaves. The firebird Alani breathed life into dips toward the Revenir as a torpedo would its target. Swift and cunning, it brushes its long-flamed tail against the Revenir's head, then kisses the Revenir behind us. Flames engulf them, ridding them of all the intimidation they forced onto us. They wriggle and scream, then drop to their knees. They're burning alive.

"How'd you do that?"

Alani peers up at the phoenix flying off into the distance. It crosses the moon and fades dark. "I felt an urge to do it in a SIM once…this was my first time manifesting it."

"That was amazing. Did you see where Kyle went?"

"I don't make portals, so no."

We jog and move to help Nate up. Parts of him are still changing into something less human along.

"I'm turning," Nate says through a swollen mouth.

"We're gonna take care of you. Just need to get home," I reassure him.

"You took care of those guys." Nate nods to the smoldering Revenirs.

"That's all Alani."

"Oh shit," Nate says in shock.

"You seriously thought *I* did?" I say.

"No, behind you!" Nate clarifies.

Alani and I dare to follow his line of sight. There's no good news. Just Revenirs reforming, regenerating. Limbs cracking back into position, allowing their arms to build their sluggish bodies upright.

"C'mon!" I run off. I don't know these woods from the next, but I know I don't want to die in them. Alani and Nate lag behind me as we cross between enormous redwood trunks. Another body is gaining beyond us. How long can we keep this up? What can we do if Revenirs don't die?

"Nate, hurry!" Alani yells back at him as she catches the Revenirs picking up the pace again. This is getting tiring…all this running and defending ourselves. Thinking on our feet. It feels like throwing spaghetti at the wall. This massive energy suck of trying something…anything to save ourselves. SIM Class makes sense suddenly. It's not just about control over our gifts, it's about skill. Fighting with abilities is a dance. It takes more than I thought it would mentally and physically. A clear, calm, and sharp mind. A creative mind in the face of danger. That's what I need. And even though I know my tokens, I'm missing the other pieces. My friends seem to do better. I look back to check where Alani and Nate are. I can spot Alani, but not Nate. I've lost him in the night, but I hear his tired grunts of pain, then a forceful boom. The earth shakes us over like bowling pins and the loudest cracking sound I've ever heard splits the forest in half.

A titan of a redwood falls. Nate is left where it stood. He did that.

I gasp. "Whoa." Nate's ability is breathtaking. All that power in one boy, courtesy of the energy he sponges around him. What a gift.

Exhausted and sick, Nate bends to his knees to catch his breath. That's when I see them. The two Revenirs. They leap over the fallen tree and rock the ground as they land.

"Nate!" Alani warns.

Behind him, the Revenir stands close. Nate turns around. I'm sure he's scared. How could he not be? But he doesn't let it get in his way. He stays brave and stares the snarling Revenir in the face. Even with skulls painted on both of their faces, Nate has an innocence to differentiate him. Goodness. Courage that comes from a pure place.

"Alani…what do we do?" I ask, shaking.

She rushes her answer, freaking out just as much as I am. "I-I-I don't know…anything."

In a split second, Alani is running. I take off with her—unsure of our plan and ready to give all I can to save Nate.

Nate throws a swing at the Revenir, but his fist gets caught by the Revenir's hand. A power struggle starts. A battle of strength. Nate struggles to remove his hand from the Revenir's grip.

The other Revenir catches sight of us running and makes a stance to attack us. Nate is bending down to his knees. This is hopeless. This night is a big mistake.

Blame and guilt crowd me, and then, a cracking sound shocks Alani and me. Kyle pops out of midair behind the Revenir attacking Nate. He wraps a bandanna-covered hand over the Revenir's face and squeezes his other arm around the Revenirs neck. He doesn't let go until the struggling Revenir goes limp. Kyle drops him carelessly while Nate nurses his freed hand.

Wasting no time, the other Revenir chucks a flat disc of red light at Kyle. Alani and I freeze and scream. "Look out!" we warn him, and luckily, he is two steps ahead—teleporting out of the way and reappearing behind the second Revenir. He uses the same technique as he did with the first one. It's scary how natural this comes to him…almost as if he enjoys it. There's an ease in him. How he looks at the Revenirs as they gasp for breath. It looks like satisfaction.

Once the second Revenir's body falls limp, he drops him and a loud thud brings us the peace to collect ourselves.

"How'd you do that?" Alani asks him.

Kyle wraps Nate's arm around his shoulder and gives no answer.

The answer comes to me suddenly. "The tincture. You used it on them."

Kyle peers at me through his wavy bangs. "Had to. These guys weren't going to stop. And even if we got away, they'd remember everything."

"That was so smart," I tell him, half-impressed and half-shocked.

"That was all you," he grunts, trying his best to keep Nate up. "Let's get out of here!"

Alani and I flee to him—relieved and terrified. I check behind us for the Revenirs, scared the tincture won't be enough.

"Hey, I got you…everything's all right." Kyle reaches for me. There's isn't much of him I can see, but I know he's genuine. All four of us huddle together and get the hell out of this place.

CHAPTER FIFTY-TWO

HEIRLOOM BLOOD

THE RIVER IS FLOWING in reverse, crawling from the banks, rushing up Andre's porch and finding its way through the spaces of the door and windows. All of the same lights are on in the house. I check with Alani and Kyle. Worry is their new mask.

Nate wretches, his body hangs from Kyle like a scarecrow. "Hang on, Nate," Kyle says. "What the heck are we gonna do? He's sick as a dog." He's too late—Nate lets loose to vomit into the marshy soil. An inhuman gurgle loudens in his throat.

"He's turning," Alani says. My insides tighten. I'd rather hear anything but this. "Maybe there's too much of the chasm in his blood. He had more than us."

I look at Nate as he hurls his stomach empty. "Sorry. I didn't know there'd be a blood sacrifice," I cry. My hand is on Andre's door, but I'm too nervous to open it.

"No one is saying you did," Alani says.

"They asked for heirloom blood," I recount in shock.

Alani cuts straight to my worry. "Are you worried we'll think you knew that?"

I don't respond and try to find answers through Andre's window.

"Lex, Nate signed himself up for this," she says firmly.

With the pressure of my fidgeting hand, I somehow crack the door ajar. Water should spill out, but it doesn't. It flows into a sloshing whirlpool in Andre's living room. The old man is still sleep with one slipper missing, his mouth open, and restless eyes speeding around in their sockets. I push a low-floating soleil chandelier out the way. Murky water douses my boots as I run to take Andre's face in my hands. Seeing his eyes up close tells me one thing. "He's dreaming. That's what's happening with the water. He's calling it. We have to wake him up!"

Alani stares at me like I'm dumb. "Lex, he's drugged. He'll be toast till tomorrow."

"It is tomorrow!" Forty-two minutes past midnight to be exact.

As waves of water splash the sides of our faces, Nate suddenly pins Kyle in his grip. His regular face is a phantom—tired and shocked as it discovers the terrorizing Revenir pulling and growing from him. It roars from the side of his face. Jagged teeth drip blood onto Kyle's mouth.

Nate screams, "Help!" His hands push Kyle under the inches of whirlpool.

"What do we do?" Alani panics.

I almost answer her in the heat of chaos. Who ever really knows in times like these? But the answer comes to me between seconds, right before doubt teases me. The antidote. I hear Sage Cameron's voice: "*Virgin apples.*" My feet can't splash through the kitchen fast enough.

"Lex! I need your help!" Alani hops on Nate's back to tame him. The Revenir in him lunges face-to-face with Kyle, screeching with anger.

I clamor through the refrigerator. "It's here. It has to be!" Although it isn't. I check the cabinets and bulldoze through them. Nothing. Then memory banners in the front of my mind. "The cider!" Andre warmed up a batch for Kyle before we left. I leap to the stove and remove the top. There it is, the cider, chock-full of the virgin apples Sage Cameron said would counter the rhute leaf in the chasm. This better work.

"Lex!"

"I'm coming!"

"A teapot?" Alani frowns. She's struggling to tame the beast.

"An antidote. This could work for the both of them! Sage Cameron said a virgin apple can reverse a lot of reactions. And since this is supplemental…we may as well try it."

"Let's do it!" Alani shouts. "What is there to lose?"

How we manage to do it is another thing. Nate's Revenir is now one with him. No longer is his body fighting fusion to stay separate. It *is* a Revenir. A bruised eyed being with decayed skin that exposes regions of a browned skull in missing patches. A relentless killer.

"Fake!" it roars at Kyle who gasps for air.

Alani is trying to put Nate in a sleeper hold. That won't be enough. I head back to the kitchen for something heavy and thick. All I can find is a cast iron skillet. Goodness, cast iron has all the answers. I run back to the living room; turbulent water changes its current toward me, causing me to pick my feet up when I sprint. "Alani, drop off!" When she does, I swing violently at Nate's head, he spots me and hisses before the cast iron punches him to sleep.

"That was fucking crazy." Alani's hands are grasping the roots of her hair.

Kyle coughs and clenches his throat. The water washed paint on his face makes him look like a depressed mime.

"Should we lift him on the couch?" I ask.

"No. Do not wake that fool up again," Alani warns. "He's perfect. Just open his mouth."

Alani holds his mouth ajar. From my hands, the teapot funnels the drink inside Nate's mouth. We plug his nose, shut his mouth. Nate jerks like he's choking. I care, but honestly, I care more about the drink hitting his throat. When I see his Adam's apple bounce, I know we've done it. We let go and his mouth bursts with coughs.

I move on to Andre. He's much easier to bend and make a way with. His mouth is already open, and I can see just about every silver molar he has. The cider waterfalls perfectly. Andre even does me a solid and swallows the drink on his own.

We wait. I don't know how long we wait, though it feels long. When you're scared, seconds can be hours.

I can see the changes start to sink in. Water changes direction, searching for ways out. Marks and the skin on Nate's face rebuilds as if it were never destroyed. Andre shakes awake. His stare latches on to the four of us. The water flowing around his house startles him.

"Geez," he slurs. "What's going on?"

Kyle stands up. He looks like a drenched choir boy in a black robe. "You had a pretty bad leak in your bathroom. I called my crew to come help me fix it."

The only patch of hair Andre has sticks up. "I mean what happened to me? I feel funny."

"You downed all that wine and then you knocked out," Kyle says.

"I can't remember any of it."

"C'mon, man, you've gotta get some decent dry clothes on. Good news is those doll clothes didn't see a drop of water. We'll find you something real nice in there," Kyle tells him.

Andre walks with Kyle—wobble legged and confused.

"Are you okay, Nate?" I ask.

He slides his hands down his face. "No. I still feel it inside."

"But's it's fading, yeah? Maybe you need more of the drink."

"Maybe." He stares at the floor. "I was good the first time it hit me with the blood sacrifice, but in Pynman's…when we drank it. It felt like poured metal on my heart. Immediately. Makes me wonder: Why my blood? Why heirloom blood? There's something about it."

"Like they want yours for something?" Alani says.

Nate's frown is equal parts disturbed and spooked. "No, more like…heirlooms are Revenirs."

Alani's brows spike. "Are you serious? That's crazy."

"That guy that forced us out," Nate shares. "That was Irving Rockwell. The Grand Skull—he's an heirloom member. I see him at every meeting."

"And a guarde," I add. "He was the one that twisted Kyle's wrist that day in the Belle Rues. I remember his ring."

Alani can't help but sit on Andre's overworn couch. "That means a lot of things."

"Bad things," I finish.

"Do you think he suspected you?" she asks.

"He knew we all weren't the real deal…but I don't think he knows who we are," Nate responds.

It takes a moment for Alani to say anything else but four-letter words. Then she questions, "What about Sarai? Did you see her, Lex?"

"No…I didn't."

Alani groans and Nate's spirit crumbles a little bit more. The shit I've put them through tonight. Alani nods—almost snapping herself out of disappointment. "Well, we'll get her. Next time."

I smile with my teeth even though it's disingenuous. They believe me, I hope. They believe I'm full of hope. I've really only got a mustard seed's worth, just enough to put *myself* through this again.

CHAPTER FIFTY-THREE

DIVIDE

"You can't smoke here, you know?" Jessie Maldonado says as she crosses Alani's path. Chilled by the turnaround of the cold weather on an overcast day, I can't tell if she's shivering from the temperature, or the realization of a mistake.

Alani's lose shoelaces are flopped behind her as if they could fly her away. The growing scent of cigarettes tells me she's been lit for a while as I walk up. She takes out one of her ear buds and squints. "Can I help you?"

"Your cigarette." Jessie points, scowling.

"Mmm." Alani takes in a drag. "You should probably tell your dad. He'd appreciate the vigilance."

"Gladly. Dad, look!" The girl waves Coach Dean down on the field as she points at Alani. Coach Dean's eyes pop. Alani side-eyes him. Smoke pours from her mouth and sends Coach Dean into a dawdling U-turn.

Alani gives a satisfied grin. "Father knows best."

Jessie looks to me for saving, but I'm all crossed arms and shrugging brows. Someone should've told her. When she doesn't move fast enough, Alani pops sparks on the asphalt around her feet. "Bye!" Alani snaps.

I've never seen someone skip off so quick. Jessie doesn't even look back. "Ugh." Alani flops down on a bleacher bench. The sleeve of Nate's letterman jacket hangs off her shoulder. "Don't you wish burning at the stake would come back as a punishable sentence?"

"No," I say with obvious disgust. "How'd you manage that with Coach?"

Alani smirks and I immediately grow scared. "Anything is possible when you catch the coach running a numbers scam in the academy basement…even getting *your* boyfriend off the bench."

I can't help but laugh. The ringing of that word has my head shaking. "Boyfriend."

"Is he not?"

With a halo shining brighter than everyone else on the asphalt, Kyle steals all words in my grasp. He's a focused, beautiful mess with a crown of sweat-clumped waves. "…He hasn't asked me to Blossom Ball."

"Well, when should he? He's literally hunting Revenirs with you. You two don't really have time to be basic. Initiation is coming up. Give him some time to make a moment."

I roll my locket round in my hand. "That's actually what I need to talk to you about." Coach must have the power of advanced hearing—that or soiled underwear, thanks to Alani—because he whistles for a fifteen-minute break. The boys walk over and Alani tosses her cigarette behind her and crosses her legs. After rinsing her mouth with water and spritzing it with some kind of spray, she pops gum in her mouth, then practically bathes herself in perfume. Smoking is something she told Nate she'd quit in exchange for his full financial support for her Blossom Ball campaign. Her hair whips and I know she's checking for the scent of evidence.

"You're lucky no one knows Nate is your weak spot," I say. But the show is on and Nate's brick wall of sweat meets Alani with the usual passionate PDA.

"My turn," Kyle says, drawing a hand to my ear. His head is cocked to the side.

I grin for the first time today and palm his forehead. "Nope."

He backs away. "You're right. This is more our style."

"You're doing good out there," I say, reaching for his hand.

"Really?" As he smiles, his halo glows stronger.

"Wait, Lex has something to tell us." Alani rears her head with the worst timing.

"Oh, there you are, Nate." I wave.

Kyle spits out his water.

"All right, you've got the floor." Nate laughs.

"Okay…umm." I crack my knuckles in my nervous palms, instantly tilting the energy in our circle. "I hope you all know I'm so grateful for you. Having you with me the other night was a relief…a security, and I'm indebted to you for it. But it was also… terrifying? I don't know if that's right to say. It's how I feel…I just know you won't want to hear it, but I have to tell you. Because I can't do it again with you. I can't risk your lives and your health."

Instant frowns are served. "You don't want us going to initiation?" Alani asks.

"I need to do this alone."

"You would've died if you did Passage alone," Alani firmly replies.

Kyle nods. "She's right. We got you out of there in one piece."

"But we almost didn't make it out in one piece. Especially Nate! Look, this is my problem. Let this be my problem. I'm not going into this expecting the best. I'm mentally prepared for the worst. But I'm fine if it means Sarai will be okay…same for you three."

Coach calls everyone back with his whistle. A light rain, tears I'm holding, fill the sky. I can barely look my friends in their faces. Over Kyle's shoulder, in the distance, two mahogany blurs stare from the ivy-ridden academy: Sage Cameron and Greta. My stomach churns. They're here for me. They want me to know it. I expect to hear Sage Cameron in my head summoning me, but my own thoughts call me to her.

"If you care about me, if you truly do, you'll listen." I breathe out slow although it doesn't feel like I'm breathing at all. As I pass Kyle, I squeeze his arm. He doesn't return to his place on the court. He doesn't turn around. The cold of his shoulder overcasts the light he sparked in me a while ago.

CHAPTER FIFTY-FOUR

The Standoff

From the feels of everything—the slamming of Sage Cameron's office door and closing of the drapes sans hands—I won't be getting any sort of break in here. "Are either one of you going to say something?" I ask.

Greta cuts eyes at me. "Something? I've got a whole lot of something to say to you, child. Sit down."

"What?" I glare.

Sage Cameron's mind scoots a chair into the bend of my knees. "Sit down, Alexia!"

I reluctantly obey.

"Now, I'm only gonna ask you once. Okay?" Greta leans over the desk, her palms are pressed into the wood. The scent of her trip into The Grove is still in her threads. "What were you doing in the canals?"

Shit, I forgot about the locket. "The canals?"

You heard me, Greta's attitude speaks.

"Answer her." Sage Cameron paces back and forth.

"I was with my friends."

"What friends?" Greta interrogates.

"…Some friends outside of Malveaux."

"Is that right?"

"I met them at the Belle Rues a while ago."

"And you went to the canals with them?"

"Yeah."

"And y'all hung out?"

The two sisters lock stares. Sage Cameron throws her ring-laden hands up, leaving me to Greta again.

"Tuh." Greta shakes her braided head. "I know we look young. I'll take that compliment, but don't take me for a fool. I wasn't born last night. No good business goes down at the canals, just make outs and mischief. Which one were you doing?"

Lies are burning my throat. A pressure suddenly nears my temples. It never sinks in, but the push is there. I look over at Sage Cameron, and right as she shifts her gaze, the pressure disappears.

Greta rolls her eyes. "Don't even answer that."

"This is stupid! I was just hanging out! Who are either of you to say what I was doing?"

"Women who've helped build this place and protect it for decades," Sage Cameron interjects. "Women who can read through lies."

"Don't read *too* hard. It won't be ethical."

She softens, pulling back on the pressure she's telekinetically sent near my skull again. "Are your friends the kind you wanted to find? Did you get the answers?"

"Yes, actually."

"The conspiracists?" Sage Cameron checks.

"Mmhmm, the conspiracists."

"The worst thing you can do is lie to me. You know that, right?" she says.

I huff. *There are worse things.*

Sage Cameron loses patience with me and storms to her floating keyboard where she slams her fingers dow. "You will not be leaving this campus without mine and Greta's permission."

"What? Greta doesn't live in this realm!"

"Hey," Greta warns.

I cross my arms. "You haven't even told me how my family is doing like you promised."

Greta looks convicted. "I've been very busy, Alexia. I'm sorry."

"This situation is a one-way street." I turn away, shaking my head.

"Back to the subject at hand." Sage Cameron clears her throat. "The school will be armed to ensure you stay put. Additional security will also be deployed."

I lean forward. "Hold up! You're getting security because of conspiracy theorists?"

"Yes, conspiracy theorists, radicals you've exposed your identity and location to."

"I have nothing that interests them."

"You have everything, and you don't even know it!" Sage Cameron shouts.

"I don't even have a fraction of what I want." I stand up.

"What you want?" Sage Cameron sighs to the ceiling. "There's nothing else I could possibly give you."

Heat bubbles in my chest. It urges my fists to clench. "Admit it!"

"Admit what?" Sage Cameron asks.

"Revenirs are real, and you both know it! You both know they are the ones deep in the canals and you're afraid that's where I went!" When I'm done shouting, my breath has outrun me. I'm scared but too angry to apologize—too fed up to backtrack. They need to say it.

Greta's eyes are blank. "If you need any goods. You will tell Dama Hadley and she will make note and order them for pick up." Sage Cameron keeps typing like I've said nothing.

I scoff. "Can I go now?"

Greta says no, while Sage Cameron affirms I can.

I sling my book bag over my shoulder and storm to the door. "Thanks for wasting my time."

CHAPTER FIFTY-FIVE

GOING ROGUE

WHEN NIGHT FALLS, I prepare. Lights are low in the dorm. Every candle Alani has ever acquired is lit. It smells like a flower market and burned sage. "You're going to set the building on fire," I tell Alani as I weave sections of my hair into cornrows. Keeping clean and less descript stands to be the best for anonymity among Revenirs. No one will know my curls this way.

"True. That could be a thing if I weren't the mother of fire itself." Nicotine gum pops in Alani's curling mouth and the room goes black. On the count of three, every flame is relit, setting her aglow.

The final night curfew bell rings, demanding that we not only stay in our dorms, but resist using our gifts past this hour. Another way Sage Cameron has killed our teen bodily autonomy, and it's all because of me.

"You know what I'm talking about. What is that on the balcony?" I point to the silver tray set Alani threw out on the balcony floor. It's scorched, so are the leaves on it.

"Sage. I was burning sage."

"You were *torching* sage. That's not how you do it."

"It's how *I* do it." She shrugs. "I was hoping it'd cleanse your feelings about tonight's initiation."

338

I pretend I don't hear her, then sigh. "You know I'm not going to budge on this, Alani. I'm doing this for my friend."

"I'm your friend too."

"I know. That's why you're staying home."

"You're so stubborn. I can't deal with this."

"Then don't!"

Alani pops up. "Are you kidding me right now? I'm getting heat because I want to protect you. We helped you at Passage. You would've been done for if we didn't."

I pack my small bag with a small mirror, shell paste, coal paint, a makeup brush, and my dagger. I make sure to go sans the locket and wrap it in my silk headscarf. "Nice to know you think of me this way. That I'm weak and clumsy…a danger to everyone I love."

Alani's face wrinkles. "I never said that. What's going on?"

Our curtain panel flails from the wind and laps around my neck. I toss it away and head toward the balcony. "You don't have to say it, but it's what you're thinking. It's what all of you think."

"Alexia, stop!" Alani follows me.

I pat the outside wall. An invisible metal cloth catches my hand. Vinman netting. If Lucie is right, and if Nate identified my blade correctly, my dagger could cut through this. I grip the net in my hand and slice a hole down the side till I feel the trellis nailed in the wall beside the balcony. *It worked!* The trellis is wet from the light rain, but still sturdy and bolted to the ground and building. I can manage the climb down, I'm sure.

"Are you listening to me?" Her raspy voice breaks.

I study my route down. Beneath the grip of my combat boots, the marble balcony rail is slippery. One wrong move from it and this operation could be over. Only now do I realize Alani is still ranting and has been this entire time.

Rain slicks her tresses to her cheeks. "I've never thought of you that way. I swear. You're not some feral Varien."

For a moment, guilt pierces me for fighting with her when I'm really fighting my own demons. How can she color me her best friend when I've never shared all my shades with her?

"Maybe I am."

Alani wipes at her eyes. "She's doing all of this, you know? She's got the other spot Variens keepings tabs on if we use our gifts past that BS curfew she made—which is in twenty minutes, by the way. The layout outside…it's different. It'll be hard to get out."

I nod solemnly—even though I had no idea these weather and earthly changes were the *security* measures Sage Cameron meant to enforce. "I know." A served goodbye is somewhere in there. I head down with one leg and arm reaching toward the trellis. My fingers wrap around its metal. I swing my body to its base. Finding footing between so many doused ivy leaves and branches is awkward, but I find a rhythm as I climb down, concentrating on where to put my limbs, and not Alani.

"Be careful," I hear her say when I touch down on the lawn. "You've got to be careful."

Malveaux grounds feel less like home. Less permanent summer sanctuary prep school; more cold, dark, overgrown, rearranged, and watchful. The Knaves labyrinth and the topiaries have stretched around the entire campus. Something about the trees and earth below screams to my senses. Does the land have tabs on me?

"Got you!" someone says behind me. I turn. My stomach flips. It's Kyle.

CHAPTER FIFTY-SIX

LOVER, YOU SHOULDN'T HAVE COME

A PERFECT PICTURE COULDN'T be taken at a more imperfect moment. The guy I love sneaking around with is here when I *specifically* said don't be here. "Kyle, I don't need this right now." I hold up my hand between us and walk on, but the hand betrays me and folds as soon as he offers his touch.

"You're doing it again. You're scared." A light flashes from the window to the right of us. Kyle grabs me and we creep under windows till we get to the shadowed bank of Lake Moody. Something about the water doesn't vibe right, not with it bubbling.

"Don't do that!" I sneer.

"Do what?"

"Don't show up and screw up my plan."

Wind twirls the ends of his wispy hair exposing the lowliness of his brows. "What're you talking about? Wasn't I in the plan?"

"No."

He shakes his head. "That won't work on me."

"I don't care." I push away and walk toward the end of the academy. "I'm going to get what I need done so I can stand on the right side of history boldly this time, and I'm going to do it alone."

"Okay, this badass thing you do…shutting people out, it doesn't fix anything. The problem just gets worse. That's how you

341

end up regretting things." He bulldozes through the grass behind me. "I used to feel that. I'd be too afraid to ask for help or accept it because I didn't want to lose anyone else. Maybe they'd think I was crazy…maybe they'd get hurt or hurt me more. So, I shut down and my aunt forced me into therapy for years. And the most valuable thing I could've taken from it was to take the 'life jacket,' accept the help."

I stop in the shadow of a stretching oak and face him. His hands are in his pockets. He's freezing in his black thermal, yet still prepared with a backpack, ready to follow through on his promise with me. I've wished for this help for *so* long—from everyone—that having it registers as fragile to me, something I want to place on a pedestal and admire on a Sunday afternoon. These ride or die friends, these coveted collectibles, they're who must be preserved. It's a hard trap to escape from.

"You sure you feel like risking your life again tonight?" I pass my surrendering off as a joke.

"I'm finishing this thing with you, then I'm taking you to Blossom Ball."

"You don't want to take me." I shake my head.

"I do…more than anything."

"Well, I don't want to go."

"Why not?"

"I'm not in the mood." I fight the idea of keeping these words caged. "Because…my mom will miss the moment."

"I see." He drops his head then gets back to being watchful. "What's she like?"

"She's…elegant, everything I want to be in life. The best therapist. There's nothing I couldn't tell her. Most people are afraid to come to their parents when they're in trouble or wrong. I never felt that way with her."

"Until now," Kyle corrects.

What an incredibly dry pill to swallow. "Yes, until now."

"Have you thought about how she feels? Must be pretty hard for your mom to lose her daughter. Same for your siblings. Does letting them know you're all right ever cross your mind?"

All I ever do is think about my family—especially my parents. Knowing I'll never see them again and have their forgiveness kills me. "Honestly, Kyle, I'm sure they hate me."

"They hate Set."

"No, you don't get it. It was me. I injured my dad beyond repair. ME." Kyle's face drops, but I've been holding this in for so long, I can't stop the words from spouting. "It was an accident. I tried to get Set. So I ran! And if I go back, the country will hunt me down. My father's legacy will be—"

"Fine. Maybe after all this time…he's healed, and your family may end up accepting you and loving you unconditionally. Maybe they'll understand."

"You don't know Sylvia and Senator Edward Jacobs. They aren't simple people," I tell him.

I don't want to continue the conversation. So, I look up at the night sky and let my face meet the sprinkling raindrops before the ground does.

"Look, Lex, I'm not trying to push you into something you don't want to do. But I do care about you, and from what you tell me about your family…I don't think…well…I know they miss you. Maybe the distance and space has made them rethink things. You being a Varien is better than the idea of you not breathing at all. *You* know you're safe here. *They* have nothing. Trust me, ignorance isn't bliss. Not when it comes to things like this."

Here I am, running away from a family that's always protected me while my boyfriend would give anything to know his. I'm horrible. I have no choice but to fold. "I'll think about it…," I tell him.

"Good. Where you headed to first?" Kyle asks me with such softness. I fight the impulse inside of me, the one that urges me to take on these wars alone.

"Lucie's."

There's a grin on his face—the match that lights the prickling in my chest and warms the dead caves of my heart. He steps closer, then vines his hands around mine. A kiss in the dark sets me completely free from the enemy of me. I take the life jacket, and we creep around from the lip of Lake Moody to the doorstep of Lucie's madshop.

CHAPTER FIFTY-SEVEN

THE MADSHOP

"WHO GOES THERE?" THE door to Lucie's madshop is cracked, giving us a peek of her packrat space.

"Luce?" Kyle unwraps from me and moves the door aside. An animal screeches. Kyle checks below. Much to our shock, there's a robotic cat with its paw squished under Kyle's sneaker.

"Excuse you!" Lucie dashes over to collect the metal cat. She cradles it as if it really witnessed pain. "Are you okay, Perry?" she coos. The cat has one screen for eyes, all it shows are two *x*'s.

Kyle is confused. "Does he need some oil?"

"He's not made of tin, Kyle." Lucie rolls her eyes.

"What're you doing here anyway, Lex?" Kyle pushes me to explain.

"I hit Lucie up earlier to cop a few things to help with tonight."

Lucie is a bit more irritable than I'm used to. Very serious and not her giddy and enthusiastic self. I don't think I like her this way. "Does he know about everything?" Lucie nods at Kyle.

"Huh?" I'm confused but catch on quickly. Lucie still doesn't know what we really have going on—so my lie about manticores is still my meal ticket. "Oh…that. Yeah. He knows."

"Ohkayyyy…" Kyle's eyes widen in surprise. "Interesting. Hey, Luce, how'd you get past Dama Hadley tonight?"

"If I told you, I'd have to kill you." Lucie's serious face stiffens. "Well…more like maim you, but you get the idea." She glares at Kyle.

I take a look around as we make our way inside. "So, this is the famous madshop?" I say.

"Yeah…I don't really like that name. People only gave it to me because they think I do weird things in here."

One person's weird is someone's regularity. Hard to imagine how one could view things like Swiss army pocket watches and spoons as mobiles or old metal beakers as an IV of compost for plants, but Lucie does. "What would you prefer it be called?"

Under the dim ceiling light, she winds down and sets her robot on her pool table/working desk. "My basement."

"Well." I smile. "I really like your basement."

"Thanks."

"How'd you get your own office here?" I ask.

"It helps to be rich." Kyle cups his hands like he's whispering but says everything loud. After Lucie huffs, she stays quiet, allowing Kyle to elaborate. "Her parents built an entire wing of Malveaux in her honor when we were little and made a room just for her to have once she got admitted."

"Oh." I try to hide my shock. "Well, you're lucky. It's cool here. Reminds me of Greta's."

"You've been there?" Lucie's enthusiasm all but jumps from her.

Kyle obnoxiously clears his throat and kicks my foot with his. "Lex, what is up with your feet right now?"

I frown. "You're the one that kicked me."

"Only because you're about to *walk* into something we don't have time for." He winks harshly.

"Okay?" I don't know what he's up to now, so I ignore him and get back to talking to Lucie. "Yes, I came through there after she found me. Have you?"

"Oh, no." Lucie's freckles begin to sparkle like a calibrating machine. "I never have a good enough reason to go on realm leave. I made a self-driving car just so I could travel out during full moons, because I can't drive and the trolley system can't do what I want it to do. That's why this will be a game changer." From an old trunk, she pulls the neon lit backpack I've seen her lugging around the academy.

"What is that?" I ask.

Kyle mumbles, "An hour of talking that we don't have."

"The Midray! It can transport any party to and from realms without dependency on the moon."

"Of course...," Kyle mumbles. "It's never been tested on any Varien for safety and hasn't been approved for use...but yeah, it's genius."

"Why do you always say that, Kyle?"

He throws his hands up to shrug. "I'm just looking out for you, Luce. Don't want you going to juvie or anything for accidentally hurting someone."

Lucie shrinks in the wake of that sentence and tucks her Midray machine back in its home. "I can tell you about it another time, Alexia...just don't bring him around."

"Love you too, Luce." Kyle smirks.

Sweet Lucie mouths, "I love you" back like it's painful yet true. "So, what's up with you two? Is everything okay?"

"Yeah, I was just wondering if you had any fermented virgin apples. There weren't any in the apothecary when I checked this morning," I say.

Lucie doesn't even need to ponder. "Are you kidding? Those things are essential. I've got a closet stuffed with them."

"Perfect! Can you spot us a jar?"

"For sure! Is this for the manticores?"

Kyle leans his head forward, gobsmacked with humor.

"Yeahhhhhhh...I found a pack. I know exactly where their den is," I answer apprehensively.

Lucie nearly catches the Holy Ghost and throws her hand to the ceiling. "Dah! You'll need this tranquilizer gun. Both of you! Fermented virgin apples act as a sedative in manticores. You won't harm them this way, and they won't harm you. Oh, this is so perfect."

"I'm sorry…did you say manticores?" I see Kyle's teasing smile and urge him to control himself before Lucie turns back around. He's too amused but diffuses at the sound of a cocked gun. "Whoa! Luce! You said no harm."

"Sweet Lucie" turns around looking more like Rocket Racoon on a power trip with one gun in each hand. "These are harmless. What do you mean?"

There's a drying effect in my mouth. The idea of holding a gun, even with a supernatural power given to me, seems like playing God. It's not an organic weapon or gift. It's something man-made with one purpose.

"That's a gun!" Kyle holds his hair back.

"Oh, this isn't a gun, silly. Well, it essentially is. I mean, I found some information on the IVnet and made a blueprint and basically got carried away with scrap metal. It's constructed to dispel injected bullets, like these." Lucie holds a handful of needle-pointed bullets in her hand. "I filled these with the fermented virgin apple elixir and they're good to go. Precise and effective."

"Hmm…perfect. You scare me, but this is perfect." Kyle takes the guns and bullets as Lucie slides them across the pool table and hides them into our hips.

"Is that all you need?" Lucie inquires.

"Yes," I respond.

"Wait, no!" Kyle's brows knit together. "Lex, how do you expect to get there?"

"Umm. I was…going to nab your bike."

"My *bike*?"

"Yes, that's your bike," Lucie chimes in—because she can never mind the business that pays her.

"I have no choice," I clarify. "Andre's is pretty much not an option after the flood."

"The flood. What is this, Genesis? It was just a small stream." Kyle takes a deep breath. "Lucie, I have one more thing to ask," he says.

Lucie shares another braced grin. "Yes, anything you want."

"All this stuff is great, but my bike is conspicuous and loud. Manticores, yeah?" Kyle goes on. "They'll pick up on the sound. So, right now we're nothing without the bird."

That's when Lucie's smile drains from her face. "You're not asking me to give you—"

"Yes, I am."

"Can't you teleport?"

"I can teleport a lot of places, but teleporting there isn't an option…I've never seen this other entrance. So, we have to follow another set of instructions. It's kinda dangerous."

"But the Hoverwagon hasn't been used since my robotics championship. You know it can't run without a computer operator, right? You would need me to come along."

"Yes, I know."

"Kyle, that's a big ask. I-I-I must decline."

Her denial makes this mission more complicated. As I cover my sighs, Kyle soothes me with a back rub. He knows I'm losing optimism I'm afraid I'll never get back. "We understand, Luce. Thanks anyway," he tells her.

"Wait, I can do it!" Lucie declares. "There's a way around this. I can hack into the system with my powers and control the car from here. Take the Hoverwagon…take it."

"That's a lot, Lucie. Wouldn't that tire you?" I ask.

"To an extent, but I want to help. You two are my friends."

Kyle pulls Lucie over the table for a hug. "Why didn't you just say that? Phew!"

Lucie pats him on his shoulder. "You guys better get going. The Hoverwagon is locked in the shed next to the menagerie. I highly suggest taking this map drone. It's not smart to teleport out of Malveaux right now. Sage Cameron…she's moved things around and has spot Variens monitoring if we use our powers on campus, so I don't recommend teleporting until you make it through to the main road. You could get in a spiky situation…pun intended! Better get a move on before day breaks."

Kyle and I, a duo of chance and courage, take the map drone, slip out of the small basement, and thank Lucie.

"Of course. Oh…and what's your diversion?" Lucie inquires. She waits for our response but we are two deers in headlights. We most certainly do not have a diversion—which causes Lucie to face-palm. "You need a diversion! The flora will snitch on you in a hot minute!"

Kyle and I exchange glances. Great, one more obstacle. How did I miss this?

"You're so lucky to have me," Lucie plays. "I'll donate my physical presence this one time. I'll go out there a few minutes after you make your way. The plants will have definitely alerted Sage Cameron by then, and when she or another teacher show up, I'll tell them I left Perry outside earlier somewhere and can't find him. And if that's the case, his battery would have him moving for hours without me powering him down. Therefore, the plants will keep warning Sage Cameron about a foreign body on their grounds, but Sage Cameron will tune them out some because it's most likely Perry."

"Uhh…Perry?" I ask.

"My cat!"

"Your robot," Kyle corrects.

I reach over and cover Kyle's mouth. We don't need to lose our arsenal ally. "That's right." I look down at Perry the cat as he purrs and curls his artificial tail around Lucie's ankle. "But…won't you get in trouble for being out? I don't want that."

Lucie swats the air with her hand. "I'll be out looking for my AI cat. That's about as innocent as you can get. They'll go easy on me." She smiles like she knows this all too well and uses her veil of naïveté (and money) to her advantage often.

"Thanks again, Lucie," I say. "Honestly, you just saved us."

"You're helping The Grove by doing this for us," Kyle tags on. "We may be the ones facing these—"

"Manticores!" I burst before he slips up.

"Manticores...*yup*. We may be facing these *manticores* head on, but we wouldn't be able to get where we need to be without your help. Thanks for being a good friend."

Lucie's cheeks wrinkle back to her ears. A smile is permanently etched into her face.

"How can we pay you? We can't take this for free," I say.

"Baby, no." Kyle tucks his mouth in before turning to Lucie and pointing at me. "We can absolutely take the Hoverwagon for free."

"One: don't call me baby. Two: she's going to be moving a piece of machinery with her mind for a big chunk of time."

As we ready to debate, Lucie makes things easier. "I don't need the money."

"So what do you prefer?" I ask.

"I was hoping you could do my makeup for Blossom Ball, Alexia? And maybe you, Kyle...could get me a date? With Erik Townsend?"

If mischief could be a person, it'd be Kyle. "Done and done!"

We shake on it and make way into Malveaux's storming wilderness.

"Wait, who will teach me how to dance? I'm not too physically inclined," she says over the sound of cracking thunder, scurrying behind us.

With a head full of dampened wavy hair, Kyle whips himself around. The moon's light touches the bow of his lips, highlighting the smile I love. "Don't worry about that! You made a deal with the greatest," he replies, pointing at himself.

THE KNAVE'S LABYRINTH

THE SWIRLING SKY IS the only constant outdoors. Stained in shades of violet and obsidian, I wonder if Sage Cameron wants the sky to swallow everything below it. Each step and I make through the coarse grass along Lake Moody makes the weather change. It's clear our presence on Malveaux's lawn screams intrusion and the elements waste no time deterring us with heavy rain, lightning, and wind. "How are we supposed to get out of here? I can barely make out a clear view." I squint through the rain.

Kyle takes the map drone from his pocket and checks its screen. "Let me see…try this." He guides from the back of my hand and helps me toss the drone above. The machine spins and camouflages in the air before landing back in my hand. It folds back into its handheld hexagon shape with a projecting screen that shows us a local map.

Kyle throws his hood on and checks the screen. He leads me to a familiar and strange site, the Knaves labyrinth. "To make it to the main roads, we need to head through here."

"Are you serious? The labyrinth?"

"Well, according to the map, we don't have many options. If we go through the front gate, the faculty will catch us in record time. And neither of us have the guts to brave it through that crazy moat surrounding the other half of the school. The labyrinth is the best out of the three."

"It's true!" Lucie jump scares us. We turn around and there she is, short and bell shaped, drenched with a yellow raincoat that flares out at the ends. Her thick tortoise shell framed glasses are fogged up at the end of her wide button nose. I almost forgot she was our cover. "It's the only way through."

Kyle reinforces the option. "Look, I'm not happy about this either," he says. "Teleporting would be my first choice but… I can't. If you want to go back, we can."

The labyrinth, and its spilling fog, towers a few feet over our heads. Branches protrude from the boxwood topiaries and cast abstract shadows. Right-angled hedges are now jagged with untamed foliage, and what used to be a clear path down the middle is now reshaped with curves and sharp turns. I stare at the dark and deep nothing of the labyrinth's passageways.

"It's your choice." Kyle speaks between gulps of rushing wind.

With one foot planted in front of the other, I've already made up my mind. "Let's go!" I shut my eyes and press onto the marshy, padded lawn.

Lucie shouts, "Good luck!"

Kyle follows two faithful steps behind until we're in the first corner of the maze.

"What's up? Why aren't we moving?" he says.

I'm too busy fiddling with the map, restarting it in hopes of it correcting itself. "I-I-I don't know. It's weird. It's like the labyrinth is changing."

Kyle studies the hologram map. "What do you mean changing?"

"At first it told me to turn right. Look to your right, there's nothing but hedges! Then it said to turn left up ahead, but the same thing happened. There's nowhere to go but straight."

"Then let's go straight," Kyle says matter-of-factly.

A sound alerts me to check behind us. "Wait…wasn't the entrance over here? It's closed!" The view of the academy's distant lights is no more. What's left is a shadowed path leading to a wall of ivy and boxwood.

"That's interesting," Kyle faintly says.

"This is exactly why I should've had a better plan. Sage Cameron has gone nuts. She's created a damn botanical security trap! The plants are against us."

"That's ridiculous. We live here. The plants know who we are rig—"

A swarm of searing arrow-headed darts shoot past our heads and stab the green wall behind us. I scream in terror. Touching the newly sliced skin over his Adam's apple, Kyle swallows his remaining words. He squirms at the sight of his blood-stained hand. The dart nicked him good, not too deep, but just enough to make an impression.

"What the heck?" Kyle pats above his head to remove one of the many threatening objects. "It's just my imagination, yeah. I'm psyching myself out," he sings. It becomes harder to believe this once his hands find the offenders. Kyle draws his arm down and inspects a shark-fin-size thorn pinched in his fingers.

"Please tell me that isn't what I think it is," I cry. "Now would be a great time to run." I look to Kyle for our next move. After all, he's my partner in crime, the hero of all teenage heroes.

"Uh, yeah…okay," Kyle pants with the heart of a wimp before bolting into the deceiving darkness. Taking advantage of the map, I run ahead of Kyle, as it guides us through the labyrinth before the hedges rearrange themselves. We're outwitting our botanical foe with each stride, but the labyrinth thirsts for our fall and won't stop chucking throngs of thorns till we give in.

"Argh!" I wail upon getting struck. Kyle drops down to help as I yank the hooked thorn from the middle of my thigh.

"C'mon, Lex, keep it moving," he encourages me.

Another thorn grazes Kyle's cheek before he catches a second one in his shoulder. An earth-splitting rumble shakes under our feet and scatters us from one another. I crouch on my pad of broken earth to shield my face from windswept branches and leaves. Through the space between my forearms, I see a pack of gargantuan vines sprout from the wet soil and stretch to the sky. We quiver as the vines curl under themselves and aim down. Like ropes, they wrap and constrict their green stalks around us.

Thunder mutes our screams as the vines' movement jerk us through the air. Once the vines shrink closer to their roots, their predatory velocity slows. Kyle and I wriggle to free ourselves. "Where are we?" I glance around.

Humid, wild, and saturated with ruby-hued flowers, the setting looks like home and a foreign land all at the same time. Flickers of lightning illuminate the space, giving Kyle all the answers. "We're in the rose garden!" he says.

Refusing to get squeezed to death by a damn plant, I try my hardest to ignite the pads of my fingers. Living is the first priority, after all. I can't save Sarai if I'm dead. "I think I can stun them into letting us go."

"No!" Kyle reprimands. "Do that and it's over! Sage Cameron will be here in minutes! On top of that, are you crazy?"

"Crazy would be securing the school with meat-eating plants! Crazy would be waiting to get killed!"

"We gotta think of something else!"

"Like what?"

"I don't know! Think of something!" A rattling noise grows louder as fanged rosebuds move closer. Venom slides down their saber teeth as they hiss.

"I may…there may be something!" I holler as the vines squeeze around my chest.

"Do it! Hurry!" The roses, studded in spikes and loaded with rows of pointy teeth, proceed with their attack.

"Uh-uh-I-I'm Alexia Jacobs. This is Kyle! We-uh, we go to this school! Don't you remember me? I sit here and read all the time."

The rosebud facing him remains unchanged. It unhinges its jaws like a snake and edges closer with the speed of honey. The putrid smell of devoured raw meat gusts from its mouth.

"Lex, these things don't remember you! Next plan! Next plan!" Kyle says anxiously. He keeps a steady eye on the roses and trembles.

"We were just here the other day…uh…studying. Right, Kyle?"

"Yes!" Kyle shouts. "Hurry!"

"It was warm but cloudy and we had books around us…and… we had music…" The longer I wait, the faster their momentum grows. "M-m-music playing from my watch." Suddenly, my brain floods with details of that day in the labyrinth. I have only one other thing to try. It's so ridiculous but trying is the only way out of this. "We played a song you all loved. Do you remember? 'Ghost in the Machine' by SZA?"

The rose in front of me comes closer.

"Alexia!" Kyle screams as the roses accelerate, bringing their faces down to our level. The buds snap their jaws.

"Just wait!" I flinch. "I'll sing it, okay?" A song rings from the fears in my heart. There isn't much room to breathe through the notes as the vines rope around my rib cage. I don't sound the best. My voice is cracking and speeding through parts SZA lingers on with so much ease. The roses cringe with each off-key note. I just do what I can with what I have, because Sarai is there in my mind's view again. The one this is all for.

The rosebuds' velvet petals fold over their fangs as they move backward. Something about the melody tickles their senses. They *do* remember! Showing its fondness, the rosebud opposite of me tilts its head and welcomes me to continue. The rose that holds me loosens its grip some. I go on and crank out the sweet chorus. The rosebuds face each other and break out into sounds of endearment and applause. Kyle is speechless. When I hit the closing note, the now docile vines bow their heads, untie us from their grips, and place us on our feet. I notice the wind is a light breeze and the sky has tightened up its downpour into a sprinkle.

"Hey, thanks!" Kyle winks at his petal-faced plant. In an instant, he also claps at me. "That's my lady right there."

"Thanks," I say to all of them. Mutters of relief bounce between Kyle and me as we prepare to pave our path to the main road.

Something nags at me and demands addressing. "Oh, uh… excuse me?" I turn back to the rosebuds. "Can we keep this between us? I'm sure Sage Cameron told you to squeal at the first sign of intrusion. I respect that. I really do. But snitching makes our plan difficult. Nothing will work if we get stopped. Please don't tell her we're leaving the academy."

The buds huddle together and deliberate. Luckily for us, they promise by nodding and return to their business.

"You're the best. I'll sneak you some compost when I get back!" Kyle jokes and clicks his tongue.

Fighting through a list of wounds and aches, we navigate to the bridged main road. Although the labyrinth isn't nearly as crazy as what the Revenirs have in store, its danger serves as the proper warm-up for the main event.

Kyle gives me dreamy gaze and nudges my arm. "What can't you do?"

I let out a dry chortle. "Sing"

"What? Stop…you're a siren," Kyle quips with a smile. He mimics a broken note. "That's how you lured me in, isn't it?"

I punch him twice in the shoulder. "You wish."

CHAPTER FIFTY-NINE

THE NIGHT PARADE

"LUCIE, HOVER DOWN! SLOW creep! Slow creep!" Kyle's voice cracks into a holler. Kyle's trying his hardest to remain supportive of Lucie and her navigation skills by only giving her directions. She's a genius for what she's accomplished—a flying, old mini-wagon with turbines that runs on solar energy, much like everything in The Grove, and lunar energy at night. Genius. Other than that, there's nothing else nice to say, and it's best to leave harsh criticism unsaid. After all, Lucie did us one hell of a favor by telekinetically hacking into her creation and steering through the thick of a strange forest. No one else would've been willing to do the same. I just wish she'd handle the car with a little more finesse.

"Everything is spinning," I groan through my fingers.

The bulky car rockets a few feet past our destination, causing us to thrust forward.

"*Sorry,*" Lucie apologizes sweetly through the radio.

Kyle drops his head between his knees. "It's cool, Luce."

"*Do you want me to quiet the engine? I have a mute feature!*"

"Oh, not now. It's not like we were asking to be undetected or anything," Kyle jokes.

I take over and plead into the car's radio. "Land into that dip ahead, please. Park right over there between those two bent redwoods."

"You got it, Alexia." We finally fuse back to land and tell Lucie to stay close in case we need a return flight. Kyle tells her to get some rest and Lucie agrees. *"Start the radio when you get back. I'll be married to mine, so I can hear you. Go get 'em, guys!"* She unlinks her mind from the motor and dashboard. Kyle pockets the car keys. Everything deads.

"Married?" Kyle mouths.

I giggle and work with the moonlight shining through the window to paint him as a pretty corpse. My balance is still tossed, making the lines and shapes less human and more revenant. The paint is always fitting on him, like an old body of skin.

When it's my turn, he complains about covering my beauty marks in paint. Before he strokes the coal and ivory shades over my mouth, he kisses me—a nice firm, soft, tight hug of a kiss. "I hope we'll get to do that again," he says, his voice low. I fight the urge of another round and let the brush of cold paste make me a villain.

"What time will the caravan be here?" Kyle asks.

I rummage through my satchel for my watch. "Eleven thirty. The cadets named the landmarks they'd pass on their way in. Twisted Towers were named for that time."

Kyle checks out the window. Two amber redwoods weld around one another like curling vines. "Should be easy to teleport back to."

"It's eleven thirty-four."

He hears the anxiety in my tone. "Give a few minutes, there's no way we could miss them. You've got everything you need?"

I've got the tranquilizer gun in my hip, Kyle has the other, and when I search back into my satchel, I wonder if my dagger should join it.

"Take it. Take everything you need…," Kyle tells me.

As I admire the blade, a spot of white shines on it. I turn back and crawl to the window. Floating, glowing orbs—petite moons, I think—grow closer, and behind them a parade of skeletons bodied in black.

I hike up my dress to secure the dagger into its holster. "That's them. Let's go."

We cloak up, inch around massive tree trunks, and make way till the tail of the young Revenir recruits sliver by. From the tree's shadows, we move, and sew ourselves onto the end. Two agents of change hiding in a Trojan horse, ready to burn it all down.

CHAPTER SIXTY

MIDAUTUMN'S NIGHT

THE MANY FEET IN the caravan scratch against the dirt—a sound bite so fitting against buzzing cicadas and ominous songs. "From underground we come, for Eve's will be done," they hum. The words don't bake in my tongue. I don't mean them and being in the back takes away the pressure of saying them. Kyle learns the song as parts repeat, and I check to make sure he is him and not an authentic recruit. We walk for what seems more than a mile, till trees circle a clearing of mounded ground. Vines rope over the top like clamoring snakes. The recruits at the head of the caravan partner in speaking the infamous greeting at the vine ridden mound.

The hanging vines squelch, shrink, and crawl until a dark entry way is visible. Shivers rock my spine when the déjà vu hits. We were just here, the four of us—and we were lucky to make it out.

In the fog, our parade follows the buoyant little moons inside what seems like an old sewer—a direction we didn't come through the first time. Rats scurry across the edges. A stench of sour, humid waste steams into my nose and I battle between holding and stealing breaths. Can't look too dramatic. Can't show I'm soft.

The pale moons usher us through the sewer, and into the foyer where the Grand Skull interrogated us. I screen around for

361

him, but there's no lingering Revenirs mixing like before—just the shadow of lonely flames dancing against the dusty ground. Now, in single file, we funnel back where we started: the cavern.

Drips from dangling, broken, defunct pipes and stalactites echo like instruments through speakers. The thick air is damper than I remember. Uncomfortably warm. The puddle we wade through is murky, a browned scarlet red with a hint of zinc, all of which makes my skin feel scratched at.

Set's *Midautumn Night's Dream*, maybe. He waits on the ridge of the balcony, cracking pistachios open. I study him for a few seconds—maybe he's not hiding all his cards. But then his hungry, mismatched eyes catch me, and I panic to run back out of his web.

"Look ahead," Kyle tells me with master level ventriloquism. I can barely see his mouth moving. I spot Set fly down from the balcony. Those wings of his could be beautiful with their long span of gold feathers, except there are gaps in their rows. Stains and dirt smudges, blood on the tips.

"I should apologize," he breaks through a smug grin. "The minutes got away from me. Got a little excited with the offerings." A trickling sound grows louder in my head. I scan around and find a stream of red spilling from the balcony and into the pond.

Sarai, please God, tell me it wasn't Sarai.

A Revenir sloshes by for the stage and I snap back sober. There are Revenirs bordering the pond—knees to the floor with their hands in the red water.

Set traces their perimeter. His brows are boastful above the bowed heads. Crazed humming rocks the cavern so loud, vibrations send ripples through the pond.

"For the reclaim, the right, the riot, live by night!" Set starts the chant. His wings fan crests and waves into the pond till the red dust I wish I could forget seeing in Mercy Bay mists from the water and swirls into each Revenir's nose. They shiver and convulse. Some wretch. Then little by little as Set's eyes color crimson, the Revenir's veins blacken. One of them stands and raises a hand at the torches and moons and vanquishes the light. Another across from him ignites it back. A woman Revenir forms an arm of rock and goes to clock her neighbor but causes a big bang when her fist meets an igneous hard face. They cackle madly. Fucking cult.

Set's eyes cut around. He's happy to have an audience tonight. The grin has yet to leave his scarred face. "Don't worry. If you're worthy, you'll be here soon," he says. "Splicing is a Revenir's lifeblood…an intimate process. You've got to know what you're doing—how to cut the right veins…you've got to know why." He lights a cigarette. "Do you?"

The drip from the broken dangling pipe sounds louder now.

No one in the pond speaks fast enough. This alarms Set and causes a stir with the other Revenirs.

"Because a Revenir is a soldier." Kyle steps from the shadows. "A soldier is only as good as his weapons. Louis Malveaux believed there's no greater weapon or species than an elite Varien."

Set's chin juts to keep hold of the cigarette between his lips. "Man over here is right. There's nothing better than an elite Varien. We came from this thing, we built it up…but we don't own anything. Not with Wonts choking our resources, drugging us, muting our cells, and sectioning us to badlands." He palms a mini moon in his hands, grazes a stare over it, then blows smoke right into its face. The moon goes translucent and disintegrates into a sea of stars.

"There's no space for mediocrity in the realm we live in. There's no in between either, only our side and theirs." The bleeding stars chalk up to the dust rain that piled in my hand at the Belle Rues. They sculpt into mounds and thin in other places. A hand holding a gun is formed and a bullet bursts from its barrel at a figure the dust rain creates. Set controls this from the palm of his wind-generating hand. He stirs scene after scene of Wonts fighting in the streets and in wars. He conjures images of trashed oceans and the natural disasters built from their pollution. Corrupt politicians speak from podiums and rile crowds. I spot presidents and prime ministers, but my heart thuds when the dust washes over into the form of my father.

"The greater good must be protected!" he echoes. On and on, the sounds tune like a radio. Revenirs seep from the walls of offices and bedrooms while their depicted victims are sleep. They kill. A snap of the neck or suffocation. I shut my eyes to save myself from knowing all their ways.

There's applause to which Set bows his head. "Our most prized jobs. We've kept Varien worlds safer by exterminating the corrupt, avenging sins, but there's higher levels to reach. Cleansing must be brought to the Wonts. Their systems are contaminated with corruption, so much so, they've sought the only ones capable of quenching it—us. That's where all of you will be needed. We'll do their bidding. Take their hit assignments. Come out the cage when they want…for now."

Their bidding. Was my dad part of the bidding that day in Mercy bay? Is that what brought Set to us? The spiral his information throws me in is steep, but I can't go there. I can't spin out of control, so I refocus and clear my head to think only of Sarai.

The dust Set manipulated curves in waves and draws an army of monsters charging and eviscerating the Normal government's military with their powers. Explosions turn the dust aglow, blinding all recruits as the little moon Set broke reforms.

Cheers erupt and a chant of "Reclaim!" rattles the floor. Kyle joins. I'm apprehensive. Set's colleagues name him a genius and praise him. They raise their hands above and rejoice like he's really the reason and way for a Varien revival.

Set waves for their volume to fade. His pleased face stiffens. "The time will come…if we're smart, patient, and ready. The time comes closer with every splice."

"Mother Eve's splice!"

"Mother Eve!"

"Her blood is our right!"

"Is it true we'll never have to splice again?"

Rogue hoots and claps are mixed among the black of the cavern.

The Revenir beside Set, with a thick, scarred neck, nods. "Yes. Her cells have no ceiling, even after transferring to us. They'll evolve till we die. Imagine that, the list of capabilities you'll have in minutes till you meet your maker."

"We want it now!" a Revenir yells.

Set walks to a place that cloaks half of him as the other half is tinted bronze beneath the little moon. "Soon…the wait isn't much longer." I catch his head turning toward the balcony with numerous lined strikes on its exterior. A countdown of sorts. Five numbers remain…to what? Nadir?

"Till her blood rains down this cup and fills us," someone shouts.

I stare down at the end of the balcony. What Set calls a cup is a bulb-shaped structure stained in the mixed blood of other Variens. A drain connects to the end of the cup and continues draining blood in to the pond. I grow nauseous. Ringing punches my ears.

"The other bodies will do as we wait. Grand Skull," Set calls. The Grand Skull I know as the creepy guarde, Irving Rockwell, comes forward. I pray he doesn't notice us from afar. "Show them around the sacrifice inventory. The cells are almost full. Each finalist from tonight has their choice of first splice."

Rockwell's smile stretches crooked. He summons us to follow with the click of his tongue. I shudder—from the damp chilling air and the stabbing reminder of blood soaking into my ankles. Recruits walk in a line that curves like a snake. I'm the last slithering piece to pass Set.

"After you," he says as I go, yellow eyes hooked on me.

CHAPTER SIXTY-ONE

DETOUR

OUR SERPENT'S LINE HAS two heads. One Revenir at the front, and another at its end. We trail on through the cells. Imprisoned Variens are curled inside like wounded animals. A rancid stench of urine overwhelms my nose. Blood splatters are stained into the concrete beneath my feet. Loud clinking noises echo through the hall, adding to the cacophony and sobs. With all that we've seen, there's no Sarai. Where do they have her?

"Go!" a Revenir commands Kyle, nudging her head forward to put him in check. Other recruits turn to stare. Kyle is going to get us killed.

"Bio break," he states.

"What?"

"May I have a bio break? I drank a good load of water before getting here. No way will I make it through the night with a swollen bladder."

"Then you may not make it at all," the Revenir mocks.

"Ah, hmm." As Kyle processes the Revenirs bladed words, the Revenir with the neck scar approaches.

"First Skull, everything okay?" he says.

"I think so, Skull Sargeant. This recruit forgot his place and asked for restroom access." Her coal lined lips purse.

366

The man beside her folds his hands together. His hooded cape is lined with grey silk. "Isn't it everyone's place to use the restroom?" he asks. The paint on his face is less smooth, it's cratered in patches. When the First Skull fails to respond, the Skull Sargeant raises his eyebrows. "We're Revenirs, not a damn day camp."

"Right, Skull Sargeant." We see him break off and enter a tunnel on the right. Kyle nearly jumps to the restroom. *What luck.*

"Would I be able to go also?" I ask timidly.

The Revenir huffs at me.

Kyle swings right into the restroom. He's waiting for me. I know it.

"One at a time," the Revenir checks me.

"I don't think I can manage the wait."

When I step away, the Revenir blocks me. "One."

"First Skull," a rumbling deep voice grows near. The scar-throated Revenir, he's back and walking toward us. "Are you intentionally ignoring my advice?"

"No, Skull Sargeant. I simply intend to keep my eyes on this end of the recruits. It wouldn't be wise to allow more than one recruit in the restroom."

"Are you calling me an idiot?"

"No, Skull Sargeant."

"You are. You must think I'm a fool."

"I…I'm merely enforcing protocol."

"And I create the protocol. Don't question me again." The Skull Sargeant glares. The muscles in his face tighten like a fist. This is not a problem the First Skull wants. It's not a problem I want to be in the middle of. The Skull Sargeant steps aside, allowing me to pass.

I scurry before he changes his mind, and when I barge into the restroom there are no feet belonging to the legs of Kyle Pereira-Phoenix in any stall.

A dull pop sounds behind me. It rattles a stall door.

"Hello?" No answer comes, only the slushing of dripping water. Out walks my boy.

"Yeah, I really just teleported foot first into a toilet." His boot squeaks when he walks, and his right pant leg is soaked.

"Well, we were just standing in bloody water…I'm not sure which is worse."

"All of it is worse, Lex. Are you calling me an idiot?" He morphs into the Skull Sargeant who shrunk the First Skull with the pitch of his voice.

"I knew it was you. Smart."

"You didn't. You could barely move." The comedic light inside his head clicks on. "Ah, because you knew it was me."

Our minds get on the same page. I don't need instructions or a warning to hold Kyle's hand. He squeezes mine and teleports us right outside of the pond's cavern—where we initially came from. The smoke he brings is a loud, gaudy feature that threatens the mission.

"I can't help it," Kyle says as my hand waves away the smoke. Only, he isn't him anymore—he's the Skull Sargeant again. Another Revenir walks by with no face paint, just the pallor of pale skin and black veins. Kyle fakes a few lines about the building, "teaching" me the origins of Revenir headquarters. It's annoying, much like his Malveaux tour, except the stakes are higher. We stroll on as low-key as we can.

I press the button on Lucie's infrastructure viewer. Knowing where we're going would help.

Down the way, I hear shoes scuffing. "Skull Sargeant?" The passing Revenir circles back, doubt tilts his chin.

Kyle tries not to glance my way. "Yes?"

"Done with labs? I didn't expect to see you out again till Nadir."

"Well…sometimes procrastination hits. I like observing the recruits. They have a good energy."

The Revenir tilts his head. "So locking yourself inside was said in jest?"

"More or less."

"With a recruit?"

"Oh. This one is a straggler. Somehow, she lost her way and I'm trying to locate Rockwell."

The Revenir teases a face of suspicion. "Grand Skull," he corrects.

"Yes, the Grand Skull. Excuse me. Isolation has already done me in."

There's no response this time from the other Revenir. The back and forth has stopped and is replaced with a cold sizing up.

"As you were…" Kyle nods, leading me around the bend of a wall.

"Hey!" I hear the Revenir shout as we're in transit. But we are gone, running farther from where we started, and by the sounds of the stomping, in trouble. An alarm wails.

"In there. Hurry!" Kyle pushes me toward a random steel door below a teal light. We hurry over to it. I yank at the knob. When it gives in and opens, relief takes the weight from us.

"Yes," Kyle whispers. On the other side of the door, the room is vacant. Kyle morphs back into himself It takes a while for us to become whole again, to reclaim all the confidence we lost down the hall. "Did you see Sarai?"

"No. I don't get it. Why wouldn't she be in the cells? Where is she?"

A half-shadowed figure shuffles from behind a mounted wall of swords. With an arm outstretched and a threatening gifted hand aimed at Kyle's chest, the silver haired man creeps closer for a better look.

"Hands up! Now!" he yells. "I can break your bones without laying a hand on you. Hands up!"

Kyle's eyes widen as he brings himself to surrender. His body is practically preparing to disappear on its own. I can feel it.

"Calum?" the man queries, bringing his hand down and squinting his brown eyes. "Phoenix, is that you?"

Kyle's confused. "Have we met before?"

The silver haired man lowers his arm and studies Kyle's face. "Been a long time…"

The end of a blade pokes the right side of my neck. I'm dead where I stand. "Alexia?"

"…Sarai?"

She's well. Fresh-faced. Hair slicked into a high-braided ponytail. Skin free of bruises, gloriously pigmented by the baking sun. Not an ounce of flesh has thinned on her. She's clothed in a fitted turtleneck and matching black leggings. Sarai is well and she has never looked better.

Tears pool in my eyes. I'm breathless. Sarai drops her knife.

With his arms still raised, Kyle slides his back to the left of the wall, moving farther from the man.

"Even in all that paint, you look just like your father, Kyle."

Those words sizzle into my ears like acid.

CHAPTER SIXTY-TWO

THE WIZ

IT'S TRUE. KYLE DOES look like his father. Both share the same brawny jaw and cushioned bottom lip. And when Kyle skips a haircut, his hair hangs identical to his dad's and loosely curls at the ends. He's Calum Phoenix's clone and hearing himself called by his father's name is nothing new. It's a common thing to hear around The Grove, just not from a Revenir.

"What?" Kyle breathes heavy.

"I never thought I'd see you again. I mean—"

"Who are you?"

The man stands under the light and exposes the thick scar tissue around his throat. The same feature I've seen on him three times today. His face is almost clean of the face paint he wore earlier, but still stained with black smudges on his forehead and mouth. While his skin boasts a healthy shade of brown, he appeared decayed earlier, like his fellow Revenirs. "I'm Timothy Oswell. Your parents knew me as Oz."

"I don't think so. My parents wouldn't have known anyone from this sick place."

"Sick place?" Sarai frowns at Kyle, ready to gather him all the way up.

I'm confused right now. I want to cry so hard. I want to hug her, but the *her* I want is not *who* I'm staring at. We aren't linking like we used to.

Oz lets out an amused chuckle. "My man, so much you haven't been told."

"Sarai, why are you acting like this? Is he forcing you to be on their side?" My voice breaks.

"This is your sister?" Oz asks with an examining brow.

"She was like one." There's no delicacy in her movements anymore, no play in her voice. When she walks to me, she doesn't even waste a moment on my eyes. She grabs my wrist. "We need a word."

"No! No! I'm not going anywhere with you till you tell me what you're doing here. I've searched for you for so long! Risked everything to take you back home and you're in here…with him? Pointing a knife at me?!"

Guilt reshapes Sarai's face. She's there underneath it all—a drowning victim trapped beneath a floor of thick ice. In an instant her arms are wrapped around me, hugging me the way I've dreamed. I've found her. My girl. *I've got you.*

A booming knock at the door breaks us apart. It's loud enough to startle us over the alarm.

Oz motions for Kyle to stay. Sarai pulls me out of sight on the other end of the room.

"Apologies, Skull Sargeant." I hear when Oz cracks the door. "Checking in. Two recruits are missing and nowhere to be found. Skullman Reed reported a suspicious conversation with you. Everything okay?"

"Yes. Just working." Oz goes to shut the door and is blocked by another Revenir's boot. It's the Revenir who chased us in the pond.

"Skull Sargeant," the Revenir says.

Oz grumbles. "Let go of the door will you, Skullman? Unless you want nubs for fingers." The door slams and startles me.

Sarai offers me a chair beside a block of surveillance screens. The seat she opts for is a rolling stool. Less informal, her body language reads too comfortable. She knows where everything is. She's not afraid of Revenirs knocking at the door.

"Why're you here, Alexia?" she sasses me.

"You serious?"

Sarai cocks her head. Her full lips purse. "You will not make it here."

"And I don't want to. What the hell does that mean anyway?" I spit. Then it all clicks. "Sarai, do y-you live here?"

With the help of one hand, she cracks the knuckles on her other. She stalls, spacing out at the floor beneath us.

"This is not your home!" I tell her.

"I don't have a home anymore."

"So what is Sacramento then? What about your *mom*? What about *me*?"

Sarai's elbows press against her knees as she leans forward. "Gee, why don't you ask your dad, Alexia? Yeah, ask him about my mother! Ask him why she had to be arrested for sheltering me, a minor, her child. Ask him why I was never innocent till proven guilty—a girl he was fine claiming as his own till her blood muddied. Ask yourself why you never asked these things."

"I've always wondered these things. I've never stopped thinking them. That's what got me here…not being able to look myself in the mirror." I shake my head and wipe tears from my cheeks.

Sarai's eyes are void of sadness, as if she's exhausted all her tear supply. This is not the Sarai I've known. The thought of her change sends me spiraling and my hold on my tokens drops. A small ray of starlight peers from my jaw. The sensation pops me and fades back into my skin.

Sarai scoffs. "You're not really all here for me…are you? Looks like your blood is just as muddy as mine. That'd be the only way The Grove would have you. Let me guess, Daddy threw you away too, huh?"

"No, he was changing…"

"Bull."

"Stop." I can feel the force in my voice. "Do you even hear yourself? So my dad is full of shit but these assholes aren't? They're a cult! They kidnapped you."

"They saved me."

I close my eyes for a moment and try to massage what I just heard into my ears. "No…they're going to slit you open the first minute Nadir starts because you're their 'Mother Eve.' You'll be sacrificed! Tell me you're not this crazy!"

Sarai stands. A sparkle hits her eye. Satisfaction molds her mouth. "Not anymore. I used to be, though…when I believed in Wonts. They were the ones who poisoned me and tortured me for hours…locked me away without a thought. They weren't the ones that hurt my mom. Do you know what an Echo is, Alexia?"

"What do you think?"

"Girl, listen, stop being so damn hardheaded. In our society, an Echo is a Varien with genes like the Eden gene. They don't continuously evolve, but they can mirror the abilities of any Varien near them. That's what I am."

"I thought you could move through solids."

"Only because I was around another Varien with that ability." She tunes a TV screen for a shot of a different location. As she flips through, I notice the locations Kyle and I visited with the other recruits. Some are littered with Revenirs searching for us, while the cavern pond is vacant. On another screen, shots of captives make a grid. A familiar face topped with mousy thin hair is in the upper left box labeled cell 13. His head rests on the back wall and right when my brain tells me it's Bill Murray, it resets. Andre! Andre is in the cell!

I catch my breath and straighten up when she turns back to me.

"They swooped me in a case of mistaken identity. I was terrified of the Revenirs at first…but you know what? They never stopped valuing me. Even when they thought I was the one, they were grateful and kind. It was Set who insisted I stay and train with them…go to school."

"School? You go to Knox-Oxley?"

"Where else would I be?" She folds her arms.

"At a better place. Maybe a school that isn't full of elitist lunatics."

"Holding Varien strength to the highest regard is not elitist."

"It is when you believe everyone at the bottom of a hierarchy Louis Malveaux made is expendable."

"Knox! Louis Knox," Sarai corrects me. "I see you've learned a lot. You go to school?"

"Yes."

"Where?"

"I'm not going to get into that."

"That tells me enough. Malveaux… You always did like diet-lite shit. That neutral nonsense. Anyway, the Black Coats were cool with me rotting. They never once showed an ounce of mercy at so-called Mercy Bay."

"You think what Revenirs do is mercy and grace?"

"I think its clear Wonts know nothing but the opposite. They're a disease."

"Sarai."

"And their spread has to be stopped."

"Their spread? This isn't you! Just…please. I'm sorry, okay? I'm sorry about everything. I'm sorry I didn't do enough. If I could go back, I'd do everything to fix it. *When* we go back, I will do everything. I'll help your mom. I promise. You two can be together again. The three of us could leave then!" If my powers could break me into small fragments of matter, I'd fall away to the floor. This all hurts so much. I'm growing hotter and I can't see my dad.

Sarai folds both of her hands around mine. She squeezes them tight. "It's too late," she whispers. "Always has been…I just woke up."

"Come with us. Please, don't stay here." My tears fall onto our hands, a stream I can't turn off. Although Sarai has been hardened in a way I may never understand, something tells me she wishes things didn't have to be this way.

She wipes my eyes and a smudge of black and ivory transfers to her fingers. "Don't cry. I'm all right. I'll be okay."

"I'm sorry."

"I know." She takes me back in her arms and we hug tight. "I need you to be okay too. So, listen and leave me."

I break away, heart stunned one too many times to still beat. Sarai is serious. "They'll find you if you don't get out of here. They'll kill you. I'll do my part to help you. Oz runs surveillance normally, but he's been taking breaks for his labs. He says I've got an eagle eye, so I pull my weight and help sometimes and alert the crew when I need to. But there'll be no need today. You'll walk right back through the pond and go back the way you came. I'll lead them elsewhere and keep them out of your way."

"Why?"

Sarai doesn't waste a second. "Because you're my best friend."

I sniffle, growing sober from that morsel of comfort. It's short-lived, and Sarai makes sure to remind me. "But I can only do this once. Make sure you don't cross us again."

Us. I remember when we were "us."

I wipe my nose on my sleeve and nod. Sarai is a Revenir now. She's made the same vow I've made, drank the chasm, now she lives the part. So little time has passed, and yet, even in front of me, Sarai still seems worlds away. I leave her to her literal devices—the screens, buttons, and lights just as she's left me. We're even now. An effort for an effort.

I come around the wall and find Kyle sitting face-to-face with Oz. "I have a lot of questions for you." Oz smiles. "All this." He points at the wall of screens where Revenirs are searching frantically for us. "This is all your doing?"

"No." Kyle watches me take my place at his side.

"I see. Partners in crime, huh? Still, don't belittle yourself, son. You have a talent."

"I have heart. I did this for my own reasons…for her. We did it without much of an organized plan. Getting here was pure luck…"

Oz scratches through the hair of his short-peppered beard. "Luck only works for the talented. No one succeeds at anything for no reason. Whether the reason is dignified, minor, or huge, the accomplishment is a result of talent."

Oz's demeanor is throwing me for a loop. "Your father had so much charm, heart, and wit. He could talk to anyone and make them feel whole. I saw that in you back in the day." Oz grins. "You also have your mother's compassion, free spirit, and craving for justice. I knew this all when you were a boy, and I see it more clearly now." Oz stares at us in silence, his mind working in ways I hope to be merciful because getting through to Sarai is only one part. He looks away and fiddles with a gold ring on his pointer finger. "How do you expect to get out of this, son?" he asks.

Sarai edges around the corner. "I'll cover them out, Oz. I can call every Revenir out of their path."

"Oh, no need. The boy teleports. Haven't you heard?" Oz's dark eyes light up in amusement. "And also…you cut that deal with the girl. She's half the equation."

"We go together!" I affirm.

"Not by my command. *You* made a deal. Sarai doesn't even hold a proper rank yet, love. I'm the superior. Now what do you say we really get you out of here alive? Hmmm? Otherwise, I could kill you both without raising a hand."

As I try to hold myself together, Kyle flexes a strong face—one that knows defeat when he hears it.

"That's what I thought. So again, how will you two get out of this? It isn't just a matter of getting out anymore. You've poked the bear and it's on the hunt. Child's play won't do the trick when you want to sleep peacefully in your own bed in a few days."

"Teleport and then…to be honest…" Kyle drops his head. "I've got nothing."

Oz nods. "I'd hate to see something happen to you, Kyle. And because I care about you, I'd hate to have someone hurt your girl. If you weren't so special to me, I'd have killed you on sight. I don't have it in me to watch you fall," he says with a heaviness. "I do, however, have a moral code I must comply with."

"What type of moral code would someone like *you* have?" Kyle asks Oz.

Standing up calmly, Oz fiddles with the Knox-Oxley crested ring on his finger. "If this works out per my offer, you leave alive and well. She leaves alive and well. I'll grant you immunity and you won't be hunted. I'll assist Sarai in reeling in my men—they're already searching through the forests for you two. Once you teleport outside, I'll squash this entire thing. This must look a certain way to work in my favor, so until then, Sarai and I will trick them into running in the opposite direction."

Kyle sucks his teeth. A reason must live behind Oz's kindness. "What are the conditions?"

Oz turns to a cork board of black and white pictures. "They're quite complex," he sighs as he glazes over the old photographs. "When your parents died…I snapped. I became angry and vigilant. Your father was my best friend, and never in my life had someone risked their life for me so many times…" His voice trails off as he looks at a photo of himself and Calum. Both of them are casually dressed with beer mugs in hand.

Kyle and I curiously walk behind Oz. The image is something familiar, something I'm sure I've seen. Then a rush of heat floods down my body. The both of us look like we are ready to shoot stars through our fingers. The photo is his. An exact copy of the one resting in his wallet. The same photo of his father he showed me at Adieu Lagoon. Oz is the man whose hair was once all black with just a strip of silver.

I can hear Kyle's throat tightening. "What're you saying? Huh? That my father was some zombie prick? No!"

Oz attempts to put his words together before facing Kyle. "Yes."

Kyle's teeth clench. "No, that's not true. Don't disrespect—"

"Haven't you wondered why your temper runs wild once you let it loose? How about why this all comes natural to you? Haven't you wondered where your relentlessness comes from? Or why you feel alive in all this. It's in your blood, son."

"Don't call me that! No…no!" Kyle wipes the tears from his face. I am chilled, heartbroken, and aching all at once. Even Sarai's gaze is aimed at the ground.

Oz proceeds without mercy. "I'm on the cusp of finding the trail to your parents' killers. They're here, you know? One of our own called the job on your family."

"Don't listen to him," I tell Kyle.

"Hard to do when no one else has been honest with you. No one can because everything happened here. They don't know."

Kyle gives in to curiosity. "What don't they know?"

"They don't know that after a particular mission, your father was planning to separate from the Revenirs and take you, your brother, and your mother to live far off the grid somewhere. He wanted me to do the same, but I was too afraid. Then I had decided I would take the leap. Gather my own family and travel along with yours. And that was the day they wiped your entire family from their home. I found them there…and I see that scene every time I shut my eyes. I've had more survivor's guilt and PTSD than anyone can handle. Only thing that's made it better has been coming back and piecing the clues together. Figuring out who did it and why. I'm so close, Kyle…so close I can taste the victory. If you join my campaign, it'd only ensure the downfall of those people."

"Campaign?" Kyle shouts. "You want me to become a killer? No!"

Oz slams his hand down on the desk beside him. "You are collecting a debt. A life that should be taken for their lives!" he spits. "There must be a price for what was stolen from us! You feel it every day, son. Don't you? I know you do. It's there when you itch to hear your mother's voice on the phone. It's there when you notice your friend's parents in the bleachers at your ball games. It was there every time you fell off your bike and it will be the bottomless pit when you walk down the aisle and marry the love of your life. What we do is *kill*! We do not murder! We simply seek revenge in defense. We bring punishment for crimes when the rest of the world is too stupid and cowardly to do it. An eye for an eye. Your parents' lives were priceless and priceless items must be avenged! This can't be avenged correctly without you!"

More tears fall down Kyle's face. Oz has hit a nerve. All those feelings have been in Kyle before—and perhaps every day. And when those feelings surface, he runs. He's never confronted his demons head on.

"Fine." Kyle sniffs. "Fine, I'll do it."

"No," I gasp.

Oz relaxes. "I'm happy to hear we will be a team, but, Kyle, I must stress the value of your word. It is your lifeline. Honor is all we Revenirs know. Tell no one what we talked about! You fail to come back to me at the end of your senior year and you're as good as *dead*. That includes the girl. It saddens me to draw this line with you. You mustn't take this on with cowardice. Do you understand, son?"

Oz waits on Kyle.

I imagine what Kyle must be thinking of—his parents, his pain, his friends, and our times at Adieu Lagoon. What he'd give to be there instead. To still be naïve and wet behind the ears.

My insides feel dead in so many ways. There's too much coming at us.

"Understood," Kyle promises.

What? I cry a sound I've only made upon injury. "No! No, Kyle!" There's no reason in his face. He's immovable. *It's done.* I'm speechless, running water from eyes, too shaken to stand. When my knees buckle, Kyle's arms are there for me.

"Don't worry," he whispers.

"No! You can't do this!"

"What else can I do?"

"You could not make a deal with the devil!" I am trying my hardest to hold myself up as I cry when all I know is shattering. Through the teary screens of my eyes, I see Kyle in a dead stare. He lifts his focus to Oz.

"We need a minute…," he says with a low voice.

"One minute," Oz enforces and nods before busying himself near the screens Sarai is watching.

"Lex," Kyle reaches out and whispers. I shrug his hand off me.

"Don't touch me. Don't you dare. You made a deal with the devil," I repeat.

"I made a deal to keep us safe."

"Wasn't everything else enough? Sarai and your father being Revenirs…now you? How could you do this?"

His breath tickles my ear. "I need you be okay. I need you to be safe."

"Don't put this all on me. I can take care of myself. You're doing this because you believe him. You *want* to do this. Be honest. It isn't all about me." I wipe my face and straighten up from the drunk feeling of devastation. I can't let it impair me. We have things to do. "How do you know you can trust him? You're just going to commit your life to him off a promise? No. They're getting off too easy."

"What're you getting at?"

"The price has to be bigger. They let us go *and* they release Andre from their cells."

Kyle's brows wrinkle. "Andre? What?"

"They have Andre, Kyle."

"How do you know? I didn't see him when we went down there."

"Because we didn't go all the way to the end, but I saw him on the screen. It's him. Same balding pattern on the top of his head."

"Well, we don't know why he's here."

"*He shouldn't be here.*"

Full of skepticism, Kyle shakes his worry-filled head. "We're done here. We found Sarai. We've got a deal."

"No. We don't have a deal," I say loud enough to alert Oz.

Kyle roams his eyes over me. "Wait," he begs.

But Oz is a loyal audience. He homes back in without much effort. "No deal, huh?"

I turn around to face him. "You have a prisoner we're interested in."

Oz squints. "We have a prisoner you are interested in?" This intrigues him and makes him chuckle. "I'm curious…go on."

I walk over to the screens and ignore Sarai. "There," I tell Oz and point to the screen showing Andre with his head perched against his cell wall. "This is the guy. What's his name?"

Through a side-eye, Oz checks the screen. "That is Andy Navarette. He came here not too long ago."

I give Kyle an "I told you so" look and focus back on Oz. "Why?"

"Is that really any of your business?"

"If you want Kyle, you're going to have to work a little harder to earn our trust. Why is he in there?"

Oz waits a beat before responding, "Corroboration. The heirloom passage in his family wasn't sealed and that poses a great danger to us. It allows access…which now makes so much sense to me." Oz's face lights up. "You two? Oh, that's good. You were the ones. You're friends of his?"

"Yes, and we aren't leaving here without him," I affirm.

Oz and Sarai bounce their gaze between Kyle and me. Bitterness is washed over Sarai—a child who knows discipline is coming but doesn't want to give in.

And Oz, he's enjoying every bit of this for some reason. A slight smirk is stamped into his rich brown face. "Of course not. You want me to let him go. And in doing so, this will be enough for you to see I am being honest about going against my brothers and sisters here…my Revenirs?"

I nod. "Exactly."

"I see." Oz ponders. "And how will this work?"

"That's for you to tell us."

A deep sigh blows from his mouth. He tilts his head to the left and raises his brows and replies, "Well…it could work. I could call the guards away from the cells. You two teleport there. We open Andy's gate and from there, you jump back to where you came from. It can be easy, but you'd have to be fast."

Finally, Kyle speaks up again. "We will."

A proud smile cuts across Oz's face as he extends his hand out for a shake. "Then we have a deal, my boy!"

The two shake hands and seal a deal I hope will never come to fruition. Oz's strong eyes stare right at Kyle. The dim white light shining overhead builds haunting shadows down his face and scarred neck.

"You know, you said getting here was pure luck…but now, I don't think so. Getting here was just *her* will." He laughs against the raucous of the alarm and shakes Kyle's hand faster.

My will. Our deal. Here's hoping the two are enough to get us back to Malveaux—our home and a sanctuary I will never take for granted again.

CHAPTER SIXTY-THREE

ROBBING THE POND

AFTER OZ MAKES A round of calls and commands to his peers, Kyle wraps an arm around my waist and turns our bodies into molecules that scatter and blink from Oz's lab and snap back together in the deep of the cells we explored earlier with other recruits.

I take a look around for Andre, but I don't see him. So, I jog farther down with Kyle until I find our frumpy mess of an old man slumped over with his elbows rested on his knees.

"Andre," I whisper. "It's Alexia and Kyle…from Malveaux."

Our friend drags his head up, changing faces from being tired and distraught, to surprise. "What're you? Why're you?" He looks us over—covered in paint and dressed in black. We don't look like innocent kids. We're Revenirs to him.

"This is just an act. We can't talk much…" I grab the bars on the iron gate and study the surroundings. A camera where the ceiling and wall meet tips me. I stare into the lens and wait for Oz's promise. One. Two. Three. Four. Five seconds, and the gate whirs at the lock before making a clinking sound. It gives way to the loudest noise possible when the gate clicks open and slides into the wall.

A promise kept. Andre is free.

Even with the noise of the alarm, all is quiet under the weight of what is happening. The other prisoners around us have stopped their whining and chatter.

Andre's eyes widen and he stands. The legs of his dingy grey jumpsuit flood over his feet. "What is this?"

"C'mon. We're taking you home," Kyle assures him. "With us…to the academy."

"I want to go with you!" the prisoner behind us shouts.

"Take us too!" another yells.

"Shh!" I order them. But they're crazy and desperate, determined to get us to rescue them. They scream and clank objects against their cell gate. "Please! Just stop!"

A figure builds in my peripheral. A barefaced Revenir guard is at the end of the cell hall. His face scrunches tight as his body anchors to set off and launch toward us. I grip Kyle's hand.

"Andre, c'mon! Hurry!" I shout.

"I don't know what to do!" Andre replies.

Down the way the Revenir guard grunts and takes off running. Bit by bit his body fades, as if God is taking to our reality with an eraser.

"Oh shit!" Kyle shouts. He takes the initiative and grabs Andre and we evaporate. Except there's no regularity in the sensation. When I first teleported with Kyle, I felt disoriented. Not as bad as I did when I plane jumped with Greta, but dizzy. Eventually those dizzy spells turned thrilling. Exciting like the dip on a roller coaster. Now, binding is all there is. I feel tight and stuck. Bound and pulled under like an ill-fated mafia member with cement shoes. *We are almost home…just hang on. Hang on*, I say in my mind.

Our surroundings are stretched and slow moving in transit. We're in limbo. Drowned in static and tight discomfort. Things sharpen from smeared watercolor to dark fine lines. Liquid cool is thick around my feet when we land. Lake Moody? Why did Kyle drop us here?

All is dark on top of me. All except the opening of a skylight that lets moonlight in. The air space around me is damp and humid. I hear a scuffle. Sounds of punches hitting flesh and bone. Kyle's hand is missing from my grasp. He was just here. Right next to me. A cold shiver spirals down my back as I search frantically. There's nothing on me. No Kyle around anywhere. No Andre. The cold continues to wrap around me. *Is this anxiety?*

"*It's submission,*" a deep voice answers in my head. There's no one anywhere I turn. Just sprawling darkness and the wet drip of water diving from the cavern's broken ceiling pipes. I see ripples reaching far. Somewhere in the epicenter is something.

"How long do you think ol' boy and that old man can hang before their organs crush their lungs?" Feathered wings graze against the pondwater. Set steps into dusk light. And suddenly, the sounds of my boyfriend and Andre—struggling to move—as they dangle feetfirst from the ceiling stun me frozen.

We're not back in Lake Moody—we're back somewhere much, much worse.

CHAPTER SIXTY-FOUR

SET AND THE REVENIRS

"TEN HOURS? TWENTY-TWO? LONGEST anyone's managed is twenty-eight."

"Leave him alone," I order Set.

Set drags from a rolled cigarette. Smoke plumes from his nostrils. The yellow of his eyes is a predatory glow—a black panther lurking in tall grass. A force tugs at my bones. "Not in the plans… but now I'm wondering if you should join them." He sizes me up, teasing me with telekinetic yanks at my insides. My arms shoot up as he commands them with a nod. Too many seconds go by as he circles me. "You got a name, girl?"

I've forgotten everything. I can't even conjure the faintest star. I feel nothing. No power. Just the sensation of a wet wick in its place. Sounds of Kyle and Andre struggling knots my stomach. I don't know the extent of Set's torture. He could be doing much more than he's letting on. I've never seen a Varien this composed and capable—manipulating more than one target—without breaking a sweat.

"There's a mythology lesson here, yeah? Some parallels flying around the periphery. All it takes is a sweet face to stir up chaos. Shit, that and the perfect pitch. Eve sold Adam into shame. Helen of Troy saw the city burned in her favor. The face that launched a thousand ships…"

Set stands center stage beneath the cavern's skylight. He stares into me like he did on the night of Passage. "Are you our Helen?"

Trembling, I battle his magnetic hold to speak. "N-n-no."

Set laughs. "Lying will only piss me off. Death will be a slow dance, so be smart. Are you Helen?"

Set's telekinetic hold on my throat lifts.

"No, I swear to you."

"Then who are you?"

"Not Helen…more the Trojan horse. The boy was only trying to stop me." Lying feels like the only way out. The only thing Set could buy. "I wanted to rescue my friend. He followed me when I went rogue from the group…only he was too late."

Set walks to the side of the room where blood still funnels from the moonlit bloodbath of an earlier sacrifice. The Revenir that found us in the cells is there. Silent anger bubbles underneath Set's surface.

"What do you think, Skullman?" he asks. "Do you think this girl here is our Trojan horse?"

"Both of them," Skullman's deep, husky voice answers. "I think they're both trouble."

Set kneels and scoops a handful of water. His head drops and several Revenirs enter the pond. I'm still pinched here, a taxidermied butterfly beneath the pins of his hold. I stretch my eyes as far as possible above me. It's hard to see Kyle and Andre without lifting my head, and in the black of the ceiling, they camouflage perfectly. I wouldn't be worried if I could still hear them moving.

"Skullmaster?"

"Yes."

"We've been infiltrated."

"So quick of you to notice," Set bites. "Perhaps we wouldn't have if you'd have upheld our measures."

"Great apologies, Skullmaster," another Revenir says. "Somehow, we became disoriented. What should we do to protect the soil now?"

As Set rises from his knees, he examines his cigarette. "There was only one way to eradicate the threat of the Trojan horse." He flicks his cigarette, with sharp eyes cutting through me. Then he steps close to me, and sneers, "Burn her."

I spit at his face.

Seething, his mind loses grip on me as he brings his hand to wipe my insult from his skin. In seconds, his body starts turning from man to wraith. The monster within him screeches as his bones break down and sprout from his skin.

I reach for the tranquilizer gun Lucie equipped us with.

A Revenir sets his entire body into a human sun. Too bright for this room. Its heat is great. One without color. Blinding me and cracking me with burns from several feet away. I take blind shots and hear the feral squall of a Revenir. Hopefully I landed a bullet. As the sun-blaring Revenir's heat ramps up, I brace myself to die quickly. Except the moment never comes. It stalls. Then the heat shrinks. A ruckus clatters ahead of me. Grunts and "oofs." Bodies hit the floor. Set is yelling. The Revenir's sunlight goes out. I try squinting my eyes into recognition, but the brightness is still stamped in my sight.

"Lex, on your right!" Kyle materializes from a portal of smoke. I can see the best of him, the pieces of him that throw another gun my way.

"Andre, duck!" Kyle orders around me. A banging follows with another body drop.

Set, wounded on the floor, continues to slowly turn. The reaper inside of him shrieks. Convulsing and contorting his body into the pond. Bones break in the wake of larger ones building. His muscles mold like sculpted clay.

"Hit the trigger!" Kyle shouts around the pond, patching himself in and out of view as he beats several Revenirs with a pipe.

I see Andre running around swinging his arms like a wild man who can't fight to keep Revenirs at bay.

I aim down. Set rattles me with another shriek. Chunks of his flesh peel from his cheekbone and jaw. His neck bends long and unnaturally, a trellis for the black veins to climb. One eye closed, I shoot once, twice, then land when the third darted bullet pierces near his neck. The giant creature tearing out of Set shrinks and cries in pain. He bends down in the pond—a cat on his seventh life. Relief leaves as soon as it greets me. More Revenirs enter the pond, more are turning.

I waste no time shooting, and then let the bullets fly. Andre runs to me and I give him a gun. Together we stand back-to-back and shoot. Kyle is still a machine. He zips around, swinging an old cast iron pipe from the ceiling into their skulls without mercy. They're throwing abilities at him. Spikes, charged blasts, and stretching limbs to catch him midair, but he's too much of a menace to let them succeed. Darts take a handful of Revenirs down. Some before they can turn, the others as they're turning. Then something happens…my gun clicks empty. No matter how many times I frantically knock the trigger back, nothing else shoots. Andre keeps shooting around us before he runs out also. The Revenirs around me know what that means. We're out of luck. I remember my dagger and yank it from its holster.

"What now?" I mumble as I threaten and point its blade. But another Revenir answers for me, yanking my crown of hair and dragging me through the bloody water. I hold one hand over their grip to fight. I'm unsure if my head could pop from my neck, but a Revenir would be the person to make it so.

Revenirs mob around and cheer as I'm thrown into the center of their circle. My dagger is pulled from my hand and thrown in the pond. The hand on my head forces me under water. I squirm and reach around for leverage. Nothing helps. I'm suffocating in the dark. Suddenly my head comes up by the Revenir's command. Air has never felt so good, so missed. I could choke taking it all in. With their hand still gripped in my hair, the Revenir brings my face to theirs. It's Set. I shiver, and for a moment, I wonder if he's stolen the air from my lungs. With a low brow, eyes that could melt me down to a pulp, and a sneering mouth that spits black blood in my face, he tells me that's just the effect my fear of him has. I wipe the fluid away and hide behind my hands.

"No. Hey, hey! Look, here. Look at me!" Set takes my will and powers my body. My hands flop into the water at my side. Both of my eyes are pried wide open. This time the hold isn't as strong as before. Shreds of my energy push Set's control out of me. Maybe the tranquilizer bit him harder than I thought.

"Ay!" Kyle bats the pipe against the wall. "Touch her again… and I'll kill you." Manic in his tone, I know Kyle means it.

"My guy." Set stands and claps his hands together furiously. Both Kyle and Andre are shoved against the cavern wall behind him. Kyle's hands raise around his neck, scratching for whatever's squeezing his throat closed. Set raises a hand above his head, and with it, Kyle slides up the wall like a magnet to metal. "I don't know what kind of venom she's got, but trust me, it ain't worth dying for. Don't let your hormones get you ripped apart."

Revenirs around us laugh. Under Set's controls, Kyle and I focus on one another. Early daylight is breaking through the skylight now. I can see him better. Even with gritted teeth and pain, his eyes feed mine. We understand each other and what needs to be done now. I know what I have to do. Go deep in my head till I clear the sound of the water sloshing around the Revenir's ankles from my attention. Ignore the damp air and the deep belly of Pynman's Den. No one here matters. No one here is who I need.

"Baby girl?"

"Dad?"

Beneath the skylight's bleached violet glow, Dad looks over at me.

"How're you here? Unburned?" I reach out to touch his face. Smooth and stubbled at his chin. Classic Dad.

He grins nonchalantly. "I couldn't stay that way. I had to change it."

"What? Change? You can't change that."

Dad pokes his bottom lip out, halfway holding in a rebuttal. "You can make anything possible if you do the work. I did the work."

"I guess…," I mumble.

Troubled, Dad looks around us. The Revenirs are on mute, but they're heckling screams. Set has unleashed spores of red from his skin. The blood dust from Ren's house. It sawed right through the bodies of Black Coats. It'll do the same to me in seconds.

"How're we going to get you out of this?" Dad looks worried.

"I need you to say…your poem…our poem."

"That's it?" Dad's brows arch. "No choppers, grenades, machetes? Just a poem?"

"I know it's weird, just follow me…yeah?"

"I wish I followed you a long time ago…so, of course. Ready?"

I grin bittersweetly. A tear crawls down my face. "Yeah."

Dad starts his self-penned poem, "And when you're in trouble…when the breeze of your mind blows down your last restraint, and pain comes flooding in, remember you have me, and I've always got you."

Love begins to coat me in power. I join in with Dad to double the dose. "No adversary is strong enough to break through. Not even time or distance. Remember you have me, and I'll move a mountain. Remember you have me, and I'll spread my love on the wind."

No words and no time, Dad nods confidently. "You got this, baby girl."

"Thank you, Dad. I love you."

"I love you too." He fades into my mind's static. The token charges my veins, racing to pour into the pond as the blood dust makes my acquaintance. The earliest remnants of the newborn sun peek down on us from the skylight. We've been going at this all night. It's time to end it.

Shocked, Set stands still. His blood dust malfunctioning—spinning and spinning. That crooked mouth of his is ajar. *Why? Because he knows he's been outmatched by a lesser than?* Quickly, I spot my submerged dagger and hold it tight. I command and conquer control of my own body, hunching forward with both arms elbow deep into the water. A lit root grows and sprouts through my fingers, toes, chest, and eyes. A flow of white starfire streams from my hand through the dagger blade. Shooting stars knock down every target. Sparks pop the surface of water. Flesh is cooked. Smoke scents the air. Bodies break through the water; I see them fall before I watch Kyle and Andre tumble from Set's grip.

My heart sinks as I race to find Kyle. Somehow, he finds me first, wraps an arm around my waist with Andre tagged on to him, and vanishes us home.

CHAPTER SIXTY-FIVE

SANCTUARY

THE SECOND TELEPORTING JUMP is the charm. It brings us right home to Malveaux. Our bodies pop through the air and settle into a room with blue-and-tan-plaid wallpaper. Jolting an unexpecting Nate from reading in his bed.

"Whoa!" he exclaims. "You made it back." He sounds surprised and Kyle looks offended. But honestly, making it out was an act of God. We are so lucky.

"Who is that?" Nate asks, looking strangely at Andre.

Kyle and I bring Andre to sit on what I assume is Kyle's bed. "He's a friend we found in the prisoner cells there. He needs sanctuary. He can't go back home."

"What do you mean I can't go home?" Andre breaks a word in.

"They will be waiting for you to come back." Kyle throws a set of dry clothes from his dresser at him. Oh, how the tables have turned. "They won't touch you here. Malveaux is sacred ground bound by Marcel and Louis's pact."

Andre slides a shaking hand through his hair. "Wait a second. Wait a second! I didn't even ask for all of this. You kids drugged me to get into my cellar which apparently is a vessel to a Revenir hub! Because lo and behold, my ancestors were Revenirs, and Revenirs aren't just some urban legend! They are a real society. And my mother never told me. So, I had the luxury of getting kidnapped and tortured for something I had no clue of and no part in. You two rescued me but tell me my home is no longer my home. My new home is a place I haven't lived in since I was eighteen! Do I have that right?"

Kyle, whose face paint is smeared and missing in random chunks, puts a hand on his naked chin. "If the sedative we gave him was herbal, could it be classified as a drug per se?" he sarcastically asks Nate and me.

"Don't piss me off!" Andre pops up.

I place both my hands on his shoulders. "No, wait. You do have it all right, Andre. We were wrong. Absolutely. Everything just blew up in our face. We only did this to save my friend from being sacrificed…but everything just wasn't what I thought it was. We messed up, and we treated you horribly."

"You ruined everything!" Andre exclaims.

I tear up hearing his anger. Andre has become the actual affected party we didn't intend to be affected. "Yes. We're sorry. I don't know what else to say…but we brought you here to stop things from getting worse." I look over at the boys. "Nate, could you please go get Dama Hadley and tell her we have someone here who needs sanctuary. She'll get Andre settled, and between her, Sage Cameron, and Greta, they'll know what to do."

Andre holds his hands up. "Stop right now…you're telling me Dama Hadley still works here. I'm gonna jump out the window."

"No, don't do that. Sage Cameron wouldn't want you to do that." Kyle shakes his head.

Nate runs off and in a cluster of minutes, while the three of us take turns changing out of our wet clothes behind a privacy screen. We keep things silent—processing the timeline of events, and a grip of emotions we probably don't have the sanity to name.

When Dama Hadley comes through the dorm door with Nate, she's too stunned to see her old student in dire need of her help to give us any grief. It's the only time I've seen her nurture come out instead of her discipline.

"Oh, Andy dear," she consoles him as she prissily guides him out the room. "Let's go get you taken care of."

Damo Ben enters when Andre and Dama Hadley exit. "Phoenix, let me look at you," Damo Ben tells Kyle. His mechanical arm whirs and takes shape into a cylinder that flashes light from it. He draws it up to Kyle's eyes. "Okay…give me your arm…"

"Why?"

"I've gotta check your blood pressure…"

"Are you the school nurse?"

"I'm a first responder…you know this. Stop with the games—"

Greta and Sage Cameron swing the door open. My mind is immediately shaken up. Memories of the last few hours are stirred through. Sage Cameron has entered my head and the last ounce of optimism and relief dries up. There is only accountability now. There's only truth. And judging by the tension in their flared noses, uncomfortable conversations and punishments are also in my future.

Sage Cameron's scent smells like cinnamon today, a real change from the calming floral oil I'm used to. The dark circles under her amber eyes tell me she didn't sleep well last night.

"Alexia," she tersely calls. "My office, now."

CHAPTER SIXTY-SIX

MEETING WITH THE CAMERONS

ON THE WAY TO Sage Cameron's office, through Leona Hall, students peek through doors. Malveaux's security guards are peppered all around. I see Kit, Lucie, Raquel, and Erik at various points, in between gusts of images in my head I'd rather not drum up. This time, all I see are images of my dad ripped apart by Set. The visuals come into my head like a stab wound. Painful and distracting. It's not something that's been on my mind, so the intrusion of it is strange, especially in the middle of this spectacle. Even the faces in Leona Hall's murals seem to judge me and stare. It is an academic walk of shame.

Sage Cameron's mind maneuvers everything. She opens doors ahead of me before I can meet them. She shuts the dorm doors belonging to those nosy peeking students and moves anyone walking in our path out of the way.

Once we get into her office, with the muscle of her mind, she commands the blinds down and the curtains shut. The wood logs in the hearth spark a flame to warm up the chill that's made its way from outside. Soleil lamps turn on, and a chair scoots out for me to sit in. Sage Cameron practically scoops me into it—pushing it into the back of my knees until I fall onto it.

Greta comes from behind me and slams a folder on the desk. She hones in on me. "Please tell us you didn't go where we think you went."

"No need, Greta. I already know, and it's exactly where you think she went." Sage Cameron stares at me with disappointment.

Greta wrinkles her eyebrows. "Do you want to die?"

"W-w-what?" I stutter.

Greta presses her palms into Sage Cameron's desk, leaning forward so there's no mistaking what she's asking. "I said do you want to die?"

"No!"

"Well…I can't tell. You've done just about every knuckleheaded, dumb thing possible to die in the most sinister and excruciating way," Greta sneers.

I shake my head, pent-up sarcasm and anger bubbling to the surface. "Maybe if the two of you were honest with me from the jump, I wouldn't have!"

The whole jig is up at this point. I see no reason to tiptoe around what happened tonight and why it happened. I want to see Greta's and Sage Cameron's faces as I tell them the truth and seek the truth. All killer, no filler.

"I told you I was looking for my friend and I promised myself I'd do whatever it took to find her!"

Greta's arms are folded. Sage Cameron is still locked quiet, sitting in her chair.

"And what did you find?" Greta asks firmly. "What you're looking for…I hope."

"I did. Revenirs…they're real. And you two have been gaslighting me this entire time…making me think I was crazy. Greta, you were even there to see Set the day you rescued me. And still…nothing about him or what he does and who he works for! Nothing! You've both been fine with me wondering the worst and feeling the worst for the rest of my life. You've been fine with them human trafficking, playing like they're just some conspiracy. But the moment I get back from their headquarters you storm in and bring me here and ask me if I want to die. That tells me everything, that you've always known…"

"Of course." Greta doesn't budge. "Did you stop to think there's maybe a reason we know and don't share any of that with you?"

I roll my eyes. "I didn't have time to think about that. There are people dying by their hands every day. I had to work."

Sage Cameron and Greta pass one another looks.

"You mean save the day," Greta responds dryly.

"I mean help people who need help."

"And did you?"

"Yes."

Greta fakes a look of surprise. "Oh, how so?"

"We found Andre in the cells…the Revenirs had him. And if I never went there looking for Sarai, I wouldn't have known that, and Andre would be dead and gone."

"As grateful as we are for that," Sage Cameron finally speaks. Like a kettle before it screams, she's carefully releasing steam to prevent herself from blowing up. Her nostrils are still tight and slightly upturned. Her eyes wince with attitude. Words sound sharper coming from her mouth, rougher in tone. "You do understand how much danger this puts the school under? Your elders, friends, and peers? They're safe here on Malveaux grounds, but what about outside school hours when they go off-site? What about holidays and summers? As Malveaux's Sage, what am I supposed to do then? We can't protect them or their families. You have put a target on everyone's back…more specifically, yourself."

"I voluntarily put myself on the line to find Sarai," I snap. "I knew the risk. I accepted it because I don't agree with leaving anyone behind and letting them die so everyone else can live."

"Funny," Greta retorts. "That's really funny."

I almost curse when I speak. "What's so funny?"

"The punchline is you being so disobedient and self-righteous to the point where you serve yourself on a platter—giving those

Revenirs what they want—all while being blissfully ignorant but convinced you know it all."

"What?" I scoff. "I don't get it."

Greta leans closer over the desk. "Then let me say it a different way so you can understand. You haven't changed a damn thing. One will still die and lead to more death. You didn't stop the operation. There are people still there locked up. The Revenirs will keep doing what they do, and they'll never stop pursuing you until your blood lives in theirs."

My eyes drift down to Sage Cameron as I try to figure out Greta's context. "What is she getting at? I know they'll be after me now because of what I did…why is she acting like I'm dumb?"

"Because you are!" Greta shouts.

Sage Cameron jumps up and motions a hand down while placing the other on Greta's shoulder. "Please." Suddenly all the quiet, pleasant sounds Sage Cameron garnishes her office with become front round noise. Noises I don't remember hearing when we first entered: the dripping water of her fountain and bamboo cup that bows as the water spills over. Crystal windchimes knocking against one another outside.

"What am I missing?" My muscles tense as I wait for clarity.

"Your final lab result came in. We found something in your DNA…," Sage Cameron goes on, facing me with clear focus. "The Eden gene. A gene limitless in its evolution—"

"I know what it is!" The emotion inside me slips through my eyes and breaks my voice. When I open my mouth, I can taste my tears. "…That's wrong."

"It would be highly unlikely to obtain this kind of inaccurate result," Sage Cameron regretfully shares.

"I want to test again."

"That'd be really unnecessary," Sage Cameron tells me.

"Not if it means getting it right!"

"The results are right," she says.

"No…mistakes happen all the time."

Greta cuts in and overpowers me. "Alexia, the results are what they are."

"According to a test! I want a second opinion."

"The test was your second opinion," Greta replies, face stoic.

"What? What does that mean? You knew before the labs… that the *Mother* is me, that I have the Eden gene?"

Greta and Sage Cameron stand elegant, like two priestesses, in posture. Regal, with proud necks weightless upon such heavy shoulders.

"From the day I saw you…yes," Greta says.

"How?"

"Your halo…it bleeds violet."

"And? I can't be the only one who has that, right?"

"Right…," Greta agrees. "Echoes, Variens with the power of mirroring other Variens' gifts, have violet halos."

"So there…maybe I'm an Echo."

Greta is still firm. "Your blood says you are not."

"Why didn't you tell me this? Why did you keep it from me?"

Sage Cameron takes her turn. "Telling you before confirming anything didn't make any sense. You've already been through so much. The weight of that worry would've been too heavy."

Shock is setting in. Every nerve I have feels worn to threads. "So what else do you know, huh? Greta, you lied to get me here. And you, Sage Cameron, I sat here in this room waving my arms and going off about Sarai being sacrificed for Nadir…you told me I was searching for things that truly did not exist. You both lied."

Sage Cameron's face softens. "Those lies were only supposed to protect you. Not hurt you." She sniffles and beads of tears start to puddle from her eyes. "I'm sorry. We only tried to protect you and the world the best way we could."

I can't help but think of my dad's words about the greater good. He felt he was doing the lesser of evils and taking care of the greater good. That was his assessment, and he thought mine was juvenile, just like Sage Cameron and Greta. Never, until this moment, have I ever agreed. Why couldn't I just accept a lie? Why couldn't I spend my whole life wondering about Sarai till her absence turned to a scar I only notice when I see it?

As I sit in regret, Sage Cameron motions me to follow her and sit on a spread of floor cushions with her. Her long skirt drapes over her feet, giving her the illusion of walking on air, while Greta actually does—to the top shelves she goes, rummaging in books and folders.

Sage Cameron sits on the assortment of burnt orange, cream, and olive cushions. I take a seat next to her, relieved from holding myself up as I deal.

"There's another reason we didn't keep things honest," Sage Cameron shares. "It hits close to home because we see a lot of ourselves in you. When Greta and I were young, we believed in activating the community to fight corruption boldly and explicitly. Not within the Varien Country's government system or to its liking. We believed you had to be loud and unapologetic with everything."

"Everything," Greta echoes.

"The protesting, marches, fundraising, and hard questions… they helped and changed so much here in Varien Country. But it seemed as we kept digging for the root of these issues like classism, sexism, and supremacy, it seemed as though we hadn't even gotten close. We'd cut off one head and three more would appear. And it puzzled us…me and my partner at the time. We formed a group to investigate the fraternity."

To which Greta fiercely drops a thick-spined book from twelve feet up. This draws Sage Cameron's irritated eyes closed. "As I was saying, together, we found an ancient cancer had been growing right under us all for a very, very, long time. A quiet society of elite Variens born from what they call heirloom families—the oldest documented pure Varien families with top-tier abilities. Together, they've been the puppet masters of Varien Country, and they were led by Louis Knox till his death. Their goal never changed: They must return to all realms and reclaim. The earth to them, is about checks and balances, and the Revenirs make it so."

Greta descends the air steps, handing Sage Cameron old, folded papers. "If you're a bad person, they get you for your crimes. There's a price to pay for doing bad things, and they believe it is their job to collect the payment karma demands. The payment is death," Greta explains.

Sage Cameron nods. "Things happen to people and explanations go unanswered. They've even taken care of things for our government. If there isn't an answer for a disaster, or if something doesn't add up, it's them."

"Political assassinations," Greta comments.

"Greta!" Sage Cameron gently claps.

"Too much? One moment she's got baby ears, the next she's a mature audience. Now she's a baby again?"

"You never could pace yourself or read the room." A huff wipes Sage Cameron's slate clean. "As I was saying, same goes for weak Variens who scale The Grove and Varien Country out of balance. Per Louis's word, it must always be elite, so we are always ready and worthy to be what we were—the originals, the dominant ones. They achieved this by splicing. Taking a Varien's cells and fusing them to their own, giving them a growing list of powers to become the best weapon."

Sage Cameron unfolds the thick browned papers. Illustrations are scribbled on what takes the shape of a map. "This is their road to reclamation; they call it the Varien revival."

Sketched in ink, the map details the steps in a series of illustrations like a dark version of Candyland. Symbols and drawings of the terrain color the spaces. Sage Cameron points her fingers to those completed. "Spill into Varien Country law and government, build alliances in Wont government, rally the pure…" Her slim hand scoots across the paper to a female figure draped in cloth. A flower crown is on her head. She's circled inside a moon. "Bathe in anointed blood." Then down the way: "Reclaimation War."

I don't want to see the papers anymore. I know what this all means. They want me dead. They want to use me to bring about the end of Normals.

"Is it sinking in now?" Sage Cameron leans closer. "We received your labs, which confirmed our suspicions. We couldn't only rely on your violet halo. We had to learn the precise details of your condition, because with you, their list of powers is infinite for all of time, unlike what a regular Varien would give them. Their powers stick to them for a while, but the body fights the fusion and eventually, those abilities disappear."

Greta waits for me to react, then adds. "All of this is very important. It's why we brought you here. It's why we must protect you. If they have you, they are one step away from war."

All I can think is how I have played this completely wrong. Each step of the way. I pursued my best friend only to find she is no longer my best friend, but a Revenir, and in doing so, I have offered myself to them. I walked into the lion's den as the prey they always intended to hunt. Set and his crew, their faces before I attacked them, and his crew, suddenly makes sense. *How did I go so far off?*

"I…I have to tell you guys something," I stutter. "They know me. They're coming. It's only a matter of time."

"Who is?" Sage Cameron asks.

"The Revenirs…I think they saw my halo."

All expressions of terror appear in Greta and Sage Cameron. They both talk over each other: "What do you mean they saw you?" and "Alexia, be completely honest with us" to which I want to quip and say something smart like, "*Oh, because honesty has been the best part of this relationship.*" But sarcasm isn't going to save my ass or anyone else's, so I come clean about the last piece of my Revenir story, my valiant and dumb effort to save Andre from being murdered because we used his secret entrance at Passage.

Greta shakes her head. "Your halo burns regular with your locket…which you didn't have on…which is why we couldn't track you. You're the only Varien I can't see without it," she mumbles herself through her thoughts.

"I didn't want to be tracked. I'm sorry."

Sage Cameron's hands cover her mouth, but I can see the rest of her tight brown face. She is made of stone. The caution she exercises is still in a league of its own. "I'm not sure what to do…," she whispers.

"I messed up. I'm sorry."

We sit silent for a while, meditating to the sound of my sniffles and the wind creeping through a window telekinetically opens. Sage Cameron's locs sway like cattails touched in the breeze. The whites of her eyes shine like handblown glass.

"Fear." She wipes her tears away. "That's all that is. I've seen too many friends killed at the hands of those monsters. Each death took a toll so large…I'm still paying for it. The fight just wasn't worth it anymore. See, I did what you did—fought it up close, tried to get everyone on board and it just…imploded. It's better to fight from afar. I'm not sorry for caring and protecting you. I just wish I handled it better. Wish I'd told you sooner."

The three of us sit below the windowsill, backs against the wall, legs laid like sitting dolls. My head hurts. My heart hurts even worse. It pulses flares of starfire on and off as I think of the shambled life I have, how short it will be, and the things I'll never get to say to make things right. Let alone the regular things I'd love to experience before I die like driving on my own, going to college…maybe even getting married. "I wish there was some way to rewind, or fast forward…so I could fix and feel things," I tell them.

Sage Cameron turns her resting head to look at me. "I don't know about the fixing, but you've got forever to feel all the things you want. Malveaux will always be safe for its students, and that's a bound oath. The Revenirs will never hurt a student on Malveaux grounds."

I can't help but laugh a little. "Rules were made to be broken." When did they become so noble? "What makes them so afraid of Malveaux?" I question.

"Their word," she answers. "Their word is their bond. Louis promised his brother, Marcel, that neither he nor the fraternity would ever bring harm on Malveaux's grounds. It acted as a truce in the wake of Knox's banishment. The Revenirs' code weighs heavily on their word."

The fact that these bastards are so hung up on pinky promises infuriates me. Criminals who value their word? *Mythical.*

"I'm not seeing how a society like this could follow such a moralistic code," I say.

"Well, to them…a man is only as good as his word," Sage Cameron goes on. "If he can lie to his foe, who's to say he's true to his friend? A foe has not one positive expectation of you. Why conceal your motives? It's overkill…and besides, Marcel packaged the oath with consequences no one knows. There's a lot of red tape."

Red tape may be worth cutting through when I think of not just who I am, but what I did. Sage Cameron isn't asking for all the details yet, maybe because she can hear them inside of me. I paint a blank space in my mind to protect my story—how I escaped campus, and found Revenir headquarters, and most importantly, Kyle's agreement with Oz. I drag my knees to my chest, asking myself how I got here, and why me. Together we sit. Less like pupil and teacher, more like friends—knowing that any future time won't ever be the same because we've been caught running from the past. We've been so afraid of it swallowing us whole, we forgot to really love what the present has given us. It's all that is guaranteed.

"Do you think things will settle? Go back to…the way they were?" I sniffle, naïve and desperate.

Sage Cameron sighs, a tired, not-so-believable optimist. "Time always tells…but I think it'd be best if you stay on grounds. You keep it low-key…in a few weeks, Blossom Ball will be here. I'm sure we'll be wondering how we're able to dance again."

CHAPTER SIXTY-SEVEN

A New Nirvana

"WHAT IS THIS STUFF? Lip balm?"

"That's primer, you cavewoman!" Alani fusses.

I've asked her a mountain of questions about her makeup bag all morning because it isn't my thing. I rarely wear anything besides a little mascara and lip stain. Sometimes I even get around to adding a little eyeliner. But primer? That stuff is for the big girls—like Alani. She's a vixen. She doesn't need any lessons or help getting prepped for the Blossom Ball. She's got everything on lock, even what *I'm* going to look like. When it comes to following through on the undiscussed empty promise her cousin made for her to do Lucie's makeup in exchange for her arsenal, she's quiet— which is how the makeup brushes landed in my hands.

"Doesn't primer go under paint?" I ask Alani, with an eager Lucie sitting on the stool in front of me—lips and eyes closed as if I'm ready to take her from Lucie to Lupita at the Oscars.

"I'm going to pretend I didn't hear that." Alani slides her hand down her face. "How do you feel about going with smoky eyes and a nice neutral lip? It pairs pretty hot with the cocktail dress you can borrow."

"A cocktail dress? Kill me now," I whine while moisturizing Lucie's rich and dewy brown skin.

Somehow, in the midst of this tornado of suck called life, I forgot about finding my perfect dress. It wasn't until yesterday, when Alani suggested I try my dress on, that I even realized I had nothing. And there's no use in bouncing off to the Belle Rues when I've been sentenced to "school arrest."

"Lex, this dress isn't so bad. It matches what Kyle's wearing," Alani reassures me.

"How do *you* know what he's wearing? I don't even know!"

"I'm a girl, we talk about these things."

"You never talked about them with me! How else am I supposed to learn how to be a woman?"

"Lots of ways," Lucie spouts off.

She's too sweet for me to roll my eyes in front of her, so I give it a shot with my lids pulled over.

Nia and Mom would teach me. I need them right now with every fiber of my being to show me the way. But more than anything, I need Mom to meet the beautiful person that holds my core together. She's missing this time and I'm missing her.

Wishing I could chicken out on the ball, I fall into my bed and gaze out of our window.

Lucie's bad posture shrinks her. "Did I say something wrong?"

"Everything you say is wrong," Alani mumbles as she holds her gown and observes it on the hanger.

"No, nothing is going how I want it to. Lucie, you're either going to look like an alien with foundation painted over her eyebrows, or like I couldn't decide between the eyeshadow shades in Alani's palette and said to hell with it. Kyle hasn't even talked to me about the ball since we last spoke on it. I don't even know if we're still going."

"You seriously think he'd do you like that?" Alani asks.

"I don't know. He hasn't really spoken to me much, and his sweetness has changed…even his humor."

"Yuck…but honestly, Kyle just gets like that sometimes. He goes dark, it's just a matter of why, and I'm sure the cloud you've also been sulking under influences things. He'd ghost you if he didn't care for you anymore." Alani's right. I *have* been different. I don't know how to act with the information I have. How do I tell my friends *I'm* the one with the Eden gene?

The steam brewing from Alani's hand creeps to the ceiling. She's been steaming every wrinkle out of her cobalt satin dress and I'm tired of watching. God answers my prayers when Alani's phone chimes.

"Speak of the menace, Kyle wants you to meet him in the Great Room," she says after reading her messages.

"Tell him I can't. I don't have time."

"Why don't you have time?"

"Because I'm getting ready, doing Lucie's makeup…and he hates me."

Alani folds her arms. "You know I'm not going to let you make a fool out of yourself, right?"

"…Yeah."

"If you trust me, you'll go downstairs and meet Kyle. When you come back, I'll make you into the most stunning girl to ever attend the Blossom Ball."

"And what about Lucie's face?"

"I'll take care of Lucie."

As hard as I try to fight a smile, I can't contain it.

Lucie loses her mind and embraces Alani as if there's never been any boundaries between them. "You're the best! I like you, Alexia, but I've always wanted Alani to beat my face…as they say. Will I be the most stunning girl too?"

"Eh, well…after me of course, and Lex." She winks. "We're going to take the night from these self-centered bitches."

I hop out of bed, take off my head scarf, and put on my favorite pair of hoop earrings. "I can't wait to see what that literally means."

"You will. We have twelve hours till take off." She smirks.

"And no smoking while I'm gone. I'll find out!"

"I'll keep an eye on her!" Lucie interrupts again, with courtesy no one asked her for.

Alani mocks me and gets back to steaming her unwrinkled dress, swatting Lucie's hand away from touching it, as I step out the door. I think of taking the elevators, but they don't move fast enough.

I run down to the Great Room against Dama Hadley's orders to stop. I'm too close to slow down. The fact that I can outrun her doesn't help either. I lose track of so much: who I pass, the route I take, and even the pressure of my feet pushing against the ground. Nothing matters till I find Kyle behind double doors.

He radiates light, a turnaround from the partial gloom of the last few weeks. Some days he's short with words and touches—dry where jokes brought flavor. He's easy to read today, and beautiful. This is exactly how I prefer him. Light stubble along his jaw; outgrown, wavy, dark hair; and most importantly, a smile on his face. My heartbeat doubles. I race to plant my hands on him, then stand on my toes for a kiss.

"You must've missed me," he says.

"Too much to admit!" I want to stay like this all day, sitting in sweats by the grand fireplace. Oh, and kissing also. That's extremely ideal. "Can we skip out on the ball and stay here? Or leave to Adieu?" I ask. I want him all to myself.

Kyle brushes my fingers against his lips. "You're crazy! It's freezing out there."

"I don't care."

"Yes, you do. You hate being cold."

"I'll wear a coat."

Kyle pauses for a second, the corner of his top lip curls in a smirk. "What if I don't want to see you in a coat tonight?"

I feel a fluttering in my stomach and an uncontainable burst of energy.

"I have a confession," he says.

"Okay."

"I know things have been weird. I've been distant and that's probably why you've been off too. So, you should know, on our free days...I've been leaving Malveaux."

"Oh."

"After everything at Pynman's...that talk with Oz...I've kinda been wanting to speak to someone about all of my issues. They're bigger and louder now...and I handle them well on my own, but I know they could eat me alive at any given moment. So, I looked for a therapist."

I tilt my head. "Okay? We have therapists *here*."

"Yeah." Kyle nods. "But I wanted someone who doesn't know me or my life here. Someone foreign to my little orphan story."

"Okay...that's good. All I can think about is what happened, and we haven't talked. You shouldn't keep your feelings in. It must feel so horrible."

"It is, and I don't want it to change me. At first, I searched far out areas of The Grove. But then, with the help of Lucie, I searched for someone and found a practice hours away under the name of Sylvia Jacobs." Kyle looks into my eyes.

"My mom?"

"Yeah." He backs away from me as though standing close prevents him from speaking freely.

I fiddle with my locket, scratching my thumbnail over its etching. "Why?" *To tell her where I am and send a mob after me?*

"Just listen...the first time I met her she was sweet, just like you. She sat there, taking me in and listening, never jotting down notes. Anyway, when I left here on Thursday after the game, it was to confront her. I planned to tell your mom about you. But for some reason, she opened up to me first. She showed me a picture of her amazing family. I strategically commented on how breathtaking 'this one in the middle' was. Almost instantly, she broke into sobs. When I asked her why she was crying she said, 'Life took my daughter away.' I didn't know what to do. I mean, everything sounded great in my head before I came and then...

whoosh! All I could say was, 'She's taken care of. She found a safe home.' That's when she stopped. She wanted to know what I meant and how I knew. So, I just told her everything. Then I told her who I am: this Varien kid who can morph and teleport and do all the 'terrorist' things Normals accuse us of—"

"Kyle, you scared her?"

He corrects himself. "Nah, I didn't say that verbatim! I'm not stupid. I just handed her the gift of knowing her daughter is alive and fed, sleeping under a roof in a warm bed. She was happy to know you're still in school. I don't think she could even focus on your powers. You're still her daughter. That's all you'll ever be to her."

My joints lock stiff.

"…And you'll be happy to hear your dad misses you. He's not angry…he understands."

Tears roll down my face in record time. The only instinctual thing I can do is sit before I combust.

Kyle guides me to the couch. "Obviously, he suffered from the burns, but he's been able to treat them with skin grafts. They hope he can run for governor in the next election. Until then, he's taking his time focusing on recovery."

I cry through his entire explanation. I'm feeling a mix of so much: relief, more guilt, happiness, loss, and despair.

"Everything is okay, Lex," Kyle assures. "Your family, they want to see you. They miss you so much. Do you think you'd be able to meet them? Maybe at Greta's. That'd be the safest option in their realm. I'd be there, and maybe Sage Cameron can set up security. I don't know if it'd work right now with what happened to us in Pynman's. It doesn't matter, though. I'll get this figured this out. I'll get them to you."

I take a moment to soak all this information in. "Hold on… how did you even leave campus? Security follows us everywhere and we still have that curfew on our gifts."

"Yes…but you taught me well by going to Lucie. I know she doesn't like it when we call her crazy, but her mind really is crazy. That Midray really works."

"You used the Midray? And you're in one piece?" I pat his torso down. "Alani is going to kill you."

"Doubt it. It's been sixteen years and she hasn't managed it."

"How'd you pull this off?"

"Well, Lucie, like I said, is a mad genius. Apparently, she's got these hidden tunnels all behind the walls and floors of the academy. I went through the air vent in my dorm and exited into the library. There's a tunnel behind Marcel Malveaux's portrait. Lucie met me at the halfway mark of the tunnel and gave me the Midray."

"And no one knew you left? The Spot Variens didn't pick up on it?"

Kyle shrugs. "I guess the Midray does this thing where you occupy two places and two different times. You know how Greta can move between planes?"

I nod.

"It's sorta like that, but I was still here physically at Malveaux, in bed for every bed check while being in the Normal realm during daytime hours."

"Kyle, you idiot. You let Lucie experiment on you for me?" I sigh.

Kyle giggles. "It was dumb. I know."

"The things you do for me. I just don't deserve them. Thank you isn't enough."

"You do. I couldn't let you live with that weight on your back anymore. That was an accident, not an attack. You've been working too hard on punishing yourself for it, like you have to suffer forever. But you deserve every good thing." Kyle wipes my eyes and tells me he has one last thing to reveal. He walks to and from the back of the couch for a black gift box wrapped in a satin white bow.

"When I told your mom about Malveaux, the ball came up. Loads of questions about all your girly stuff were asked. I sort of threw up my hands and told her we don't talk about that stuff. She wanted me to come back before the ball, so she could grab you a little something. Because I was in the Normal realm, I didn't want to screw things up and draw attention to myself, so I didn't use my gifts at all. I had to take a bus and walk to get around. I told your mom I didn't have enough bus fare from the money I made selling the cuff links Nate gave me to sell at a Normal pawn shop. I couldn't make it out again. When she offered to pay for my trip, I couldn't take her money, but she insisted and told me to take it for her baby, not myself."

Damn, that definitely sounds like Mom.

Kyle places the box in my lap and sits cross-legged on the floor. "Go ahead, gorgeous. Open it."

I wipe my eyes with the side of my sleeve. Pulling each tip of the bow, the ribbon falls loose from the edges. I peel back the shimmering wrapping paper inside to find a champagne chiffon gown. "Oh my gosh! This is an Elie Saab gown!"

"A who-eee whab what?" Kyle mocks.

"He's a genius designer I learned about on Pinterest."

"Pinterest?"

"An app from home. It helps you find ideas in images. You can save them for inspiration. I used it for theater costumes. I always blew my allowance at the fabric store so I could make my own low-priced knockoffs. They never looked like anything but scraps of fabric safety pinned together." I laugh between sniffles.

With a delicate touch, I remove the gown from its box. Sleeveless with a cape draping down to the floor from each strap, it's perfect for the Blossom Ball. The front points into a V with an embellished gold and silver waistline. When the last bunch of the fabric leaves the wrapping, a note falls to the bottom of the box. It reads:

Alexia,

My girl, oh, how I miss you. I'm over the moon to know that my flesh, my walking heart, is still on this earth. I know it's been rough and there are many things unsaid, but always remember that I will protect you until the world's end. I am overjoyed to know you are safe and even happier to know that even though life dealt you unfavorable cards, you're living as a teenager should. I heard about your school dance and figured Cinderella can't go to the ball without the perfect dress. You have your Prince (he's fine and fantastic by the way), and now you have your glamour. Take loads of pictures. Mommy will see you soon. I love you, no matter what.

A salty tear soaks into the beige paper and the marked ink bleeds through.

I have nothing else in me at this point, nothing else but the purest and most potent emotion in the world. "Kyle…I love you," I breathe.

He grins sweetly. "Oh wow. Alexia, I love you too."

A relieved laugh pushes out of my chest. *LOVE.* I now have love.

He picks me up and spins me around, moving the chiffon dress, wedged between our chests, to carousel around his legs.

"You don't know how long I've waited to say that," he whispers, trying to tame his smile.

"I think I do."

He stares down at me and places me back on my feet. "Can I say it again?" he asks.

"Yeah."

He tilts his head and moves close to the pulse of my neck, kissing the area softly. Then, he travels to my collarbone and plants another kiss there. The magic of it all makes my knees weak. He breaks away from my neck and palms the side of my face. I feel exposed under the light of his gaze, but I welcome the thrill. My true self and all my mistakes are accepted by the most important person in all realms. I'm lifted.

"I love you," he tells me again.

"I love you too."

We close in for the kiss of our lives. His hands sweep under my shirt and rest in the dip of my back. I shudder and repeat my first thought upon entering the Great Room, "I want to stay."

This is all I want—to forget about Eden genes and whether I should tell Kyle, skip the dance, and build on our milestone. But now, the ball is important. It's a symbol of so much, not only because of Kyle, but also my mom and Sarai—who can't live out the things we always planned. I owe it to them to have a great time. And maybe, I guess, I owe it to myself for overcoming everything. I start to believe what Kyle said earlier, I deserve happiness.

What a time to be alive.

I deserve good things. I deserve to be in love.

CHAPTER SIXTY-EIGHT

REBEL IN A BLUE DRESS

I WEAR THE SCENT of Kyle's cologne like a crown. It lingers on the ridges of my nose and lips. Each inhale sends me back into the Great Room—to the return of those three big words. In and out of a dream, somewhere between Kyle's magic and Dama Hadley's Blossom Ball roll call, I wander.

"Diaz? Diaz? Lucida Diaz, where are you?" Dama Hadley hollers shrewdly. She's always stressing herself out. Even simple things like taking roll make her angry. We're only halfway in and she's having a conniption.

"I'm here, Dama Hadley." Lucie trots through the ornate Divine Hall, searching for her place in line with the rest of us. Dama Hadley huffs like a fighting bull and returns to her roll sheet. The entire hall rolls off in gasps, a stark change from the usual scoffs Lucie pulls with her misting gadgets. She is carved from onyx, lit by warm candlelight that gilds the tip of her round nose. Pearls are embedded in the chunky twists of her bun. Russet colors her lips. Between the union of both her inner beauty and glamour, she is the eighth wonder of the world.

"You did an amazing job," I whisper to Alani. "Thanks for doing this…I know you didn't want to."

"Eh…" Alani—in all her 1940s pinup waves and glam—plays her excitement down. "Seeing her smile like this makes it worth it." Lucie's beams are enough to brighten every nook of this historic building. Lifting the front fabric of her powder-blue dress, she hurries to the front of the line, passing Alani and me on her way.

A winter ball makes for a frigid setting. The academy, and all its stone, wood, and brick, is damn cold—too damn cold to be wrapped in chiffon and diamonds.

"Want some hot cider?" Alani rasps into my ear. "You're shivering like mad."

"I can't stop. I'm too cold…and nervous."

Out from the cups of her strapless dress comes her flask. "Told you it comes in handy. Here, it's still warm."

I grab it and go for it before instantly regretting it.

"Don't spit it out!" Alani reprimands quietly.

But how can I not? Either I spit fire and burn a hole into the ground, or my esophagus is no more.

"Quit the drama," Alani snaps.

I down it, and I've never regretted anything more—and that's saying a lot. "That isn't cider!"

Alani takes the flask back with the best shit-eating grin. "Nope, it's whiskey." She takes a sip.

"Uh, what is wrong with you? Dama Hadley is going to kill you."

Alani shrugs. "Hey, I'm here for a good time, not a long time."

Dama Hadley claps her white-gloved hands. "Places, everyone! As your name is announced, please take the arm of your partner at the end of the stairwell. Remember, greet with eyes and a grin, and stroll to the ivy quarters."

Beneath oversized painted portraits of our ancestors, the entire line straightens up along the wall of Divine Hall. Bodies of fluff and fabric ruffle as Kit hurries to scoot in behind me.

"Sorry. Excuse me," she whispers.

Alani peeks over her shoulder. "Queen Punctuality. Guess there's a first time for everything."

"Chill. My zipper got snagged on to my gown," Kit explains.

Kit's face goes from beautifully neutral to a smeared bleed of brown, peach, and pink, before my eyes. Just hers. No one else's. Mindful of the eye makeup, I squint instead of rubbing my eyes into focus.

"What's with you?" Alani says, swatting my reaching hand down.

"Something's wrong…Kit's face."

"Thanks, Alexia," Kit snaps.

"No, not like that!" I defend. "Or maybe…do you see? Her face is all mushed."

Kit rocks her neck back and blows raspberries. "I'm fine, Alexia. What did you give her?" she asks Alani.

Alani gives me a cut-and-dry look. "Damn, you're such a lightweight. It was only a sip."

"Really, Alani?" Kit rolls her eyes. "Booze her up for her first ball, yeah. You're the salt of the earth."

"That can't be it. Can it? Oh, God. I'm drunk." I fan at my warming face. "Am I sick? Should I lie down? I'm sweating and I just silk pressed my hair."

"You got her drunk?" Raquel—an underworld goddess in a strapless black mermaid gown and gloves—scoffs from ahead.

Alani flips her hands up. "I can't right now."

"Yes, you can and will. Fix this!" Kit demands.

"Okay, fine. Alexia, listen to me. You need to breathe and just think of embracing the wonderful possibilities the universe has in store for you right now."

"I can't tell if you're serious." I frown.

She goes on anyway, Alani the yogi. "Do it like me." She lifts her hands, tracing the outline of one with the other. "Breathe in, breathe out. Breathe in, breathe out. Why are you two looking at me like that?"

Kit's blurred head shakes. I hear her tongue click. "I bet if Sage Cameron weren't Kyle's godmother, you'd have been expelled by now."

"Say it louder," Raquel agrees.

"What? His godmother?" I say.

An affirming flash of guilt seeps from Alani, followed by the roll of eyes. "All right, I'll dump it when we get outside, Judas."

The whimsical melody of the violin against the voice of an announcer turns my attention back to the ball. I don't know what's up with Kit's face or my eyes. But at least I can see her as she is again. I fuss over the edges of my hair, gently tapping them till I'm certain all baby hairs remain laid. Every rhinestone is still glued in the middle of each swoop. The announcing of couples continues. I see Kit's date, Rylee, they're waiting on the first floor for her to complete her elegant steps down the stairs. Alani and Nate are next. And right as my open-toe heels touch the edge of the marble staircase, Nate greets Alani with a tasteful peck. Dama Hadley, who's now huffing, is displeased. Her instructions were to take arms, not lips, dammit.

I giggle under my breath and brace for my name to be called. "Alexia Jacobs and Kyle Pereira-Phoenix," the announcer calls out. This is our moment, another milestone on our map to forever.

The end of my cape leaves a train of chiffon behind me as I move down the steps. I feel larger than my regular life, like a princess gifted with one night of magic.

Then, I see him.

Waiting in a tux and bowtie, postured and proud, he wears his heart on his sleeve and drops his jaw when our eyes meet. I reach out and push up his chin.

He holds out his arm for me. "I'm the luckiest guy in the world."

I hook on to him and return his glow. "And I'm the luckiest girl."

Outside, the rain doesn't touch the glass torches lighting the walkway through the topiary. It's an odd thing to see, raindrops falling around the perimeter of the ball, leaving each attendee dry as a bone.

Kyle brings his mouth to my ear and ends my curiosity. "Thank God for Sage Cameron."

"She's always clutch," I respond. "By the way…when were you going to tell me she's your godmother?"

Kyle gives a surprised smirk. "Probably at the next family get-together when she starts pushing everyone to try her vegan ambrosia."

We walk through the courtyard. Between the torches' lights, I spot crystal and pearl strands hanging from a row of oak trees. At first sight, they appear as they always do, but with a second glance, they wear long, black, gaping faces on their trunks. Their horrified eyes and mouths elongate. I shake my head and peer. *What?* Stretching beyond recognition, the faces melt from the trees, and in an instant, the horror is no more. All is as it was. The rose garden, which normally closes for slumber at this hour, behaves like a show choir and sings an old jazz melody. At the tail end of their song, we enter the ivy quarters—a large dome netted in twinkling ivy vines. Heaven on earth is what we're living in. A scene my psyche could never put together in my dreams, and yet, the high of it brings me low in an instant. Above us, a neon blood-orange moon hangs—a mark I can't believe I'm seeing.

"You good?"

"No," I say faintly. *Why tonight? Why now?* Instead of Kyle's voice, I hear my frantic heart. "I need to sit."

"Right here?" Kyle looks around. "Are you sick?" I don't respond as I'm just trying to breathe. To think. But my other half gets it after the slightest glance at the blood moon. It is the night of Nadir.

Kyle squeezes my waist and pulls me closer. "Hang on to me. I've got you."

I'm safe. Nadir can't happen if they don't have me. I can't be attacked here. I've outsmarted them, I tell the anxiety consuming me. In the blink of a moment, I've been robbed of a full evening of happiness and beauty. Outside doesn't seem so perfect anymore. I'm not sure if it ever was, but I see things differently. Mud streaked on blades of grass. Buzzing flies. Dead lilies and fox gloves. Grey foliage on the ground. The death winter brings.

I keep my head down and close my eyes. "It's a little too early to be so tired at your age, Jacobs. She all right?" Damo Ben aims an inquiry to Kyle.

"Yeah…small headache. Too busy today, she forgot to eat."

The cold contact of Damo Ben's metal limb is on my shoulder. "Hey, don't get lost in this. You need to recharge." When I peer up, his hand rebuilds itself into a flashlight and floods over my eyes. "Pupils are dilated."

"Because you're shining a light directly in her eyes…call me crazy."

Damo Ben spotlights Kyle. "Be good to her. It's a sketchy night." Kyle and I know what that means…but does Damo Ben know? Is he in line with Sage Cameron and Greta? "Table nine, kids."

Inside the ivy quarters, candlelight illuminates the ballroom. Garlands dangle above tables topped with crystal candelabras and flowers. Hues of rose gold, blush, ivory, and muted yellow paint live in every corner, along with a soleil lantern-adorned tree that stands in the center of the ballroom. To seal the night's glamour, iced confetti floats in midair and dissolves into a smoky vapor at the floor. A Shakespearean sonnet come to life.

The clock ticks away, but the night stays young. All of Malveaux dances till our feet ache. I, on the other hand, must make sure I eat something before I keel over. Kyle rounds up saucers of fruit until crab cakes and pasta are served for dinner. Beside me Nate plops into his chair. Bits of his clothing are undone after dancing—if you can call it that, and I bet Dama Hadley wouldn't—with Alani. All the gel that had been in his hair forty minutes ago has sweated out.

"Does it ever disgrace your parents to know you two are joined at the mouth and genitals?" Kyle jokes.

"Only when they consider our offspring would be related to you." Nate smirks and clinks glasses with Alani. Her waves have dropped into one vixen-like swoop over her eyes.

When I giggle, Kyle massages my back. "Feeling better?"

"Lots."

As if it's possible to outdo that answer, Nate offers me whatever is in his flute. "It's just hard cider," he says.

"You two really are made for each other," Kit sighs from across the table. "Alani already beat you to the punch and liquored her up."

That's when Kyle's eyelids peel back like old-fashioned blinds. "What the hell, Alani?"

"It's okay, Kyle. I'm fine…," I tell him.

"Can we stop acting like I'm the source of everything that's wrong? No one is pure enough to be shitfaced from a sip of…" Alani checks around her. "Whiskey."

"We're talking about it because Blossom Royals don't behave like this," Kit replies.

"Well, here's hoping I don't win so I won't have to live as a square for twelve months."

"At least you know who you are," Rylee, Kit's date, backs Alani. With slick hair and a charcoal suit, they're too stylish for Malveaux. They and Kit—whose dress looks like smoke in the midnight sky—are by far the best-looking couple here.

Our table gets back to talking between bites of our food. Nate is going on and on about his fight to wear an old suit instead of a new one like his mother preferred. "Grants are never second-rate!" he mimics. Raquel empathizes and shares her own laments of her parents' expectations. Erik escapes to the table from Lucie. He's fresh from the dance floor, doused in sweat, in serious need of water, but not quite free when Lucie and her giddiness recapture him.

"I studied this dance for two weeks! C'mon, hurry!" Lucie cheeses and pulls Erik back to the dance floor.

Nate is amused. This is something he'll never let Erik live down. And right next to us, the Phoenix cousins are using their strange and unique ways to communicate. It's a mix of hand gestures, lip reading, frustrated squinting and sighing. Honestly, it's having an argument on mute—totally ridiculous. But I pick up the hard sound of "Nadir…Nadir!" when Alani is having trouble reading what Kyle pretends to speak. I soothe him by holding his hand. His tension loosens immediately, and he stops. Alani's got watchful eyes on me from her end of the table.

"I feel really good," I tell my friends. "Even better if we could dance a little."

"Let's go!" Nate sprouts up first, then Alani.

I follow suit while Kyle delays making one more quip. "Who'll hose those two down if I go? Serious question."

Not our problem, say my two hands. Like Lucie did her date, I grab on to mine and whisk him away from fast talk and sarcasm to the dance floor, where he can be mine.

It's just a matter of time…whether it be me…or them, my mind teases. *The Mother has to bleed, and you are her.* I've been so afraid to tell my friends this, and Kyle also. He's been so heavy until this evening. I'd rather keep fighting myself from weighing him down with worry.

We become lighter when we focus on the music. Under the lights, is my love's face—chiseled by God and better than any bust man could carve. The waves have stopped crashing in my head and I focus—on him, the sound of a slow dance beat, the bass in my chest, and the arms I'm in.

"I'm so happy right now," he leans in and whispers. He's close enough to kiss, so I make the trip.

"Nah-uh…six inches apart!" A ruler points distance between us. Dama Hadley couldn't be terser if she tried. "Keep it wholesome!" Off she goes to find the next offenders, although we can't understand how Alani and Nate keep going unnoticed. There's not an inch or centimeter of air between them. People have even skipped dancing to watch.

Music I've never heard before goes on and on. Outside of the songs Alani plays in our dorm, and the music Kyle plays while we study, I don't know much about Varien music. So, when the realm rockstars Home on Saturday take the stage to perform, I'm not greyed out in our field of color. I'm excited too. All of Malveaux dances, and when we want to retreat for a rest, we fight through the pain.

"Good evening, everyone. Welcome to Malveaux's annual Blossom Ball!" Sage Cameron takes center stage and commands the attention of the crowd. Zipped in a lilac gown cluttered in floral embroidery, she's doing justice to her formal look. "You all look so lovely tonight. I'm inspired by the respect and love we continue to harness for our land. We see its gratitude daily, as The Grove flourishes and grants us a safe and majestic place to reside. The Blossom Ball, a celebration that stands community wide, will always remain our covenant of appreciation to Mother Nature. Let us also learn from The Grove, by remembering to show love to one another while we have time. It doesn't take much to observe how far its nourishment has carried us. This is also true of our relationships. We stand here because we are loved by so many."

Applause warms the ivy dome.

"Moving on, shall we begin our Blossom Royalty ceremony?" Sage Cameron asks the crowd. "My final nominees, please make your way to the stage. Remaining students, fill in the dance floor. Dama Hadley, the stage is all yours."

Kyle teleports us next to Nate as Alani shoots past us.

"It's showtime," she mumbles, switching her hips through the crowd.

The final nominees parade the stage and stand to the side of Dama Hadley, who now has the microphone. We can hear her complaining to Sage Cameron about Alani's dress code violation. Sage Cameron pleads for her to carry on.

"Are you sure that split isn't cause for disqualification? It's two inches too high," her shrill voice mutters. She clears her throat and turns on a happy front. "A Blossom Royal has the social responsibility as the muse of both spring and summer. They're the ambassador of flora and fauna and a liaison for Varien-nature relations. This is no small feat; great responsibility and compassion come with the title. Thus, the one who wins Royal today will take the first step into a ring of social achievements. So, without further ado, allow me to introduce the runners-up."

Dama Hadley opens the envelope in her hand. "Please give a congratulatory hand for your new Lily Blossom Royal, Jess Maldonado!"

Third place.

"…And Cherry Blossom Royal, Alani Akina-Phoenix!"

Second place. Not what Alani was aiming for at first, but it's what she preferred knowing she couldn't uphold the Blossom Royal standard.

The band plays a new number. The crowd claps and rumbles as Alani and the other Blossom Royals kneel for their floral-gemmed tiaras.

"If I had a potato sack, I'd put it on her right now," Dama Hadley mumbles again, holding the microphone at her stomach while she reads the contents of the other envelope. "Now, here's the one you have been waiting for. This year's Blossom Royal is…Kirath Kaur!"

Kit shines brighter than ever and gasps beneath the halo of the crown placed on her head.

"I knew it!" Kyle shouts.

Dama Hadley hands the microphone to Kit, but Alani snatches it away.

"Thank you for all that you do. Dama Hadley, everyone!" She raises her arms.

Dama Hadley reaches out to grab the microphone back. Alani dodges her and moves center stage to deliver a passionate speech about the pitfalls of respectability politics before Dama Hadley finally drags her away.

Once Kit finally gives her monologue of thank yous in the background, Nate scratches his head. "What just happened?"

"Hurricane Alani," I answer.

Even though her antics threw a wrench in the Blossom Ceremony—and probably sentenced her to a month's worth of detention—the ball is far from ruined. Home on Saturday returns to the stage and knocks out another show. The waterfall works as their backdrop, rushing along with the strength of the guitar and bass, growing stronger and changing colors through mighty solos and choruses. The night is ours, especially for the young and in love. We all happen to be both.

Later, in the thick of the band's second set, in the midst of spinning around with Raquel, a sick stench sways me into nausea—waste and decayed food. Blinding lights pierce into me yet again. I need something. A sip of water, or a splash, before I empty my stomach right here.

"I'll be right back," I tell Kyle. "Just gonna head to the bathroom."

"I'll come with you," Raquel says. I don't stop her. All I can think of is holding myself together till I get through the bathroom door. "Are you sick again? Did Alani pass you the flask?"

"No…it's that smell. It's too strong."

"Smell? I don't smell anything."

I push through the girls' room door. Raquel goes into a stall.

"The smell," I talk myself through. Things are spinning and I hold on to the sink for stability. "The smell from the caverns…" Realizing it is enough to end me. What the heck does this all mean? Is my body fooling me through my trauma? The caverns smelled of death, nothing close to what the ivy quarters is filled with. Quickly, I splash water on my face to get cool and calm. "You're home," I say to the girl in the mirror. "Home is safe."

But the girl in the mirror is me with frightening details—half her face is missing with skin and flesh peeled back to her hairline. Black blood spills from her mouth and rains down her neck. Fear is strangling me is so tight, sound won't leave me. I'm so locked, I've forgotten to turn the water off. I can see it filling the sink as the drain is too slow to empty it. Only as it fills to the brim, its contents turn thick and tarry black. Strings of muddy ooze drip to the floor in overflow. A matter of some sort, a skull atop shoulders fights to form inside of it.

In seconds, I'm all sound. From mute to 100. Raquel bursts from the bathroom stall. "What's wrong?"

"I don't know! It's them, I think."

"Them?"

"They're coming. They've been telling me this all night, maybe. I know it."

"Alexia, hang on! Breathe. You're losing it.."

"Dead! I was dead or dying…half of my face was ripped off." Saying it makes it real, and reality is turning me into a body of energy. I could blow this entire room up if I don't calm myself enough. In between thoughts of my dad by my side, I make up a plan. "We have to get everyone out of here. They will die with me here."

"What do you mean everyone will die? What's wrong with you?"

"Please listen to me! We need to get everyone out of here. Trust me! There's no time to explain. Not even a second."

I become aware of seconds that never arrive once the stalls begin to rattle. Raquel grasps my arm. Lights blink.

"Oh my gosh!" She startles.

"C'mon!" I shout and lead the way out the bathroom. I pull the fire alarm on the way out. It's quick. It's loud. It moves everyone from the ivy quarters and rushes them back toward the academy.

Hand in hand we race to where we were on the dance floor. Kyle spots me and reaches out. He knows everything without hearing a word. But then the ivy quarter's lights shut off as a great chilling boom blows at our ears. Raquel's hand is yanked from mine and all at once a shriek from the depths of her chest rocks me.

"Lex!" I hear Kyle amidst feral screams. He pulls me to his chest.

"Wait! Raquel!" I say to him, feeling around for her. Light exposes the obvious. Raquel is gone. "We lost her!" I tell Kyle.

"She's probably in the academy." He pulls on me. "C'mon, we've gotta go!"

A startling wash of rain slams down from the once shielded walkway. I look for the one person responsible for our protection from its wrath. Given the terror inside of me, she must know. There would be no way she wouldn't.

It's the wrong ending to the sweetest night. A misleading bite into half-rotting fruit. The dichotomy that's followed me to The Grove. Nothing good, it seems, can stay.

CHAPTER SIXTY-NINE

GASOLINE

RAQUEL RAVENWOOD IS THE one name void of response during roll call. Dama Hadley's jaw trembles in the wake of silence met. Every student in the academy knows she's missing, but only I know her absence to be a kidnapping by the Revenirs. She was with me one moment…in my hands. Pulled away the next. A terrified cry is all she left—the only memento or clue to pocket on the night of this Nadir. I can't think. Can't act like I believe those sounds and events were freak happenstance when they were acts of terrorism. Terrorism meant for me. So why is Raquel the one they took? Did they intend to grab me?

Across the auditorium, I spot Sage Cameron cutting through the crowd.

"Sage Cameron!" I hike my gown up and rush over lounging students. "Sage Cameron! Did you find her?"

"Who?"

She's apprehensive and barely making eye contact. "Raquel!" I shout. A change in pitch does nothing as she makes her way out of the auditorium. I dodge and bullet through to keep up, desperate to grab her attention. "Hey!" I call out one more time and grab her forearm.

Dama Hadley's eyes nearly melt from her head. "Oh no! Hands off!"

With her shock, I catch myself and immediately let go. "I'm so sorry, Sage Cameron…I need to talk to you."

"You need to have a seat," Dama Hadley snaps.

Sage Cameron intervenes. "Dama Hadley, it's all right. Alexia, come with me."

Come with me, she says. But her walk is nearly impossible to keep up with. An ache in my foot dulls with each swift step. "Do you know where she is?"

"Who?"

"You know who."

"Raquel."

"That's right, you said that already."

"I know."

A beat passes. She thinks, heels clink.

Greta comes out from an office room and joins us. "The board is expecting us in fifteen…"

"What does the board think? Do they know where she is?" I aim my inquiry to Greta. Maybe one Cameron sister will respond.

"No, but all schools are being informed by the guarde and required to create emergency response." *Bingo.*

"Knox-Oxley too?" I add.

"Greta," Sage Cameron warns as we continue the pace.

Greta never makes eye contact with me when she answers, "Declined the invite."

"Greta!"

Looking ahead, Greta argues, "Alexia is not in the same position as the rest of the children, Maureen. Treating her as if she is will only exacerbate the situation."

Sage Cameron stops abruptly. "You are exacerbating the situation."

"I'm not giving away details."

"Greta, you are feeding details! We don't need any escalations."

"What could she possibly do?"

"Drug Andy Navarette for the second time! Intercept Pynman's Den! Storm Knox-Oxley!" My friends pull up as Sage Cameron retorts. Her head turns to the right slowly, as if the neck it sits on is rusted. "You four will give up your phones, head to your rooms where security are positioned outside."

"But no one else is honoring curfew right now," Alani scoffs.

"Everyone will be dismissed to their rooms shortly. All halls and rooms are closed for the night." Sage Cameron looks to her left and summons a man waiting on her a few steps away. "Lamont, please escort the children to their dorms. I would like for you to take up post permanently outside the two boys' rooms to ensure no one teleports out of our facility."

"Yes, Sage Cameron." Lamont nods with both of his huge hands clasped together. He's muscles scooped on top of muscles with a clean face and a smooth, shiny, round, bald, mahogany head.

"Lamont's gifts can bleach the gifts of those in near proximity to him. I'm grateful for his help on this night as it will help me focus on these other urgent items."

"What? Sage Cameron!" I shout. "Bleach?" I repeat, confused and surprised. Lamont wastes no time in showing rather than telling. A coolness drips through my body and I feel empty in my stomach and chest. Empty in a way I never knew I could be empty before.

Alani snaps her fingers and no flame sparks.

Nate punches at a locker without kinetic charge.

I push for stars to leave my skin, but that burning feeling is iced over.

And Kyle, our only hope of getting out of this, closes his eyes to teleport only to find he's still here.

Proud of his power and his service, a pleasant smirk stretches Lamont's face. "To your dorms."

CHAPTER SEVENTY

One Way Out

Locking me in a room with a living version of fire was probably not a good idea. Lamont, or "Bleach" as Alani calls him, dropped us off at our dorm first. We were surprised to find a security guard outside our door, but relieved to know they are at least staying there and not coming in. A double shot of relief came after Lamont walked off to the other end of Fates' dim hall to check the boys in to their room, where he'll set up shop for the rest of the night.

Our blood is warm again and the stirring flares of heat I occasionally feel in my chest and stomach are back. But the fact remains—we are in a cage. A five-star cage—but a cage no doubt. And while we complain and groan and fill our room up with bad moods, Raquel sits in real danger somewhere. Her only saving grace is the group of school boards and our corrupt guardesman who are moving at the most glacial pace and having meetings.

There's no time for their kind of plan. Not on the night of Nadir. Not when an age-old pact has been broken and a child has been attacked on Malveaux grounds.

So much for Louis's promise.

"I want to burn everything down," Alani seethes. She's going to burn a hole in the ground just from pacing back and forth. Her dress is in a heap on the floor and her gloves are living on opposite ends of the room after she spun them like helicopter rotors and threw them.

"Alani, please," I beg her. "I'm already worked up right now. I'm angry and scared too. You're not helping." I change out of the beautiful dress my mom got me, hang it up, and zip a protective cover over it. Kyle's black hoodie and leggings—my outfit of choice—remind me the magic is over. I had it for a moment, a brief and vibrant one...at least.

Alani tries her best to sit and perches herself upon the armchair Nate made her. Her hands go back to searching around the drawers of her nightstand. "There has to be something somewhere."

"Something?"

"Matches. A lighter!"

I click my tongue and tilt my head. "Alani, you cannot burn the building down. Stop."

Alani slams her hand down and dramatically sits back. The oversized olive crewneck she wears hangs off one shoulder. "Why aren't you mad? You of all people should be the maddest. They took Raquel and probably meant to take you in retaliation. Don't you feel guilty? Aren't you pissed you can't do anything?"

"Who says I'm not?" I snap back. "Just because I'm not ranting about burning the only place I have to call home doesn't mean I'm not all those things."

Alani catches herself and settles down. She slouches in the bend of her armchair and looks out our window. "I'm sorry. I didn't mean anything..."

"I know. I know. We'll figure things out. We just need to stay calm so we can be clear."

"You're right...it's just how clear can we be to get out of here? There are no options. No way out the door. No way out the window. No annoying teleporter to get us out of our problems. We're cornered."

Cornered. It's a word I don't want to hear right now. I take a block of bubblegum from my nightstand and unwrap it.

"Got another for me?"

"Yeah," I say.

Alani comes over and takes the gum, then cuddles up right next to me in my bed. "Things are getting bad, aren't they, Lex?"

She has no idea how bad things really are. I've told her what the Revenir headquarters were like, how Sarai is a Revenir, but I never told her the worst part: that her dear late uncle was once a Revenir; and her cousin—whom she's so protective of—made a vow to soon be one too. Kyle hasn't said a word about it either. Then, there's my Eden gene secret. "I'd say so…"

We sit in silence and the amber glow of the ceiling's soleil light. It tints the cream butterfly wallpaper and linen curtains tan. I never noticed how beautiful and cozy it is here. Never thought of how much I'd hate to never see this place again. That must be all Raquel can think about, never seeing Malveaux again. Never stepping foot in the dorm she calls home during the school year. Never breathing again…

Faint pressure sends tears from my eyes. Poor Raquel. I can't think of her without crying and I can't not think of.

Rustling sounds come from the side of my bed. I turn to Alani, whose head is on my shoulder. "Is that your feet making that noise?"

"What?" She sits up. "No."

"It sounds like it."

"Lex, you would see me moving if I was moving my feet."

We stare at one another puzzled. Not sure what either one of us heard.

"It's me," a voice from below whispers.

"What?" Alani and I gasp in unison.

"I'm in the vent."

"Who's in the vent?" I ask, crouching.

"Marcel Malveaux," the voice sarcastically delivers.

"Kyle!" Alani and I whisper in surprise. In an instant, I grab my dagger and start unscrewing the metal cover. When I'm finally done, I place it to the side and a head full of wavy, floppy, dark hair hangs out. There he is, handsome and resourceful, even in the craziest of times.

"Follow me," he orders.

He doesn't have to tell Alani and me twice. I snap my locket from my neck and leave it on my bed. We squeeze our bodies inside the vent and crawl behind him, finding there was one option when we thought there were none.

CHAPTER SEVENTY-ONE

KYLE OF BAKER STREET

KYLE WAS RIGHT. LUCIE is a mad genius. The same route that brought Kyle to sneak off to the Normal realm, brought us through the vents, in between walls, and out from behind the wall that houses Marcel Malveaux's portrait in the library.

In the dimly lit space, Nate startles us as the wall opens and we find him front and center. My heart drops then settles when I hear his husky voice say, "I was getting worried."

After hopping out the hole in the wall, Kyle gives me and Alani a hand down. "So you stand right in front of the portrait? I almost went into cardiac arrest."

Nate apologizes, and to our surprise, skips the PDA with Alani.

"So what now?" Alani asks.

"We've gotta get organized so we can rescue Raquel," Kyle answers.

Nate chimes in. "Okay, and how do we do that?"

Everyone brings their focus to me.

"What?" I answer. "I'm just as confused. I have no idea where they took her. She could be at headquarters. There's no guarantee she's anywhere, so…we have to choose the most likely location."

"Which is?" Alani drags her voice.

"I don't know. I just know Nadir is held somewhere separate. At least that's what I remember the DeuxCadets said in an old video. And Knox-Oxley's faculty declined the emergency conference call because they're obviously guilty but also occupied. So, odds are, she's where their ceremony is."

Alani waits a beat. "Do you think this means Raquel has the Eden gene? I mean…you were haunted all night…but isn't that to be expected after what you and Kyle did? You said Sarai doesn't have it. What if Raquel is the one?"

My head drops as I know I have to lie. I have to wear this weight in a time that makes carrying on with it unbearable. "She could be…," I reply. "And that's why we need to hurry and figure this out. C'mon, before we get caught."

The minutes don't pass like normal. As I'm scouring books, I can't help but feel as though time is slipping away like granules through a sieve. These are old devices—of mine and Kyle's. We know how to work together, where one is weak and one is strong and how to save time. But with Alani and Nate tacked on to our sleuth work, taking flight likens to a wobble-legged sparrow leaving the nest for the first time. We can't find our current.

"Okay, I don't understand why you think you'll find something in any of these books. It's the library." Alani smacks. Her hands run over dull book spines.

"Have you read every book here?" I question.

"No."

"Then shush and scour." I lodge a textbook in her hands.

"Great. *The Grove: A Photographed History*," she reads mockingly. Still, Alani isn't done arguing. "Alexia, Marcel Malveaux hand approved each book that references Knox-Oxley ages ago. You're not going to find blatant content about Revenirs and Nadir."

Her practicality makes me sweat. "That may be so," I say. "But there could also be breadcrumbs that lead us closer."

Alani shakes her head. "…She's going to die if we stick to this."

"Who's going to die?" Nate chimes in from the other side of the aisle.

I storm off for some solace. Some place to focus like mad. Equipped with a flashlight, Kyle sits at a desk with his gaze on yellowed pages. He pulls out a pilled houndstooth chair beside him. "There aren't any texts here with maps of the school."

"Nothing online?"

"No."

We stare at one another, emphasizing how odd that sounds.

"I know," I tell him. "They declined the board call, remember? And they're the only school without a map for public consumption. Something is happening there."

"Nadir."

"Yeah."

"Why don't we just go then?" Nate creeps behind us.

"It's not a dream of mine to be fileted, but you're free to go on…" Kyle huffs.

"You two aren't going to find anything by being assholes," Nate jokes.

Kyle cuts his eyes. "That is *exactly* how we've found everything."

Alani passes Nate a book in my peripheral vision.

"*On Intention: The Narrative of Louis Knox and the Architectural Law of Attraction*…yes…fun." Nate stretches the sarcasm out. He's so committed to being annoyed; he nearly knocks over the marble bust capped at the head of the aisle. "Everything is basic."

Alani, who makes a seat on the floor, can't stop the wheels in her head. "We need to really think about things. I can't be the only one thinking Raquel has the Eden gene."

"No, you have a point…I'm starting to wonder the same thing," Kyle responds. "We need save her before they have their way with her."

My ears ring hot. I've got to tell them before I send them walking in to the lion's den. "They meant to take me," I dive right in.

All three of my friends lean in. Ticks from a distant grandfather clock bother the pit of my stomach.

"Sarai doesn't have the Eden gene...I do."

Kyle and Nate's faces are stuck.

Alani seems to have trouble breathing. "Your labs...you already had the results."

"Yes...I guess there was another one that came after the first chunk."

Alani shakes her head. "How long have you known this?"

"Not long...a few weeks."

"A few weeks? And you didn't tell us?" Alani hisses.

"I was processing..."

"Alexia, we should've known right away," Alani scolds.

"I could barely wrap my head around it. Sage Cameron told me, and I literally have felt like I've been running full sprint since."

Kyle drops his head. "That explains everything. You were off because they told you what this means." The low warm light from the overhead soleil lights hits his scabbed knuckles. A reminder of the course we've battled. There is so much between all of us. My friends wipe their faces. The sound of sniffles fills our space. Pain and fear swell larger, making little room for much else.

"Look, I'm sorry I didn't tell you all. But you have to understand how hard this is for me. I wanted us to move on and enjoy what we have."

"You can't make decisions like that for us," Alani replies.

"She can decide what to share. It's her information." Nate takes a seat in an old leather armchair. "None of us should feel entitled to any of it. Didn't we sign up for the cause on our own?"

Kyle nods. "True...but when you care about someone...it's just nice to know."

It is too quiet here. Too cold and warm all at once. Too much hurt and discomfort to stomach. "I'm worried they grabbed Raquel as they intended to grab me," I go on. "I know it's good to be here... to be safe and all. But they could return for me any moment."

"Or they could be using her as bait," Alani says. "Knox-Oxley promised to never harm students on Malveaux grounds. There must be some loophole we're missing. Let's think this through."

"Yes. I understand they promised not to harm students. But they did, and what do I do? Hope and hide forever with this looming over me my entire life? I can't. I could barely sustain these last few weeks."

"Lex," Kyle breathes. "What're you saying?"

A sole tear slides down my face. "I'm saying I have to go to the lion's den again. I can't wait for them because doing so means I will die. But if I'm smart and I come to them on my terms, I have a chance."

As I catch my tears and hold back the pour of others, Kyle sniffs, pulling in his own sadness.

"Nadir is happening, and Raquel," I go on, "who no one in this school cares enough about, is in the middle of it because of me. She *will* die. I have to go in her place…either to stop it all or…I have to go."

Alani looks around before speaking, "And you know we'll be with you…" Nothing more is said. Just exchanged faces of confirmation.

We scour pages as best we can, putting our four heads together to build pieces. Much of what we find is light and superficial, not a revisionist history, but an opaque canvas of academic life post Louis and Marcel's separation.

"Only five books here on Louis…and nothing worthwhile." Nate shakes his head. "Except this guy was a pure narcissist with a penchant for fêng shui. He named his mansion Turnstile."

Kyle lets out a 'hmph'.

"What?" Nate replies.

"A turnstile is a gate that allows one person in at a time. Fitting." There's a flicker in Kyle's hazel eyes, a sudden shot of fuel which travels up his spine and powers him to jump up and point his flashlight at the book. "What's that photo up there?"

"That's the house," Nate responds.

"But the inside…are there any exterior photos?"

Alani and I perk up to the sound of Nate flipping pages.

"There! What's that?" Kyle points.

"An exterior photo…"

"What's that beyond the mansion?"

"Mountains?"

"C'mon, Nate…that spire. That's not part of the mansion."

In seconds, Alani comes closer for a look and agrees. "Right… it looks like the ones atop the institute." She points at a picture from the book she's holding. "What does this mean?"

Kyle shares his deep thought. "When Alexia and I went to the Montparnasse, our guide defined Nadir as a 'turnstile of death to seed all life.'"

I shake my head in disbelief. "How do you remember that?"

Kyle ponders and Alani breaks in the conversation with simplicity. "He's a freak of nature. It's not a power, but he remembers everything for infinite amounts of time. Always been that way."

"It just stood out and stayed with me," he clarifies.

"You're so sharp, Kyle." I smile. "I think that's it. Revenirs communicate cryptically. They do this for Passage. Why wouldn't Nadir be any different? It can't be coincidence. The Turnstile Mansion on Knox-Oxley acreage…it's probably working as a gate or filter of some kind and the actual location of Nadir. All this time we thought it was in Pynman's Den, but there's more to it. The turnstile of death to seed all life is the Turnstile Mansion!"

"We don't know for sure!" Alani makes this clear.

"But Greta let on that Knox-Oxley faculty are in on something when I chased Sage Cameron down. They declined the emergency district call and Sage Cameron did not want me to know any details. Greta downplayed the repercussions, while Sage Cameron named me storming Knox-Oxley to be one. Why would she do that if Knox-Oxley isn't the epicenter of all of this? We need to get ahead, and we need to go now."

Alani slaps her hands on the sides of her thighs. "Going would be great, but that's another question: How do we go? We can't just make things up as we go."

"Who says we will?" Kyle points his flashlight under his chin with a stoic face. "When you have friends in high places…you don't have to. Let's go." He motions for us to follow him and we go back the way we came. Behind the dignified image of Marcel Malveaux, ready to fight the ongoing legacy of his estranged dead brother.

CHAPTER SEVENTY-TWO

Gang of Rogues

"**I** CAN'T BELIEVE THIS," Alani rants as we make our way out of a large cement tunnel—a piece of the route Kyle walked to get to the Normal realm with the Midray. Through Lucie's own quirky excursions through the walls of Malveaux, she found a defunct floor of rooms that let out into a defunct basement which was connected to the edge of Malveaux's property line and some other zoned area. It's a maze on its own. But thanks to the infrastructure viewer, things have been smooth. "Why does Lucie know this shit? Sometimes I wonder about her. She's always thinking big. It's like she's preparing for something," Alani rambles. "Like what does she know that we don't know?"

"That should be obvious," Nate tells her. "Everything."

Kyle agrees, "Yeah, she hasn't steered us wrong. You're wrong about the Midray too. It works perfectly."

Alani stops in her tracks. Her mouth hangs open. "How would you know how it works? Did you...use it?"

Nate acts as if he doesn't hear anything and takes big steps ahead of them. I jog to catch up with him as Kyle and Alani bicker in the background. Alani's voice box is completely fueled as we make way to the Hoverwagon. It's tucked under a tree, concealed by bushes as tall as Nate.

"She should be reported," Alani nags.

"We're not reporting her," Kyle says.

"Well, the ancestors would say otherwise. Their guidance should be the only way in and out. Not some experiment. It defies the rules of our land."

I look over my shoulder. "Since when do you mind rules?"

"Since two minutes ago…when my bonehead cousin admitted to offering himself up to a kid scientist. He may show up with another nose on his face tomorrow or watch his eyes slide down his face during breakfast now."

"Would that be the worst thing?" Nate jokes as he slides open the door to the Hoverwagon.

"Stick your tongue down her throat and shut her up." Kyle begins to crouch into the front seat.

We follow his lead under the amber moon, creating a chain of shadowed bandits entering the vehicle.

Kyle whips out a key from his pocket. "Call her up, Lex."

Kyle had to let Lucie in on things in for a hefty price: rooming with Alani and me for senior year. Those were her terms. When Kyle told us what he promised, Alani's mouth ran with expletives. But steep rewards are born from steep favors.

"We're here, Luce," I announce.

Headlights on the Hoverwagon click and flash. *"She's ready, and I'm connected."*

"Thanks," I reply.

The odor of burning wax gusts as the engine rattles the doors. Alani rolls her eyes. "Is this thing going to make it?"

"Of course! It has enough soleil energy to get you there… I don't believe it has enough to get you all the way back, though." Lucie's voice comes through the speakers.

Alani lunges from the backseat. "What?" She checks the energy gage. "Why would you offer this piece of crap if the fuel is low?"

Poor Lucie pauses then stutters to answer. *"A-after Alexia and Kyle used it last time, I never brought it back to Malveaux. I didn't want it to get taken away from me. So…I drove it here and hid it. Which explains my inability to refill its soleils."*

"Ughhhhh," Alani groans and flops back.

We tell her to chill, and Kyle goes even further, explaining his plan is to teleport us back home anyway.

Upon launch, the Hoverwagon makes it into the winter night sky. A man-made UFO above the trees. None of us know the way to Knox-Oxley tonight, but the Hoverwagon does. It cruises like a fine helicopter.

A thin screen ejects from the dashboard between where Kyle and I sit. Round face in full glam—it's Lucie. *"I never got to show you this feature! Like?"* She laughs when we jump. *"I probably should've warned you. I get too excited and forget everything."*

"If you forget anything while we're up in the sky, my firebird's got you," Alani says, pulling forward from the back.

"You're hilarious." Lucie shakes her head. *"Activating stealth mode for invisibility. A new feature I programmed for ultimate privacy!"*

Slight relief relaxes my spine. "Lucie, you think of everything…"

"Thank you," Kyle finishes.

"It had to be done. I knew we'd team up again at some point…for a more dangerous mission." A half smile tugs at her cheeks in an all-knowing way. At this point, she's proven herself an ally—someone who has given me the devices to at least put up a fight and get answers. She's never snitched, and for some reason, I know she never will.

As we fly on, we paint each other's faces with the coal and shell paste I left in the Hoverwagon weeks ago. The personas we assumed at Passage and the last initiation still live. And thankfully, the boys brought black attire and gloves for Alani and me to change into. We blend in with them perfectly, but the vision of us, these gothic painted kids, reminds me how quickly the night turned awful by forcing us out of our formal wear.

"There it is…" Nate points at the front window. An angular and sharp building with warm lights pooling from windows and streetlights. Knox-Oxley. Beyond it, a batch of hillside wind turbines spin at a low speed. A chateau property down the way is bathed in midnight and blood orange. The Turnstile.

"Drop us into the woods, Lucie," Nate tells her. "Keep us in stealth mode and drive a little closer. I'll walk up the rest of the way."

"Seriously? When did you start leading all of this?" Kyle quips.

"Since I became the one who could get you all into these things," Nate replies while studying the earth below us.

We descend as planned and park somewhere foliage can hide us. The three of us rogues making way to the Turnstile Mansion, with an heirloom blue blood as our admission.

CHAPTER SEVENTY-THREE

THE TURNSTILE

A BLANKET OF THICK fog rolls through the forest and encircles all of Knox-Oxley. It makes midnight a sinister hour. The fog can be an advantage, but it can also enable our foes. I don't know how anyone would be able to spot Lucie's invisible Hoverwagon among the trees, but this is Knox-Oxley and the Revenirs we're talking about. I won't allow myself to get too comfortable.

Alani checks her watch incessantly. "It's been too long. He hasn't said anything. Something's wrong."

Under heavy brows, Kyle's hazel eyes scan our old 3D map to track Nate's movement. "He's in. He's just pacing himself. Blending in."

"Nate?" Alani calls after tapping the earpiece Lucie equipped each of us with. "You're scaring me."

A beat passes. Static starts. *"Don't be. I'm inside."*

"Did you take the chasm again?"

"No. Admittance was simple. Just had to show my heirloom coin."

"Ah. I've never been so grateful for nepotism." Kyle nods.

"Should we teleport now? Where to?" I ask, reviewing the 3D map.

Nate's voice breaks up but clears quick enough for us to hear. *"Cloisters on the east side. They're closed off, open, and dark. Ceremony is in the amphitheater. Raquel's got to be in one of the room's attached to it. That's where I saw a bunch of Revenirs go in. Hurry."*

Alani and I set sights on Kyle. "You think you can do it?" Alani says. "Get us in safe just from studying the map?"

"This is the third time you've asked," Kyle scoffs.

"Well, I want to be sure."

"*Well*, it's making me anxious."

"He's got this," I break in before giving Kyle a reassuring look. "Okay? You've got this."

His posture resets—an affirmation of my statement. I don't waste a second to lock hands together. Kyle gifts me with a kiss on the back of my hand in return.

"Ugh…gag." Alani scoots closer to an annoyed Kyle who rolls his eyes before gripping her palm and vanishing us from the Hoverwagon. When the smoke clears, we're in the corner of an open area…a courtyard bathed in overhead light.

I sink closer to Kyle and Alani. "This is wrong. Get us out of here."

"I know," Kyle says, looking around. A group of older students are walking ahead.

"Kyle!" Alani scolds in a whisper and yanks his arm. We teleport once more and appear elsewhere. This time on heels of a tall man and woman draped in black.

"Sorry!" Kyle exclaims.

Alani is quick on her feet with a reply right as the skull-painted man sniffs out the scent of Kyle's smoke. She makes a straight face and plays things off. "All good, I just hope I didn't singe you." She holds a fireball and presses her hands together till nothing but smoke remains. "It's a cold night."

"Sure is." Kyle nods.

I agree and smile.

"There are warmers near the floor of the amphitheater. Grab your seat quick so you can be close to them," the female Revenir encourages.

"Thank you," Alani says.

The three of us behave like strangers as we walk off separately in the same direction. I wonder what those Revenirs must be thinking as we move. Are we even headed in the right direction? We must be giving ourselves away. We carry on through a garden full of large topiaries when a large wall of jasmine grants us the privacy to teleport again.

"Get us there. No more fuckups!" Alani spits.

"Shit. I know."

We take hands. I close my eyes. All of my matter evaporates and reappears. Once I feel the ground beneath me, I open my eyes. A hall of darkness and the silhouette of arched eyelet columns. The cloisters.

"I think you did it," I whisper.

"Yeah, it only took three tries." His voice is doused in disappointment. The hardest critic. This will be something he'll obsess over for weeks…if we're alive.

"C'mon," I tell them. "Follow the fire light over there." We move fast but quiet. When we arrive from the cloisters, the image of our trio has changed.

Alani pauses on the stamped gravel. Her smart eyes roam over the figure between us. "You look just like him."

"I am him," Kyle corrects her in Nate's voice.

"I mean even down to the scar on his chin."

Kyle slaps her hand when she reaches out to touch him. "Seriously, right now?"

"I'm not trying to kiss you."

"Could've fooled me."

I keep quiet and let my feet do the talking. We have somewhere to be, and our game faces need to be on. Our minds must be solid and focused. "Nate, we're en route. Are we still good for the back entrance?" I page from my earpiece.

Static sounds, then his voice comes clear. *"No. Plan B."*

"Plan B? We didn't talk about a Plan B," Alani panics and power walks beside me. "We don't have time for you to explain a Plan B."

"But you have no choice. A group of Revenirs went in…take Plan B."

Alani's jaw juts out as she shakes her head and glares. "We took too long."

"Where do we go?" I ask.

"There's a room that was unlocked. Some sort of twisted custodial closet. It leads out to some dumpsters out back on the west end of the amphitheater. Can Kyle teleport to them?"

Alani and I wait on Kyle to confirm, but he's hesitant. "It took a few tries the first time, and I barely know the layout there…"

A couple Revenir passersby size us up. "Evening," one of them nods and speaks. Their faces are smeared in coal paste, streaked in ivory lines—as if their fingers rushed down their skin. It's scarier than the skull faces of Passage. "It's a promising night," the Revenir says proudly. "An heirloom's night." He gives our fake Nate a wink, then smiles at me.

We return a mix of nods and pleasantries until the shadowed duo is behind us.

A warm sensation of needles peppers my throat. I'm lighting up inside.

"Kyle," I whisper and wedge between him and Alani. "We need to hurry. I think that guy…he recognized me." I look behind us and all seems to be well.

"You do have to hurry…I don't know what the heck all of that meant but it ain't good." Nate comes through our ears. *"Do you see the dumpsters on the side?"*

"Yes," Kyle replies.

"Just teleport there. If you can see it, you'll be all right. I'm inside and I'll let you in."

"Are you sure?"

"One hundred percent."

Without a word, Alani, Kyle, and myself are linked. We vanish and reappear behind the dumpsters with ease.

Alani breathes heavy. "We made it, Nate. Nate?"

A rustle nearby sounds. "Yeah?" Our dirty-blond herculean friend comes around and reaches out to Alani.

We made it. We actually freaking made it.

CHAPTER SEVENTY-FOUR

THE FOOL

BODIES AND RUMBLINGS ARE just outside the closet. A group of Revenirs talking no doubt. This changes things a bit. Saws, tools, and a variety of blades are pinned to the brick walls. The undulating light spilling beneath the door changes shape as feet step about. This wouldn't be an ideal place to be caught or seen leaving.

"Kyle, you have to move us," I demand. It's "move or be moved" loud in my head, hot in my flesh. "We need to go."

"How? We can't walk out that door."

"Shit. This was a mistake." Alani shakes her head.

"Hang on. We just need a minute," Kyle explains.

"A minute is not promised. We need to do the plan accordingly," she says.

I shake my head and turn back to face Kyle. "Remember how you phased out to the pond? We were in the hall outside of Oz's but were still moving. It's like we were mid-transport."

His wide hazel eyes draw up then close shut when he recalls. "I don't get how I did that."

"You can do it, though. It's exactly what we learn at school. You just have to pull. What were you feeling in that moment?

454

What was in your head? There's an emotion there. You manifested that ability through a token you hadn't used."

He's trying hard to trace back. Fighting through the noise pollution outside and the sterile scent of medical and industrial tools inside. "I was in shock…I guess. Everything was moving fast. I was thinking of my parents and how my dad could've been intertwined with those guys…"

"What guys?" Alani's voice breaks his focus.

"Shh," I whisper.

The sole of a heavy shoe plants on the other side of the door. More rummaging. The search for keys.

Kyle closes his eyes. "Scared about…losing you, Alani, and Nate…my world."

I see his image thinning into transparency and jump to grab his hand. "Keep going, Kyle," I encourage.

Alani and Nate take hold of him as well. The four of us are departing, but not fast enough. A key slides into the lock and the sound of grooves turning causes Kyle to open his eyes. The door slowly draws open. My heart races and drops all at once. I can see someone entering…then nothing. White noise. The same static as before. We are moving, jumping from space to space without fully materializing. We keep jumping. We even jump back to the closet with a view of a Revenir in a white coat, loading tools into a leather bag. But we keep moving on and on. Teleporting in and out of different places. Searching and searching the Turnstile amphitheater rooms until we see her. A pretty corpse. She lies on a bed of mint velvet. Hands and feet tied to the gold posts. I don't have to tell Kyle to materialize. He does it on his own. Piece by piece we make the transition from the static to Raquel's room. Limbs heavy like lead make me trip. Nate stumbles. Kyle pauses to catch his breath. Alani looks like her head is swimming.

"She's alive," Nate tells us with his hand on her pulse. He retrieves a knife from his boot and works at the heavy rope around her right wrist.

I fight through my clumsiness and make way with my dagger. "Raquel," I whisper once I'm placed on the other side of her. "Raquel…please wake up." I cup the side of her warm face with my hand. Her cheeks are flushed, the same rose pigment as the tip of her nose and lips. The ballgown she was kidnapped in has been replaced by a silk garment that reaches her ankles and drapes from the bed.

Alani and Kyle make it to the foot of the other posts when she wakes.

"Alexia…," she mumbles. Once her sapphire eyes stretch wide, she groans. "No…no!"

"It's all right," I say. "We can get you out of here."

Raquel shakes her head in protest. "You shouldn't have come. No!" Tears well and stream down her face.

Nate cuts her left wrist free and moves on to the post holding her ankle.

With her gift of fire, Alani works on the ropes around the other.

"We've got you. Okay?" Kyle assures her. "As soon as they get you out, we're gone. I'm gonna get us home."

Raquel shivers into a nod. Her trembles make me wonder what could've happened in the window of time they've had her. As the board of education met and the guarde pretended to investigate, she has been ruined. A quick prayer comes and goes in my mind while I focus on cutting through the ties holding her wrist. *May we all get home. May we all have peace. The Revenirs will end.* With a few more motions, the ropes unwind and fall to the Persian rug on the floor.

"You're a bit early, aren't you, Bel?" Set comes from the shadows of the other end of the room. Only his yellow eyes are visible. The tips of his wings second. Then his smile hits the light. "And you've made it a party." He nods in amusement at my friends.

Raquel cries and leaps off the cushions. Blank on a plan. Thoughts racing.

I turnaround and shout for Raquel to run with us. She proceeds, then abruptly stops. Alani grabs her but she yanks her arm away. Her black hair whips. A closed smirk dawns on her plump lips. The shape of her face, the sharpness of her cheekbones is a menacing mask I've never seen her wear.

"What're you doing? You can't stop him!" I shout.

"Raquel, let's go!" Kyle shouts.

She says nothing.

Set stands still.

Raquel stands still.

We fall out of form at the realization of her eyes fixing on us. We are in the middle.

"Oh." It comes to me. The ick of embarrassment. The wound to the heart. Betrayal is both of those feelings occupying the same space. Alani brandishes flames on both her fists. Kyle and Nate have changed stances, ready to fight. Yet I can't help but crumble within her gaze. Our trust was built on fraudulence. A trail of breadcrumbs to lead me here.

"Why?" Kyle demands. "Why are you doing this?"

Barefoot. Step-by-step, Raquel comes closer. Once an angel, now fallen, her movements are foreign. So different from the way I knew her, very much a Revenir. Confident, cool, otherworldly. Almost extraterrestrial.

"Say something!" Kyle yells.

Raquel laughs—half scoff, half giggle. Her rose colored mouth parts to respond, right before her eyes flit over to me. "Oh, Mother...may I?"

CHAPTER SEVENTY-FIVE

THE BAIT

Arrows shoot from the porcelain Greek statues peppered around the room. A pinch tweezes at my neck, and I fall cold. I palm at the site of pain. Something's been shot into our skin. Nate grits his teeth. Kyle sets eyes on me, then Raquel.

"Can't have you teleporting about anymore, lil' friend." She shrugs. "Or flambéing us where we stand. We definitely can't have you using kinetic energy to bring buildings down." She walks around us, delighting in our everchanging reactions. "Wait, you thought you actually beat the system? That you were so smart?"

We don't respond.

"You did?" Raquel feigns shock. "How cute."

"Raquel, what're you doing?" I say.

"Why are you here?" Alani adds.

Set doesn't let her finish. "She did what she needed to do… find you. *And,* without breaking any old blood pacts. That's the beauty of staging your own kidnapping." Before I can calibrate his next move, he grabs me by the neck. My friends shout while I swing and fight the dullness inside of me. My gifts are out of touch. Dead. "You were our Maltese Falcon. And I would've never known if you hadn't revealed it to me yourself in the pond. That violet halo…can you imagine? Can you put yourself in my shoes and hear the symphony of that moment? Thank you."

He squeezes tighter and a whimper comes from my throat.

A scuffle behind me clamors. I see Set raise his other arm. "We did this already, my man," he lectures. "You got lucky the first time. That won't happen again."

Kyle is screaming. Crying in pitches I've only heard that evening at Ren's. Alani cries and begs for Set to stop.

"You really are crazy. We gave you a chance, you know?" Nate shouts at Raquel.

"Aww, Nate, sorry to ruin our friendship. But when it's your time to go…it's your—"

"Stop it, Raquel!" Nate interrupts. "What do you want? Money? I can give you whatever you want. You know that."

Set's face grows amused.

Raquel giggles. "Oh…yes, Nate. Please. Throw money at it. As if money holds such great value. And…wait…I'm sorry, but do your parents know you're here? Wouldn't they be disappointed?"

Nate freezes as Raquel grows tickled. "I see them sometimes. Throwing their pocketbooks about the way you just did. Real chip off the ol' Grant block."

All of our weapons wiggle from our waistbands, pockets, and ankles. All but my dagger flies to Set's feet. Raquel catches it in midair. I throw punches at Set's arm and can't help shedding a few hopeless tears myself. Finally, his hold loosens, and my body drops with Kyle's. I turn around, coughing for short sips of air as I run to him.

He's holding his shoulder. Between the spaces of his fingers, I can see his shirt has been ripped through, and so has his skin. Blood is soaking through.

"Bitch!" Alani yells. She slaps Raquel's face. A clear and clean pop echoes in the room. "You set us up! You lead us here to die! You fucking bitch!"

In an instant, Alani's hands are pulled back by Set's mind. Nate is shoved to a wall. Kyle and I are pried apart. The four of us dragging about as though marionette strings are looped around our joints. Where my friends go, I separate and watch them drive up a paneled wall and disappear as it flips around and fastens shut.

"No! No! Bring them back!" I order.

Set nods at Raquel. "Get her ready for the ritual."

Raquel nods back. "Yes, Skullmaster."

The menacing cold eyes I've feared reach over to me one more time. "Don't make this harder for yourself. Your blood *will* be ours."

CHAPTER SEVENTY-SIX

TRANSPARENCE

A PLAIN WHITE DRESS. That is what I am ordered to change into. Made of linen. Full of wrinkles. My face paint must be wiped off. A clean face presented. All jewelry—the four piercings in each ear, a ring my parents bought me one Christmas with my initials—must be removed and placed on a catchall.

Raquel watches me complete each requirement. I've never seen her look at me in such a way. She is stoic, yet resentful. No care behind her aqua eyes. No warmth in that mouth she used to encourage me with during SIM Class. Her skin in this cold room is the color of milk. It wraps in her frame, which I'm noticing has grown sinewy since the day we first met.

"Sit."

I shoot a defiant glare.

Raquel's brow perks. She closes in on me. "Either you sit, or I make you."

My mind says back down, but my body does another. I spit in her face—with a heaping amount of saliva. It's the disrespect she deserves. And for a moment, it is absolutely worth the punishment. A slap hits my face. I shove Raquel and she falls steps back. When she gains her footing, I step up to her again. But she is handy.

A speaker from the wall beeps, *"Reinforcements needed?"*

"I don't know…" Those fox-like blue eyes ask, *Are you done?* The question comes with the pinch of a blade aimed at my stomach.

I cave and fold into an ornate wooden chair.

"Good girl," she taunts before telling the speaker, "I've got it. Thanks."

Raquel scoots an ottoman toward my feet and takes a seat. Her gloved hand picks up my bare hand, studies it, and turns it 'round till my palm is up. I fight the urge to knee her in the nose or give her the two-piece knockout she deserves.

She grins. "Such tiny veins." My brain goes in a whirl as to what that means. Raquel reaches for items on a three-tray cart.

"Mmhmm." A sinister grin on her face. She taps my arm. "Ah, there we go." A packaged needle is in her other gloved hand.

I squirm at the sight of it asking, "What're you doing?" as though we still have some sort of dignified friendship.

Raquel humors me with elbows on both knees and the now filled needle aimed at the sky. "Puritine. Cleanses your blood. Increases the number of red blood cells and their quality. You're gonna be our prized heifer." She winks, cleans my shaking arm with alcohol and pokes into my skin. "We can try as many times as you'd like. I'm not a phlebotomist. But I did learn about intravenous procedures on the commune. We did our own medical. I suggest you calm down and let me get it right."

I grit my teeth as the needle comes out.

Raquel examines the area and tries again. "Ah, there we go." Little by little, the liquid disappears from the needle's reserve. A coldness surges at the sight of the shot. It is polar. Painful like a frostbite. When I grimace, Raquel gets up to throw away her used gloves and trash—she acts like a doctor. Washing her hands in a sink behind a cloak of curtains. Like she's done this too many times.

I hunch over. So much is happening. How did Raquel fool us all for so long? How has she been right under our noses? What is going to happen to me? I don't have an ounce of a plan, or that mustard seed's worth of faith I usually carry around. I am void of the good things and filled with bad. The worst being the cold pain traveling through my body. As it moves, my veins grow visible. I gasp in horror as I take them in. They have turned black and swollen so big, my fingertips can feel them beneath my skin.

Raquel returns with a bowl of steaming hot water and a sponge. She wrings it out and draws its heat across my collar bone and arms, then cleans the coal and shell paste from my face. The action does alleviate some pain, but I know this is not intentional. The Mother must be clean for sacrifice.

When she moves to my back, I cover my face with my hands. "You've been with them this whole time." Spills of stress, shock, and sadness fall from my eyes. "I was your friend."

"Hmmm…but was I ever your friend?"

"It doesn't matter. You set me up. You betrayed us all. You lied!"

"Lied? I never lied. Well, I did lie by omission. I couldn't tell you that my mother and stepfather were both Revenirs. Legends among their kind. But really, the writings were always on the wall, Alexia. They were just…painted over." We come eye to eye. One of us disgusted and the other thrilled by her power move. "You never even cared to know what my abilities are. Ever think of that?"

Sudden embarrassment hits me. I sure didn't. Why didn't I? Was I that consumed? She never used her powers in SIM Class. I never asked about them.

"Nightmares and intrusive thoughts—they were all me. My illusions. If you were smart enough…you would've seen all of this. I had to antagonize you to push your buttons. Fears always hold answers and tell truths."

A montage of all my feral fears and the odd SIM sessions. *It was her.*

"Why else would a pariah come to such a school?" Raquels says it like it's obvious.

"A sane person would want a clean slate. A different life from her mother's," I snap back.

"Wrong. A sane person would show up to prove themselves worthy of value. She would correct public opinion by showing what she's capable of: tact, being unassuming and resourceful."

"Couldn't you have just initiated yourself like everyone else."

"Did you hear what I just said? Do you get any of this? I said I'm a pariah! No one believes in me after the Hundred Mile. I was thrown away!" She rattles off but quickly gets herself back together. "I was a pariah. I'm not anymore. But because I *was*… other measures had to be taken to determine my future."

"The sacrifice of another person to get ahead," I snap.

Raquel throws the sponge into the water bowl. "As if you had any real plans. You hold the cosmos in your DNA and it means nothing to you. How sick is that? You'd sooner get rid of it and be an insect for the rest of your life. You never worked for it. You don't deserve it. I deserve it. I was supposed to be you."

Heartless. There is nothing inside of this girl but contempt. It's a contagious emotion. I feel it rushing through me at this very moment. I'm drunk with enough of it to act out. To leap from this seat and choke her…perhaps bludgeon her with a vase. Foreign and nasty thoughts. I don't like it. But if this coup has brought me to feel these things, it's not hard to see why this anger is a second skin for Raquel. It has been her mental diet ever since she was shunned.

"You hate me." Her straight face molds. A curt smirk cuts her cheeks. She bends forward. A scent of cashmere whisks. "I hate you too."

A battle inside of me rages harder. I only manage to prevail when I think of the fate of my friends. I'm also outnumbered and on Revenir turf. I need to tread carefully.

"Oh," Raquel says to the quick swinging door. "Just in time." Three figures enter. All of them are young girls. Knox-Oxley students, I'm sure. Two of the girls look identical to one another. Blond hair styled in a short blunt-cut bob. Nude bodysuits. Very athletic builds. Catatonic in the face like the Manson Family.

They're here to follow orders. They believe in this mission. "She has nail polish on her hands and feet. Remove it as well," Raquel orders.

"Yes," the twins say in unison.

The third girl comes behind my chair. Her hands work through my straightened tresses. In my peripheral, I see her brown hands. She works through my scalp like its familiar territory, drawing lines with a fine-tooth comb and sectioning chunks of hair with clamps.

"Do your best braids, Sarai. Yeah?" Raquel perks a single brow. She gives me another shit-eating grin. "I remember you telling me they're her favorite. She sure did wear them often."

I turn around. Sober from anger by heartbreak. She can't be part of this. She can't hate me this much. I study her for signs. Sarai is the same as I last saw her. Hardened, but still Sarai. Not a complete zombie. Still, how do I read her now? As she braids my hair in cornrows pretty enough to die in. How? Once my sister, now my foe. She's not only purchased a ticket to my downfall, she's made it possible. While she may be trained to show little to no emotion by now, I am not. I sob a cry so great and wounded, it chokes me. I am not a whole person sitting in this chair anymore. I am a girl that has been broken down to her soul. A mosaic of something I once knew to be beautiful. I wish I had more time. I wish I could go back. I wish I never met Sarai.

CHAPTER SEVENTY-SEVEN

Nadir on Stage

Nothing matters. None of the good I have done. None of
the regrets I've had. None of the wrongs I've tried to right.
I have wasted so much time pouring into someone I loved until
minutes ago. But she's so twisted, so poisoned by bitterness, she
would never receive my efforts as acts of love. She'd see some silver
lining of selfishness. Some reason I took the risk for my own gain.
And this disdain for me—my inaction—is enough for her to want
me dead? I can't understand it. I can't live with it.

We say nothing to each other as she braids my hair. Her hands
aren't only light, or only heavy. They're the same as they've always
been, a decent mix of grip and ease—most careful on my crown,
the sore spot. I wonder what this means for a moment before
determining it means nothing. It is a job.

"All right, done," she says.

Raquel nods and buzzes the speaker on the wall. "Moving on."

The words order two male Revenirs at the door. They wait for
Sarai to cuff my hands, then we're off. In a formation of seven,
I am surrounded. A Revenir positioned at the front and back.
Raquel and Sarai on either side of me. The twins at my back.

Numbness swells larger inside of me as the seconds tick. I throw
stares at Sarai from time to time, searching for some familiarity or

remorse. Yet, there's only the glint of fire from the wall torches in her eyes. An urge overtakes the numb feeling, and I give in to it.

"Sarai…," I whisper, ignoring the tears crawling into my mouth. "Do you really believe this? Why are you helping them?"

Sarai rolls her head back and tucks her mouth. A curious whirl hits my stomach. *She reacted. That's something…*

As I spiral into interpretation, I realize everyone has stopped walking. Raquel and Sarai look ahead, but the head Revenir at the front glowers at me. He steps closer and his cloak drags against the graveled ground. One step. Then two. On the third, he stomps and a wave of air gushes through me. All wind is knocked from me, and when I work my mouth to cry out in pain, no sound comes. I tremble when I realize what he's done and fall into obedience—to move on and continue the walk to my death. Void of all autonomy over my body and stripped of my voice.

We arrive at a door when the hallway lets out. The stadium is ripe with noise and buzzing energy. It's a wonder I made the walk the way my nerves feel—splintered at the ends, worn into threads. Through sore, swelling eyes I can see the stage floor as I venture onto it. Large, with stamped golden sand, a ring of fire burns the perimeter of the stage. A stone chamber is in the far back of the stage. We stop as we come to the left of it when Set appears from its mouth.

Raquel, Sarai, the twins, and Revenirs kneel. I don't move. The crowd grows louder—a bunch of dry faces painted in white.

"Bow! Get down, girl!" I hear one Revenir spit. She is gaunt and wiry with tinged teeth that camouflage with the flesh of her mouth. My gaze drags down her row. Across more shouting and flailing attendants dressed in tactical gear. Three faces are recognizable. Three innocents in a field of tarnish. My three—Kyle, Alani, and Nate. The only people with despair wearing on them. Tied to their chairs, they're helpless with no ability to do anything but shout my name and cry. I turn my head. I cannot look at them. I cannot face Kyle as he watches me die, another person he loves. Alani and Nate will never be the same again and I hate all the Revenirs for making it so.

At this point, the audience of many grows more volatile and begins throwing items on the stage. Cups of liquid. Clumps of mud. Food. I stay strong and unmoved. Set is three steps away from me now. He's slowing down, almost giving me a chance to correct myself. If only this was something to obey. I won't be doing any bowing or worship of any kind. Not while I can breathe. I keep testing him—staring him dead into his eyes with each heavy footstep.

"Hardheaded," Set says, realizing. "Till the very end." He breaks away from me, faces the jeering crowd, and raises his arms. The jeers turn to roaring and cheering howls. The blind allegiance is so bizarre, a stranger would mistake the Revenirs for rabid football fans. The only difference is the extremism. How far they're all going for their system of beliefs. This is not feuding fans duking it out in the stands. This is not the heckling of an opposing team. This is a group of people, many of them adults believing that a child must die tonight.

"She's ours!" Set's voice carries through the stadium. The bare skin of his chest and back turn bronze near the ember-colored flame of the fire pit. His wings are richer and cleaner—a regal hue of gold.

In the middle of observing, I'm pulled to a stone figure shaped like an hourglass with a post down the middle. The two Revenirs are rough, yanking my arms away from my body as I resist moving forward.

Sarai! Please! Help! Help me! Don't let them do this! I am shouting through my body and still nothing can be heard. I drop all my weight and fall to the floor. Revenirs huddle over me, ready to reassume control. The two break apart, as Set pushes between them, and gathers me in his hands like a doll.

No! Don't touch me! Get off! Get off! I say from inside. Yet, he takes off in midair. The launch stiffens me and brings me closer to his chest. Not soon after, we descend, except we don't land on the stage floor, we sit right into the cup.

"You're scared." Set grabs my face, speaking quietly so only I can hear. "I know it isn't fair…" For once, he's less menacing, and that somehow makes him scarier.

"But we didn't make it this way…people like your pops did. He's the bad guy. Wonts are the bad guy. Those big shot politicians, they're the ones who put a hit on you and the old man the day I turned up."

"What?"

"Seeing your clean face…I remember you."

"Who wants to kill my dad?"

Set grins. "Wanted. They pulled the hit after seeing how things turned out. Guess they felt his karma was enough." He giggles. "Don't make me the bad guy. I just want to bring the balance back. The world as it was. You're going to give us that, okay? Your sacrifice won't be in vain." Set props me up and begins tying my arms to the post's 'T' like branches. The entire crowd is quiet now, all except my friends and their cries, and the crackling of the fire pit. "One life for a utopia."

I cry as the ropes around my chest, wrists, and ankles are tightened. When Set is done, he jumps down to the stage and addresses the crowd again. "This is not a gluttonous sacrifice. I do not take what we are about to do lightly. A life—undeserving of death—will be lost. We take lives, yeah? But from the corrupt. The soiled. Not from children and innocents. It is the cycle of karma that we operate on. Every dog has their day, and we give it to them. The Wonts…are dogs." To this, the crowd rises in excitement.

"We hide. We don't live proudly. And we should. We are made in God's true image. Their bloodlines lost the Varien genes as they took them for granted and became greedy, bitter, vain, and careless. We shouldn't be here…hiding. We shouldn't yield to live beside them. We should be over them. Leashing them to move when we say move, eat when we permit, and involve themselves with us when we allow. The game is all wrong…," he says while pacing, then he stops and faces me. "But not for long. Not with our Mother."

The audience erupts and Set kneels down to the cup. He's shouting now. "We are humble at your feet! Receiving every cell you shed! Your breath will become our breath!" Pulling a thick knife from the sheath of his holster, he continues, "We are grateful and receiving of your loss to breed victory! A victory! A victory for all time!" The blade is wielded, and Set is amped, crouched with veins protruding from his neck.

The crowd is the most ravenous it's been since I stepped out. All I see are yelling mouths and white faces. Ghosts. A cult. My chest heaves with my cries and I stare above, over the stadium seats at the stars. They will be the last thing I see. Not the Revenirs. Not my friends. Not Sarai or Raquel. Certainly not Kyle. I won't do that to the ones I love, and I won't give the satisfaction to the ones I hate. A mass rises, a Black body sprouting gold. Set. He is in motion. Wings flapping. Blade posed to strike where the red moonlight touches my neck. His arm extends, and I am ready.

I've given myself a chance to correct my mistakes. I've gone on a journey for someone else, but I have fallen in love with the person I am. I know what it's like to be loved and to feel love. I ended up with true friendship with people who weren't afraid to go down with me. My family still loves me. I have lived and accomplished all I needed with blessings. Dying, for me, will be a gain. I believe it. I trust. I'll be okay.

Set's body glides closer to me, till he is all I see.

I am ready to die.

I close my eyes tight.

I open them seconds later, when the blade should have met me. Set's hand is empty, and he has floated back, looking to his right.

The audience collectively gasps.

I follow their focus, the line extending down to stage right. She is bursting with an aura void of sunlight. Shiny, jet-black hair blowing in the wind, milk white skin aglow with the blade tight in her grasp. Blue eyes brooding under a low brow as her chin tilts. Raquel, the dark horse in my life, has hijacked Set's move.

CHAPTER SEVENTY-EIGHT

HER HAVOC

SET'S EYES BLACKEN. HIS skin begins to tear. Flesh chunks fall to the ground. The Revenir inside of him is breaking through. It shrieks a battle cry as Set's wings flex.

Raquel is immovable when Set takes off, and as he torpedoes toward her, foreign incantations dance from her mouth. "Montovel!" Her hands swish and conjure their own current of wind. Then, she stops abruptly. Feet apart. Eyes locked on Set as she hangs her mouth open for a spill of tar to exit her body. The sight is shocking. The crowd sounds sick and disgusted. This fluid is volatile in its movement, burning as it puddles and eats anything it touches. Fumes billow from the ooze and engulf Set's body until he can't be seen.

I can hear him. He's hollering and grunting in pain, but there's more to the sounds. It's almost as if he is also terrified. Shivers hit me when I try to fathom what would make a Revenir cower like that? What could bring such an embarrassment? How is this young girl throwing a wrench in everything?

It isn't long before the Revenirs around us begin to turn. Those unnatural sounds break through their chest. One by one in the crowd—their bodies change. Flesh peels. Bones break and grow. Monsters are where people once were. Raging and stomping, they charge the stage. The two Revenirs behind Raquel have grown to scale over her with raw, decayed skin and spikes sprouting from their spines. The tar around her creates a protective barrier as it bubbles and splashes on to them, eating them alive and sending gusts of smoke to the wild Revenirs fixing to attack her. A cloud of smoke expands until it blankets all in attendance. More sounds. More cries. Choking voices. A total cacophony. I don't know what's happening. I think of Kyle, Alani, and Nate. This can't be it for them. This can't happen in front of me. My chest aches as helplessness fills me. Which cries are theirs? What are they feeling? And what is Raquel doing all this for?

I close my eyes again. I try to picture myself free.

We'll be okay. We'll be okay. It will end…

I can't see anything but my reality. I can't hear anything except agony and writhing. All I see is fire and blanching smoke.

It will end…, I tell myself, looking up. Shuddering, I keep at meditating. This will end. All things do. I will be home again. We all will be.

The smoke is swelling, inching closer.

God, please, I beg. *Please don't leave me here.*

My tears balm over my eyelashes as I face the night sky again. The stars are strewn across as their dots are connected in a straight horizontal line. I blink and let the tears burn down my face, and the smeared starry sight glows brighter. A piece of lacerated sky bleeds white light. It strobes over me and peels back, giving way to the silhouettes of three figures. Two on the left drop down like falling stars. Their rhythm matches at the start, then differs as they fall closer. One is making their way toward the ground as if the air were solid matter, a series of declining stairs. The other is zooming, gliding atop some kind of vehicle that blinds my view with its headlights. I turn away and look back at the third figure once the lights have passed. It is still airborne. Hovering with its arms spread as wind floods from it. The wind is colorless, yet powerful, causing the smoke fence Raquel conjured to clear and everyone in the audience to crouch for protection. As its power grows, I hear the warping of the metal benches in the audience. The popping of bolts and screws. The wails of loss of control as the cyclone disposes of Revenirs and other guests. Bodies launch into the distant forest.

I look over to find Raquel. She is defending herself against the two Revenirs who walked me out here. They're fighting all out with their powers. Black venom shoots from her mouth as one Revenir takes the form of a behemoth made of boulders. The other may be disadvantaged with their powers, but they are still a fully-formed monster. For a moment, it has the better of Raquel, then she finally lands her attack: her venom hits his face. It burns and smokes and brings the Revenir to its knees.

While distracted, I feel a rough hand grip round my neck. I scream as a blade cuts through the side of it. The pain is bold, then it dulls once the blade exits. Wings show up in my peripheral. Set. He is still intent on his mission. Tonight is Nadir. I still have a fate to meet. Adrenaline burns into my heart as the mental fear of dying again takes me, but then shock sobers me as the figure begins untying me from the post. The wings are attached to a small and dainty figure. "Sarai?" Her name breaks from my voice box in brittle pieces. I can speak again. I wonder how, then quickly remember Raquel took down the Revenir who stole my voice.

"We can't talk."

"What're you doing?"

"Getting you to a safe place. Take that chip out of your neck. I cut the area for you. Hurry up."

"You have wings?"

"Not for long. I was able to echo Set's abilities when I crossed him. C'mon!" She holds out her arms for me. Her face is warm with intention. I know in this moment, I can trust her. This is the best friend I came here for. I latch an arm around her shoulder. The two of us take off. Blackbirds on the rise to the heavens, leaving the chaos on land. It is filled with bundles of fighting and scurrying crowds, making it too hard to find my three friends. I hope they're okay. I'm sure they are. They have to be.

Sarai is working hard to fly against the cyclone winds. She wobbles from time to time as it breaks her strides but she always recorrects herself. Moving us on. Moving ahead. A trickle of guilt passes through me the moment a bit of security hits me. This can't end with just me making it. Kyle, Alani, Nate, and I all have to make it. It is all or nothing.

"My friends!" I shout to Sarai. "What about them?"

"Your friends will be happy you're alive." She gives nothing more.

We fly on, passing to the force sourcing the cyclone. It's her. The one I would never anticipate rising: Sage Cameron. Even through the distance, I can see her divine regality. I stare, hoping she will follow us. She stares back, but I can't make out her face. She doesn't follow. I start to wonder why, and how she could figure I'm safe with Sarai—a stranger to her. When I look back toward her, she's flown away. Still battling those below, and the Revenir in midair pursuit of her, Sage Cameron is a sight. An example of the control and power we train to harness in SIM Class. Dodging all threats coming at her and meeting her offenders with the blaze of lightning. She's got this. She will be all right.

Our flight continues over the Turnstile grounds toward Knox-Oxley Institute. We descend quickly—a small plane without breaks. Luckily, Sarai gets the hang of slowing as we land on our sides inside the bell tower.

"Ow!" I yelp, rolling over the dusty, cold concrete floor.

"It wasn't that bad," Sarai tells me. She gets to her feet and retracts her black wings into her back. "Let's go! Follow me." She gives me a hand and we make our way down stories of slim spiraling stairs. The winter chill gives me goose bumps. Suddenly, the boringness of my routine is realized as a luxury. My bed and the crisp plush softness of my comforter. The smorgasbord of food Malveaux's chefs whip up three times a day. The two-in-one shower-steam rooms in the girls' lavatory. They were all guarantees.

Who needs those things when you're dead? I shrug off the whispers in my head.

"Is this safe?" I ask Sarai.

After creeping around Knox-Oxley's gothic industrial-like halls, and dodging the sights of passing students, she shimmies at a doorknob. Pushes the door ajar. Grabs me quickly, then rushes to shut the door once we enter the room behind it. A force blocks her, and soon, we come to see the pale hand responsible for the power struggle. "Luca! Go somewhere!" she yells.

"With the campus under siege? I don't think so," Luca retorts coolly.

Sarai gives way to his weight and falls back. She snatches up my arm.

"Who is this?" Luca interrogates. As he leans closer, in the dark of what seems to be a classroom, my hip runs into a desk. Only the light from a bubbling fish tank burns—exposing Luca's hollowed cheeks. A chill-inducing look takes him over as he examines me.

"This is our sacrificial guest. I had to move her before someone else took her out," Sarai answers.

Luca arches one eyebrow. "Tempting."

"Exactly. You can't tell anyone she's here."

"That's exactly what I should do. She is the Mother."

"Yes. Yes. Luca, I know. I mean, you can't tell just anyone. I need you to go get Oz and bring him here. I'll turn her over to him."

Luca is not immediately convinced. He's a statue in the dark, weighing things in his mind and making me nervous.

"Luca, please," Sarai begs.

A beat passes and a response comes with expected curtness. "I like seeing you desperate. I guess I can help. Stay here," he warns as his boney fingers release the door.

I ask Sarai if she believes him, and I'm not so sure she does. "Luca," says Sarai, "looks out for Luca. But I'm hoping he'll be happy to play some part in this. He loves clout. When Oz gets here, he'll know what to do."

Not knowing Oz, I don't feel relief in hearing that. Yes, he let Kyle and me go free during Passage, but under certain conditions. Conditions Kyle is still bound to. At the end of the day, Oz is still a Revenir. I am still the Mother of all. The key to the Varien revival.

Sitting in silence with Sarai makes me a raw nerve. She and I have scores to settle. Things time won't fix. Last-minute acts of goodwill will never outweigh her betrayal. I gamble whether speaking up will win in my head. I settle with "no." Not on her turf, when she is the reason I am here. She is a Sarai I still don't know.

A festering ache in my neck draws my hand up to it.

"You still got that chip in there?" Sarai questions.

"We've been moving so quickly."

"Better move quicker and get it out."

I'm no surgeon, so I have no idea how to remove it. The thought of really trying makes my head swim. I press down on the wounded area and shiver once the pad of my finger finds a hard protrusion. The chip.

"That's Oz," Sarai says to the creaking door. She passes a breath of relief that dies almost as soon as she births it. Something is not right. Her body language signals my fear to flare. "That's not his walk. That sound. Oz limps a little…this sounds different. Like heels."

And the sound's owner is here, in this room. A cloak of the darkest onyx—what the sky's hue would be if the moon abandoned it and the stars retired. Sarai and I are still like bricks, edged in a corner. Me behind her, her arms are expanded at her sides—gating me from whatever unexpected presence that has just entered the room.

Faceless, the darkness moves a few steps. "Hmph," they mumble.

And suddenly, we know…

Sarai bends, bracing herself to extract defenses from inside of her. The darkness steps closer, right into the fish tank's wedge of light. Pale skin illuminates. That cold ivory. Nothing could stop her from finding me. She's a force I never anticipated and the fact that I don't know anything about her affinities, her gifts, terrifies me. I can't fight a foe I don't know.

Raquel cuts a grin. "Feels good to come out of hiding. I'm bored with being who the world wants me to be."

"And who is that?" I dare myself to ask. "Who do they want you to be?"

"Depends on who you ask. And that really doesn't matter because I've failed every-fucking-body, really."

"Then who do you want to be?" I ask.

Raquel's teeth sink into her lip as her eyes form into a glare. "You," she answers.

"Me?"

"The extraordinary piece of you."

"I don't get it." I shake my head.

"Don't say that!" She slams her hand on a desk. "If you can't feel it, you don't deserve it. But you have it, and you ignore it. I would never! The things I'd do…the way I'd carry myself…I'd wear it better than you. I'd act like the Mother!"

"Raquel, it's okay," Sarai calms her. "How you feel is valid. I understand."

This doesn't quell our villain into submission. It doesn't trick her either. In fact, Sarai's intent ricochets off the mental shield Raquel has put up—allowing her to spiral into a full-out breakdown.

"Did I ever tell you about the Hundred Mile ceremony? Huh?" Raquel wipes at her chin—where dozens of tears collect.

"No," I respond.

"It was fucked up, so fucked up…but it was more than that. The commune thought I was the one. I fit the prophecy and they believed I'd be chosen as the Mother during the ceremony, but I was never chosen. Fate and God gave what was supposed to be mine away…and I was shamed and shunned by everyone for years. You have no idea what happened during that time. You wouldn't believe me if I told you two now."

I don't know what to do: fight it or talk her down while she's her weakest.

"They called me a false promise…a lie." Raquel's tongue licks at the tears near her mouth. "The Malveaux brothers spoke of a Varien so anointed, she'd move mountains with her fingers, cause quakes with her steps and shine light back to the stars. The Mother Eve. She'd come to lead the Variens and save them from what they've become. Her marker would be her birth on The Grove's birthday. No other Varien can be born on that day: April 22 in the eight year of the new millenium. That was me." Raquel breaks from staring off at the window and faces me. "…Till you were born on that same day."

"I am not…I'm…I'm." I shake my head. "Look, Raquel, you can't do this. You can't be mad at me. I wouldn't ask for this!"

"Exactly. You don't give a shit. You would gladly give it all up to be a mucus-filled Normal who's blissfully ignorant. It makes me sick! That's why I stopped feeding the Revenirs information once I learned more about you. I couldn't serve you on a platter when I could just make my own destiny!"

"Get down!" Sarai forces me to the floor as a canon of yellow light hits where I was just standing. Sarai throws a chair, then charges at Raquel. I can't tell them apart in the night. But I can hear their struggles, Sarai's struggles. I find reason in my panic and remember to move—take the chip from my neck, and hurry! I hate the feeling of it, that rawness, touching the inner workings of my own body. It makes me sick. I grunt and dig my bare heels into the cold floor to deal with it all. Even in a dark room, I close my eyes to cope with the pain and hone in on what must be done. For a span of seconds, I focus on hearing nothing. Because if I'm going to save Sarai, I need all of me. I need my memories. I need my dad and the replays of "I love yous" from hours ago.

My finger finds the small pill-shaped chip and guides it out till it finds its exit wound. When it's out, I hold it between my shaking fingers and drop my arms. Somewhat ready to pass out, but gamefaced to finish this madness. I close my eyes again and pull my tokens. I call the warmth in my stomach and remember what it feels like when it comes to me. What those burning stars do when they launch through my veins. I feel it igniting and heating up. Never have I ever been so happy to experience its surge. I hold on to my memories as the heat travels through my limbs and throat.

I'm going to see my dad again. I'm going to keep being loved by my family and friends…and Kyle. This is not the end of my story; I haven't decided it. This is the end of my beginning.

I'm making damn sure of it.

Sarai is lodged into the air, thrown into a cabinet nearby. She is down, but Raquel lunges toward her to make sure she is out and will never get up again. In breaks of Sarai's grunts, I hear Raquel call out incantations.

Just a few seconds, Sarai. Hold on.

Heat floods my face as light pours from my eyes. The ground beneath my feet quakes. Star rays shoot forward as I steer them toward Raquel and miss. My aim is off. The nerves, I'm sure.

"What?" Raquel snaps. She whips around. "What're you going to do to me?"

As I try to keep my footing on the shaking floor, a white star forms in my palm, and I chuck it at her. Raquel ducks, sings an incantation, and the same star turns yellow and shoots right back at me. I react, my reflexes bring my arms up and a rush overcomes me, manifesting into the form of a sheer violet halo that covers me. I've never felt this way before, so clear and pure in emotion.

Raquel hisses, spitting ooze from her mouth. She's violent and persistent, hissing and spitting multiple times, until it hits her.

She can't hurt me. Through this force field, nothing can. I smile. Butterflies fill my stomach.

"You want my gifts?" I ask her firmly. "They're yours, *right?*"

"Yes!"

"Then take them all!" I shout back.

As Raquel hesitates, I send a cluster of shooting stars to devour her. They rain, sprinkling her in fire and lighting the classroom in blazes. A body of flailing flame-covered arms and legs is all I can see. Cries of agony are all I can hear.

"*Rem nou jin!*" Raquel calls out, and like a dying ember, she fades to burn out and vanish.

"Alexia!" Sarai wraps an arm around me.

"I've got you," I tell her. "Let's go!" I maneuver my best around the sprouting flames. They're too mighty for the erupting sprinklers to wipe out.

A tall body bursts through the door. "Sarai! Sarai!"

"We're over here, Oz!" She shouts.

Two strong arms paw us through a wall of smoke and fire, guiding us through a path to safety. Deep coughs plague me and Sarai. My lungs burn. I've cheated death, again. Maybe for the last time.

CHAPTER SEVENTY-NINE

GILDED CAGE

"MY FRIENDS!" THROUGH BILLOWS of smoke and coughs, I shout at Oz. Kyle, Alani, and Nate—they're all I can think about. "Did you see them?" Last I can remember, the three were sat bound in the midst of chaos.

Oz finds a place to stop. After scurrying us through door after door, farther away from the eyes and curiosities of Knox-Oxley students, we land in a strange courtyard of statues. White marble, but the night's sky darkens them.

"What happened in there?" Oz shakes Sarai's shoulders. "The girl. Where is she?"

Sarai is jumbled, trying to get her words out. "I don't know. Alexia defended me and summoned her gifts. I thought she caught fire, but then she vanished."

Oz huffs.

"You think she's out there?" Sarai asks.

"She's not dead," a disappointed Oz responds.

I fight a shudder and ask Oz about my friends again.

He faces me sharply, almost annoyed but understanding. "I'm sorry. I wasn't checking for them." A beat passes and his eyes drop down then find me again. "We've got to get you back to Malveaux."

"Not without them," I affirm.

"Are you crazy?" Oz frowns. "They're more likely to make it okay. You stay any longer, you're good as dead."

"I'm as good as dead without them!" I storm off, but in my quest to face an army of enemies, I recognize something, something that freezes my bare feet to the pavers. The ridges of my ears burn. So do my eyes. My head is light. Her likeness is in the middle of the courtyard, a white marble statue—dainty and delicate. Crowned in flowers, posed with one hand extended and a light dress draped to bare ankles. Completely bathed in the red moon, I'd know her face anywhere, those sharp cathedral-like angles. That sleek curtain of hair. Otherworldly, as if she were erected from this figure's stone. Raquel.

Behind me, I hear Oz, "You see it...don't you?"

Frantic, I ask him. "Why is this here?"

"She was the one...the prophesied...what everyone in the last century had been expecting."

"Everyone?"

"All the way back when Louis prophesized her: 'A girl who calls to the terra and cosmos and sees them answer, will become them. Land will quake under her feet, her eyes will shine back at the sun, and stars will burn in her blood.'"

"Wait..."

"And she will arrive in the eighth year of the new millennium on April 22, at the eleventh hour in a world region apart."

"A prophecy? That's supposed to be about me?"

Oz goes on as though he doesn't hear me and the world around us isn't burning. "A citizen of both worlds, she will have keys others do not and return our home to what it once was."

"Stop! This makes no sense. Why would Raquel want to be this only to die! Why would she want to be raised for slaughter?"

"Slaughter?" Oz's brows knit. "Nadir isn't the end...it's a beginning. It fills the Mother with the desires of those nourished from her blood and evolves her into another form—an energy a bit more removed from this life."

"That's not death."

"For you, it is."

I've dropped ten stories and shattered every bone in my body at this moment—at least, that's how I feel the more Oz speaks.

"Oswell, stay away from her!" Sage Cameron storms from the other side of the courtyard. Her hands are down, but her stance and rhythm read as nothing to play with.

Oz welcomes a chuckle. "You never told this child who she was, but I'm the one who should stay away?"

"You know damn well why I didn't. That's not her. She is a treasure, yes…but so are all of my students."

"Is this what you tell yourself so you can sleep at night?"

"She is a child, Oswell."

"She's not the same as you and me, or the rest of these kids and you know it." He waves his arms around. "You've failed her! We aren't all destined for the same things, Maureen. Put our different beliefs aside, you should've told her."

"Are you listening to me? You've got the wrong person. This little girl is an Echo, easily mistaken for an individual with an Eden gene, but no Mother."

"You're saying this is coincidence? You know the prophesy."

"Yes, you never did let me forget when we were married…" Sage Cameron cuts her eyes at Oz. "Coincidences happen. You haven't checked her blood, the actual determining factor." She looks over her shoulder. "Alexia, do not move. Greta is planing, she'll be here any moment to take you back home."

"Oh, Sage Cameron…" Yellow eyes illuminate in the thick dark ahead of me. "She won't be going anywhere."

Set is here. Barefoot. Strewn in blood. Still thirsty for mine.

"Stop the pursuit, Set. The girl is not what you think. She's just a girl. An Echo who unknowingly made contact with the person you are actually seeking and projected their traits."

"It pays you to lie."

"It'll cost you everything to be wrong. All of this devastation… and no reward? The embarrassment waiting for you will be hard to live with. You're a leader. Act like it!"

"Serving her blood to our people…what could be better?" Set glowers.

Sage Cameron aims her arms in front of her and the wind wraps around her. "Another move and I've got your number."

"Now, now…that don't sound like the kumbaya you used to preach to me." And with no hesitation, Set plants a foot down onto the concrete. A taunt Sage Cameron responds too quickly. One arm posed straight ahead; she sends a bench into his back. Her other arm commands me with a magnetic pull—twirling me around to face her.

She focuses on my eyes. "Everything will be all right," she says, dangling a gold item from her hand. My locket. Sage Cameron lodges it in the air and takes hold of it with her mind—arrowing it my way. A foreign heat hits me. Liquid on my chest. Seeping into my skin. I try to fall to my knees, but Sage Cameron's gifts are holding my body straight.

I scream and hold on to my chest. That's when I feel it, hot metal under my palm—my locket fused to my bone.

The pain continues as Oz has his turn, pulling Sage Cameron's back with his own telekinetic abilities. This drops me from Sage Cameron's hold and sends me to the ground.

I spit and grip at my chest. The pain is searing. So much so, I am too weak to fight Set when he grabs me. And with Sage Cameron wrapped up with Oz, there's no other defense for me to depend on. I watch Sarai in the distance, her face lit with worry and restraint. A stream of students breaks through the doors, running from the burning area of the school, to become spectators.

Set gets to his two feet and throws me over his shoulder. The end seems near again until reality tears for the second time today. The very fabric of this plane we exist in is being cut open as if it were just a theatre backdrop. A kept promise in progress atop a chopper, Damo Ben and Greta, appear. The rev of Samo Ben's engine alerts Set, and he turns around. I know his game, and he starts his move with extending wings.

"Greta!" I shout upon launch.

Greta jumps off the bike, staring as Set flies higher into the air.

"I got her!" Damo Ben shouts. He makes a fist and aims his forearm in our direction. The metal on it shifts, transforming into some grand artillery. Damo Ben fires and spinning metal objects whiz by. Another cuts Set's lower back and throws him off. Damo Ben takes another and misses, and I begin to believe nothing will be all right.

The thought is brief, as Damo Ben makes the right shot. A spinning blade cuts right down the joint of Set's left wing.

"Ah!" Set hollers. He tries to re-center himself and adjust. He flaps the right wing more, then attempts to coast. None of it will do. Set and I are going down.

Still in her sight, Greta charges up to the sky as if she's rushing her way up the stairway to heaven.

"Let me go!" I shout at Set. "It's just going to get worse!"

"For them." Set accepts his downfall and turns to face Greta in midair. His skin warms and the red particles I've seen reduce a Black Coat to a pulp pours from his body and takes form to saw into Greta. I beat into his body, closing my eyes, thinking of my tokens in defense. I imagine the heat rushing inside of me exiting. Filling the air with threatening temperatures. I can feel it on my face…but in a different way…like it's separate from me.

When I open my eyes a blur of flames flies by and incinerates Set's murderous dust. A piercing call echoes from the flames. Alani and her firebird! A shot of hope fills my heart—the push I need to power my gifts. My hands glow and I beat them in to Set's back. He tilts in impulse. I slide from his shoulder, freefalling down toward the courtyard. This was a good idea initially, but I didn't think of anything afterward. Not smart. Not at all. I flail and remember the force field I manifested moments ago. But who can remember anything right before they die?

"C'mon, Alexia. C'mon!" I yell to myself. "This is the worst way to die!"

A pop cracks in the sky. Smoke. The scent of blown matches. "I can think of a dozen worse than this," Kyle jokes, catching me midair, and teleporting back to the courtyard grounds.

A full-out battle is breaking out around us: Revenirs, some Knox-Oxley students, and our small Malveaux crew. Alani is a sensation. She and her firebird tag team their opponents creating little fires everywhere to further feed the main buildings burn. Where Alani falls short, the firebird fills in, dropping down to kiss a Revenir or drag its tail against the institute's rooftop.

Kyle teleports in and out, avoiding punches then landing his own. Circling Knox-Oxley idiots like a hummingbird and chin checking them to sleep. In a matter of seconds, he gives the illusion there is more than one version of him fighting.

Nate is behind him, fighting his own battles while intervening when Kyle is double-teamed. I can tell he is stuffed with the surrounding kinetic energy. His fists radiate, and when they make contact with screeching Revenirs, he sends them through stone walls or six feet below.

As Damo Ben zips around on his bike, shooting and bending bullets at Revenirs, chills rock me. The sight is something I've never fathomed. This is all because of me. I can't see how we will get out of this. Will we have to fight till morning? Will reinforcements come? Could there be surrender? By my logic, surrender would have to be ours.

The fire eating at the four sides of the building shows me otherwise. We are in an arena of flames. Closed in. No way out and no way in at this point. The battle is what it will be, and knowing this, there's a spot of hope for us.

"Got you!" A vicelike grip cuts the air from my throat. I gasp. Heart beating in overdrive. My feet dangle as they leave the ground.

My neck, in the hand of a Revenir, is pressed so tightly I'm afraid I'll meet my end in seconds. Foaming at the mouth, it turns me to its face and laughs. My hands clutch around the Revenirs fingers to pry them off.

I have seconds left. Seconds before the light inside me dims.

The Revenir hisses. It takes its other hand to remove mine. Slowly, it forces it down to my side. I'm shaking, trying to hold on but I don't see how much longer I can.

A piercing stab slides down from my shoulder to my elbow. No scream can form in my throat, only more suffocation.

Set is bent before me. Eyes rolling in relief and glory, splattered in my blood.

The Revenir drops me to the ground. Something inside my neck pops open. I choke on the air I've missed.

Broken. Sliced. Mangled. My body has seen the worst tonight, and with Set succeeding, it will be something I won't recognize soon.

It's over. Everything we've fought for…it's over.

The Revenir that choked me transforms back to size—a tall and stocky man balding all the way to the back of his head. Rockwell, the guardesman from the Belle Rues. He stands beside a euphoric Set and sops my blood from the ground floor with his hand and licks it.

"Your breath will become our breath," they chant in unison. "A victory for all time."

Everything around us stops. The fighting. The battle cries. The running.

I'm growing faint. The blood, it's leaving me too fast, pooling beneath me and bleeding into the white linen dress.

Other Revenirs rush around me to bathe in my life. They pick up the chant as if they were always part of it. Like zombies, their thirst doesn't seem like it can be satiated, and I wouldn't put it past them to indulge in feasting on my flesh.

"Get away from her!" Kyle runs up with Damo Ben—who scoops me in his arms.

I cry in the nook of his chest. "I'm sorry."

"Nothing to be sorry about, okay? You're a fighter." Damo Ben massages my head as tears I never knew he could shed fall.

Kyle comes to the other side of my view. "Lex, no! Stay…look at me."

"I am," I say. Even through my blurring vision he's still the most handsome. The only one I could ever…fall in love with. He works fast. Removing his shirt and ripping pieces from it to wrap around my arm and end the bleeding. He ties each ribbon tighter than the last.

"Ow," I whisper.

"Kyle, too much pressure." Alani voice comes from somewhere overhead. "Too much!"

"She needs it," Nate chimes in. "Leave him alone."

"We've got to go home," Sage Cameron, who stands before us all, commands.

I can feel the hope draining from Damo Ben. The weariness in his breath. "What? We're too late, Maureen. She won't be herself soon. It's midnight."

The bell tower rings.

After the words leave his lips, everyone—the Revenirs, Knox-Oxley students, all but Sage Cameron—stare up at the red hunter's moon. Giddy smiles infect Revenirs one by one as they wait.

Set reaches to the sky. "Her blood is our blood now!"

Bizarre sounds of euphoria and devastation clash.

Time goes on. Sobs stain joys. *Ticktock.* Wide happy mouths are mixed among morose shaking chins. *Ticktock.*

The minute passes and everyone wearing my blood is as they were. Realizations start to bloom. People check in with each other, even my Malveaux crew. Still faint, but not any worse, I sit up a little as the fact gives me a light second wind. What is happening?

With his arm stretched in front of him, Set wonders out loud, "Why aren't we turning?"

"I feel nothing."

"She is the one…right?"

"Set?"

All eyes trail to him.

Sage Cameron has never let up on him. He's been at the other end of her gaze the entire time. Regal, and more powerful than the woman she was that one day in her office—when she spilled her fears of Revenirs to me—Sage Cameron raises her head. "Don't say I didn't tell you so."

Set is seething and confused, yet his posture admits defeat. In exchange, Sage Cameron conjures rain from the clouds, a mercy they don't deserve.

The broken fools in inglorious blood watch us leave them behind as Greta tears into the plane, taking us through a passage between worlds that leads home. One by one, Sage Cameron, Alani, Nate, and Kyle all enter. Damo Ben picks me up, and before he walks through the tear, I spot Sarai and Oz beyond their horde. There is something all-knowing in Oz's face. As if an answer lies in each wrinkle age has given him. He gives a pained look at Sarai, who would've cried if something this catastrophic happened to us a year ago. Instead, she's more complex than I've ever known: this dichotomy of love and hate, respect and disdain, my villain and my hero. I wait for her to show me something, but she is stoic. It isn't until Damo Ben has one foot out of this plane, that she pats the center of her chest and nods.

My sister.

A stranger.

Greta enters the in between last and sews the tear behind her. The worst chapter in my life finally closes, while the stings in my arm and chest remind me how much further I have to go.

CHAPTER EIGHTY

The Two Madonnas

DOCTOR LANGLEY FACES ME. Six months have passed, and still, I am one piece. "Your flesh is fusing to the gold just fine. No infection. No poisoning," he tells me. "I'm pleased with the progress of healing. The wound looks beautiful."

Wound. A four-inch slice on my arm and a golden locket cauterized to my chest. Deep brown scars have grown over my cuts, and my skin has finally healed from my locket's burns. I wouldn't say they're beautiful, but they're me now. Just tattoos of survival.

"Thank you." I smile.

The doctor asks if I have any more questions for him after plopping his hands in his lap. There are things I wonder about, like the stinging I feel in my sternum occasionally and the exhausting dizzy spells I have—but I'm already on iron for anemia, and I visit Dr. Langley every couple months to ensure the locket is still fusing with my body peacefully. Things are better left with the shake of my head.

I'm dismissed and free to go, except the doctor reminds me of my mental health check with Sage Cameron in one hour. "Taking care of your brain after a trauma like that is just as important."

This lecture, I know. It's part of Malveaux's principles. But what no one talks about is how much work mental health really is when you're so out of shape…like I was when I came to Malveaux. You can condition yourself out of that state as much as you want, but sometimes, the darker side of you comes in nonthreatening ways to turn you back—through sleep, busy schedules, or silence. That's my current captor: silence.

Kyle, Alani, Nate, and I talked about Nadir only one night: when, after a few blood transfusions and care, I was well enough to live outside a hospital room again. We met in the Great Room, where Alani manipulated the perfect fire. Everything got laid out then between us. How scared we all were. How scared we still are. We learned that heirloom blood is more vulnerable to a Revenir's chasm—which is why Nate turned into a wraith so quickly. He's had to sit through many sessions of holistic medicine to flush the impact of that night from his system. I shared my truth too. And ever since, we've never muttered one word of Nadir, Revenirs, Raquel, or Sarai.

THE HALLS ARE a little too loud for my liking today. That's no surprise on Fridays—especially as summer break looms. I find quiet past my peers in an area where powers can get you expelled.

Malveaux's art gallery is a huge spectacle to have wedged in its corner. So much is here: art installations, sculptures, paintings, shadow and silhouette art, and a low backdrop of jazz. It is the history I didn't understand when I first came here, but now I know. The paintings are my favorite. So many Black Varien faces in Romanticism—their stories properly told. I can read them better than ever before. Glory and decadence coated atop tired and stubborn resilience. Make a way or be moved. We are here. This is our land, and we will build a safe haven here by our rules. Because I'm more familiar with myself, I know them better. Each painting, especially *The Two Madonnas*. When I first laid eyes on it, I only saw myself split in two. A warm smile on one side, perfectly kept room, well kempt hair and clothes, eyes that say, "Everything's fine," while the other half shows a woman miserable with tears and the background of no home or city, just a barren plot of land. That was me if you asked me then, yet now, all I see is Sarai and myself—different paths chosen from different cards we were dealt.

Suddenly, my Mary Janes aren't the only shoes making sounds on the polished stone ground. From behind, Sage Cameron glides in the gallery. The soleil chandeliers above dim as she stands beside me. "A penny for your thoughts."

"I *was* going to show up today."

"How would I know?"

"Because I was."

"Well, with the last three appointments you've rescheduled, it's hard to tell." Sage Cameron observes me as I stare at the large painting. Malveaux's historic bell chimes at the hour and the miracle of sun-kissed stained-glass shines on the floor.

"How was your meeting with Andre?" I ask her. I've thought about him every day since we've brought him to Malveaux, but I rarely see him. I don't know if that's intentional or out of his control. Makes me sad no matter how I slice it.

Sage Cameron perks up. "Very well, actually. I think he needs to be in a place like this. I wish it didn't take a bizarre situation for him to find that out. He was lonely for so long and now he says he doesn't feel that way anymore. I'm thinking about having him teach art history next year."

"Really?" I smile. "That's perfect...I hope I can take his class." I drop my head and Sage Cameron nudges me with her elbow.

"Of course, you can," she reassures.

My eyes find the painting again and get lost in the brush strokes and clashes of color.

"A penny for your thoughts," she tries again.

"Really, Sage Cameron?"

She nods playfully and insists, "Really."

"Okay...I see this differently now. I used to see one person and now I see two...makes me wonder."

"Hmm. Art is funny like that, isn't it? It's for everyone—even all your different versions. Your current, past, and future. This is why I argued with Dama Hadley over placing detailed background information of the painting near them. She wants everyone to learn, whereas I just want you all to feel as much as possible. You can't feel if you know a piece was inspired by the first batch of imported pineapples."

"Please tell me this wasn't."

Sage Cameron giggles. "You have my word. This piece, painted by Jules Olivier, is not inspired by the pineapple. It's a narrative of the genocide. How two sisters were made and broken by it. Their outcomes birthed other outcomes."

"Like me…"

"And Sarai?"

"…We're enemies now."

Sage Cameron is pensive for a moment. "The love can't be totally lost. If foes are just envious of the other, that means admiration is between them. And, in your case, where does that old love go? Honestly…does it die? Or is it dormant? I ask myself the same thing."

"Maybe it just freezes in time and stays where it should," I respond. We leave *The Two Madonnas* behind us and carry on in the octagonal hall of sculptures—many carved in marble, and bronze. "And I don't believe all foes share a sort of love. What Raquel did to me isn't love. That's something much more heinous."

"Are you sure? You don't think she had an admiration for what you are?"

"Sage Cameron." I click my tongue. "See, this is why I didn't want to have these talks. I don't want to bend my mind over things that aren't things. She wanted to kill me and that's it. There's nothing deep there."

"But she had motive, didn't she? Something to gain from you?"

"Okay…my Eden genes. I forgot to state that."

"Your genes in which our Creator chose for you to inhabit. Your life went one way, and hers another because she was not what the prophesy promised. Sounds like another Madonna to me. All her trauma did was birth another outcome. Another chaos agent to burn the streets."

Fear twists itself around my stomach. "She's still out there. Her and the Revenirs. Every night I pray to not mull over them so much…but I…I'm not there yet." A tear rolls down my face.

Sage Cameron is there to catch it with her handkerchief. Her eyes drift to where the sun meets the gilded spot on my chest. "Your genes are concealed now. That's why Nadir didn't work. Remember? It wasn't for nothing…it ended the worst of it."

Having mulled over Nadir for the past few months, I shake my head. "We fooled the Revenirs, but for how long? I don't think Sarai was ever convinced. And Raquel knows who I am…she'll come back for me until one of us dies."

"We won't let that happen here."

"But I can't live with that over my head. Everywhere, every single day and night…I can't settle with knowing anyone will fight for me and get hurt. It's too much. Remembering you all in the center of a battle…no one, no one knows what that's like!"

All of her features suddenly hang low. "You may be surprised." A sentence bearing a bruise from heartbreak I have no idea of. I don't dare press it, because I know the ache it can spread to the rest of the body. "When I worked to dismantle them, I was sure I could do it once and for all. Revenirs are calculated fools, but they didn't have the brains I had. And many of them are not omegas on their own. That kind of gift—the kind you have, the kind I was blessed with—is different when the Almighty gives it to you. You don't need an army, just your faith. I thought that was enough, till they killed people I loved and made an orphan of the child who was lucky enough not to be home."

Instantly, I want to cross in and ask her more. Why were Kyle's parents killed if they were working within the Revenirs? But that, and the pact he made with Oz, is a taboo discussion, one we still need to have.

"Move on is all I ever did—all I could manage," Sage Cameron goes on. "Smart and careful. That's what we will do. Raquel pursuing you at this point or showing her face in The Grove makes her dead where she stands. She broke her contract with the Revenirs, and that is something no one can do without a large bounty on their head the next minute. The nastiest of them are tailing her now, I'm sure—if she hasn't been caught already."

"How do we know if she has?"

"Seeing as access to those sorts of answers led the monsters right to you, it's best to not know."

"I can't live that way."

"It can be done. You have no better option at this point. Leave it alone. Leave them alone. Their trail has gone cold, Set is surely a pariah for letting his people down, and your halo can't be detected ever again. To find their way through all of that will be a feat, especially as you've just newly manifested."

"I don't know what I can do with it. It's too much. Just like the stars."

"Too much? Was it too much when you saved yourself against Raquel? When you summoned the earth to quake under your feet and a force field to cover you? You needed that 'too much' then."

I aim to the stained-glass window and see other kids going on about their Friday. Their regular life. "I mean, I get it…but it is too much when I want to be like everyone else here. When I want to be the same kind of Varien."

"I can imagine it feels like you fit nowhere…but I believe you'll be at peace one day. Time is the remedy."

"Guess I've got a lot to learn over the summer." I shrug sheepishly.

"You know? When I look back on your journey. You don't always follow the rules, but you do the right thing. You've learned to defend yourself and master your gifts. I'm not worried about you learning to love yourself the way you deserve. My concerns more so lie with your counterpart."

"Kyle? What did he do?"

"Well, I'm sure he knows I read your thoughts after you two broke into the Revenirs' headquarters. He knows I know about the pact he made with Oswell."

As she says this, I cough and feel my chest getting tight.

"He's found every possible way to avoid me. Instead of meeting with me, he's opted for meetings with Ben. I respect Ben very much, but he is not a qualified psychologist. As Kyle's headmistress, it's my job to worry about him. As his godmother, it's second nature. I need him to open up to me and explain why he did that. Oswell was my husband, yes. He was Calum Phoenix's best friend, but, he's not a good person. He hasn't been for a long time. Kyle can't give himself up to him…I don't want him to end up like his dad." For a moment, Sage Cameron is lost in her memories. Frozen with an arched brow. "Maybe I could renegotiate and reason with Oswell…"

I place my hand on her shoulder, halfway tempted to tell a story that isn't really mine to tell. "Should I push for him to meet with you?" I suggest.

"No." She snaps out of her trance. "I'll get us where we need to be before school's out for the summer. Just keep an eye on him. If anything stands out, tell me."

"I'll do my best. We haven't really discussed Nadir or Revenirs. We both prefer to act like it's behind us."

"Hmph," she laughs. "Avoidance, the old friend and foe. I'm not sure you have room on your plate to do that."

"I don't, which is why I think it's time to make room." I bite my lip the moment Sage Cameron's brows hike with curiosity. The space is so stylishly quiet. Bright with piano rhythms and nothing more. Just art and academia around us, inside us. "You always say time is the remedy…you just said it, actually. And well, I think maybe time has made it possible to reunite with my family again.

Just me, in this skin. I want them to hear me and see me as I am…
and I think I'm ready for the world to do the same too."

"The world?"

"Yes." I breathe deep. A stone angel behind me—a tired, yet
persistent expression on her face as she carries an earth-size orb
above her head. "I want everyone to know what happened to
Senator Jacob's daughter, and I want them to hear it from me."

CHAPTER EIGHTY-ONE

INFINITE

"*I*'*LL PROTECT YOU FROM the world if I have to.*" Words Dad once said echo loud today. Before these stars grew outside of me and shocked him. The memory of how I left him douses me in shame—the raw, red peels of skin, the busted vessels and tears that trailed to his demolished left ear. I'll meet those scars soon.

The raised patch of hives on my skin reminds me of how out of it I am for not thinking this through. When I decided to meet my family here at Greta's, I thought I'd have better composure.

"Please save me," Kyle blurts, clinging to the back of Greta's office door.

"Ugh! I was afraid you chickened out and went back to Malveaux," I tease.

Kyle wipes the colony of sweat from his forehead. "The only thing evil enough to run me out is more dusting of places Greta's too lazy to clean." He morphs into her likeness. "Kyle, get all the blades on the fan. Oh no, baby, you missed a spot. Get up on top of that bookcase! Watch out for those widows. I forgot about those!"

As soon as he ends his mimicry, Greta pops her head in the door. "Ay! Are you crazy? No powers! Someone might see you...I heard everything, by the way."

"I meant for you to!" Kyle shouts back as Greta closes the door. "So, let's hear this script, Lex. Whatcha got?" He gives an enthusiastic clap and sprawls himself across a jade chaise. "Go on, present for me. And by all means, picture me naked if you must."

"There are huge brown recluse webs on the sides of Greta's china cabinets. Did you get those?" I say.

"Did you hear anything I said? You get to picture me without clothes on…and without any of my judgement."

His humor ricochets off my bundles of nerves.

"You're not laughing. I might not be funny to everyone, but I always manage to make you laugh." He follows in my pacing steps. "Are you having a problem memorizing things?"

"No. I think I got it down. "For now…"

"For now?" Kyle glances at his watch. "You're going live in a few minutes. You should be reciting that thing in your sleep."

I look away from him and gnaw at my jagged thumbnail.

"Alexia?" Kyle calls and bends to my eye level.

"Yes?" I peek out of one eye as he takes both of my hands.

"I'm going to take a wild guess and say your anxiety has everything to do with the parentals. Never mind the live video that'll connect you to thousands of people…"

"Well, you guessed right, okay?"

Kyle sets a hand on his chest and mouths the words, "I'm right?"

I groan.

"No, I'm serious. Because if this is a trick, I don't need to be right," he clarifies.

"Fifty fifty odds of it being a trick," Lucie adds with her back turned to us. She's been the savior to all my roadblocks. The girl with a way out of The Grove outside of full moon hours—thanks to her Midray. And now as my jailbreaking wonk, hooking up a used phone so I can log into my old social media apps and send the video I've envisioned in my head for weeks. All this, and the addition of keeping the device untraceable.

"You see, this is why Alani didn't want her to come," Kyle mumbles.

"Well do you have a physics-forward machine that could've jumped us through realms without the moon's permission?" Lucie says matter of factly.

I snap my neck forward as Kyle looks stumped. "Exactly," I laugh. "Look, Kyle, I just need you to hear me because I'm freaking out right now. All I can think about is my family. What if time doesn't heal all wounds? What if things aren't the same? What if they don't love me anymore? I can barely manage one thought at a time and now there's this speech—"

Kyle clamps his hand over my mouth. "Lex, stop. Do you see what you're doing to yourself? It's unfair. Things won't be the same. You knew that the day you ran away. Change happens to all of us and your family chose to greet it. They want to be here so they can be a part of who you're becoming. How can that be anything less than love?"

He waits for my reply. "Oh, yeah," he giggles, remembering I need an uncovered mouth to talk. "I'm going to let you speak now, only on the condition that you stop marathon worrying."

"Moh-kway," my voice muffles before he removes his hand.

I sigh and pout on the jade chaise. "Why is it so hard for me to hope for the best? It's like I'm trained to anticipate the worst."

"You think that way because you've had to. You're tougher than you know. I mean, six months ago, you cooked Revenirs on command. Today is nothing compared to the big fish you've literally fried," he jokes.

A snorting laugh honks out my nose. It's the first time Kyle's referenced Knox-Oxley without flinching in awhile.

"Finally, a laugh! I'll take it, even if it's out of pity. My bruised ego needs it," he says.

Greta props one foot inside her office and squeaks into the heart-shaped door. "Alexia, sweets…they're here. Can you believe it?"

I open my mouth to speak but can't.

Kyle massages my knee. "Everything will go like you dreamed. I'll be right out that door rooting for you with everyone else." His arms slide through my fingertips as he leaves. Time. I need more of it, even if only for a span of seconds.

The click of the closed door lodges a pit in my throat. "Lucie," I cough. "Do I look all right? Is there sweat or anything weird hanging from my nose?"

She throws me a once-over look as she tightens a tripod. "Negative."

"I don't have sweat anywhere?"

"Nope."

"What about my teeth?" I cheese. "Any lipstick on them?"

For the first time, Lucie is the one fed up with me. "Alexia, you don't have to save the world. Just do what you want to do. Be that person…that's what I do."

…*That's a vital suggestion.* "Wow, that helps a lot. Thank you, Lucie."

"You're welcome. Gonna start charging you soon!"

"Can't we compromise?"

"If you think bringing me a manticore is fair…then yes." A tilted grin and wink follow. "Any minute now, captain."

The rigged phone facing me is clamped in a tripod. The camera shows my nervous face. "I'm on now?"

Lucie slaps a palm against her forehead. "Yes," she whispers. "And your live numbers are climbing. One thousand people on already!"

My made-up face stares into the void of profile names joining the live. So many I don't know. So many people ask, "Where are you?" or write in some exclaiming burst, "OMG! Ur alive!" I'd forgotten just how overwhelming it is to have a phone. To live online versus living in life. All of it is just another sad dichotomy. A familiar pang knocks me in my core. Two-faced. Two ideals. I could never go back there.

"Hi, everyone! Thanks for tuning in," I tread gently into speaking my piece. There is no smile, and there is no overt strength. There is only me in my awkward vulnerability. Awkward because this is new to share, but nothing far from true. "I don't want to take too much time saying what I have to say but wanted to come on here and share it with you all because I think it's important."

Two names I grew up hearing in the walls of my home scroll up on the screen.

@Nilesjac has joined

@itsniaj has joined

I resist the urge to blow chunks where I sit. I'm nervous. Slightly sick and scared, I remind myself that none of this is about Nia or Niles. It's about no one but me.

"I just want you all to know I'm safe and doing well…it's been a long time. A LOT has changed for me, and I just didn't feel right continuing without giving you all some sort of answers and closure. I don't know what the consensus is about me, or what rumors there are…but I want you all to know that I'm in good hands and making it on my own."

"But what happened to you? Were you kidnapped?" I read aloud in the comments. "No, no…I left on my own, which is what I wanted to talk about. I wish I could say my leaving didn't stem from the threat of imminent danger, but, it did. In more ways than one, actually. Yet, the driving force behind all danger at the time came from my identity: as Senator Jacobs's daughter, and also as a young Varien girl in hiding. I manifested months before disappearing and kept it a tight secret from my family, friends, and coworkers. Who would I be if I became the Varien daughter of a staunch anti-Varien politician, you know? I wouldn't be—that's the answer. I wouldn't be able to exist. So those were my options: to rid myself from the world or lie. And while I seriously had many days of considering the former, I chose the latter. I learned how to be a con artist. How to sell a narrative I'm biologically against because I'm the aberration in question. I wore the mask and it felt like hell." Feelings, old thoughts, and memories play around me. Sarai. My father. The battle at the Turnstile. They are confining. Shackles on my feet. A coffin engulfing me alive. "I didn't choose for my cells to change, but I want to stress that even having a choice in anything that steers from one person's norm shouldn't grant open season either. If there is no harm being done to anyone, I don't see how who we are as Variens is anyone's business. And everyone makes it their business. I am a witness to that and various debates over dinner regarding what rights Variens should be allowed. It's insane...."

Did your family disown you?
Fuck Senator Jacobs!

"No!" I squint and lean in. "No! Let me make it clear. I love my dad and my entire family. They all have been incredibly supportive in ways I never imagined. And I do believe if I had had the support I needed and craved from society, I wouldn't have questioned if my family had my back as much. They operated off influence and brain. That's helpful and smart and can definitely help one out at the right times, but it doesn't answer what happens when tribulation knocks on your front door. Think to yourself for a moment. What if someone you loved manifested? Would you stop loving them on command? Society would tell you to. Except, the heart, the same anatomically constructed heart beating in all of us, would say no. Love is too great to fall victim to the formalities of things like cells and genes."

In the comments, my brother leaves a ton of hearts and a fullness starts to well inside of me. A few feet away, Lucie gives me a thumbs-up and wipes tears from beneath her glasses.

"While I existed in the Normal world, I was alive. But just breathing isn't enough. It's the basic function we need to carry out each day at our best. And leaving home, and finding others like me who are allowed to live free with human rights introduced me to the heart of myself...to my optimum potential.

"By knowing my truest self, I'm happy with the smallest things. Yet somehow, my existence in this world is the antithesis of peace. Like so many of my Varien friends, I wonder how that's possible. Guilty even when innocent—how can we wear that brand? Doesn't everyone know we never asked for this? We have never started wars, we have only ever been employed by Normals to finish them. Sometimes I cry trying to understand it, other times I'm angry, but the truth is always right in front of me: divide and conquer. It's a powerful strategy that ignites mass hysteria and segregation. This is a huge problem. When we stop asking questions and empathizing with the next person, we have enormous reason to worry. We must know we are only executing a hidden agenda.

"A solution can't be found in brick and mortared walls meant to shut us out. I guarantee it won't be found in false convictions, like the one given to my best friend, Sarai Baker, whose youth and innocence decayed in a prison somewhere, or the deduction of health care. These places and actions don't breed love, and we, the people of the world, need its light to coexist. We need you. We need your help to see things through, to end the pain and suffering. Work with us to find balance. Promote therapies, programs, and facilities to protect the gifted as we always come to your rescue when needed. All those things are reflective of humanity's true light. I think it's terrible I've only found this same light in a hidden community of 'freaks and monsters.'" I pause and think of my roster of friends. "These freaks you plan to exterminate are capable of love, feeling, and empowering one another. *We* are so much more. We are righteous. We are valuable and…I don't want to be anyone else. So, on behalf of Sarai Baker, and per my own beliefs, I'm calling for the release of Miss Paulette Baker. She has been convicted as an accomplice to a Varien a.k.a. a loving and protective parent to her child who chose not to turn her over to the government the moment her cells flipped. Miss Baker has done no crime. How could this be such a crime? This is the true aberration. Miss Baker only wanted her daughter to live a life where she is able to pursue happiness and liberty. I see no crime there. Lastly, I declare my stance against the California Screen Bill and its further deduction of human rights. You should too, because at any moment, you could easily become Miss Baker or her daughter. Everything seems distant until injustice knocks on your door. Thank you all for listening. I'll see you around…maybe."

My lips close. Lucie ends the live recording.

Applause and proud remarks creep through the door. I even hear Indy barking.

Lucie is still wet faced, an adorable glaze over chocolate skin. "Where in the world has all of that been hiding?"

I shrug. "Under layers of mental slush."

"Really, you're a natural. What you did probably saved someone's life today."

I smile behind my hands and shut my eyes.

"Oh! Don't make yourself a mess yet," Lucie gushes. "I'll go tell your family you're ready."

The door closes and resets the archive of feelings I put aside for the speech.

I go back to nibbling on the nails Alani manicured, then move myself into the next habit. Standing then sitting. Sitting then standing.

Hinges creak and the heart-shaped door pushes opens. Will they be furious after what I said? What if my words work as dried pine to an already raging fire?

"Baby girl," my mom coos in the doorway. Like a dream wrapped in a chiffon jumpsuit, she graces the room. Mascara stains the apples of her cheeks.

I whisper through a growing sob, "Hi…Mom."

"I'm so proud of you," she says.

I fold over, except this time in the safe arms of the woman who gave me life.

Niles, my brother, fresh with a newly barbered cut and moustache, hugs the two of us. The last time I saw him his face was chubbier.

"I don't know why I put on this makeup today." Mom dabs her under eyes.

"I told you not to put all that on your face," Niles playfully scolds.

"Please, you don't tell *me* anything," she corrects.

A knock on the open door turns us away from each other.

It's Dad.

He may as well have risen from the dead. I imagined him decrepit from my damage, covered in fractal shaped scars and deformed skin. He looks the extreme opposite, rested and tranquil. Despite the wrinkles lining his forehead and eyes, his mahogany skin is still rich.

He shows no love lost by gathering me in his arms.

"I'm sorry." I sniff.

Dad lifts his head and steps back. "No, baby girl, I'm sorry. I made you afraid."

"But, Dad, you didn't know! It's not your fault…this is just how the world works."

"I'm not the world. I'm your father," he rectifies.

"That's right," Mom adds. "Baby, you did what felt natural to protect yourself. All that anti-Varien talk you grew up around… we gave you no choice."

Dad agrees, "Sometimes people can't understand what's foreign until it happens to them. But not you…you've always been transparent. Such a soldier."

I feel redemption. This is all I ever wanted and needed to hear. There's only one thing missing. "Where's Nia?" I ask.

Mom, Dad, and Niles lock eyes.

"Nia isn't quite there yet," Mom explains. "She's had some trouble accepting everything."

"Oh." Hearing that is like taking a cannonball to the gut. Maybe I should've expected it. Everyone can't be won over. I just never expected my sister to be the one.

"Don't stress about her." Niles wraps one arm around my neck and smiles. "I think it's dope. When do I get my Varien gene?"

A piece of me wants to tease him and pick up on my sibling tendencies. Lucky for him the mood doesn't welcome it. Only positive vibes live here.

THE DAY RUNS into the evening and the evening brings a platter of Greta's homemade treats: lavender scones drizzled in raw honey, po' boys, creole stew, butterscotch tulips, custard cakes, and rooibos tea.

My two worlds, the Jacobs family and the Malveaux Academy crew, blend and roll through the hours like they've been old friends. The sight is surprising, but Van Gogh couldn't have painted a better scene. Indy—who I've missed so much—runs over from person to person and begs for belly scratches. Ultimately, he's fallen in love with Lucie, and I completely understand. Niles tries his hardest to give Kyle a tough time by flexing his big brother machismo. When really, even he can't deny my boyfriend's charisma. Nate is losing to Greta at Spades. Alani and my mom model antiques from Greta's inventory. Like a pair of giddy girls, they shimmy in strands of pearls and Victorian pinchbacks, sipping tea with perked pinkies and pouty lips. Every now and then I hear Alani in awe of her actions. Using the Midray with the rest of us. "I can't believe I did this…" she reflects and zones out. Turns out, Alani's Achilles heel is being left out from her loved ones—which explains a lot about her.

Highly intrigued by the inner workings of our parallel world, Dad clings to every wise word Sage Cameron shares. He says he's inspired to change his platform with the intention of molding a more tolerable world for myself and the Varien community. He even wants to help Miss Baker and get her exonerated.

"Today," he says, "is a spark of fire for humanity's future."

Just when I think I may die of euphoria, Greta encourages us to get going before wanderers hit the streets.

"Ooh, Eddie, you need to drive us home. I had too many of Greta's B-52s." Mom prissily trots through the shop's yard and jingles her keys. "Thank you for having us, Greta. We had a great time. Maureen, don't forget…girls' night soon. I've been waiting to hit the floor with the wobble!"

She breaks into the electric slide and shuffles across the grass.

I grip both of her wrists and forbid her from continuing. "Mom! Mom! Dial it down…and you're not even doing the wobble."

Niles hides the side of his face with his bent hand. "She always gets them mixed up."

Mom nudges me away and beelines for my boyfriend. "Now, Kyle, you take care of my baby. I want you to swear it."

"I've already sworn to do that with my life, Mrs. Jacobs. Haven't I done a good job so far?"

Dad nods. Mom gives him a hug. "You have. I'm just giving you a hard time. The maternal voice inside me keeps saying, *What if she's in the wrong place at the wrong time. What if some bad people get a hold of her?*"

Kyle pats her back even though he's the one choking. "Oh, that won't happen again."

Mom giggles at his last sentence. *If she only knew.*

Everyone gives their goodbyes till it's finally my turn. I smile through bittersweet emotions. Again, Kyle was right. One year of life changed my family. And with Niles off to his first year at UC Berkeley, and Dad plotting his campaign for governor, I feel selfish for not being around. It's becoming clear I'll never be content with the way I have to live now, even with my family rallying in my corner.

"Lil' Revolution." Dad holds his fist up. "I'll get to work on finding Miss Paulette as soon as I get home. We'll get her back…Sarai too. Promise you'll call and write. We're behind you, no excuses."

His mention of Sarai touches a wound I'm unsure will ever heal. I want to tell him, but that's another saga to share another time. Today is only about our truth and progress. Sarai is somewhere beyond that now. "I'll do better, pops. I promise."

"And get me a Varien girlfriend," Niles jokes. I slug his shoulder as he dives into the car.

Mom presses on the car door and avoids facing me.

"You okay?" I ask.

She blinks, tears pooling her in eyes. "You're not coming home, are you? Ever?" Her voice breaks apart.

This is a moment I didn't plan for, discussing my permanent residence with my parents. "I have to stay…Mom."

"You're not even eighteen yet. Do you know how unnatural it feels to not be with my child?"

Dad sighs from the other side of the car, "Solo."

Mom taps her foot. I forgot she does that too.

"I want to come home," I cry. "I never wanted to leave, Mom. But…what kind of life can I have there now? Where will I work? Will I even be able to with a Varien academy diploma? Dad's political enemies would pawn me against his campaign and hand me over to the state."

"We can make it work. We always do," she weeps.

"Solo, what we have to give will end up hurting her," Dad chimes in. "She's doing the right thing. It was written before it happened."

The whites of Mom's eyes are a shade of pink. "All right," she surrenders. "Stay. You know better than anyone. I'm not going to force you to come home. You'd be a caged bird, looking over your shoulder, unhappy with being a fraction of yourself." She looks me over. "You grew up, baby girl…I can sense it. Maybe I'll sleep better with things this way."

"I'm gonna miss you, Mom."

"Not for long. I'll be back to see you at Greta's as much as I can."

Our goodbye stings—almost like when I was a kid and chased my parents' car as they rode off to vacation for a week. If only it were a week instead of forever. At least I have them back now.

I worry for my parents when I remember what Set revealed about someone putting a hit on my father and me, then revoking it. How safe are they? What can I do?

The wind-swept fragrance of Kyle's cologne gives him away before his hand wraps around my waist. "You sure you don't want to go home for the summer? I'll survive if you change your mind. I won't be excited, but I'll understand."

"It's better this way." I watch my parents' car turn the corner. "Especially with Revenirs around."

"Well, I'm sure they're at peace with you at Malveaux after meeting all of us and Sage Cameron."

An awkward smile grows on my face at the mention of our headmistress's name.

"Why the gremlin smile?" Kyle squints and tilts his head.

"I was waiting for the right time to surprise you. I haven't told anyone besides my family about this yet but…Sage Cameron invited me to stay at her house for the summer. I decided I'm going to accept."

"Thank God! I thought I was going to have to move out of my room for you."

"Kyle!"

"I'm kidding, I'm kidding. I'm stoked you're going to be close this summer. The moment you turn around I'll be clicking my heels like some corny leprechaun." He pantomimes a shoddy little river dance and stiffens his face like a doll. "Please don't tell me you're overthinking again."

Bingo, Phoenix.

"Spit it out," he says.

"I know, it's silly…" I pause, fully aware of how neurotic I sound. "I'm just thinking about everything I love at Malveaux: you, me, Alani, and Nate. I want things to stay the same. No changes. Me staying in town this summer is gonna change stuff… don't you think?"

"Lex, do you listen to anything I say?"

"Eh…sometimes."

"Forget about the what-ifs." He steps closer to me. The pale pattern of freckles on his lips are close enough make out. "You can worry all you want, none of it is promised anyway. None of it except you and me…we're constant. We'll always be."

Kyle amps the beat of my heart and wraps his fingers with mine. Every bit of him is so devoted. He seals his statement by cradling the side of my face and kissing me. As always, he's medicine.

"Did you not believe us when we said you're stuck with us the first time?" Alani shouts from behind us. Lounged on the banister of the porch, she reclines against Nate's chest. "We made a promise, remember?"

She crosses her heart. Nate flips a smile.

"We've got The Grove at our feet for the next three months," Kyle says. "It wouldn't be the perfect summer if we didn't stomp through it. Let's be present for each day." I ogle where the cotton-candy-colored sky and the edge of him touch. Sweet, warm, and bright, he wraps me in a hug.

Time is arrested. My anxieties turn back to ash. Old stifling habits scamper back to their graves. And right here, in the crook of Kyle's chest, I can't help but know this:

We'll always possess the light to cast out the dark.

I raise my face to my love's and beam. "That's all I want to be," I say.

Acknowledgments

I have often dreamed of this moment. At times, I knew what I would say and how I would fashion my words to encompass a labor of love that has been gestating for over twenty years. But times have changed, which has made me and this story change—and for the better.

On many occasions, I feared I would never cross this finish line. I have shed so many tears over this book and the stable space required to make it. Stability hasn't always been a constant, so the very fact you are now holding this book is through the grace of God.

This achievement would not have been possible without my Heavenly Father. Whenever I thought there was no way, a path appeared, bridges were built, dead ends were paved over. I've been covered every step of the way, and I'm so grateful for the love, guidance, patience, and security He has given me.

Mom, I did it! After all these years, you never have to ask, "When are we releasing this book, girl?" The moment has arrived.

Whenever I felt like I was sinking, you found me, gave me a life jacket, and pulled me on board with you. As your child, I know nothing I could ever do is enough to pay you back, but I hope you feel how treasured you are by me and our family. We see you. Thank you for believing in me first, loving me always, and never giving up on yourself—or your girls.

I love you, Mama, my world.

Dad, there was always an anxious ache when I thought of hurrying this book so you could live to see it printed. Spiritually, I think I always felt the clock was ticking faster, and we'd have to say goodbye soon. You may have left this earth, but your presence as my ancestor is felt daily. Your likeness is in all these pages—along with the passion you've given me for imagining and creating. Thank you for loving me and always trying your best. I wish you knew how important you were to us all. I hope you do now and are proud of the promises I have kept and how far I've come. I miss you terribly.

I love you, Dad, my muse.

My sisters—my first readers, my playmates, my best friends, my band members, and sometimes unwilling accomplices—this book has covered me from childhood to the present—so much of the spirit of what kept us bonded and afloat lives here. I get so emotional when I think of our adolescent need to escape, naivete, and happiness. Our tenacity and how hard we ride for one another have been my favorite things about us. The March sisters have nothing on us, and one day, our lives will look like the final scene of *Little Women*. Thank you for being my sanctuary and the mirror I need to see myself as I am.

I love you, my sisters, my pillars.

My daughters, you have shown me so many things about myself. You remind me how vital and warm a safe and loving family is. Your existence has made everything brighter, sweeter, and louder! I wouldn't have it any other way. You two make me feel alive. I'm so proud to be your mother, and I hope you will look proudly upon me as you grow. You motivate me to take on the universe and bring you the stars. You deserve it all.

I love you, my girls—the greatest heroines I will ever create.

My husband, we've had the luxury of watching one another grow up. How beautiful! You are my time machine—who can relive my golden days with me. With you, I'm forever young. Forever safe and loved. The best part of my days is when you come home through the door. Many times I felt I'd crack from what life was throwing us, but you stayed right beside me and never wavered in your care and protection. I don't know if I've ever said this, but I made it through grief because of you. You have supported this book boldly—replacing old raggedy computers and creating all promotional items. What a champion you are. I'm so lucky to have you as my partner in everything, down to ride and choose sides—the love of my life.

I love you, my husband, my rock.

My Godparents, while living far away for many years, your influence, love, and guidance have comprised so much of my moral DNA. Thank you for being my mentors.

My bonus parents, thank you always for your love and support.

My girlfriends—my inner circle, thank you for being here, for growing up with me and believing in me when I have not believed in myself. Like Alexia, I would cross realms for you! I love you all.

Miss Linda, my beloved village and cheerleader, I will never not hear your voice telling me to go my own way. I am so grateful for you. Thank you for encouraging me to be a rebel.

Mr. Josh Stein, my English college professor—no one stayed on my back like you. You are the reason I take writing seriously. Before knowing you, I didn't even know being a writer for someone like me could be possible.

You once said, "I've never seen someone with so much talent waste their time." I've been awake ever since.

My lovely editors: Kyle Hiller, who chose me! My brother, you came into my life and buried imposter syndrome, poured into me, taught me, and gave me a manifesting vision to do what I felt was best. Thank you for being my mentor and friend. I'm so happy you're in this world.

Sydnee Thompson and Johanie Martinez-Cools, ya'll are my behind-the-scenes arsenal. My team! Thank you for brilliantly sculpting this book to its fullest potential. Sometimes edits were stressful, but you stayed faithful and committed to my talent and this story. Thank you for pushing me!

Clara Gaby Rose! The artist you are! The beautiful person you are! I knew I had to collaborate the first time I saw your work. Then, after speaking with you, I knew you would be my close friend. I treasure our bond and hope this is the first of many iconic collaborations.

Rena Violet, who formatted this book, designed its interior, and created the cover layouts. You are a gem of a person and an absolute professional. Thank you for fitting me in and always being so kind and accommodating.

My critique partners, Issa Hessa and Liz Giles, thank you for being there from the start in this book's infancy. You both kept me moving forward and provided encouragement and feedback as I grew in my craft. Writing can be lonely, but you two gave me my first solid community.

Karly Dizon, thank you for always being there to dream big with me. So proud of who we have become!

My work family, the environment you've all created blows my mind. Thank you for giving me a safe nest to thrive in when I'm away from home. It keeps my mind healthy, and a healthy mind assists in my dreams moving forward.

My Kickstarter community, this book is here in all its glory because of each one of you. Thank you for taking a chance on a woman with a dream, an unknown author, and betting on me. I am still blown away and forever grateful for your contributions and support. Look what your contribution created!

Extra thanks to the backers who donated above and beyond: Devona White, Kenya White, Regina Mack, Robyn Hughes, Tiara Kinnison, Deja and Rocket Stingily, Erin Brethour, Brianna Welch, Noel Tyler, Christina Harris, Grecia Macias, Sherry White Young, Mark Cho, James Moore, Teena Sanders, Dr. Tacey Rodgers, Karen

Wilson, Stephanie Siverling, Amy Robinson, Rochelle Van Tassell, Brian Bohnet, Amanda Routh, Amy Cancryn, Tasha Williams, Ayreka Williams, and Saira Qureshi.

To my biggest literary creative inspirations: Sabaa Tahir, Tracy Deonn, Dhonielle Clayton, Angie Thomas, Nia Davenport, Zoraida Cordova, and Claribel Ortega, thank you for paving the road in this complicated publishing world. You are forces to be reckoned with and very kind people who have shared the wealth of information you've learned along your paths. I've learned so much from you and believed I could accomplish my dream because of your achievements. Thank you tenfold!

The literary ancestors whose shoulders I stand on: Phyllis Wheatley, Toni Morrison, Octavia Butler, Langston Hughes, James Baldwin, and Maya Angelou, thank you for stitching me up after the battle of some bad days.

To the black girls around the world who never feel seen and heard, who never feel protected, who never feel like they have a place, you are in my heart, and it is my dream to make limitless spaces where you can be yourself and be cherished. I hope to make you proud. This is for ya'll, fam.

Additionally, Malveaux Academy is also for any and every outsider and outcast. It's for the tired and weary, the wanderers still searching for *their* place. It is for you, dear reader! Thank you for being part of my new world, life, and community. I love you all!

Alright, ya'll…off for a good cry.

To the stars we go!

See you in book two!

Love,

T

TATIANA WHITE GREW up on a creative diet of comics, poetry, film, essays, and books.

An advocate for diversity, Tatiana studied the mechanics of film, creative writing, and journalism to alter narratives and imagery imposed on black youths and adults. She earned a bachelor's degree in Mass Media Communications and worked for various Bay Area media staples before returning to her first love: storytelling.

When Tatiana's not toiling over her computer, she's occupied with her life as a wife to her college sweetheart and a full-time role as a mother of two and a cantankerous schnauzer.

For writing updates and more information visit
www.tatianawhite.com.